Talking at Night

Talking at Night

Claire Daverley

PAMELA DORMAN BOOKS · VIKING

VIKING
An imprint of Penguin Random House LLC
penguinrandomhouse.com

A Pamela Dorman Book/Viking

LIBRARY OF CONGRESS CATALOGING-IN-PUBLICATION DATA
Names: Daverley, Claire, 1991– author.
Title: Talking at night / Claire Daverley.
Description: [New York]: Viking, [2023] | Pamela Dorman Books.
Identifiers: LCCN 2022054455 (print) | LCCN 2022054456 (ebook) |
ISBN 9780593653487 (hardcover) | ISBN 9780593653494 (ebook)
Subjects: LCGFT: Romance fiction. | Novels.
Classification: LCC PR6104.A8395 T35 2023 (print) | LCC PR6104.A8395
(ebook) | DDC 823/.92—dc23/eng/20221201
LC record available at https://lccn.loc.gov/2022054455
LC ebook record available at https://lccn.loc.gov/2022054456

Printed in the United States of America
10 9 8 7 6 5 4 3 2 1

Designed by Alexis Farabaugh

This is a work of fiction. Names, characters, places, and incidents
either are the product of the author's imagination or are used fictitiously,
and any resemblance to actual persons, living or dead, businesses,
companies, events, or locales is entirely coincidental.

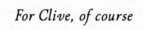

For Clive, of course

I wish I'd done everything on earth with you.

BAZ LUHRMANN'S
THE GREAT GATSBY, 2013

Talking at Night

◖

Their lives cleave apart on a Tuesday night.

This is something her mother fixates on, in her breathless, not-yet-grieving denial, under the stark lights of the hospital hallway. The tiles are scuffed gray and the sky fringes scarlet through the blinds. It is almost dawn and Rosie stands by the glass and feels half of herself retreat to a place that she didn't know existed.

But it's a Tuesday, her mother is saying to the doctor. He doesn't go out on Tuesdays.

And the doctor is kind and well practiced and reaches out a hand to touch her mother's elbow, and Rosie notices how well kept his nails are, so smooth and round and clean. She wants fingernails like that. She wants to be as kind and good and gentle as this doctor; she wants to be able to touch her mother's elbow, to steer her home once this news, this unbearable, unendurable news, has settled, somehow, absorbed.

But it will be years, of course, before anything feels like home again, and Rosie knows this, right then she knows this, as she looks at the doctor's hands, at his shirt cuff buttoned in place. Nothing will ever be right in the way that it had been before. Nothing can be ordinary or blithe or routine again, even though it was just Tuesday, even though she has a music lesson in three hours, even though his keys are still in her jacket pocket.

She thinks about his fingerprints, all over them.

How she hopes he hadn't felt a thing, when he fell.

before

one

◖

Will realizes there is something about Rosie Winters the night he meets her at the bonfire.

When he tells her that his mother left.

They are sitting beside each other with the blaze lifting into the November darkness, part of a broken circle of sixth formers. Fingerless gloves, beer cans. Distant waves beyond the pines. He doesn't know Rosie, really, despite sharing a school and some friends, but tonight, they are talking. A little.

Small talk, at first. Insignificant. Until his friend Josh—her twin brother—makes a comment about their parents, and Rosie laughs, barely audible above the bonfire, and before he can think what he's doing he's told her he doesn't know his own mother. It is something he's never said out loud before. Navigated, usually, with a dip of the head, a passing of the moment. But he finds himself telling her, this girl, with her split ends and untamed eyebrows, and her pale, slender hands. That his mother walked out, years back, while he was watching cartoons before school.

She looks at him when he says it, the flames held in her eyes. There isn't sympathy or curiosity in her face; no frown or twitching mouth, reactions he might have expected, if he'd had time to think about it.

Where do you think she is, she asks him, after a moment.

He pauses. Looks at the sky, patched through the gaps in the trees. The smoke from the fire curls upward, and there are stars, with one larger, whiter, than the others. A planet perhaps, or a moon.

I don't know, he says to her. Anywhere.

And Rosie Winters repeats the word back at him, like she's really thinking about it. Like she's wondering what anywhere might look like.

It is early winter and the wind slices through the forest, but still they remain outside. It is better than being at home, warm yet uninterested in the television.

This, their skin turned blood orange in the firelight, is new.

It sets something burning.

They spend the night talking, their knees almost touching. Saying very little, though he has never known himself to be so attentive, so desperate for another sentence, so surprised by the words she chooses. People drift away in pairs, to touch one another behind the trees and fumble in the sand, or to seek out late-night noodles, chips in oil-stained paper. Only he, Rosie, Josh and two others remain. One of them gets out a guitar and strums, alongside the dying fire. Will watches the bark glowing red, the salt-and-pepper peel of the ash.

It is down to its embers when Rosie begins to sing.

Her brother asks her to, at first. Has to encourage her, then plead, until she concedes with a small tilt of the head.

The wind has dropped. The air, without the fire, is like glass, cold and still. And when she sings, it is a sound unlike anything Will has ever known. Choral, and pure.

They listen until the fire dies and their hands go numb, and then they all part ways. Will pulls his helmet on, clips it beneath his chin and kicks his motorbike into gear, thinking that it'll be a onetime, memorable night where he spoke to someone's sister and she sang a strange song and there was nothing more to it than that.

But her voice keeps him awake that night.

And again, the night after that.

He rises late at the weekend. Pulls on a hoodie, trying to ignore his simmering need for a cigarette as he pads down the stairs in his socks. Dave accosts him on the bottom step, pawing at his knees, and Will knuckles his wiry head before he skitters back to the lounge. The dog spends his days curled on his grandpa's old chair. Like he's waiting, Will thinks, for him to come home.

His grandmother is frying bacon in the kitchen. It smells of hot oil and broiling fat; of salt and pork and toast. She trills at him when he passes through the doorway.

Afternoon, she says.

It's only ten, he reasons.

And you're only eighteen once, lad, she says. No point wasting those cheekbones of yours hiding under the duvet.

I wasn't hiding, he says, and he heads for the kitchen table, pours himself a glass of water from the jug.

Amber's been to swim club already, his gran says, her back to him. *And* finished half her homework.

Good for Amber, Will says.

There is a short silence in which the bacon spits, the winter sun blanched on the walls. His sister is nowhere to be seen. Barricaded in her bedroom, he's sure, color-coding notes with gel pens, organizing her life with heart-shaped paper clips.

You look tired, his grandma says. He doesn't answer just yet, takes two triangles of toast from the table and moves to the back door.

I'm fine, he tells her, as he turns down the handle. She is saying something else as he slips outside and closes the door on her, makes his way to the garage.

He feels bad, for the briefest of moments.

Knows she'll seethe for a while, then bring him bacon, later, for lunch.

Inside, he flicks on the lone lightbulb hanging from the ceiling. It's a windowless space with a concrete floor, an aerial-pronged radio on his grandfather's old workbench. It smells of sawdust and long-ago diesel, and there's a toolbox in the corner, a pile of unused timber lying on the ground. It is the only place where things feel somewhat right to him, where everything has a purpose, and nobody talks or doubts or expects things.

His new motorcycle stands, stripped back and unfinished, just where he left it.

He lingers in the doorway and eats his toast dry, scanning the floor for the tools he needs. And then he gets to work, without switching on the radio. Just him and the bike. Repainting mudguards, tightening headlamps. Hardly thinking of the Rosie girl while he works.

Only a little.

*

Rosie stays late in the music room. She meant to just practice her scales, to duck out after fifteen minutes. But an hour goes by and then the cleaner is there, with the swirl of her mop on the tiles. Rosie hears the drag of the bucket, the slosh of the water, and says shit, quietly, to herself, before shuffling her sheet music away. She shuts off the light, lets the wooden door thud behind her. Calls goodnight to the cleaner, who is always kind; always smiles at her when they pass late in the halls, like they share some kind of secret.

Outside, it is already dark, and the air feels cleansed, the kind of cold that foreshadows snow. It is not a night for bare legs. For running under strip lighting.

But she promised her mother, and so she goes to the gym. Changes into her kit and sprints on the treadmill, but only for half the time she should, because she forgot, because the music took over, because she was wasting her time, yet again.

The sweat musses her fringe and burns her eyes, and she wonders, as her feet pound the belt, why she is always trying so hard. Who she is trying for. Why everything matters, all of the time.

She gets a stitch halfway and stops, has to lean on the side and catch her breath. She hopes that nobody notices. That nobody's looking at her. And afterward, she heaves her bag back onto her shoulder, zips up her jacket and begins the short walk home, her hair hanging damp at her ears. Stars scatter overhead, and cars move past her in a stream of headlights. She counts her steps, and recounts again. Avoiding the cracks in the pavement.

At home, she finds her twin brother lying on the sofa.

You're late, he says, without taking his eyes from the television.

Not by much, Rosie says, glancing at her wrist, only to see that it's bare. She's left her watch in the music room again. Can't write when she's on the clock.

Mum'll be mad, Josh says, and she pushes his head down with her palm, leaves the room before he can throw a cushion at her.

Her mother is not mad; only distracted. She is in the kitchen on the phone, and she holds a finger up at Rosie, her habitual way of saying hello while also saying wait, I'm doing something important, and you understand, don't you, you know how things are.

How was school, her mother asks when she hangs up. She doesn't make eye contact, instead turns around to open the oven.

Good, Rosie says.

And the gym?

Hard.

Well, good, her mother says. It's supposed to be.

Have I got time for a shower?

Her mother glances round, takes in her shining face and uncombed hair.

I should say so, she says. Can't be sweating like that at the dinner table, can you, darling?

Rosie looks back at her, for a second too long, then nods and heads for the stairs.

In the bathroom, she turns the water on so hot that it nearly scalds. Her skin turns a livid red, but she stands there and endures it. Counting, not her steps this time, but the seconds. Elongating the numbers, over and over, in this way that she does—like blood flow, unable to stop.

When she's out, she wraps her hair in a towel, grateful for the steam that hides her reflection in the mirror. Then she dries herself off and wanders to her room, where sheet music scatters her desk and books line her shelves, tattered and tea-stained from being handled so often, trailed over like old maps. Patti Smith. Oliver Sacks. The Sylvias, both Patterson and Plath.

After tugging on some clothes, she lowers her blackout blind. Stands, for a moment, with her hands on the windowsill. She is hungry, in every sense of the word. She thinks about walking out of the door, with her hair wet and the snow about to fall, straight into the Norfolk night.

How was school, her mother asks again, once they're all seated at the table. She has dished up squares of shop-bought lasagna, passes the plates to Rosie's father and brother, says careful, they're hot. Rosie takes her plate with two hands, notices that her own square is smaller than everyone else's.

Earth to Joshua? her mother nudges. How was your day?

Good, he says, through his pasta.

Rosie?

I handed in my history coursework, Rosie tells her. And finished a classics paper.

How'd that go?

Okay, I think.

Good girl.

There is a minute more of silence, knives squeaking on plates. Rosie takes a sip of water, and then her mother launches into a story from work, something about her client surrendering to his wife, not putting up the fight that she knows she could win for him. Again, nobody speaks. The kitchen clock ticks. White sauce oozes on their plates.

Maybe it's just too much, Rosie ventures.

Hmm?

For your client. Maybe it hurts, his marriage ending like this. And he just wants it, you know. Over with.

Her mother pours herself another glass of wine, spears a tomato with her fork.

Let's not presume to know his motivations, Rosemary, she says, after she has swallowed. Josh catches Rosie's eye, soundlessly asking her why she bothers, and she drops her gaze to the table. Her father is doing the crossword.

When her mother rises to clear, Josh scrapes his remaining lasagna onto Rosie's plate, and she finishes it, fast, before standing to help, knocking his shoulder with hers.

A sibling thing, or a twin thing.

She doesn't know the difference.

And it's as she's rinsing the salad bowl that a new melody starts up. Like early birdsong, those first, tentative notes that nobody is around to hear. She is barely listening as Josh mentions revising tomorrow with Will White, from his further maths class, because she's trying to hold the notes in her mind.

Repeating them, over and over, before they can fall away.

Marley rings her early the next morning.

Rosie is awake already, picks up on the second ring.

You're up, Marley says.

Couldn't sleep, she says. She wishes, for a moment, that her friend would ask her why. That someone would notice, or care.

I was thinking we could do something tonight, Marley says, instead. Rosie says that'd be nice, but she's got revision to do.

So? *I've* got revision to do. We could revise together, even. Imagine that.

Rosie turns over in bed. The morning light is pale through the curtains, like cloudy water dipped with paint.

You say that, she says, but then you'll put on a film and we'll end up doing nothing.

Inevitably, I guess, Marley agrees, and Rosie hears the smile in her voice, familiar and slightly taunting.

I could do with a break, though, she reasons, swapping her phone to her other hand. She has ink on her palms from her late-night songwriting, all crossings out and attempted riffs.

Good! says Marley. How about we do something this weekend, then? A Saturday night treat, or something equally tragic.

Why is that tragic?

Because we're seven*teen*, Rosie. We shouldn't need Saturdays as an excuse to see each other, or go out, or do something remotely exciting.

We go out! We went out the other night.

Yeah, and all I got out of it was a bag of chips and a snog that tasted of Tic Tacs.

Rosie snorts. She can hear her mother getting ready for work, the drone of the coffee machine downstairs.

Who'd you snog? she asks.

Never you mind, says Marley.

Fine. It'll be someone new next week, anyway.

Are you calling me easy, Rosemary Winters?

Would I ever?

I guess not. But only 'cause you're a vanilla virgin.

Good name for a nail polish.

It *is*, isn't it? And Marley laughs, her big, swooping laugh, so that Rosie has to pull back from the phone. This Saturday, then. I'll buy a mountain of popcorn and a packet of those old lady sweets you like.

Werther's are not old lady sweets.

And we can replay all the Leo scenes as many times as we want. Or the Patrick Swayze ones. I feel like we need some arousing pottery in our lives.

Marl!

What?

Arousing pottery?

Doesn't have to be pottery. Some dry humping to Solomon Burke. Tabletop sex to Berlioz.

I'm hanging up now.

Prude.

I'll see you Saturday.

Knew Berlioz would get you, Marley says.

Rosie thinks about what Marley said to her as she walks to school. Josh left early for basketball, so she is alone, her coat zipped to her chin against the cold. She is a virgin, and she is vanilla. She tries not to be. But she can't care enough to be more than what she is, which is, essentially, one of the good girls.

She has never had a boyfriend. She's kissed someone, or rather, was kissed, badly, her shoulders pinned against a bathroom door at a friend's house party. The handle bruised her coccyx, and the boy tasted of over-chewed gum.

She's never been drunk. Never snuck out. Never smoked a cigarette or lied to or even sworn in front of her parents, though she's not sure they'd notice, or mind.

But there is time for all of that, she reasons, as she steps off the curb to cross the road. Seventeen is just the start. She will work hard, she will do all that she is supposed to do, and her life will be good and right and whole, filled with music and poetry and wine and sex, and life-altering moments that last longer than three minutes, and don't leave her with bruises down her back.

That is her plan.

She has to cross the road once, twice, three times on her way to school, tapping her foot on the pavement until she can stop, and that is when the snow begins to fall. Lightly, at first, more of a fine rain. It clings to her sleeves like salt.

two

◖

Josh tells him he doesn't get it. They are both staring at their further maths textbooks, the snow swirling outside the classroom window.

They are the only two in class, the only two in their year who study this subject. They knew each other before, had shared a few lessons throughout school, but now, in their last year of sixth form, Will supposes they'd call each other friends. His other mates are more break-time acquaintances; they don't ask him questions, or seem to care, at all, about his life, which suits him just fine. But Josh is different.

What's your first choice, then, Josh had asked him, back in their first class.

First choice of what, he'd asked, and Josh had said uni, and so he'd had to explain that he wasn't going.

Josh had looked up from his worksheet at that.

Come on, he'd said, and Will had said come on what.

You're like, really smart.

Thanks.

Seriously. If you knuckled down, mate, you could get in anywhere you want.

And what if I don't want it? Will posed, and Josh had looked at him then with a crease at the bridge of his nose, like he didn't quite under-stand.

Now, though, they're both staring at a page of hyperbolic functions and hoping it will make some semblance of sense before the lesson is through. Their teacher, Mr. Brookman, has already left. He quite often uses their class as an excuse for a prolonged break in the staff room, and in Will's mind, this works both ways.

Let's just call it a day, Will says.

Josh leans back, tilts his chair onto two legs.

I can't, man. I need to get this before our mock exam.

Why, Will asks, as he sweeps his pens into his bag.

Why what?

Why do you need to get it for the mock? You only need to know it for the real thing, in the spring. You've got ages.

Mocks matter, Josh says, still tipped backward on his chair. For the provisional offers, and stuff.

Right, he says.

You're really not going to uni?

Nope.

What you gonna do instead?

Work, he says, hauling his bag onto his shoulder. Travel, maybe.

That's cool.

I'm not trying to be, Will says, because this is what people think about him, he knows, with his motorcycle and his school record and all that trouble he got in, years back. It was so long ago, now, but it's all anyone remembers. All they ever want to see.

You still coming over, later? Josh asks.

You still need me to?

Definitely, Josh says, letting his chair drop back onto all fours. I'm on

Crescent Gardens—you can park on the street. It's the white house with
the blue door.

Outside, Will makes his way through the courtyard, snowflakes landing
on his hair. The school looks like a chalk and charcoal drawing, shape-
less and smudged.

He doesn't give it much thought, the fact that he's heading to Josh's
house that night, to help him revise. And that he happens to be the
brother of the girl that he can't stop thinking about.

This isn't unusual, for him. He thinks of girls often. What is unusual
is the content of his thoughts; nothing about the soft, wet parts of her,
the weight of her thighs around his. Just her voice, and her eyes. How
intensely she listened, and held all that he had to say.

You're sure you can stay for dinner?

I'm sure.

You're sure you're sure? You've not just assumed?

Gran, Josh *said*, come for dinner.

You won't get hungry?

I doubt their cupboards are empty.

You can't eat like a horse round someone else's house, Amber pipes up
from the table. Like you do here.

She is swinging her school-socked feet, scribbling something in a notebook.

Thanks for the tip, Ambs.

It's rude, she adds, with a flourish of her fluff-topped pen.

Home by ten, his grandma says.

Might be ten thirty, he tells her. Depends how long Josh takes to get it.

Remind me who this Josh boy is, his grandma asks, following him out into the hall.

Will sighs as he shrugs on his jacket, pats down his pockets for his phone.

Josh Winters, he says. He's the other kid in my maths class.

Further maths, she corrects him.

Further maths. And he needs help with this module, so I said I'd tutor him, like I told you. He's a meat-eater, possibly a Gemini, and he doesn't smoke weed. I think his shoe size is a twelve, but I couldn't be sure. Oh, and he—

His grandmother cuts him off with a whip of her tea towel.

Home by ten thirty, then, wise guy, she says, and he says yeah yeah, grabs her car keys and shuts the front door behind him.

The house is a similar layout to his own. Semidetached but painted white, with a perfect lawn and potted olive trees saying things that his gran's front garden does not, with her gnomes and her overgrown grass.

There is no trace of Rosie when Will arrives. Upstairs, all the doors are closed, and he has no idea which room would be hers, so he puts her from his mind and turns to the logic of maths. Something familiar, and consistent, like an engine.

The night is long. Josh takes several hours to understand the system, to accurately answer four mock-exam questions in a row. They eat dinner in his room, at his large corner desk, when Josh pleads with his mother that they be excused—*we're almost there, Mum, please*—and it is close to ten when he sits back, rubbing his eyes, and says he's finally got it.

Took you long enough, Will says, and Josh flicks him, hard, on the arm.

It's confusing, Josh says.

I never said it wasn't.

S'all coming together, though, Josh says, and he sounds almost glee-ful as he leans back in his chair, stretches his arms over his head. He is tall and gangling, reminds Will of some kind of cartoon. Limbs too long for his body, like he still has some growing to do.

Gonna smash that exam, Josh says. Get into Cambridge, and boom.

What's boom?

I don't know, Josh says, and he laughs. Just boom. Just the way things go, you know?

I guess, Will says, though he doesn't know anything about how things are going to go. He plans for the next day, the next weekend. The next part he needs for his bike.

Thanks for coming, man, Josh says, after he's packed up his things. Can we do this again, maybe? You're better than old Brookman.

Not hard to be, says Will. He doesn't think Josh needs an answer, but he's looking at him, as if he's waiting. Not taking his eyes from his face.

You can come to the workshop after school, he suggests. I'm behind with my woodwork project, so I'm there sometimes. Wednesdays, mainly.

Maths, further maths, and woodwork, says Josh, ticking them off on his fingers. That's the weirdest combo of subjects.

Will shrugs. Not if you want to be a civil engineer, he reasons.

And do you?

God, no.

What *do* you want to do? Josh asks.

It's late, mate, Will says, because it's true, and because he has no de-sire to get into this. I'd better go.

Out on the landing, the walls are adorned with childhood photos; Josh in dungarees, Rosie picking up shells. One of her at the piano. Will feels strangely alert as he follows Josh down the stairs, aware that she is somewhere nearby. He wonders if he'll see her. If she'll say hi.

He wonders why he's wondering this.

Downstairs, all is quiet; just the murmur of the television from the lounge. But after he pulls on his shoes and tells Josh he'll see him tomorrow, he opens the front door and is greeted by a world of white. His gran's car is wedged against the curb, topped like a Christmas cake, the snow sifting down like sugar.

Whoa, says Josh, as they both squint out of the door. I guess you're not going anywhere.

Mrs. Winters is overly apologetic. Says she hadn't noticed how bad it was, that all the curtains had been closed. That she's *so sorry* he has to spend the night here. Will gets the sense that she's sorrier for herself than for him; her face is pinched, two spots of pink high on her cheeks. There is something feline about her, he thinks, as she fusses in the hallway. She is well kept and hard-edged and she looks at him with vague disapproval, like she knows something he doesn't.

They make him a bed on the sofa, and Mrs. Winters tells him to help himself to the filtered water in the fridge; her words imply that this is all he should help himself to, and he thanks her, before she heads upstairs.

Comfy? Josh asks, as he punches one of the cushions. He has given him a spare T-shirt, and Will tugs off his school shirt, pulls it on. Josh looks away while he does it, as if suddenly fascinated by the carpet.

All good, Will says.

Cool. Well. Night.

Josh stands there for a moment too long. Goes to say something else, seems to decide against it, and flicks off the light on his way out. Will hears him clump up the stairs, then pulls out his phone to see five missed calls.

Sorry, he says, as soon as his grandma picks up. I didn't know the snow was so bad.

You're staying, presumably?

Yeah. On their sofa.

Be on your best behavior, William.

I always am, Gran.

There is a silence. He looks at the glow of the streetlight, blurred through the slats of the blind.

You know what I mean, she says. No funny business.

Goodnight, Gran, he says, and he hits the end call button.

*

Rosie cannot sleep. She'd gone over some revision before bed and now it is whirling around her brain, snagging on names and facts that she cannot, must not, forget. She sits up after a full hour. Checks some things. Decides that her mouth is dry, that she needs a drink of water.

She pads down the stairs in the dark and jumps when she sees a boy sitting at their kitchen table. William White, the guy from the bonfire. The aloof, brooding boy from school she hadn't exchanged one word with prior to that night.

Sorry, she says, even though it is her house, and even though he was the one to startle her.

He raises his eyes, very slowly, from his phone, his face tinged blue in the light from the screen.

For what? he asks.

I didn't know you'd be in here, she says.

It's the snow. Your mum said I could stay.

I know that, she says. I knew you were here. I just. Forgot.

He raises his chin, as if all the better to look at her. She is keenly aware that her feet are bare. That her pajamas are a faded pink, and arguably much too young for her. But then she remembers that it is dark; that he will hardly be looking at her feet, or her clothes. Or at her, generally, at all.

I just came down for some water, she says, unable to keep the apology out of her voice.

There's filtered water in the fridge, he says.

My mum told you that, did she?

She did.

God knows why we can't drink water out the tap like everyone else.

Well, you could, he says.

She pauses at the fridge door and glances over at him. She can't work out, in the dark, whether he is smiling, but she thinks she can hear it in his voice. A slight teasing perhaps, which is new to her. Like him talking, all night, by the fire.

All right, she says. I will.

And so she goes to the tap and fills her glass and takes a mouthful, looking out of the window as she does it. The garden is lost beneath the snow. So pretty, she thinks. So perfect and untouched, for such a short while.

So? Will asks her.

So what?

The water. How is it?

Oh. She looks down into her glass. Entirely comparable.

He laughs at this, so quietly he could simply be breathing, and something floats up and through her.

She has thought of him once or twice since the other night. It was odd, to her, that he barely moved from beside her, and she was self-conscious about the way he kept looking at her, even when she looked away.

She's always thought of Will White as detached and standoffish, despite his popularity and long list of girlfriends. Gold-brown hair, gray, unreadable eyes. It's laughable, to her, that these sorts of people really exist, like in the films she and Marley spend their weekends watching. And yet here he is, looking at her again, in her kitchen.

Well, night, she says, and she turns in her naked feet and heads for the door.

Rosie, he says.

Her name in his mouth.

Yeah?

He has put his phone down, its screen still lit up where it rests on the table. It deepens the shadows on his face, the rings beneath his eyes.

I don't know what I was going to say, he says.

She tilts her head.

I wanted to say something, he corrects himself. But I don't know what.

Okay.

Sleep well, I guess.

I never sleep well, she tells him, because she thinks she should be honest, and because he's being strange, so perhaps she can be her strange, most honest self in return.

Me neither, he says. Not at other people's houses, anyway.

They look at each other across the kitchen, the light silvery soft with the snowfall. The fridge breathes its low, barely there sound.

Are you hungry? she asks.

Always, he says. He leans back in his chair, and for some reason at this moment she remembers that he is a smoker, and that he is undeniably attractive. Two reasons to end this conversation now, to leave him to his phone and his sleepless night. She has a mock exam in the morning. She needs to try to sleep. Her mother would not approve of the late hour or, indeed, of him.

She pours them both bowls of cereal.

They talk until the early hours of the morning. Rosie has turned on the light above the oven, and it bathes the kitchen in gold, the underfloor heating warming the tiles, the slipperless soles of her feet.

They eat cornflakes with cold milk and she watches him dribble a spoonful down his chin, and this makes him seem less intimidating, especially when he fails to notice. She tells him, eventually, with a small laugh, and he wipes it away with the back of his hand, says that's embarrassing, and when she asks him why he shrugs and grins, his canines pointed, sharp-looking.

He doesn't try small talk. Doesn't ask her about school or subjects or being a twin. He asks her, immediately, why she rarely sleeps, and this is what does it; this is what catches her, places him in her sphere in a way she wasn't ready for.

I just worry about things, she says. Sometimes.

What things, he asks, and she says stupid stuff, and he says surely not, if it's keeping you awake.

All normal things, she says. School. Grades. Life.

One and the same, right? he says, and she wonders if he's mocking her.

I told you it was stupid.

Did I say that?

She says nothing, lifts her spoon out of the milk.

We're taught to care so much about all of that, Will says. Like every decision we make will lead us down a particular path.

And you don't think that's true?

Nope. I think we have a path, but it doesn't change based on the decisions we make. It's a path that leads to the same place, anyway.

She sips the milk off her spoon. It tastes sweet from the cornflakes, reminds her of late-night study sessions and her primary school breakfast club, the years spent rising at 5 a.m. so her mother could get to work.

What do you mean, she asks.

What do you think I mean?

She lets his question hang in response to her own, sees his eyebrows rise, just slightly.

Dying, she says.

Right.

Will leans forward in his chair, as though it's no big deal, which she supposes it's not, when you're seventeen. When it's so far away, so implausible.

I figure we're all dying with every day, he says. So we might as well do what we want, before it happens.

He is looking at her as he speaks, and she drops her eyes to the table. There is a crescent of milk, from the bottom of her bowl. She dabs her finger into it, draws it out in a line.

That's kind of morbid, she says, and he shrugs, says it's true.

So what do you want to do, then? she asks him. She doesn't add *before you die*, though she thinks about it.

Guess I'll figure that out, Will says.

Rosie nods, her fingertip wet from the milk.

And what do you want, Rosie Winters?

She looks back at him. He is smiling, again, but barely. The edges of his mouth are lifted, his eyes soft, lamp-like, in the semidark. The use of her surname seems either aggressive or affectionate; she cannot quite work out which.

I want all the things you said I shouldn't, she says. To do well at school. To get good grades, have a good life. All of that.

You think those things will get you a good life? Will asks.

I think they'll help me *get* to the things that will, she says.

He holds her eyes. Doesn't argue, or ask her about it again.

She lowers her spoon, watches the milk ripple.

It is half past three in the morning when she says God, it's late, and Will follows her gaze to the microwave clock and says that technically, it's early.

I should go, she says, rising out of her chair. She rinses their bowls under the tap, and Will watches her as she does it. Her hair is dark and mane-like, falling just beyond her shoulders. He can see her ankles, so pale beneath her pajama legs.

He doesn't want to be interested. Doesn't have the time or the inclination for that, not if she's going to university. Not if she's Josh's sister. Not if she'll be too desirable, which he's sensing, already, that she would be.

That song you sang, he says to her, raising his voice so she can hear him over the running water.

What about it, she says. She shuts off the tap, turns the bowls upside down to drain. He wants to tell her it was beautiful. That her voice, that she, is beautiful. But it is so far removed from what he would ordinarily say, so daring, even, to think.

I can't get it out of my head, he says.

Like an earworm, she says. She has turned her back on the sink, is leaning against the counter. Looking at him, with those eyes.

What's an earworm?

When you get a song stuck in your head and it goes round and round.
I get it sometimes, when I can't sleep. Like my brain's caught on a loop.

Will considers this. Tells her it's nicer than that.

She half smiles at him then, all lips and no teeth. He wonders what
she would say if he got out of his chair now, and pressed his own mouth
to hers.

I'm going to bed, she tells him.

Night, then, he says.

She doesn't move. He doesn't, either.

It's been nice talking to you, he says.

So formal, she says, still with that half smile, and then she leaves him,
her footsteps light on the stairs. He sits there awhile, in the honeyed glow
from the oven. So many hours to go until sunrise.

He pretends to be asleep when Josh jumps on his legs in the morning.

Rise and shine, he says, bashing on his side with a fist. Will grumbles,
though he's glad it's daytime, glad he can get up and source some caffeine and maybe speak to Rosie again.

Breakfast? Josh offers.

Is the snow gone?

Better than that, he says. It's a snow day, mate.

Really?

Really! No school. Praise the Lord, or whatever deity you may or may
not worship.

I don't know how you don't get shoved into walls more often, Will
says, sitting up and massaging his temples with one hand. The room tilts
with his lack of sleep, with the too-bright-white of the wallpaper.

Just lucky, I guess, Josh says. *And* endearing.

That's one word for it, Will says, and groans as he gets elbowed in the ribs.

Pancakes, Josh declares. You like pancakes?

I guess.

You know what I like about you, Will, Josh says, as he springs up from the sofa. Your boundless enthusiasm.

Will gives him the finger, still rubbing his head. But when he looks around, Josh is gone, and his twin sister is standing in the doorway. Her hair is loose past her shoulders, and she's cradling a mug in her hands.

I thought you might want some coffee?

Christ yes, he says, and he stands and takes it from her, burns his tongue when he drinks. He is suddenly conscious of his bed hair. Crumbs of cereal stick in the craters of his teeth, and he can taste the tar of his breath.

I didn't know if you'd want milk?

Black is fine, thanks.

Did you get any sleep? she asks. He wonders if that's a loaded question, whether she's asking if he was lying awake, thinking of her.

In the end, he says.

A loaded answer.

Rosie crosses her arms like she's cold, though he heard the radiators clunk on before dawn, the water banging in the pipes. She has blue eyes, he sees now. Full, dark eyebrows that match the wildness of her hair. She opens her mouth to say something just as Josh sticks his head out of the kitchen.

Rosie, he says. There's no butter.

Use oil then, she says.

Where's that? The fridge?

She shakes her head, says it's in the cupboard, and Will looks at the crease of love in her face as she turns toward her twin.

He has never looked at Amber that way, not even when they're getting along. He holds the coffee in his mouth before swallowing, and it's bitter, still too hot.

D'you want to go for a walk, he asks her, before he even decides to say it.

Rosie looks back round at him.

Now? she says.

Or after breakfast, maybe.

What is happening, he asks himself, as he watches her question the same thing. Her eyebrows pleat together and she sucks in her bottom lip. Just for a moment, before her face returns to neutral.

Maybe, she says.

Then she walks into the kitchen, leaves him standing alone with his rumpled bed covers, in his not-slept-in T-shirt and boxers. He listens to them talking, the clank of pans, roll of drawers. It is the sound of routine, familiarity. He has distanced himself from these things in his own house, spends most of his time in the garage.

When he joins them, dressed, Rosie is mixing batter, Josh peering in cupboards and foraging for honey and syrup.

Every snow day should start with a sugar hit, Josh says, as he clunks the condiments down on the table. Rosie is quiet as she ladles the batter into the pan.

This one stresses about snow days, Josh says, nodding over at her.

I'm not stressing, Rosie says.

She had a history mock today, he tells Will. And she'd rather be in school, taking it, than sitting here eating pancakes with us.

No, I wouldn't, she says, and she cranks the heat up high. It's just more days to forget everything, is all.

They watch her flip the first pancake onto its uncooked side. The kitchen smells of vegetable oil and yolk, the windows steamed up with the heat. Will offers to help, because it feels wrong letting her cook for them both, and to his surprise she steps aside. He ladles and flips while she slices strawberries from the fridge, fills a small bowl with a mound of sugar. He tries not to notice as she dips a strawberry into it, sucks the grains off with her mouth.

*

The boys head out to do whatever it is that boys do in the snow. Throw packed ice at each other, no doubt, get their jeans soaked, stay out until their fingers turn numb and they can't put their keys in the door.

She is trying to revise. Trying to embed historical facts into her mind, and when it fails, she tries to practice her scales, but they come smoothly, and she is bored within the hour. She thinks back to breakfast, when she is sure that Will kept trying to catch her eye, and in the light of day, she decides that she doesn't understand why. She isn't interesting, and nor can he be interested. Everything felt different in the dark, the room hushed with the snowfall outside. Their feet almost touching under the table.

He'd told her he had a dog named Dave.

That he lived with his grandmother.

They talked about death and guitars and travel plans, Will's fear of rats, her aversion to cotton wool. Not once did he mention his motorbike or his suspension from school, nor did she feel she could ask him about it.

The part she's replaying, though, the part that's distracting her now, is that he told her he couldn't get her song out of his head.

Her song. One she wrote, herself, though there's no way he would have known that.

She catches up to them on the playing field. Children dressed in padded onesies drag sleds to the hillock beyond the playground, ridged footprints trailing from their wellies.

They are by the swings. Will is sitting on one, his legs stretched out in front of him. His boots are black leather, like his jacket, and his hair is laced with snow. She is this close to him, can see how it looks like dew, when Josh lobs a snowball at her head.

You came! he says, as it explodes in a puff. He bounds over from his place by the railings, his ears shrimp-pink from the cold.

Just for a bit, she says, dusting the snow off her hair. I needed a break.

Her brother takes her wrists in his hands then, and his gloves are moist, reptilian; the palms dotted with tiny grip pads. Rosie forgot her own gloves, and the air prickles her skin.

That's great, Josh says, and he squeezes, once, to show her he knows how hard it is for her to choose fun, to choose snow, over study. To ease up, like he's so often asking her to. She feels suddenly hot under her coat, wondering what he would say if he knew she had not come out for him or for herself, but for William White, and that she is not even sure why.

They lean on the railings and talk, a little. Watching the kids play, a dog on the field chasing a ball. Josh drops onto his back and makes a snow angel while Will watches from his swing, and Rosie watches Will watching him. Fixing her gaze beyond his head, as though she's looking at the trees.

I love snow, Josh says, when he stops moving.

Will catches her eye, at this, and they share something in that look. Appreciation, she thinks, or affection, for the unapologetic candor—the innocence, even—of her seventeen-year-old twin.

I don't, says Rosie.

Go home, then, Josh says, and for this, she throws her own snowball at him.

Good shot, says Will, and Rosie laughs.

They keep talking, the three of them, for almost an hour. Josh recalls a snowman they made when they were younger, how they hadn't understood it would melt. You cried, he tells Rosie. I think that was you, she says, and it is Will's turn to laugh, though he shares no memories of his own.

When the conversation has slowed, Rosie tells them her hands are frozen.

Put them in your pockets, then, Josh suggests. The snow has begun to glitter in the pale sun, emerging now, from behind the clouds.

I think I'll just head home, she says.

I'll come, says Will, and their eyes meet, briefly, as Josh tells them they're no fun.

They walk side by side across the grass-pocked snow. The trees lining the field are black and bone-like, the snow already gone from their branches.

Never lasts, says Rosie, as they step through the gate and onto the road, now speckled with gritting salt.

Thank God, Will says. The roads would be a nightmare.

And school would stay shut, she says.

Slush, on the verge. More grit beneath their shoes.

I've never met anyone who loves school like you, Will says. Her cheeks flush at this, but he doesn't sound troubled, or even amused. She is grateful they aren't seated at a table, this time; that he is not able to look at her face.

I don't, really, she says. I just like having a plan.

Will is quiet. They approach a bend in the road and have to cross, so that they're not caught by an oncoming car. They cross back, without discussion. There is a song of snow dripping off the trees, sporadic and out of time, like rain.

That's interesting to me, Will says to her.

Well. That's condescending.

He looks at her then, a half glance, and she keeps her eyes straight ahead.

I didn't mean it to be, he says. The snow still drips and a car drives past, flecking them with sleet.

I just meant that it's good, he says. That you're so. I don't know.

Naïve? she asks him, and he shakes his head.

Assured, he says.

Josh is trailing behind them some distance away. She has the strange, near irrepressible urge to take Will's hand, just to see what he would do, to see if she's reading this thing right, which surely, she isn't. But she can't test the idea, not with her brother in full view behind them.

She keeps walking, beside him. Puts her hands in her pockets.

It's as they near the corner of her street that a truck soaks them both with road water. It is icy cold, a shock, and Will lets out a roar at the same time that Rosie gasps, and they turn to each other with wide and furious eyes, and then they begin to laugh.

Twat, Will says, as Rosie wipes her face. Her fingers turned numb long ago, and the water is somehow colder, painful, even, as she brushes it away.

God, my hands hurt, she says, and Will tells her to put them under her armpits, and she says what? And it is then that Will stops walking and unzips his jacket and takes her hands in his own, placing them under his arms within the folds of his coat.

Cars drive past. Snow shifts underfoot. Will moves closer so that Rosie's palms are compressed, his hands still closed over hers. His shirt is damp, from the truck water or a light layer of sweat, she does not know. She looks up at him and observes, for the first time, the length of his eyelashes. They are longer than hers.

Yours are cold, too, she says, because her heart is stalled and there is nothing else to say, and everything is melting and frozen, all at once.

This'll help, says Will.

Her hands hurt, even more, as the blood rushes back.

She can feel the pulse of it in her fingertips.

On his skin.

three

◖

When Will stops the car in his driveway he stays seated, staring beyond the dashboard, thinking. Specifically, about the curve of Rosie's ankles, and the way she ate with her spoon. He shakes his head, laughs, a little, at the madness of it. This girl, with her perfect grades and elven ears, whom he had never even noticed before the bonfire. He rubs his eyes, then watches the snow patter off the trees. He decides that he needs some sleep, and is just about to get out of the car when his phone rings. It is Darcy, which surprises him. They haven't spoken in weeks.

William White, she says, as though he was the one to call her.

Darcy, he says. Hey.

What you doing, she asks him.

Not a lot.

I figured. Being a snow day and all.

Yeah.

So.

So.

You wanna come over? My mum's out.

He thinks on this for all of two seconds, and then tells her that actually, he can't.

Why not? she asks. Her fury is stiff and immediate, and he sighs, not caring that she'll hear it.

I just can't, Darce. I'm knackered.

Why, she asks, again. Who've you been with?

I was at a friend's house all night, he says. Doing maths.

She makes a disbelieving noise, something scornful deep in her throat, and he wonders, fleetingly, why everyone expects the worst of him, when he is only ever telling the truth.

Fuck you, Will, she says.

Well, sure. That is what you wanted, isn't it, he asks.

What?

To fuck me. That's the only reason you called.

She hangs up on him then, and he gets out of the car, his boots sloshing through the snow as it thaws.

He sleeps through the afternoon, wakes to the sound of the ignition clicking, repeatedly, on the oven. He promised his gran months ago that he'd try to fix it. He thinks it must have something to do with the damp, because the noise always stops come the spring.

He hauls himself out of bed, takes a shower, then heads down to the kitchen where his grandmother is ladling soup into bowls, his sister bent over her homework.

He lives, his gran says, as he sits down and passes round cutlery. They keep a basket of it in the center of the table, spoons with patterned handles, leaves twirling around the knives and forks.

I said hi when I got in, he reminds her.

You're right, she says. You are the king of monosyllables.

What's monosyl-bubbles, asks Amber, without looking up.

Syllables, Will says. It means the king of everything.

No it doesn't.

How was your night, his grandma asks, placing the bowls on the table. She's ground pepper onto his, crumbled blue cheese across its surface.

Didn't sleep, he says. But Josh got the gist of the maths, so that's good.

What did you eat, she asks, because this is always her question, no matter where he's been or who he's been with. When she collected him from the police station that time, they'd sat silently in the car for nine long, difficult minutes, and then she'd asked if he'd had dinner.

Some aubergine thing, he says. I dunno, we ate in his room.

In his room? Amber asks.

Put your pen down, Amber, his grandma says. Eat your dinner, now.

Why can't I eat in *my* room?

Because you need to keep your old grandmother company, that's why. So it was okay? Uneventful?

It was fine, Will says.

He thinks of Rosie as he says this, as he dips his spoon into the red soup.

Maybe you could think about tutoring, his grandmother ventures. Will takes another mouthful, careful to avoid his tongue, still raw from that morning's coffee. The coffee that Rosie had made. Held out to him, with her pebble-soft hands.

I don't need to tutor, he says. I've got the garage.

It's not a long-term plan, though, is it?

Not this again, Gran.

Fine, fine. It was just a thought.

I'm going to be a lawyer, Amber says. Miss Brown says I'd make a good one.

I'm sure you would, his gran says.

Lawyers are dishonest, Will tells her. You don't want to be one of those.

Now why would you tell her that?

Because it's true.

Not all lawyers are dishonest, Willyum.

His gran says his name like this, clipped to two syllables, when she's tense or overly tired. On the day of his grandpa's death, he is Willyum. His mother's birthday, too. At every parents' evening, every school report day, Willyum with a sigh, and a tight mouth.

I could be a dentist, Amber says.

Much better, Will agrees, not even bothering to understand the jump. But no need to decide right now, Ambs.

I've got to, she says.

How come?

For my journal, she says. It's got a whole chapter about hopes and dreams, and what I want to be when I grow up. I've been saving my gold pens for it.

He looks at her over his bowl.

You're only ten, he says.

And you could do with taking a leaf out of her book, his gran says.

It's a journal, Amber says. Not a book.

Will stifles a grin, and his grandmother laughs, a soft sound, like cooing pigeons, and then cuts them all some bread.

*

Rosie lies beside Marley on her friend's bedroom floor, a scene they've watched dozens of times flitting across the television. They untwist sweet wrappers and crunch on toffee popcorn, and her teeth feel slick with sugar.

As they watch Jack gazing at Rose on the top deck, Rosie thinks about telling Marley about William White and their encounter in her kitchen.

And then the thing that happened, the very next day, where he took her hands inside his own.

And then what, Marley would ask, a sweet halfway to her mouth.

And then . . . nothing.

He had let go, said, better? and Rosie had nodded, and they had walked back to the house, the snow softened to sleet on the pavement. Josh had caught up to them, thanked him, again, for the maths. And then Will had driven home.

On the screen, Leo is still staring, and Rosie takes another sweet, holds it beneath her tongue.

There is nothing interesting to tell, she decides, about her midnight meeting with a boy she barely knows, and a moment where he warmed her hands, because he took pity on her, was perhaps playing a game she had no interest in playing.

What is surprising, though, is how she keeps picturing him while she sits here, with her knees drawn up, her friend rustling through the popcorn beside her.

She thinks about the gray of his eyes.

Imagines him pressing her against her kitchen wall, his face, so close, to hers.

That's interesting, she thinks, as Marley yawns. That, in itself, is new.

I love this bit, her friend says, shuffling upright as Rose clatters along the deck in her blood-red, glittering dress. I wish our lives were that dramatic.

Why on earth would you want that?

It's just . . . me and you, Rosie. We're such *bores*. I can't wait until life is more than orchestra practice and good grades, you know?

Rosie looks back at the film, because she does know, but it feels like there might be something more, already, for her. Something that's changed.

She unwraps another sweet, even though she feels sick and thirsty and vaguely worried that she might be rotting her teeth.

When she gets home, full of sugar yet starved, Rosie makes herself some toast. She warms some beans in the microwave, watching the dish rotate, slow and hypnotic, through the glass.

Lyrics come to her then, about the world turning as one, and she wonders if she's stolen them from somewhere or if they are all her own. She scribbles them down on the notepad by the fridge, folds the page into her pocket. Just in case.

Here she is, Josh says, padding through the door as the microwave pings.

Here I am, she says.

How's Marley?

Good, she says. She thinks we're boring.

Who? Me and you?

No, me and her.

Well. That I'd probably agree with.

Rosie rolls her eyes as her brother leans against the fridge, watching as she pours the beans onto her part-burned toast.

Mum's got a migraine, he says.

Again?

Yeah. There's a lot on her plate, what with Josie's maternity leave.

I guess. She has seemed a bit . . . you know.

Tense.

On edge.

Terrifying?

They share a quiet laugh and she carries her plate to the table, picks up her fork as Josh settles himself opposite her. He takes an orange from the fruit bowl and rolls it between his hands, as if trying to decide whether he's in the mood to eat it.

She'll get through it, Rosie says, as she cuts her toast in two.

Super-lawyer.

Woman of steel.

Steely-edged Samantha, Josh says, and he finally splits the skin of the orange. Steely, for sure. Her and Dad seem so miserable these days, don't they? Her especially.

They don't seem any different to me, Rosie says.

Then that's *really* sad, Josh says. He holds a segment up to the kitchen light. So many pips, he says.

They're fine, Rosie tells him.

The pips?

No, our parents. Christmas will be a nice reset. Like always.

Ah, Christmas, Josh says, and there is a dreamlike note to his voice. I *love* Christmas.

I know, Rosie says, with another eye roll. Christmas, and snow, and good cheer.

And oranges, he says, tilting the one in his hand toward her, as though raising a toast.

She shakes her head, scoops more beans into her mouth. It is warm in the kitchen, and the wind clatters outside the window, throws a handful of raindrops against the glass. She is debating, as she chews, whether there is a way she can work Will into the conversation, but before she can even form the words her brother does it first.

Think I might actually pass further maths now, he says.

Oh yeah?

Thanks to Will.

That's great, she says. She keeps the beans in her mouth for a few bites too long, is struggling, it seems, to swallow. Her brother is watching her.

Seems to misread her hesitancy—her desire to seem uninterested—as disapproval.

He's not like everyone says, Josh tells her.

No? she says, keeping her eyes on her plate. Smear of bean juice, scatter of crumbs.

I know he's got a bad rep, Josh says. With his bike, and his bunking off, and all that. But he's all right. He's smart, and he's decent, I think.

Well, good, she says.

What did you guys talk about, on the walk home?

Hm?

You and Will? What did he say to you?

Nothing, really, she says, and her stomach drops as she says it, because she realizes that it's true. Josh is silent for a while, stares her down. He's abandoned half his orange.

Nothing?

He's a man of few words, she says, and he laughs at that, says yeah, he is. He reaches over for a crust she's left on her plate.

She looks back at him, her brother. She knows his face better than her own, grew beside him before they both existed. They've spoken about that, before, when they used to make forts out of duvet covers or camp beneath their bunk beds, torches on, blankets piled around them like sandbags. At what point they became human. Were they twins before then? Or only when they developed brains, or hearts?

It's a twin thing, Josh would say, whenever they knew what the other was thinking. But about this, Rosie has never been sure. She knows other twins who seem like ordinary siblings, and it is not ordinary to get a cramp when your brother gets injured on the basketball court, or to wake in the night when his breathing changes. Sometimes she'll stir, for seemingly no reason, and know that he's awake, too, on the other side of her wall.

I think you'd like him, Josh says to her, now.

Who says I don't already, she says, and she lets the sentence hang between them, waits for her twin to catch it, to understand.

He doesn't.

Want one? is all he asks, holding out an orange segment toward her, and she takes it. Spits the pips from her lips to her plate.

*

Will is running.

He has been running every other day for the past four years, ever since his break from school, ever since he was told to find a way to channel his anger. He had never thought of himself as an angry person; had not once raised his voice, never punched a wall, lost his temper with a teacher or on the sports field. But a middle-aged expert with a pine-paneled office asked him some questions after it all happened, noted things down, and told his grandma with certainty that anger was indeed the problem.

With solutions, he had said, the S whistling through the gap in his teeth. And running was the only solution, it seemed, that Will could get on board with.

It isn't easy, because of the cigarettes. He's cut down now, barely ever touches them these days, but the damage is done, already, at eighteen.

Despite that, he runs for hours. He does not track his speed or his distance. He doesn't check his watch or try to prolong his stamina. He just runs. Without music, because he likes to hear the blood pounding in his ears. The gush of the sea, and the gulls.

He runs until he cannot. Until his side sears and his knees are screaming, and he thinks, okay, enough.

Today, he is running along the beach. He isn't cold, though it is December; his skin mottled red with effort, his T-shirt patched with sweat. He passes the beach huts, the sandbank with two basking seals. The lighthouse, once white and weather-beaten, at the very edge of the wood.

When he gets home, he showers in cold water to ease his muscles, towels off his hair, pads through to his bedroom and drops, half damp, onto his bed. He stares at the ceiling, at the outlines of his old glow-in-the-dark stars. He'd torn them down when he was seven, when he'd decided he was too old for such things.

Too old for stars.

Too old for school.

Too old, already, for all of it.

And as he lies there, that feeling creeps into his chest, something he gets from time to time. A slight tightening, like a valve shrinking shut. It hurts, a little, but it's better than what came before. The slicing urge to react.

Will rubs his heart absently now, distracts himself with thoughts of Rosie's voice. He can hear his grandmother moving downstairs, the click-click-click of the oven. He closes his eyes, starts to hum what he can remember of the bonfire song.

Stops, because he feels like he's ruining it.

When the bell rings and the students pour out of the classrooms, all loud voices and hitched-up skirts and blazer sleeves rolled to elbows, Will wades against the tide. He does not head for the exit, but takes a chance, and makes for her locker.

She is there with her curly-haired friend. Rosie is listening to whatever she is saying, and then breaks into a laugh, lifting her head so her neck is stretched to the light. An abrupt, vampiric desire pulses through him, and he wonders, again, what it is about this ordinary, soft-skinned girl.

Hey, he says, when he is beside her. She looks up at him at the same time as her friend; four eyes rising to his face.

Hello, she says, and she sounds wary. He has never spoken to her at school before. He has never spoken to her friend, either, and some weird social etiquette kicks in as he realizes this, the knowledge that girls care about this sort of thing.

Hi, he says, leaning around Rosie and raising his hand.

The friend just stares at him, then seems to remember herself. She says hi back.

I'm Will, he says, and she says yes, she knows, and doesn't offer her own name in return. I tried, he thinks, before shifting his gaze back to Rosie.

You walking home? he asks her.

Yes, she says, slowly, as though it's a trick question. One of her hands is resting on her locker door, the other inside, stacking her books. He watches her withdraw and push the door shut, latching the padlock in place.

I'll walk with you, he says.

You live on the other side of town, she says.

Yeah, but I have to pick something up.

The lie is smooth, easy. He wants it to be obvious.

Rosie says nothing. She looks at her friend, whose eyes are wide, and some charged, silent exchange occurs between them. Will watches it happen, and waits. More kids skitter behind them, shoes scuffing the linoleum floor.

Rosie doesn't give him an answer, exactly. But she tells her friend— Marley, she calls her, and Will makes a mental note—that she'll see her tomorrow, and Marley tips her chin in acknowledgment, watches them as they walk away, heading for the open doors.

They are out of school and in the teachers' car park when Will pulls his bag higher onto his shoulder and tells her he's not heading her way, after all.

Oh? Rosie looks at him sideways.

I'll be at the lighthouse, later, he says. I run on Monday nights. It's on my route.

Okay.

I'll be running past around half four, I think? If I'm not crazy slow.

Okay, she says again.

Just letting you know, he says. It's a nice spot. The sun kind of lingers there, over the sea. You'd like it.

What are you asking me, Will, she says, and that pulse goes through him again, at her honesty, her straightforwardness. He has never known a girl like her. He thought girls liked mystery and unspoken invitations; long brooding pauses and veiled suggestions.

I'm asking if you'll meet me at the lighthouse, he says.

She stops walking, at that. Younger students fork past them, one boy with his tie round his head, swinging his satchel like a lasso.

Why, she asks.

He looks at her then. Into those eyes of hers, so inkwell blue. And he decides to opt for the truth, too.

I'm not sure, he says. If I'm honest.

And this, it seems, makes sense to her.

I'll try, she says, as noncommittal as when she said maybe, before. But he'll take it; is used to it, in fact, from the days when he would see his mother. When he was young and hopeful and looked forward to things; when he had stars stuck to his bedroom ceiling.

Later, the lighthouse is waiting, but Rosie is not. A mellow light glows above the horizon, the sea black and still as iron.

Will leans against the whitewashed wall, catching his breath. It's a derelict building these days, a tourist attraction used simply as a marker on the survey maps. Disused churches are called redundant, he knows, some useless snippet he's carried all these years. He wonders whether there's a word for disused lighthouses. Vacant, or elapsed. Abandoned.

He stops stretching and breathes in the sea air. The surf rolls and breaks, white-tipped and patient. His hair is damp with sweat, and he is beginning to feel cold. He will give it another ten minutes and then he will jog home, as though nothing has happened.

Which, he realizes, would be true.

But then she is there. Zipped up in her coat, a beanie hat pulled low to her eyes. She is wearing gloves today. Fingerless, and sequined.

Hey, he says, and he sounds a little wild, even to his own ears—eager and surprised and a tenor too loud.

Hey yourself, she says.

She looks at him and he looks at her and he realizes he has no plan. The sun is setting, which was all he expected. It glimmers like gold leaf on the dark water.

I don't know why I asked you here, he says.

And I don't know why I came, she says back. He tries smiling at her then, and she returns it. Two lines grooved, at the side of her mouth.

It is beautiful, though, Rosie says, and she looks outward at the view. The sunset is spilled and soft. Waves rolling in, and out, and in again.

It is, says Will. He doesn't look at the sea as he says it, and her cheeks turn pink, her eyes flicking back to him before they dart away. The wind whistles around the lighthouse walls.

Aren't you freezing? she asks, finally, nodding at his pinpricked arms.

No, he says, and it is the truth; his whole body feels alight. I mean, I will be soon, he reasons. But not yet.

So, she says.

So.

This is weird, she says.

Good weird, though?

Good weird, she agrees.

He asks her if she's hungry, but she shakes her head, tells him she wants to watch the sea. She sits cross-legged on the ground so he follows suit, sliding down to a sitting position, his back pressed against the lighthouse. They watch the dusk turn from rose to black, so gradually that they barely notice.

Josh says he'll pass his exam now, Rosie says. Thanks to you.

I don't really want to talk about Josh, Will says.

Why not?

Because I spend at least an hour a day with the guy.

Well, what shall we talk about, then?

You tell me, he says. What's in your head?

They're sitting farther apart than when they were beside the bonfire, and he can't see her face, even in profile; her hat is too low, and she has angled her chin toward the forest. He can only see the curve of her ear beneath her hat. A thread of her dark hair.

You care what's in my head? she asks, after a moment.

Yeah, he says. I do.

She says nothing for a while. The sea breathes against the stones, and a gull takes flight from the sand.

Do you talk like this to all your girls? she asks, when the seagull has gone from view.

Who?

You know, the Ashleighs and the Keiras and the Darcys.

So she knows about them, he thinks, and something sinks in him, the pain in his chest a sudden stone. But then he realizes that this surely means something. That she had to notice, or care.

I don't talk to any of those girls, he tells her.

Sure you do. You took Darcy to the winter dance last year.

She dragged me, actually.

Well, you can't have sat in silence all night.

More or less, he says. And then, before he can think not to, he tells her that being with Darcy doesn't exactly require a lot of talking.

Oh.

Yeah.

Rosie makes a small noise, like she understands and doesn't mind. A light *mm*, as if he's simply told her what day it is. He definitely feels cold now. Can't feel his toes.

But no, he says.

No what?

Can we stop answering questions with questions?

If you stop being so cryptic, then yes.

He hasn't felt this upward tilt before; as if everything inside him, the soles of his feet, his diaphragm and his deltoids, are being lifted toward the sky.

No, I don't talk like this to any of those girls.

Oh.

This, he comes to realize, is one of her recurrent words. This girl with that voice, and all of her ohs and maybes.

I had to lie to my parents to come here, Rosie tells him. I don't really go out for no reason, so I had to come up with something.

What did you say?

That I was going to borrow a book from a friend.

Original.

I thought so. Believable, too.

I figured, Will says.

Did you, though, Rosie says, and she shifts to look at him, and it is dark now, the sun dissolved, the clouds an oil spill above their heads. Do you

really get that? That I like books and school, and music, and not cool music, either—I play the flute and the guitar and the piano. The recorder,
too. Full disclosure. And I really, really want to go to music school but I'll
probably end up doing history and I'm looking at Oxbridge and I have no
time, really, for any of this. For seeing someone. If that's what this is.

She takes a breath, and again, he is astonished by her.

Why are you going to do history if you want to do music, he asks, after
a moment. The wind blows in from the sea, lifts his hair, and hers, from
beneath her hat.

That's what you got from all that I said?

Aha, he says. Is that a question for a question?

She laughs then, and it is like the trail behind a firework; it sparkles
and fades, the silence that follows left crackling.

Fine, she says. I just thought I should warn you.

Consider me warned, Will says.

She uncrosses her legs, puts her feet out in front of her. Her hiking
boots look clean and unhiked-in, and he almost asks her what book she
borrowed, until he remembers it was a lie she had told. For him.

He walks her home when the cold gets too much; when the dark has sunk
into their bones. The cobbles shine in the streetlights, restaurant windows
misted up from the inside. They pass the local chip shop, and it smells of
skinned potatoes and old oil, the queue winding out of the doorway.

Next time we'll get chips, Will says.

And you'll wear a coat, Rosie says.

And I will wear a coat.

Not your biker jacket, though. A proper coat.

What's wrong with my biker jacket?

It doesn't look warm.

So? I'll be the one wearing it.

But I won't relax if you're cold, Rosie says. I'll just keep thinking about it, and it'll be on your mind, too, how cold you are. And it might make you want to go home.

He pauses, at this, for just a few footsteps.

I'm coatless now, aren't I? he says.

Yep. And here we are, heading home.

Will cannot respond to that. He is not sure what is going on between them; neither of them has explicitly said. There has been no kissing, no touching; no baring of souls or skin. They just sat with their backs against the lighthouse and talked, sometimes falling silent, before they would speak again.

Something passes between them, now. The hairs stand like needles down his arms, the sweat blown dry down his back.

He thinks about taking her hand. Almost does.

Then, at that exact moment, Rosie slips her hands into her coat pockets.

It's not practical, she says.

What, my biker jacket?

No, she says, not that. What we were saying earlier, about studying music. I did think about it, got an application for music school, even. But in the end I thought I should do something more transferable.

Will thinks that sounds like parent-speak, but decides not to say so. They stay quiet as they turn off the high street and begin the slight incline toward the ring road, the shops and pubs giving way to cottages with flint walls, televisions flickering through net curtains. Lives, shadowed, through the windows. Plant pots. Photo frames. Figures, moving, like cut-outs.

I always wonder what people do this time of night, Rosie says.

What d'you mean?

Well, it's a weird time, isn't it? Just before dinner. After school, or work. It's like a period of non-time, where you can't do anything real.

Real?

You know. Important stuff.

What's your important stuff?

Gosh, you're nosy.

Will laughs, because nobody has ever called him that before. He wonders if it's like the anger; if it's something that lies dormant, rearing its head only when life calls for it. When a girl with thin hands asks where you think your mother might be, and looks you in the eye when she talks.

Singing. And writing, she says.

Oh yeah? What d'you write?

Songs, mostly. And poems.

He nods. There is festoon lighting strung above them, and the bulbs chime in the wind, knocking together like spoons in a drawer. They feel dangerous, to him, these sorts of conversations. Like she'll soon realize he has scars and anger issues and a history of unspeakable things.

What's yours? she asks him.

My motorbike, I guess, he says. Maybe running.

They turn the corner onto the residential streets. Cars parked in driveways, heavy curtains drawn against them.

And travel, Will says, realizing that, once more, he's sharing something he's never said out loud.

Wow, says Rosie, and her voice lifts with interest. Where have you been?

Well, nowhere outside Norfolk, he admits. Which is why I want to go, when I can.

Where're you going to go?

Anywhere, he says. Everywhere.

That's a lot of places, she says, and he tells her she's not wrong.

*

Rosemary Winters, you dark *horse*.

Rosie can't help it; she laughs down the phone. She feels as though she is filled with balloons, a pleasant pressure beneath her skin.

Nothing happened, she says.

Nothing *happened*? cries Marley. The coolest guy in school asked you out, is what happened.

I don't think he's the coolest guy in school.

He is sexy and sullen and he owns a motorbike, for God's sake.

I know. It's a problem.

A problem? Rosie! Marley sounds slightly crazed, as if she's downed one too many energy drinks. Do you think he'll give you a ride on it?

I wouldn't get on it even if you paid me, Rosie says, and Marley sighs.

That's part of his appeal, though, she insists. His motorbike, his *sad* eyes, his dark, dangerous past. You know he got suspended for beating someone up in the school toilets?

That's just a stupid rumor, Marl.

Maybe, says Marley, but can we back up, please? Will White came over and wanted to walk you home. Now. What happened before that?

I was talking to you at my locker.

No-no-no, says Marley, and Rosie can sense her flapping her hand in frustration. She doesn't need to see her to picture it; her friend, upside down on her bed, feet up against the wall.

Before that.

He just came over one night, Rosie says. To help Josh with his maths.

And?

And we got talking. That's all.

She doesn't know why she's downplaying this, when she wants to sing, to run, to let the sun in her heart pour out of her.

Did he make a move?

No.

Did you want him to?

I don't know, Marl. I'm not sure what he wants. We know what kind of guy he is, right? He's never said a word to me, and then that night at the bonfire—

The bonfire! I forgot he was there!

Well, exactly. He barely said a word to anyone. But then after you left, I don't know, we just started chatting.

And he fell for you. *Hook line.* Why wouldn't he, Rosie?

I thought I was a vanilla virgin?

Well, you are. And that's your secret weapon.

Being boring?

Being innocent and sweet and so intently you, she says, and Rosie can't help but laugh again at the fever in her friend's voice.

Sounds like you're writing yourself a nice little movie script, she says. But the timing's not right, Marley. Really. I've got bigger things on my mind. I need to focus on Oxbridge.

You need to focus on the size of his biceps, Marley says.

They squabble-laugh for another minute and then Rosie's door opens, without a knock. It is her mother. Her hair is twisted up into a towel, her face wan-looking now it's stripped of mascara, her eyeliner wiped away.

Phone off, Rosie, she says, nodding at the space where her clock used to be. She'd asked her dad to take it down when she'd stopped sleeping; when the tapping hands, once so soothing, began to wind her tight like a cog. Say goodnight to Marley now.

She closes the door behind her and Rosie tucks her chin back to the receiver.

You hear that?

Yeah. But before you go, Rosie, let me ask you one thing.

Okay.

Do you like him?

There is a silence, clockless and lamplit.

Because if you do, Marley goes on, then none of the other stuff matters. The bike or the smoking or Oxbridge, or those other girls, or what your mum thinks, or what date your classics exam might be.

Her friend's voice has changed. It is the serious Marley talking now; the Marley who likes to debate ethics, who shows up early to orchestra practice. Who replies with the utmost concentration when her father quizzes her on diseases at the kitchen table, because she is going to be a doctor, like him.

I can't, Rosie says.

But you do? Marley asks.

Rosie doesn't say it, cannot bring herself to speak. And that, she knows, is answer enough, as well as spectacularly inconvenient.

She makes a decision, overnight.

She cannot do this now. She is flattered. She is full of warm air, and she is confused about why he wants her, of all people, to meet him at the lighthouse, to be the person he shares a bag of chips with by the harbor. And she wants to be that person. She wants to hear him talk about travel and running, all his non-plans. She wants him to listen, in the way that nobody else does; like he's actually absorbing her answers.

But those things can wait.

There are other things she has to focus on. Bigger, important things that she's been working toward, for too long. She cannot slip, not now. Not even for Will White, with his cold, assured hands and his somber eyes.

So gray, and so serious.

She struggles to leave her bedroom the next morning, checking things on a loop, then another. Her clothes, her curtains, tilting her desk chair to the perfect angle, ensuring it feels right. And then she walks to school with Josh and doesn't mention a word of it and spends the day at school with the focus of an aspiring Oxbridge student and then the bell rings, and she waits by her locker, and he comes to her just as she hoped he would.

There are too many people around. Shoes squeak on the floor, blazers jostling past in a haze of blue. Dropped books, banging doors.

Can we go somewhere, she asks him.

His eyebrows rise at this. Like he hadn't expected it, from her. Like he thinks she means something else.

Just somewhere in school, she says, to clarify.

The library? he suggests.

Or the music block, Rosie says, because she can't face being in silence with him, amid the books and the muffling carpets, everything paper-soft and private. She needs stone floors. Piano edges, the brushed brass of music stands.

When they get there, Will pushes the music block door open. It's heavy, paneled in wood, and he has to lean his whole arm across to let her pass. Inside, it is dark, nobody having bothered to turn the lights on in the hall. The mismatched voices of choir practice drift from a nearby classroom, and there are thumps from upstairs, students dragging themselves to their lessons with their oboes and guitars.

I hate this building, Will says.

I love this building, says Rosie.

It doesn't give you the creeps?

All part of its charm, she says, leading him down the hall and past the teachers' office, to her favorite—usually empty—practice room at the back. The window is blocked by an overgrown hedge, so it's always devoid of sunlight, even at midday. She loves the dappled shadows on the old carpets, the slight smell of damp that never fades.

I think we need to revise your definition of charm, Will says, as she leads him through the door. The piano is in the corner. Stacks of sheet music line the wooden shelves, Debussy and Gershwin and Strauss. Her watch is there, too, on the piano stool, after she'd forgotten it again. She sits down and wraps it round her wrist. Will is looking around, at the music, the notes on the blackboard. Anywhere, it seems, but at her.

So this is your hangout, he says.

Sort of, she says.

It's freezing, he says.

I keep my coat on, usually, she says. In the winter.

Does it always smell like this?

Afraid so.

Then why d'you come here?

I like the quiet, she says, and he nods, like he gets it, and he's making this whole thing harder just by being him, and understanding. She has never known a person like him. Never felt like she's known someone, for so long, when she hasn't.

I wanted to talk to you about something, she says, because that's what she brought him here for.

I'm listening, he says. He's still looking at the blackboard. He goes over and touches the treble clef, brushes his fingers across the whorl of its tail.

I'm not sure this is a good idea, she says.

He says nothing. Doesn't ask her what she means, doesn't throw back one of his usual questions. She can see students walking past the music block, flickers of blue through the hedge beyond the window. The snow is gone. Her history exam has been rescheduled. Her heart is drumming in her chest.

You and me, she says, in case he hasn't understood.

Will still doesn't reply. He rubs the treble clef away with two fingers, leaves a cloud of dust in its place.

Why's that, he asks, lightly, as though he's not really interested in her answer.

A lot of reasons, she says.

Give me one.

Okay. You're you. And I'm me.

I need a proper reason, Rosie.

I'm just not your kind of girl, she says. I don't want to hang off you at the winter dance or sit on the back of your motorbike or fail my mocks because I'm thinking about you.

So don't, then.

Don't what?

Think about me.

That's what I'm trying to say, she says.

So you are, then?

Are what?

Thinking about me.

Well, yeah, she says, and she's getting flustered, thinks, for a heart-stopping jolt of a second, that perhaps she's read this all wrong. Aren't you? she asks him.

He doesn't say anything. Turns around to face her, and leans his back against the blackboard.

You'll get chalk down your shirt, Rosie says. He folds his arms, as if he's settling in for something long and debatable.

I need another reason, he tells her.

Fine, she says. I just need to focus on my exams, all right? I've come too far, now. I need to get the grades for a conditional offer and then, even if I do, I'll be leaving next September, anyway.

So?

Well, she says, and she casts around the room, as though the answer is written on the walls, hanging in the cobwebs on the ceiling. Is there even any point, you know? Starting something?

You tell me, he says.

I am telling you, Will, she says, and there's a heat to her voice now, the rip of a match as it lights; clipped, and decisive. You'd get bored, anyway. I care about school and grades and all the things you've made very clear mean nothing to you. You don't want to wait for me.

Is that an option, he says. His arms are still folded.

What?

Waiting for you. Is that an option?

What do you mean?

I mean, if you get your exams done, and your conditional offer or whatever it is you need, would that change things?

I'd still be leaving, though. Come September.

But there'd be a summer, he says.

Yes, Rosie says, after a short pause.

And until then, what are the rules? That we can't see each other? That I have to hide from you in the halls, stop helping Josh with his maths?

I'm not laying out any stupid rules, Rosie says.

Come on, Roe, Will says, a half laugh caught in his throat, and it is the first time he calls her that, the first time he shortens her name to something that nobody else has ever, or will ever, call her.

She shrugs, her point lost between them like the clef on the blackboard.

Do your exams, Will says. Get those results. And I'll wait.

His eyes are on hers. His mouth is set, and his tie is loose, his shirt unbuttoned below the collar. The tut-tut-tut of her watch flits in her ears. A tiny metronome, tapping out time.

You'll wait, she repeats.

Yes.

She looks at him, at the burned gold of his hair, the down that grazes his jaw. He is stirring, and silent, and that warmth is back inside her. Why, she asks him.

He looks straight at her.

You said you think about me, he says.

She nods, once, when she realizes it's a question.

Turns out I think about you, too, he says. On my bike. And at the garage. And when I'm cooking, and running, and trying to sleep.

His eyes are like fumes; they fog up the room.

And that's new for me, he says.

Rosie's throat is so dry, she could not speak even if she wanted to. She is thinking that it's new for her, too. That what she did last night, under her covers with him on her mind, that was new, and it felt dangerous, and good, and only a little bit wrong.

So I'll wait, Will says again.

The choir starts up from the other end of the building, a hymn about winter snow. They both listen, until the song ends. Some line about dawn, and morning. He hears the words, and watches her face, and she watches him right back.

four

◖

S he didn't say they couldn't be friends. Just that she didn't want to sit on his motorbike, or go to the winter dance. That he couldn't interrupt her exams.

And so they text, occasionally. He waits for her, at first, to reach out to him. She sends him songs, or the name of a place she's seen online, an island or mountain range or a city she thinks he might like, and he writes the names down and puts them in his drawer.

He messages her early, or late at night.

Asks her how she is, how she slept.

He sleeps with Darcy, once, a week after their conversation in the music room, and he thinks about Rosie the entire time and it is awkward and bumpy and it takes him too long to get hard. What is *wrong* with you, Darcy spits at him, her nails dug deep into his back, and he asks himself the same question while he tugs his jeans back on.

*

When Rosie tells Marley that she and Will are not together, Marley seems to take it as a personal affront.

She barely speaks to her for days.

Rosie is hurt by this, but says nothing, and they're talking again by the end of the week. They make plans to see each other on the Saturday, to watch *The Beach*, or *Jack and Sarah*. Rosie says she'll bring the popcorn this time; a peace offering, though she's not sure exactly what for.

And she studies, hard. She goes over everything that could come up in her mocks, staying up late with herbal tea and pages of notes and a slight sense of having started a marathon, the buzz of it, a tremor of stress and satisfaction.

Will texts her, sometimes. She checks her phone before bed, when she's closed her books and brushed her teeth, brought her ear plugs out from her bedside drawer. She tries to be clever in her replies; more interesting than she knows herself to be. And when she turns the light off, she feels fine.

In control, and on the right path, with someone who's noticed and cared.

She falls asleep with no tension in her jaw. Wakes up feeling lighter and readied, like all the tiny grains of her life are stacked just so.

I've got a date to the winter dance, Marley announces one break time.

Rosie is eating a roll, pauses with a piece raised to her mouth.

I know we said we wouldn't have dates, Marley says. That we'd go together, as always. But that was just because we never got asked, right? And now I have, so.

She seems defensive, although Rosie has said nothing to make her that way. She lowers the bread, tries to keep her face neutral.

Who's asked you?

Tom Dellow, from my art class.

He's nice.

I know he's nice, Marley says. We've been talking a bit, on and off.

Oh, right.

Yeah.

So, er. Do you like him?

Guess we'll see after the dance, Marley says, and there's a note of finality to her voice, the conversation closed. This seems unfair to Rosie, seeing as she was only repeating a question she herself had been asked. But she eats her roll, takes a drink from her water bottle.

I think it's great, Rosie says, when Marley reaches the bottom of her yogurt, is scraping the pot with her spoon. We can still get ready together, can't we?

Marley softens at this, makes eye contact again.

Course, she says. I'll blare our favorite tunes while we mix eye colors and crimp our hair.

This is how they would prepare for school discos when they were younger; when winter dances only meant the Macarena and bowls of ready-salted crisps, boys skidding on their knees along the floor. Rosie tells her that sounds perfect, thinking it's fine by her if she wants to go with Tom Dellow, although there's something pulling inside her, an invisible thread, like Marley is somehow making a point.

I'll go with Josh, she says, to make light of it, and Marley laughs. Tells her that sounds about right.

*

The week before school is due to break up for Christmas, Rosie's mother calls her into her bedroom. It is first thing in the morning, when her mum is usually dressed and making coffee, already on the phone, or working on her laptop.

Rosie pushes open the door and the room smells of sleep, the musk of her parents' breathing. Her father is a snoring mound beneath the duvet while her mother lies, small and straight, beside him, her eyes open.

Rosie, her mother says again. She whispers, which means she is not herself.

Are you okay, Rosie asks, padding across the carpet.

My head, she says.

You need water?

And Imitrex.

Rosie comes back with a glass and the tablets, pops them out of the foil for her. She watches her swallow, thinks how she's still so striking when she is sick, and only just awake. Her hair cascades across her pillows, her cheekbones sliced with shadow.

Don't go into work today, Rosie says.

I don't think I can, her mother says. She closes her eyes, attempts to put her glass back on the bedside table; Rosie has to steady it for her.

Can I get you anything else?

Can you just talk to me, for a little while?

Rosie pulls her legs up beneath her so she's sitting on the side of her parents' bed. At first, she rests her hand on her mother's knuckles, but she shifts away.

Too hot, she says, and Rosie nods.

It is wrong to admit it, and so she never has, but she likes her mother best when she has a migraine. It is the only time she seems to need Rosie's company; the only time she slows down and wants to know things, real things, not about school or exams or her weight loss.

It's not about *weight loss*, Rosie, her mother had said, when she'd laid out her new regime. It's a *lifestyle* adjustment. I just want you to be healthy and happy and the best version of you.

She wants me to get asked to the winter dance, Rosie had told Josh in an undertone, and he'd snorted like it was funny, though she had not been the slightest bit joking.

Her mother stays in bed all day; is still there after school. Rosie and Josh cobble dinner together, and their father takes his plate to his office, opting to listen to the cricket on the radio with his feet up on his desk.

So, I've been thinking, Rosie says, twirling spaghetti round her fork. It is raining outside, the drops tapping like seeds falling on the conservatory roof.

Sounds ominous, says Josh, through a too-large mouthful of food.

I wondered if I should get a dress for the dance.

Josh looks at her over his water glass, still chewing.

Yeah?

Last year's doesn't fit that well, with the weight loss, and everything.

How's that going?

Fine, she says. It's only a few pounds.

We could probably pin it, then, he says. If you don't want to go shopping.

I do, though, she says.

You want to go shopping for clothes?

Well. For one dress. Singular.

Okay. Josh puts down his fork. How come?

What?

You've *never* bought anything without being dragged to the shops by our mother, he says. Or myself.

I know. We can't all love scrubbing up, like you.

Low blow, he says.

I just thought it'd be nice, she says, standing up and taking his plate, before he's even finished. She scrapes the pasta back into the pan, clunks the crockery into the dishwasher.

It will be, Josh says, and she can sense him watching her.

I'll just go alone, if it's such a big deal, she says.

Sis. It's not a big deal.

So why are you making it seem like one?

Jeez, Rosie, I just asked a question! I thought there might be someone you wanted to dress up nice for, he says, that's all. It's not a wild idea, now we're seventeen, is it?

Not you *too*, she says.

Huh?

Marley's always banging on about how I'm a virgin and how nobody ever asks me to the dance, she says. When she's never dated, properly, either. And it's not like you've had a long line of girlfriends, Josh.

A silence, then, that stuns them both. Rosie's throat contracts, and something seeps through her, some prickling, liquid heat.

I'm sorry, she says, and sits back down in front of him. She feels suddenly, bodily, exhausted, like she could sleep right here at the table.

What's with the claws, Josh asks. He reaches over and lifts her hand, makes a show of checking her fingernails.

Just stress, she sighs. Exams.

She says sorry, a second time, and he says it's okay; puts her hand back down on the table.

Are your checks bad? he asks.

Not the worst, she says.

They listen to the rain. Rosie lets the heat fade away, waits for her feelings to ebb. She thinks about telling Josh her secret; that she has someone, that she could have had someone. The best one, maybe. And that for reasons that made sense to her at the time, she said no, and he said he'd wait, and now she finds she wants to look nice for him even though he is not hers, and it's irritating, and distracting, and maybe she should just stay home, after all. With no date to the dance, like always.

I'll help you find a dress, Josh says, because of course he will. Because he is kind, and forgiving, and the one who cares about these things.

Maybe a light blue, he says, nudging her foot with his.

Maybe, she says, and she feels like crying, though she has no idea why.

He is the only one to know, and to ask, about what they have coined her *checking.*

It is something she began doing so young that she can't remember not doing it. She thinks it was the night before her first piano exam. She was seven. And out of nowhere, she felt the need to check she had her sheet music packed in her school bag, over and over, as if no matter how many times she checked, she did not trust that it was there.

It spilled into other things. Adjusting her curtains. Touching her door handle and her desk chair. Irrational, necessary, tiring habits that were compulsory, and private, done only at night or when she was alone, before bed.

Josh could hear her through the wall. Saw her, once or twice, and accepted it, and didn't try to change it, or mock her, or question what she was doing. But he asks her, now and then, if she's all right. Something she forgets to ask herself.

*

The school workshop, after hours, is one of Will's favorite places. Like his grandfather's garage, it is quiet and functional, a place he can use both his hands and his brain, and be left alone by other people.

Usually.

Hey Will, says Josh, as he walks in with his satchel banging his knees, his tie loosened, blazer askew.

Will straightens up from his place by the lathe. He is allowed to work in here, alone, because he has a good rapport with the technician. It's officially not allowed because, Will knows, most students are stupid, or heavy-handed, or melt things in the vacuum packing machine and set off the fire alarms, even saw off the tips of their thumbs.

Will has never done any of these things. But he's never had an insistent schoolmate distracting him while he works, either.

Is this still okay? Josh asks, clearly noting something on Will's face. You said I could come revise here, on Wednesdays?

I did, didn't I, says Will, and Josh looks so forlorn that he backtracks, gives him a laugh to indicate he was joking. Sort of.

Just don't distract me too much, he says. I've got to finish these candlesticks, and I've ruined two sets already.

Okay, Josh says, and he sounds serious as he unpacks his books, gets out his worksheets and spreads them out on the workbench. No distracting. Got it.

Will shakes his head, picks up the bases he'd planed flat last week. He still needs to sand them down, but the shape is pleasing, the drill hole in just the right place. He turns back to the lathe, and mounts a stick on the driving center. One step at a time, like fixing an engine. One thing after another.

What're you struggling with, then, Will asks Josh, as he winds the tailstock in place.

All of it, says Josh, and Will sighs. Takes his chisel to the wood, just once, the noise harsh and sharp and short. He's ruined previous sets with a slip of the hand, or a lack of concentration; getting too comfortable, too soon, and scoring out more than he wants to.

He spends an hour working like this, in careful stages, coaching Josh over his shoulder. He finds Josh watching him, sometimes, when he glances back to answer a question, or is reaching for a new gouge. Like he's more interested in the lathe, or his hands, than the maths he came here to learn.

So, Josh says, after he's finished a few questions, is stretching his long arms above his head. You going to the dance, tomorrow?

Will lets out a puff of air, a noncommittal no, as he swaps to the bedan tool. He is not planning on it. Darcy has not asked him this time, and it is always hot and messy and dull, and he would rather spend the night with his bike, or sanding down these candlesticks.

Rosie's getting ready at Marley's, Josh says, so I'm going to Jack's for pre-drinks. Think we'll all get there around eight.

He says it in an offhand sort of way, as though testing him, and Will wonders, fleetingly, if he knows something; if he senses, or if Rosie has even told him, about their non-relationship. Their suspended not-quite-anything.

But then he moves on, asks about more numbers on the page. And Will pretends that this changes nothing, because he is supposed to be waiting, and she specifically said she did not want to go to the dance with him.

He isn't going *with* her, though, if he simply shows up.

He swaps the candlesticks, working more swiftly, this time, confident that he can match the design of the first. It's no good having one that he can't pair with the other; they need to be equal, exact. He'll lacquer them, when they're done. Next time. When Josh isn't here, asking him about matrices, or watching his every move.

When the night rolls round, he dresses in a shirt and jeans. Finds some aftershave at the back of the cabinet to hide the smell of engine grease, wonders why it's considered sensual to smell of dried fruit and cedar trees. He doesn't know why he's bothering. Back in the kitchen, his grandma doesn't, either.

I thought you hated school dances, she says, as she stirs a stew on the hob. Will leans over and spoons some into his mouth, careful not to drop it down his front.

I do, he says. The food is hot so he parts his lips, lets the steam curl outward like smoke.

So are you going with Ashleigh?

Two years ago, maybe.

Then who's the girl with the piercings up her ears?

Darcy, he says. But no. It's just me tonight.

Oh?

Last time, isn't it, he says with a shrug, as he scrapes more stew from the saucepan. Before everyone buggers off to uni.

Everyone except you, she says.

Yep, Will says. It ends at midnight, Gran, okay? So don't wait up.

You're not driving, she says.

How else am I going to get there?

There'll be drink, presumably, she says.

Yeah. But I won't have any.

Like hell you won't.

Gran!

I'll pick you up, she says. I'll be outside the school at midnight on the dot. Any later, Will, and you're walking.

Gran, I'll be fine to drive. *You're* the one who said I can't ride my bike in the dark, so I'll take your car, and I won't—

Have a glorious time, Willyum, she says. Avoid contracting an STD, if you can.

What's an STD, asks Amber, as she wanders into the kitchen. She is still in her school uniform, her panda slippers bug-eyed on her feet.

Sexually Transmitted Dragonpox, Will says.

Urgh!

I know, Will nods. Don't touch a boy, Ambs, not till you're thirty, at least. Or you might catch it.

Off with you now, his grandma says.

So I have to walk there?

Won't kill you, will it?

You smell weird, Amber informs him, as he moves past her to the door, and he says thanks, to both of them, for the continued moral support.

The dance is busy and loud, a jumble of paper chains and disco balls and soft drinks abandoned in cups. Will's name is ticked off on a clipboard, and because he's eighteen—a year older than his peers, due to the year he retook—he's given a token for a beer. He pockets it and grabs a Coke. Heads for the first person he knows.

For an hour, he moves from group to group, talking, not talking, drinking and not drinking. He gives his token to a girl in a red dress who keeps standing too close, her voice tickling his neck. Like it's attractive. Like he couldn't possibly resist. Like her desperation, her hunger to be looked at, is in itself a turn-on.

Get yourself a beer, he says, handing her his pass. And she looks up at him, tipsy from her pre-dance drinks—peach schnapps, it smells like— and blinks, slowly, as though he's paid her a compliment.

Stay right here, William White, she slurs, before she slinks off, and he immediately walks the other way, toward the dance floor; leans against the school stage in the darkest corner he can find.

She's not here.

The hall smells of floor polish and fresh sweat and the sweet, sticky spill of alcohol. This is the room for assemblies and drama class, carol concerts and visitor talks, hours of stifled listening to prayers and fables and rules. He won't miss it; not for a minute.

Wiiiiiiilllllll White!

A sudden bump of elbows jars him out of his thoughts; an arm is slung around his neck, a body slumped against his own. It is Josh, and he is drunk.

Steady on, mate, Will says.

Sorry, sorry, Josh says, and he takes his arm from his shoulders. Just didn't 'spect to see you!

I was hiding, to be fair, Will says, grinning in spite of himself. Josh looks even more like a cartoon in this state; his limbs are limp, and his hair looks bedraggled, as though he's been standing beneath a sprinkler.

Did you just get out the shower or something? Will asks him.

The shower?

Your hair, he says. It's soaked.

Just dancing, bud! Josh cries, and he grabs Will's hands, tries to pull him onto the dance floor, but Will resists.

I think you need some air, Will tells him.

I think *you* need to dance, Josh says.

How about we get you some water, Will suggests, and Josh throws his head back, lifts his fists into the air and does some bizarre movement that Will is sure, once he is sober, he will not want to remember doing.

Have fun, then, he says, laughing. He backs up, is just thinking he'll get some water himself, when he meets a girl in a blue dress on the stairs by the stage. He stands by to let her pass, and she hesitates, as though she's noticed that it's him.

He is used to this.

Girls acting nervous around him, as though they want to say something.

He purposefully doesn't make eye contact. He worries, momentarily, that the peach schnapps girl will be back with the drinks, and is just about to head the other way when the girl in blue says his name.

He glances back at her, then stares.

Because it's Rosie.

Except that it doesn't look like Rosie. She has clipped up her hair, done something smoky to her eyes, and she's wearing a midnight silk slip that skims her skin, falls all the way to the floor.

Roe, he says. I didn't think you were here.

I didn't think you were, either.

You look. I mean.

She lowers her eyes, and he sees her cheeks bloom with blood, even through the semidarkness. His eyes drink her up; her bare shoulders, her braceleted wrists.

Do you want a drink?

I've just had one. I was actually looking for Josh.

She holds up a cup of water, and he grins, shakes his head.

I've just seen him, he says. Good luck stopping those dance moves of his.

Oh dear, she says, and Will says oh dear is right, and she laughs, and it is like fireworks again, the spark of it, the small explosions in his gut.

You want some air? he asks her.

The night is mild for December. Near windless, with scuds of cloud shielding the stars.

There are a few couples out in the courtyard, so Will and Rosie slip behind the bike sheds, find themselves on the concrete steps outside the assembly hall. It is quieter, out here. The disco lights whirl through the windows, make patterns on the tarmacked road.

Will leans against the railing and holds out his hand, helps Rosie up the steps in her heels.

That dress, he says. Rosie says nothing; bows her head and smooths her fringe, as though trying to hide her face.

You having a good night?

Yeah, she says, and she leans against the railing beside him. Actually, no. I sort of hate these things.

So why d'you come?

I could ask you the same thing.

I came because I thought you'd be here, Will says.

Rosie tilts her head, her eyelids shimmering with silver.

Well, I came because I always do, she says.

Even though you hate it, Will says, and she nods.

Crazy, isn't it? I don't really like alcohol, for one thing. Another cool fact about me, by the way, she says, glancing at him as she says it. I just really hate being drunk.

Sensible, Will says.

I am, Rosie says. Which is so *dull*, I know.

They listen to the music blaring through the wall. The roofs of the parked cars shine in the moonlight, and some girls cackle, distantly, in the courtyard.

Can I ask, Will asks, why it is that you say these things about yourself?

They are standing an inch apart. Her little finger, close to his.

Because they're true?

They're not, though, he says. If you were dull, or you really cared about not liking alcohol, you would do something about it. Right?

It sounds like an accusation, and she is quiet.

What else don't you like about the dance, he asks her, when enough time has passed.

Dancing, she says.

A bit of a problem, he says, and she laughs, and it is the best sound, and his heart skitters behind his ribs and he turns to face her, puts his hands on her waist. She stops laughing, immediately.

Is this okay? he asks, and she nods, once, though her eyes are doe-like, caught in the spiraling lights.

Dancing can be all right, he tells her.

He has slow-danced at all of these things; or at least, the ones he's been forced to attend. The girls usually take the lead, nuzzling into his chest as they rotate on the spot. But Rosie doesn't. She simply looks up at him, like she doesn't know what to do. Like she's afraid.

Think less, he says.

I can't, she says.

Try.

Will.

Yes?

We're not meant to be doing this.

What, dancing in a car park?

You know what I mean.

She moves with him, though, despite the things she is saying. His forehead is close to hers, and he can smell the sky, the cold. The autumn scent of her hair; apples and sweet leaves. She feels somewhat taut, as well as soft, beneath the satin of her dress.

Rosie, he says. Relax.

That's like saying: Will, be unattractive.

He snorts, tells her she's funny. They keep swaying on the steps, his heart thudding like hooves in his chest.

Rosie! Rosie Winters!

Two people stumble around the corner, and Rosie breaks, turns around. It's Marley, and Tom, a guy he knows from his homeroom. Marley is waving and he hears Rosie sigh, the smallest breath of air, and then she smiles and waves right back.

Hello, she says, as Marley and Tom join them by the railing.

Hi-hi-hi, Marley crows, before taking a glug from her beer. How are we all this *fine* evening?

Fine, Rosie says, and she's still smiling, her teeth like pearls in the dark.

I thought you guys weren't a thing, Marley says, waving her beer bottle between them. She is a little drunk, Will knows; he can see it in her eyes.

Depends what you mean by thing, he says.

Marley's gaze slides toward him, and at that exact moment Tom introduces himself, and Rosie says hi. They talk about nothing for a while. The beer, and when the burgers will be ready. How they'd all have preferred pizza, really, instead.

So let's go get pizza, Will says.

All three of them turn to look at him.

Now? Marley asks.

If you're hungry, yeah.

We can't just leave, Tom says.

It's the last one, Marley reminds him.

Will lets out a small laugh. Marley frowns, and Tom glances at him, too, with a wariness he's seen in guys his age before.

What? Marley asks.

I just don't get why people are so sentimental about this place, he says.

You mean the place we've spent the last seven years of our lives?

I love this song, Rosie says suddenly. She has stepped back from the railing, away from him. Some of her hair has fallen from its bun.

Me too, says Marley, though she eyes Will for a second longer. Then she passes her beer to Tom and grabs Rosie's hands and they dance, together, on the tarmac. Not well, exactly, but effortlessly. Like they've been doing it in bedrooms for years.

You want some, Tom asks, offering him a beer bottle. Will says thanks, and takes it, but doesn't drink. Watches Rosie laughing, as Marley twirls her around.

Bit cold out here, Tom says.

Yeah, says Will, uninterested in small talk. Tom takes a swig of beer, and Will finds himself doing the same, without thinking. The first sip is lukewarm, unsatisfying.

When the song ends, Marley flings her arms round Rosie's neck and looks over at them both. Rosie says something to her, something Will can't catch, and Marley laughs, again, her shrieking laugh. Kestrels, diving, triumphant.

Are you a thing, Tom asks him, as the girls turn back toward them.

Are *you*, he asks, and Tom pauses, the beer bottle lifted to his mouth.

Me and Marley?

Yeah.

Tom still doesn't drink. Watches them coming.

I don't really know, he says, and Will says well then, and then the girls are upon them, smelling of night air and sweat; the warmth of spinning around with their arms held high, styled hair now damp at the neck.

Let's go back in, Marley says, tugging on Rosie's hand.

I'm going to stay out for a bit, Rosie says.

Oh, come on, Marley says. Come and dance.

We just danced.

It's the last one!

I know, but.

She looks at Will, and then over at Tom. Marley pouts, grabs at Rosie's wrists.

One dance, Rosie says, eventually.

So Rosie dances, even though she does not want to. Her mind is elsewhere, outside on the steps with Will who stayed to light a cigarette, but years of loyalty to Marley and her sentiment for this school keep her in the pulsing, body-filled hall of students, with the grinding and the yelling and the slopped drinks and sticky floor.

It is strangely difficult to get away, even though no one is paying her any attention. She feels hemmed in, like what she wants and what she must do are two entirely separate things; that being here, with Marley and her friends, is only right, and there is some invisible fence that keeps it so.

When the burgers are brought out, people flock to the canteen for the cheap bread and ketchup, the heat of soft flesh in their mouths. She bumps into Josh by the napkins. Her twin is drenched in sweat, and there is something manic about him; he has drunk too much, despite not being old enough for the alcohol pass. It's become a game, she guesses; people feeding him more, the drunker he gets. Because it's funny, and innocent. And because Josh is both of those things.

She takes him to the courtyard, secluded now, all the couples relocated to the dance floor, emptying their lungs to Bon Jovi.

What a night, Josh says, as Rosie lowers him onto a bench.

Looks like you've had fun, she says.

So much fun, he says. Haven't you?

Sure.

Liar, he says, and he tries to ruffle her hair; misses, and ends up patting her on the ear. But you look pretty, Sis. In your dress.

They'd spent an agreeable hour in the shopping center at the weekend, Josh picking colors and holding them up against her. That one, he'd said, as soon as he saw the blue. For your Lorelai Gilmore eyes.

His own are half closed now, which she supposes is a good thing.

You were meant to be driving us home, she reminds him.

I know, he groans. Whoops.

And then he laughs, and immediately falls asleep.

His mouth hangs open, his hair swept to the side, and Rosie wonders, not for the first time, what it will be like to live apart from him. When he is in Cambridge, and she, in Oxford or Durham or York. Wherever she ends up.

At precisely one minute past midnight, the music is cut and the hall lights are lifted. Students pour out into the courtyard, laughing and squealing; Josh wakes, and is immediately sick on his shoes.

Rosie groans. There's a fine in place for vomiting.

She tells him to get up, now, and hobbles with him to the back of the courtyard and past the tennis courts, away from the crowds and the teachers.

You're a pain, Josh, she says, as she half supports, half staggers beneath her brother's weight in her heels.

And you're the best person I know, Josh slurs. I'd think that even if you weren't my twin, you know.

That's very sweet, but you're still a pain.

I mean it, he says, dragging his feet. You see things, Rosie-Roo. You know things, because you watch. All the important things.

He is talking nonsense, and she is barely listening. Subconsciously heading for the car park, because Will might still be there. Josh lumbers alongside her, pressing his head against hers.

You know, he says again.

I know, she says, though she has no idea what he's talking about.

Do you, he asks, and he sounds serious now. The moon is full, leaves a creamy light in the sky, and Rosie ignores him.

They pass the bike sheds and turn into the car park, where two girls are taking last-minute photographs of each other. A group of guys are smoking weed; she can smell the sweet, dank stench of it. Will, it seems, has long gone.

I'm going to be sick again, Josh informs her.

Brilliant, she says, and they pass the smokers in double time as she gets him off school property. When they are a safe distance away, she rests him against a lamppost, and he sinks his way to the ground.

I'll call Marley, Rosie says. See if her mum can drop us home.

Josh nods, and puts his face in his hands.

I have to tell you something, he says. Something I've decided.

Okay?

She is tapping the buttons on her phone, pulling Marley's name up on her screen.

Not decided, actually. You can't decide these things.

She hits the green call button, waits as it rings and rings.

You're not listening to me, says Josh, and he sounds angry, and still very drunk.

I'm trying to get us home, she says. After you were supposed to, remember?

You don't get it, Josh says. He mumbles something else into his hands, then says he wants to go to bed.

I'm trying to get you there, Rosie says, as she tries Marley's number for the second time. Once again, it rings out. And once again, Josh is sick. She grimaces, lets him finish, then says it looks like they're walking home.

*

His grandma's car is parked a few feet up the road, near the school gym; the place she always waits on the odd occasion she picks him up. Because it's raining, or she's on her way home from the graveyard. He can tell when it's the latter, from her fingernails, rimmed with dirt; from the slightest sag of her mouth.

He gets in, waits as she completes her slow, shuddering three-point turn and begins the descent down the hill. They crawl past the school entrance, students emerging from the lobby in groups, sweaty and sparkling with smeared makeup and body glitter, an excess of rock-hard hair gel.

Did you have a good time? his gran asks him. Her hands are fixed at ten and two, her eyes forward as the car rolls over the many speed bumps.

Yeah, he says. He looks out of the window, at the white limousine parked alongside the music block. Same as usual. Bad music, bad burgers.

Then what's different?

What?

Something's different. In your voice.

He glances at her, feels the tug of an unwanted smile.

Nothing, he says.

Something, she says, but she drops it, and he looks back out of the window as she indicates, turns down a quiet avenue. She'll cut back through the residential roads rather than drive along the high street. It's a longer, darker route, but she doesn't like the roundabouts or the traffic lights; anything to avoid using the clutch more than she has to.

I could drive, he says. I only had a few sips of beer.

I thought you said you weren't having any?

I wasn't, he said, but then you said you'd come get me, so.

She exhales out of both nostrils. He is just about to say that's not a crime, is it, but stops himself at this particular choice of words, when he sees them stumbling along the pavement; that tall, gangling cartoon of a boy, and a young woman, her silk dress trailing along the pavement.

Stop, he says.

Excuse me?

Can you stop the car, please? Those are my friends, he says, nodding out of the window at the pair of them.

Friends, his grandmother repeats.

Let's just check they're okay, he says, and he winds the window down as his grandmother slows, the engine juddering in its low gear.

You guys okay? he asks, as they pull up beside them. Rosie has one arm around her brother's waist, her other gripping the wrist he's slung around her shoulders. She has to strain to peek over at Will, turns to the side in her heels.

Just about, she says.

What's up?

Someone overdid it, she says, and it's at that point that Josh sees the car and says, Will! Rosie—tugging on her hand—it's *Will*.

I can see that, Rosie says.

Hi Will, says Josh, raising his voice and waving.

Hi Josh, Will says back.

There is a suspended, comical moment of no more hellos, broken by his grandmother who asks in a too-loud whisper, is he a sandwich short?

Just drunk, Will tells her. That's Josh. From further maths.

Oh, she says, and she's suddenly interested. The one who needs your help, a lot of the time?

Yeah.

Who's going to study at Cambridge?

Yeah.

The boy who's going to Cambridge, who needs help from my grandson, she says, more to herself than to him. Will rolls his eyes, leans out of the car window.

He all right? he asks Rosie.

He will be, she says. He just needs some sleep.

Get in, he says. Then, as an afterthought, he turns back to his grandma. If that's cool?

She is looking at him strangely, but she nods, once, without words.

We'll drive you home, he says to Rosie.

That's really nice of you, she says, but he's been sick. Twice.

So he's unlikely to be sick again.

You don't know that.

This car's seen worse. Right, Gran?

Unfortunately, she says, and she leans forward, all the better to observe the two on the pavement. Will feels her assessing the situation, the risk involved, if any.

There's a plastic bag in the boot, she says. If you wouldn't mind.

Of course, Rosie says. Thank you.

Will helps heave Josh into the back seat, and Rosie opens the boot and comes back with an old shopping bag, tucks it between her brother's knees.

Any trace of vomit on these seats and you're walking, sonny, Will's gran says, peering at him in the rearview mirror. Josh nods, his face pale as milk. His initial excitement at seeing Will has ebbed, replaced by a weary silence.

Rosie settles in beside her twin, clips their seat belts in place.

This is so nice of you, she says again.

Least I can do, after you put Will up in the snow, says his gran, and she lurches off in the car, clunking into second gear too late.

Will meets Rosie's eyes in the wing mirror for the shortest of seconds.

Did you have a good night, his grandma asks them, and Will sees her glance back at the girl she doesn't know. I didn't catch your name?

Rosie, she says. Rosemary.

That's pretty.

Thanks. I never liked it much. It reminds me of that rag doll on the canal boat.

There's nothing rag doll about you, his gran says, and Rosie smiles at her, and it is like the sun breaking through the trees. Will feels something move inside him then, if it hadn't already been shifting; like an anchor, catching in place.

The dance was good, Rosie says. Wasn't it, Will?

I already told her it was the same as always, he says.

There is a short pause as their eyes meet again, the engine humming, the dark houses melting past the windows.

It wasn't for me, Rosie says, and it is bold, in front of his grandma, and again, she is a complete and utter surprise to him. He takes his eyes from hers, watches the night passing in the wing mirror. Pavements and front lawns, stained saffron in the streetlights.

*

Will's grandmother pulls up in front of her house, gold lights twinkling from their front hedges. Rosie can see the fir tree in the window, the faint glow from the fireplace glinting off the ornaments. Her parents have finally decorated for Christmas, a full four days before Christmas Eve.

What a beautiful tree, Will's gran says, as she parks alongside the curb.

Thanks, says Rosie, even though it is nothing to do with her. Her father buys the tree each year, and her mother has a very specific arrangement for the decorations. She and Josh learned, fairly early on, that it was best not to interfere.

You spending Christmas at home? Will asks. The car has stopped, but it feels rude to get out so suddenly, and Josh is still quiet, seems comfortable.

Yes, she says. Mum always hosts. We have a party on Christmas Eve, and then a few family members stay over. It's nice. We eat a lot. Play games.

Descend into wine-fueled arguments, she thinks, but doesn't say, because surely that's normal, for families at Christmas, and not something that needs to be shared.

Sounds like ours, Will says. Without the party.

Hey, says Rosie, you should come.

To the party?

Yeah! It's an open-door kind of thing. We have the neighbors popping in, family friends, even Marley comes sometimes. The food's good. We get these apple tarts from the bakery that I look forward to *all year*. So. Yeah. Just if you want, and you're not doing anything.

She tails off, embarrassed, suddenly, by her uncapped enthusiasm. She sees him glance at his grandma, who nods, a barely noticeable tilt of the head.

Maybe, he says.

And you must come to ours, his gran says.

There is a slightly puzzled silence, both Will and Rosie waiting on what she means. The light outside Rosie's front door flicks on at that moment; her mother must have seen the car through the window.

It's just the three of us on Christmas Day, his gran says. But I make enough to feed a busload.

That's true, Will says.

You'll have your own commitments, of course, his gran says. But if you want to join us for Christmas tea, well, you'd be more than welcome. Your brother, too. If he's conscious.

They all glance at Josh, who is asleep again, his head squashed against the window.

That's really kind of you, Rosie says, and the air in the car seems thick, too warm. It doesn't feel normal, to her, to be invited to something as intimate as Christmas Day at a near stranger's house. But it also feels special. Rare. More golden lights, glowing, inside her.

*

His gran parks on their drive and shuts off the engine. The car smells, faintly, of apples.

Are you going to tell me what that was about, he says, as she twists the key and removes it from the ignition.

I was about to ask you the same thing.

What? What did *I* do?

You're always so defensive, William.

You always make me feel like I need to be!

She chuckles, and it sounds like gravel in her throat.

Your friends, she says, with delicate emphasis.

What about them?

That's it. They're friends.

I'm not following.

Never, in all your eighteen years, Will, have I heard you refer to *any-*one as a friend. Even when you were at primary school. You certainly had them. But you never identified them as such.

You sure you're not just paying some weird Freudian attention to the language I use? he asks, and she wheeze-laughs again.

It was just nice, she says. And they seem like good kids.

They are, he says.

Both of them, she says, slyly.

Gran. Spit it out.

I'm saying nothing.

You're implying it.

I am, she says. And I liked her.

He feels suddenly gauche; brushes his palms down the legs of his jeans. The street is still and silent. His sister's light is on. She must be at her desk with her gel pens, doodling a plan for world domination.

I like her too, he says, and his voice is low.

So why not go to the party?

You know why.

No, I don't.

It's just not my thing, is it? Champagne and canapés. A girl's parents.

William White, she says, and her voice catches him hard, like the corner of a tabletop. Don't you dare.

What?

Don't miss out on something good, simply because it's different. I didn't raise you with thoughts like that in your head, did I?

No, he says.

Well, then. Go. Eat canapés and apple tarts. Fall for the nice girl, for once.

You just like that she's got no piercings.

I liked that she looked me in the eye when we spoke, she says. And that she did the same with you.

They sit there together, the way they have so many times before. His grandma is short and squat, but she has always felt so large, to him, especially in this car. Despite being three heads shorter than he is, she somehow takes up so much space, with her knitted jumpers and her unsaid thoughts.

Amber's awake, he says, eventually.

I know. Pushing her luck, that girl.

By writing in journals at midnight?

It all starts somewhere, she says, as she opens her car door. Next she'll be staying out late, sneaking sherry out the cupboard. Loitering in car parks and getting arrested for it.

Too soon? she asks, when Will says nothing. He shrugs. Finds that words still elude him about that night, or that time in his life, in general.

He wasn't right.

He sees that now.

Things had been building ever since his mother left—after she walked out and never came back. Things that he squashed into the thin lines between what hurt and what didn't, just so he could get through the day.

He loved his grandparents. They were always the good ones, anyway, always had the hot meals and fresh sheets and a TV guide which meant he knew when the cowboy films were on. So he didn't miss her, really. Didn't even wonder about her, after so many years of nothing. After the birthday cards and the phone calls dwindled and then stopped.

But things began to get blurry after he started secondary school. He would spend days wading through what felt like deep water, everything in slow motion, and it was only alcohol, a shot of something to sharpen his wits, that could make him feel any better.

He doesn't know how he first discovered this.

Maybe it was his grandfather leaving out his nightly glass of whiskey. Maybe he stumbled across the drinks cabinet, simply because he was bored. All he knew was that if he wasn't sleeping, or he felt weighted down, a swig of something grown-up would soon make everything right.

He was twelve years old, at the time.

He drank more. Made some bad friends, bad choices.

By thirteen, he was skipping school and staying out for days and nights at a time, with groups of guys much older than him, into much harder stuff and with much harder pasts than his own. He found that helped with the pain, too. The danger of it. The knife edge he walked, every night he was with them, with their cigarettes and their packets of powder and their proclivity for theft. He stole things, too, when they asked him to. When the zip of alcohol no longer sufficed, and that jolt of energy—that *aliveness*—had to be found in other ways.

He did and saw things that he no longer thinks about.

Things he's buried good and deep.

But that night in the car park—the one his grandma likes to joke about, to pretend it's in the past and not something she is deeply ashamed of him for—that is different.

It's like a dirty, pointed object that he carries beneath his skin; a splinter, or an ingrown toenail.

Something he can pull out and turn over in his hands, if and when he feels the need.

*

Rosie takes Josh a glass of orange juice and some buttered toast, taps on his door with her foot. Inside, she sees the heap of him beneath his duvet, smells the bad teenage boy breath as she crosses the threshold.

She puts his breakfast down, opens the curtains and he grumbles and says no, please, and she says yes, that he's going to be late for school.

Can't do school, he says. Too ill.

I don't think hungover counts as ill, Rosie says.

Last day doesn't count, Josh huffs. We'll just sit around watching Christmas films.

While she knows this to be true, Rosie picks up a triangle of toast and holds it out, trying to tempt him nonetheless.

Is Mum home? he asks.

No. She's at the office.

And Dad?

Finishes at two. He said he'd try to get home early.

Then I'm staying right here, says Josh, and he burrows back beneath the bedclothes, leaves his toast untouched on the side.

Josh, Rosie says.

Mmm?

What's going on? You never drink like that. You never want to skip school.

First time for everything, he says, his voice muffled.

She looks at the mound of him, the wrinkles on his sheets.

You're okay, though, she says, and there is a long, musty pause before he says yes, and so she rises, leaves him to sleep. Takes a slice of toast on her way out.

five

◖

Christmas Eve arrives lightly misted, all beryl sky and frost-covered lawns, a fog that burns off like steam. Rosie's mother has asked her to pick up the tarts, like always, so she gets dressed early, pulls on her coat from the wardrobe. Josh's room is silent, as though he's still asleep. He's been sleeping late every day, since the dance.

Happy Christmas Eve, she says to her parents in the kitchen. College carols ease quietly from the stereo, and there is a pot of coffee on the table, the smell of leeks, creaming, on the hob. Her mother is already dressed, looping napkin rings around the linen.

Happy Christmas, darling, she says, and beams at her, and Rosie holds that, for a moment, before she kisses her father good morning. He gives her the money she needs, and her mother tells her to hurry back, that breakfast is at nine.

Outside, all is still.

Early morning sun, pure and cold and alpine.

She walks to the bakery and she picks up their order, then pauses at the corner shop and buys a bouquet of fresh flowers; reds and greens, splayed like branches from the forest. She thinks about the lighthouse, the view of the sea on a morning like this. She wonders if Will is awake, and running.

He has not texted her since his grandmother drove them home. Not confirmed whether he's coming, tonight.

She is supposed to head straight home for her mother's carefully planned spread, but her watch tells her she could make it, and so she heads for the beach. Puts the cake box down on the sand with the flowers, and removes her shoes, tucking her socks against the soles.

There is a single runner on the shore.

One brave, crazy person, swimming in a wetsuit and cap.

She walks down to the water and steps in, inhaling at the rush over her toes, and she has one of those rare moments of clarity where everything feels real and right and untroubled, and the world is open, and there is relief, in her bones, for a while.

On the way home, she decides to text him first.

Merry Christmas (Eve), she types. I have the apple tarts.

Winking face: a semicolon, end bracket. Too much, she thinks, and deletes, before she adds it again, and hits send.

*

Will lifts the brass ring on the blue door, and knocks.

Rosie's dad answers. He is a tall man with thinning hair, wearing a striped shirt with an open collar. Do I know you, he asks, and before Will can answer he laughs fully at his own question and steps back to let him in, says the young ones were in the dining room, last time he saw them. He takes Will's coat, tells him to have fun, then leaves him in the hall, humming as he goes.

Will stands there, for a moment. It is like he has stepped into the film that Amber had been watching when he'd left. Garlands wind up the banisters, all foliage and twinkling lights, not a shred of tinsel in sight. Everything looks clean and shiny. He can see through to the dining table from here, to a spread of miniature food on platters, guests glimmering in the turned-down lights with golden bubbles in their flutes.

He can't see his friends, so he heads for the food. Picks up a glass of something as he does so, and comes face to face with Mrs. Winters. She is wearing a flattering black dress, her hair scraped into a bun. Square shoulders, frown lines. Like a prima ballerina.

Will, she says, and smiles. She has sharp teeth, he thinks; but then, so does he.

Hi Mrs. Winters, he says. Thanks for the invite.

I'm not sure I invited you, she says.

Rosie did, he explains, and she says yes, she knows, and tells him to have a good time, then, that there's plenty to eat and drink, although it looks like he's already found the champagne. She leaves before he can retort, before he can apologize or drink it pointedly in front of her; he is not sure which way he'd have gone.

He takes a breadstick and moves into the living room, where, thankfully, he finds them: Josh and Rosie, sitting on the piano stool, their shoulders pressed together. She is in a velvet dress. Drop earrings sparkling in the tree lights.

Her cheeks are flushed, and she is laughing. Goes from serious to joyful, so fast. Then her eyes catch his, recognition crossing her face, and he heads toward her through the tangle of people. Josh is talking to someone on his other side, so they have two short seconds alone.

Hey, he says.

You came, she says.

He's about to answer when Josh turns and sees him standing there, his face splitting wide open in delight, like a child's.

Will!

Hey, man.

What're *you* doing here?

Your sister invited me, he says, after the shortest pause.

Did she, now, Josh asks, and he looks between them, knocks Rosie's knee with his own.

What, Rosie says, and she turns a deep red. Will looks away, runs his tongue along his bottom lip. Takes a large mouthful from his glass.

What you drinking? Josh asks him.

Not my usual, Will says, and Josh jumps up, says he'll get Coke, or beer, that there's pale ale in the fridge.

That'd be great, Will says, thinking it's fine, for one night, to have a few. Josh beams and heads through the crowd.

Another great dress, he says to Rosie, taking Josh's place beside her.

Oh, she says. Thank you.

Sorry I didn't tell you I was coming, he says. He takes another mouthful of champagne, even though he hates the stuff; the way it prickles at the back of his nose.

That's okay, she says. I like suspense.

Really?

No.

They both laugh, then, and he offers her his flute, and she goes to say no, he thinks, for the briefest of seconds, but then something changes and she takes it from him, sips at the place where his lips were.

Sparkly, she says.

Like this house, Will says. It's quite a party you throw.

It's all Mum, really.

You don't pitch in?

A little, she says. Sometimes. But she likes things a certain way.

Like mother like daughter, then.

It is a joke; a gentle attempt at teasing, but Rosie says nothing. Drains the rest of the champagne, then says yeah. She supposes so.

They both watch the room. Women in sequins and satin. Men belly-laughing, all groomed beards and buttoned cuffs and red shiny foreheads.

So are you gonna show me these apple tarts, then? Will asks her.

Have you had dinner?

Nope.

Then let's get a plate. Apple tarts come after.

How come?

Because they're dessert.

And?

You eat dessert after dinner.

Says who?

. . . the world?

Nobody's policing it, are they?

She turns to him, and her eyes are creased with humor, and he feels his insides contract with something other than desire. He likes it, and it scares him.

You want apple tarts first, then salmon or pork loin later?

I want the wildest thing you can come up with, Will tells her.

Rosie shows her tongue as she smiles, curls it ever so slightly in thought.

The wildest thing at my mother's party, she says. That's hard.

You're a creative person, aren't you?

Dessert first is good, she says.

You can't have that one. That's mine.

You're so bossy, she says.

I reckon you're bossier, he says, and she shifts back to face the room, makes an *ummm* sound, her thigh now touching his.

He doesn't hear what she says next because of this.

Will? she says.

Yeah?

How about *just* dessert.

He looks into her face. Counts the freckles, like nutmeg, dusted across her nose.

Just dessert, he repeats. You wouldn't.

Just apple tarts, she says. No, no, wait. *All* the apple tarts.

You've crossed a line, he says, and she laughs again, and that feeling is back, consumes him like the alcohol used to. Seeping everywhere, all over him.

They take the entire plate of apple tarts—puffs, really, the size of plums—and navigate their way to the conservatory. Rosie stops to offer the plate to guests, then makes it to the back door and slips outside. Will follows her, as planned, soon afterward.

The garden is long and narrow; bigger than his, because they're on the edge of town. It stretches so far back that he can't see the end of it; only the grass dissolving into shadow, hedgerows swallowed by the sky.

Rosie leads him to a square of decking framed by trellis, more lights twirled along the wood. There is a small table and four chairs, and they sit down, the December air sharp on their skin.

We can't keep doing this, Will says.

Doing what?

Meeting only in the freezing cold, or in dingy old music rooms.

Or the middle of the night in kitchens, she says.

Exactly. Can't I just take you out like a normal person?

Nope. I've got my exams, remember?

You've got exams, yeah, he says. And yet here we are. With apple tarts.

He gestures to the tray in front of them.

Together, he adds.

All rules are off at Christmas, she says, picking up a pastry.

I thought there were no rules?

Just eat an apple tart, will you?

She takes another off the platter and holds it out toward him. He thinks, for a second, about eating it straight from her fingers. Wonders what she'd do, if he did.

They really are amazing, she says.

You've hyped them up, you know.

I know.

And things are rarely deserving of such hype.

I disagree, she says. The Beatles. Led Zeppelin. Beyoncé.

That's an eclectic list.

Mozart, she continues, ticking them off on her fingers. Monet. Paris. Peanut butter.

Smooth or crunchy?

Always crunchy.

See, now I trust you a little more on the tarts, Will says, and he takes it from her and bites into it.

The pastry flakes as it should, the apple silk-soft between his teeth. Fruit jam, melting into the lightest layer of custard. He tastes cinnamon, and ginger. The nutmeg of her freckles.

So? she asks.

I'll need another, to make sure.

You loved it.

Let's test again.

Just say you loved it!

It's clearly an important matter to you, Will says, lifting another off the plate. And I want to make sure I give a thoroughly researched answer.

Rosie laughs then, and bites into her own. Lets out a tiny, beautiful noise.

He shivers at that sound.

———

They stay outside as long as they can stand it; four and a half apple tarts each, cold hands, numb toes.

I kind of like it, Rosie says, when they compare their loss of feeling. When there's a warm house right there, and I know we can just step inside.

It's why I like cold showers, Will says, as she stands, picks up the near-empty plate.

God, really?

It's not as bad as it sounds, he says. You get used to it.

How did you even discover that, though? What made you think, one day, I'll just turn this cold and see how it feels?

He follows her back to the house, glad she can't see his face.

We lost hot water one weekend, he says. Boiler broke.

Oh, she says. Then I guess that makes sense.

He says yeah, but he hasn't told her the truth. Hasn't told her that he just stopped feeling, altogether, for an entire month of his life. That he tried some things. Ice-cold showers, the least extreme.

Inside, someone is playing carols on the piano, and the dining room is deserted. The table looks like it's been ravaged by seagulls, crusts of bread left on plates, sauce stained onto the tablecloth. Will grabs a sausage roll while Rosie puts down the plate of remaining tarts, positions it in the same spot as before.

Who's playing, he asks, tipping his head toward the music.

That'll be Dad, she says. He's the one that got me into the piano. Sort of.

You're better, I'm guessing.

He just plays for fun, Rosie says, with a shrug.

And you don't?

I play because I have to, she says. Because I don't feel okay if I don't.

She fingers the linen of the tablecloth as she speaks.

Sorry, she says. Marley says I can be a bit intense, sometimes.

He takes her hand then, without thinking, sees that she has a constellation of freckles here, too. Her fingers fold into his own, and he has pulled her, gently, toward him, when Josh walks in and says oh.

Rosie steps back, like she's been burned, just as Will looks up and sees something cross Josh's face.

Hi, he says, but Josh doesn't say it back. He has the blurry look of someone who's been drinking, again. Not quite as much as before, but enough to make him different. Magnified.

Where on earth have you been, he asks.

We've been around, Rosie says. You must have just . . . lost us.

She gives a tiny smile, but Josh just stares at them both. There is a beer in his hand. He puts it down on the side and says, without looking at his sister, that their mum was asking for her. That she wants her to play for the guests now.

Rosie nods.

Josh, she says. Are you—

But he's already left the room.

Well, I guess I should, she says, gesturing toward the music.

Sure, Will says.

Come listen, she says, and he says that he will, once he's eaten something without sugar in it.

She smiles at him, and lingers, as if she's going to say more. But then she slips out without a word, and Will turns to what's left of the sandwiches. He picks one up and peels the bread apart.

Pâté, a voice informs him. Mrs. Winters is standing in the doorway, a freshly poured flute in her hand.

What kind, he asks.

Wild boar, she says. Or Brussels, maybe. There were two.

Course there were, he thinks, and he takes a bite, chews it slowly in front of her. She looks remarkably neat for the late hour. Like no time has passed since she put up her hair and applied her makeup, all thick lines and bronze tones and straight edges.

Where are the twins? she asks him.

Roe went to play piano, he says. And Josh—

Roe?

There is a tight smile on her lips. The champagne hisses in her glass.

Rosie, he says, with a shrug.

You like my daughter, then, she says.

Will leans against the table and waits. Not sure if it's a question. If it's any of her business. He has the impression that this woman is used to pulling justifications out of people, and he has none for her.

She's a good girl, she says, and he says he knows.

You're not playing some kind of game, are you, she asks.

What sort of game?

The sort guys like you play, Will. Let's be real here. Let's be adults.

Guys like me?

You're not dating her for a dare, or something?

I'm not dating her, full stop, he says, and his voice is curt, and his heart has turned to rock. The pâté is thick and oily along the roof of his mouth. He hates it.

Ah-ha, she says. But you plan to?

I plan to do only what Rosie wants, he says, and she smiles properly, then, and takes a sip from her flute. Her lipstick is dark red and does not smudge, even as she drinks.

Well, then, she says. That's all I wanted to hear.

The amateur piano playing has stopped.

Merry Christmas, then, he says.

Yes. Merry Christmas, Will, Mrs. Winters says, her eyes not leaving his face.

The piano starts up again, and it is different, and softer, and he knows that it must be Rosie playing now. Her mother leaves the room to watch, and he is left with the sandwiches and the lukewarm blinis, a mushroom-rich taste in his mouth.

*

Rosie loses herself in the songs she has written, purely for tonight.

She always starts writing in the autumn, inspired by the smallest things. Pink-footed geese, flown home for the winter. The school cleaner, with her scarred hands, the peeled laminate of her name badge.

They smoke like coals inside her, for a while. She has them written by November. Then reveals them, first heard, on the piano at her mother's party, same as she's always done, same, she's sure, as she always will.

And people listen. Things go quiet; the chatter dies. Her hands move over the keys like she's blind and tracing braille; effortless and a part of her. And when she finishes, there is applause. The clock on the mantelpiece reads eleven, and her father booms Merry Christmas, and there are chinked glasses and air-kisses and thank-yous and goodnights.

Tonight, after she's done, she turns on her stool and watches as the guests leave. Waits, for her twin brother, or for Will, but neither of them shows.

When everyone has gone and the house is in darkness, when she is in her pajamas and her teeth are brushed and she has checked her phone for the twentieth time, Rosie turns off her bedside lamp.

She lies there for all of three minutes, her heart thrumming. There is an anvil on her chest, and it forces her out of bed, into her brother's room.

Josh, she whispers.

He waits, as though he's not going to answer. But then he opens his duvet and she gets in beside him. It is bodily warm, and she presses her bare feet into his.

Jesus, he says, nudging her away. Your feet are like ice.

Sorry, she says, and something in her can't quite believe that she is apologizing, for this, when he missed her playing—when he's never missed it, before.

Are you okay, she asks, after he says nothing more.

Yeah, he says, into the dark.

You don't seem it.

Go to sleep, Rosie.

He turns away from her, then, but he doesn't ask her to leave. She stares up at his ceiling and then turns away herself, so their backs are pressed together, warm and solid and unmoving.

*

Will wakes, close to 5 a.m.

He feels sick with sugar and champagne. Light-headed, with everything else.

He had listened to Rosie playing, from his place by the dining table. Songs that flowed like seawater from one verse to another. Songs he didn't recognize, and so knew they must be hers.

He did not know what to say to her, about the music.

And so he left.

Easier, that way. Before he ruined things, like he always seems to.

He gets up, though it is still dark, puts on his trainers and leaves the house. It is cuttingly cold outside, but he heats up as he jogs along the street, sticking to the pavements for the lamplight.

He focuses on his breath, the thud of his feet.

Finds himself thinking about his mother.

She liked Christmas. She didn't like a lot of things, but Christmas morning was different, gave her some kind of supple edge. Permission to slow down, to be around instead of out, doing whatever it was that she did. Before Amber was born, when it was just the two of them, she would buy him special cereal, the expensive, branded sort, and they'd eat it in bed out of the box, watching cartoons on the TV.

She liked the Disney ones. Not Looney Tunes. Too loud, she said. Too crazed.

Then they'd head to his grandma's for midmorning, and she'd sit on the sofa and drink orange juice and it would be the one day of the year when nobody argued, when they'd eat and open a few gifts and maybe walk to the park with his grandpa.

No regrets, she would say, when they'd chink their glasses at dinner, and they'd all repeat her words, even Will, who was only young, and had no idea what regret was.

When Amber was born, though, things changed. They started spending Christmas Eve, and night, and morning, at his grandparents' place, without his mother, and their shared cereal became a thing of the past. Spending nights at home did, too, but he was never told why, and so he never asked.

He remembers her snowflake earrings.

Dangly, chipped things she got out of a Christmas cracker one time, and would wear every year, without fail.

He wonders if she still has them. What she might look like now.

Runs faster, until his lungs hurt.

———

Merry Christmas, William, his grandmother says when he comes down later that morning, showered, dressed and thirsty.

You too, he says, and he pours himself a pint glass of water, drinks it standing at the sink.

That was an early one, even for you, she says, as she peers in the oven, her bird already roasting. The kitchen smells of meat juices and stock.

Woke up at five, he says. Couldn't sleep.

How was your night?

Good, he says. Decent food.

I'm glad, she says, and she doesn't ask anything more, though he's aware that she's playing him. Because if she doesn't ask questions, he'll end up telling her, eventually. He always does.

I really like her, Gran, he says. He pours himself a cup of tea from the pot on the side. Adds one sugar cube, and then another.

That much is clear, she says, and she slips off her oven mitts, takes her own mug from the counter and faces him. He takes a sip of his tea, which is strong and black and sweet.

I don't have time for girls, he says.

Since *when*? his grandma asks.

As in, properly, he says. I've got my bike, and my travel plans, you know? And she's going to uni in the autumn.

He takes another mouthful of tea. His heart beats slowly in his ears.

She told me I have to wait till her exams are over. Well. *I* told her I'd wait. I don't really know why. I don't, you know . . . want to care.

His grandmother peers at him over her mug, and for once, he can't read her expression. Her eyes are crinkled, like dates. Dark as treacle.

Perhaps you have no time for girls, she says. But you have time for *the* girl.

He wants to roll his eyes at her. Finds that he can't.

You'll figure it out, lad, she says, turning back to the stove. Is she coming to tea, later?

I don't actually know, he says. She didn't say.

Well, she says. Let's see, shall we.

Let's see, he says.

*

Rosie sees his text, late in the day, wishing her a Merry Christmas. Saying he loved the apple tarts. She stares at it, for all of three seconds, then asks her mother if she can go to Marley's.

Now? her mum asks, her eyes glassy with wine. There is classical music playing from their old gramophone, her uncle and father playing cards in the armchairs by the window. Her baby cousin is crawling along the carpet, her aunt hovering above her.

I wouldn't normally ask, Rosie says. It's just she's got this new karaoke game, and Josh is still in bed, so . . .

Karaoke?

SingStar, she says. She got the new one for Christmas.

You girls, she says. You're just a little musical duo, aren't you?

Yep, Rosie says, her stomach winding in on itself, because she is lying, and she's not even sure that she needs to. But she cannot bring herself to tell the truth about this. About him. Not yet.

As long as you don't outstay your welcome, her mum says. Her parents don't mind?

They said it was fine.

Take something, then, she says. One of the bottles in the wine fridge. Or that stollen we never opened? Don't go empty-handed.

I would never, Rosie says, and her mother smiles at her, the symphony in the background lulling her eyes to a slow blink.

Rosie, she says, as Rosie turns to go.

Yes?

Your piano, last night.

Yes.

It was sublime, she says, and Rosie is filled up with those words, and her doubt about tonight, and the self-loathing from the lies, all of it lifts, for a moment, like steam from a cup into air.

She knocks on Josh's door before she leaves. She has taken her hair out of its plaits, letting it fall past her shoulders. Changed out of her dinner dress into jeans, and a soft blouse she would want to be touched in.

Not that she is expecting to be touched, at Will's grandmother's house.

But she wants to look good. To feel it.

To have him look at her the way he did at the winter dance, like he wanted to drink the words from her mouth.

When Josh doesn't answer, she pushes his door open so the light from the hall falls in stripes across the floorboards. His curtains are closed. He's playing indie music, soft and low, from his computer speakers.

Josh, she says.

He doesn't answer, but she knows he isn't asleep.

You feeling any better? she asks him. He'd had a stomachache all day; wasn't his usual self when they traded gifts or sat down to Christmas lunch; wouldn't meet her eyes when she asked him to pass the gravy.

I'm going out, she says.

He remains silent, but she senses a shift in his attention.

To Marley's, she says, using her fingers as air quotes. If anyone asks.

Her brother raises his head off his pillow; she sees that his eyes are wet.

Josh, she says, and her voice has changed. Talk to me.

And it is her twin voice; her leveled, serious, I-am-entirely-yours voice, which finally seems to get through. He shuffles to a seated position, opening the duvet as if in invitation. Rosie shuts the door and flicks on his lamp and sits, cross-legged, beside him, so that they're both staring at the wall.

There is something, Josh says, and Rosie says she knows.

Are you okay? she asks. Are you really sick?

No, he says.

Is it uni? Do you not want to go to Cambridge anymore? Or have you just fallen behind? I can help you—

It's none of those things, he says, so she falls silent, gives him time.

What's going on with you and Will, he asks her, as if to fill the gap that he needs; some filler, while he finds a way forward. She passes her palm over his duvet cover, an ombré in navy blue.

Nothing, she says.

Doesn't seem like it, he says.

How does it seem?

It seems like I couldn't find you both for an hour last night, he says. And then when I *did* find you, you lied about it. Made out you didn't want privacy, even though you so blatantly did, standing so close, like that.

Rosie blows the air out of her mouth.

I know, she says. God, I'm sorry. I didn't mean to do that.

So then?

So what?

Are you going to tell me the truth?

She thinks he is being overly standoffish with her, for a relatively inoffensive crime. She didn't think he'd care so much about her potentially liking his friend. But perhaps he thinks more happened than it did; perhaps he's hurt that she's not told him all the details, and this is what has stung. That, during their last Christmas together, before they go away and live apart and become different versions of themselves, it seems like she's keeping secrets. And they have never kept secrets. Ever.

Okay, she says. We hung out, a bit. Nothing happened, I promise you. Nothing is happening. But I like him. And maybe he likes me, too. I don't know.

Another lie, she thinks, and so she corrects herself.

He asked me to meet him one night, she says. At the lighthouse. And we talked, for a while, and it was nice. And he does like me, he's sort of made that clear, I think.

Josh is not reacting; not looking at her. He keeps his eyes ahead.

So yeah, Rosie says. It's not going anywhere, Josh. Definitely not before our exams; I said that to him already. So you don't need to worry, he can still coach you in maths. And who knows, by the summer he'll probably be over it, you know? So it might not ever get to a place where it's awkward or anything.

She keeps talking, because she is not sure what is keeping him so silent, and the more she talks the more she thinks she is realizing what it could be, what she has always suspected, because she knows him, all of him, down to his cells and his movements and his moods, but he's never said, never shared, and so she keeps saying things to give him time, to prolong this moment where everything feels like it did last night, when she thought he was merely cross about being left out.

It's all fine, she says, because she so desperately wants it to be.

Josh nods, once, and slowly. He moves his palms down toward his knees, as if he's stretching. Exhaling as he does so.

Here's the thing, he says.

Rosie waits. The classical music from downstairs changes track; there is a pause, then a new song starts up, floats toward them up the staircase.

That's all great, he says. For you. Really.

Thanks, she says, because she's so relieved, so wildly and suddenly relieved, that this is all he has said.

It's just, I like him too.

I know you do. But I promise it won't be weird, if things go wrong. You guys can still be—

No, Rosie. I like him too.

There is a silence, their heartbeats sounding as one. It is like something clicks, even as the room slows; like shadows shifting to light on the floorboards. Waking to a day she'd been waiting for.

Oh, she says.

Yeah.

He is still not looking at her. He is studying his hands now, the whitlows beside his fingernails.

Josh, she says. Her voice a breath.

I know, he says. Shocker.

And then he begins to cry, great, lurching sobs she has never heard come from him in all her life, and he reaches his arms out for her and she holds him, like that, with the notes of Whitacre drifting up the stairs, little trees and green forests and so many tears, like the salt from the sea on her shirt. A shirt she had chosen for its softness, minutes before, like that mattered, in any way, at all.

six

◖

School starts up again, too soon. The paper chains from December are still dangling in the windows, scissor-cut snowflakes stuck to the glass.

Will sits through homeroom and woodwork and takes his free period in the library with his mates, not studying, not keeping it down, not doing any of the things the posters on the walls ask them to do. The librarian huffs at them from her desk.

He did not hear from Rosie after the party. He spent the rest of the Christmas break running, for miles, and faster than usual. Riding his motorbike, accelerating hard, taking corners lower than he should.

When the bell rings to signal the end of lunch, he makes his way to maths.

He's worried about seeing Josh again.

It's no coincidence, in Will's mind, that he found them together in the dining room, seemed oddly troubled by this, and that Rosie then stopped messaging. That clearly, Josh had a problem with it, and Will's not entirely surprised, because he knows a lot of guys, and he's pretty sure that despite their banter and semblance of mutual respect, none of them would want him dating their sisters.

A small, stifled part of him thought that maybe Josh was different. That he knew Will wasn't the guy everyone thinks he is. He feels irritated, but also kind of bad about it. Isn't sure what to say while they share a desk for the next hour.

But Josh is not there.

It is just Will and Mr. Brookman, who actually stays in the classroom for once, running through all the topics that could come up in the exam. Asking him what he wants refresher lessons on this term, as if it's an important question; as if it'll make one bit of difference to anything.

That night is his first shift back at the garage. He sweeps the floor, fits some brake cables, and then rides home on his motorbike, the air slicing past his face like sheet metal.

On the nights that he works, his gran leaves his dinner warming in the oven. She is often reading in her room by the time he's home, early to bed in the winter. But tonight, she is downstairs. Sitting at the table and reading the local paper, Dave curled at the side of her chair.

You're up late, he says.

I guess I am, she says.

How come, he asks her, as he eases his bowl out of the oven. He can just about touch it, if he moves fast. He slides it onto the table, grabs a fork and slumps into a chair.

My hips hurt, his grandmother says. Old age, I suppose.

He takes a forkful of food, looks at her as he chews.

You're not old, he says.

I'm getting there, I'm afraid.

Sixty is the new fifty, he says, and she chuckles, says she was sixty almost seven years ago now, remember?

Will blinks. He can't believe that much time has passed since her six-tieth. There were balloons, and an ice-cream cake, and his grandpa was still alive.

D'you miss him? she asks, as if reading his mind. He has a mouthful of hot potato, and it burns his throat as he swallows.

I don't really think about it, he says.

She raises her eyes to his.

You do, though, he says. Obviously.

Every hour, she says, and he stops eating, at this. She folds the news-paper in half, sets it aside.

But that's the sign of a good marriage, I think, she says.

I'll say.

There is a short silence, just the sound of his own chewing, the buzz from the lightbulbs above them.

Speaking of which, she says, and he braces himself.

What's happening with your love life?

Not a lot, Gran.

Well, that much is obvious.

He shrugs, wondering if all teenage guys are subjected to such scru-tiny from their grandmothers, and is about to say so, when she asks him what happened, that night at the party.

Nothing, he says.

Nothing, she repeats.

Nope.

Because you seemed high as a kite when you got back. And you've been a grumpy sod ever since Rosie didn't show up on Christmas Day.

Thanks a lot.

Just telling you how I see it, lad.

He picks up his fork again, nudges his dinner round the bowl.

She just never got in touch, he says.

His grandma eyes him. Says that's a shame, but it happens.

I know, he says. I don't care.

Oh, Will, she says, and she laughs, which he thinks is completely unfair, considering. I can't have you moping around like this. Going out like you've got hell to pay, coming back with a face like thunder. Let's do something about this, shall we?

I can't do anything about it, he says.

Nonsense, she says. You always can.

This is just what being a teenager is, he says, spearing a potato too violently, so the prongs clang against the bowl. You win some, you lose some.

I remember, she says. And I also remember, if I wanted something—even if it was just an answer—I would go out and get it.

Their clock chimes its cuckoo song from the front room. Will eats the potato, something building inside him.

It doesn't just apply to teenagers, she says, after a while. My own mum used to say, you get what you ask for, and you land what you look for.

So you went looking for this life, did you, Will asks her.

It is a single sentence, but the undertone is enough. His grandmother sits back in her chair.

I treasure this life I made, yes, she says.

Will spews some air out of his mouth. Puts down his fork.

I'm going to bed, he says, and she says fine, and he climbs the stairs, burning, all over. Because he wants more. Because he doesn't want to sit in a house with old carpets and someone else's kids and a sad little routine where all the days look the same, and he hates that he was her reason for that, and he won't go looking for something he wants when he doesn't know what that is, yet, exactly, when all he knows is it's not this.

———

That night, he types out a text to Rosie. It is half three in the morning, the same time they parted ways in her kitchen that time, and he is awake, and seething.

Where have you been? he types out, then deletes.

Lighthouse tomorrow, he tries, instead. At five.

And he presses send.

*

Rosie runs on the treadmill until her sides feel like they could tear open.

She has gained weight over Christmas. Like everyone, she's sure. But it hangs around her neck like a task she needs to get on top of; a mistake she's made that needs rectifying.

And as she runs, her mind is full. Not with revision and homework and music, but her twin brother, and how much he cried, and how he's barely spoken to her since.

She turns up the speed on the machine. All her feelings blazing in her limbs, calories shedding off her like skin.

The lighthouse seems lonelier than before. She remembers the sunset from last time, the neon streaks of the sky. Tonight, all is gray and flat. A seagull picks at something dead on the shore.

She is freezing. The sweat from the treadmill has dried on her skin, and she shivers beneath her jacket.

Will shows up soon after her, in his own running gear, his hair damp with sweat, but his cheeks barely flushed.

I go so red when I run, is the first thing she says to him. And you look like you just stepped out of an Adidas advert.

Going red is healthy, he says, leaning on the railing beside her. I'm just pasty because of the cigarettes. And 'cause I drink a lot of Coke.

Is that right, she says, and she curses herself for starting it like this; for saying these irrelevant things.

Thanks for coming, he says.

Sure, she says. I'm sorry for, you know. Going silent.

It's okay, he says, but he's looking at her like it's not.

I just can't do this, she tells him.

This again? he asks.

No, seriously, Rosie says, and she shakes her head, hard, as if to rid herself of her own hair, strands of which are blowing across her face. I don't know what we've been doing, Will. Being friends, really, more than anything. And that's great. That's all we should be, I think.

He keeps looking at her. His mouth has set. His stubble has grown longer since Christmas Eve.

Why? he asks.

Different worlds, she shrugs. Different agendas.

I don't have an agenda, he says.

You know what I mean.

I really don't, Roe.

She is going to have to do it; going to have to lie, just to stop the questions, to turn off this tap they've both been drinking from, for weeks.

I just don't like you in that way, she says. I'm sorry.

He looks so surprised, for a moment, that she almost laughs; doubts he has been turned down before. But she hates saying it, hates swallowing all the things she really wants to say. It's for the best, she reminds herself. It's the right thing.

The wind is brash and batters their legs; Rosie's hair still flecks across her face and neck, and the air smells of that heavy, weighted smell that comes before the rain. There is a special word for it, she knows. Or perhaps that's for after it rains; she can't remember. Will has looked away from her, out toward the sea, but then he steps forward and his eyes latch on to hers. Storm-gray on blue. And then he takes her face in his hands and says just one, inquiring word.

Seriously?

Rosie doesn't move. She can't. And his eyes scan her own, to check that it's okay, that she was lying, just now, and then he's kissing her and she forgets that she's cold, that she came here to end it, because she is thawing, all over, and his hands are in her hair, tracing the tops of her ears, and she can't think of anything except this, and how this is what a first kiss should be, and how no one has ever touched her neck, like this, before.

Everything alight.

Wildfires, inside of her, with the sea and the trees and the damp air, things softening and flaring in a moment that lasts, and lasts, and is over.

Then he stands back, and takes his hands from her face.

Didn't think so, he says, and she tells him he's unbearable, and he laughs. Leans his forehead against hers.

They leave the seafront because of the wind; trace Will's footsteps back through the forest, which shelters them from the rain.

They are talking about albums; the ones they got for Christmas, which seems too normal, after what just happened at the beach; too polite, somewhat shy. They mention Bright Eyes and The Shins. Mazzy Star, who Rosie treasures like sleep, and whom Will has never heard of.

He is walking in front of her, his back streaked with sweat from his run. Rosie has things to say, and things she can't, so she just follows him down the path, silent except for when he asks her a direct question.

She keeps her answers short, basic.

He seems happy and talkative, looks even taller than before. And she is filled up with everything, butterflies and cravings and the thing that just happened.

But her throat is tight.

She wants nothing more than to run home, now, in her tired trainers, to tell her twin brother all about it. And she keeps thinking how she can't.

Roe? Will stops walking.

Hm?

I asked what you're doing for dinner tomorrow.

Oh. I'm not sure.

I think my gran feels like she missed out, not meeting you properly at Christmas.

Okay.

So d'you want to come over? She's a good cook.

I'm sure she is.

Roe?

Yeah?

What's up? You look all freaked out.

He has turned around to face her, and the trees are tall behind him, the smell of pine and soil and darkness descending all around. She takes a step back.

I came here to end things, she reminds him.

Because of your exams, he says.

And because of some other stuff, too, she says. It's just . . . not right.

That wasn't right? Will asks, and he jerks his head toward the beach. Rosie bites the inside of her cheek. Tells him no. It's very nice, and she's flattered, but it's just not the right time, for her.

We agreed that already, he says. And I told you I'd wait.

Inviting me to dinner is not waiting, she says.

Well, fine, he says. Come to dinner in May. Or June. Whenever the hell your exams end.

Will, she says.

What?

Don't do that. Don't get angry. I've said all this from the beginning.

And you kissed me back, just now, he says. And if I remember rightly, *you* invited *me* to your fancy Christmas party. Don't make me feel like I'm the one confusing things here.

I never said you were—

Can you just tell me what the actual problem is? he asks. Is it your mother?

My mother?

Do you really care that she doesn't like me? Because I don't.

Where on earth have you got that from?

It can't just be your grades, either. I saw last year's, Roe, on the results board. I doubt you need another mark to get into Oxford.

That's not true.

Is it Josh? Was he mad?

No, Rosie says, somewhat louder than she'd intended. It's got nothing to do with Josh.

So what are you so worried about?

Nothing, she says.

Is it the smoking? The motorbike? The break from school that happened *eons* ago?

Yes, she says, latching on. Yes, it's all of that, Will. All of it. You're the wrong kind of person, for me, okay?

Will has his mouth open, as if he'd been forming an argument. But it doesn't come. Rosie watches him as he realizes what's she's saying, what she means, and her heart closes up, like a shell.

She waits. Wants to reach out, bury herself in him, take it back. But it's done. The spark in Will's face, his stormy, flecked eyes, has gone. He lapses back to the boy she'd known before she knew him, cool and distant, and still he says nothing, though she can hear so much noise in the silence between them, the lie, the hurt on both sides, because it is not fair, this is not fair, and she wants to tell him the truth, but she can't, and her throat swells as she watches him believe all that she's said. She wants him to yell. Wants him to challenge her. Instead he just nods, swallows it whole, and they stand there, losing the daylight.

seven

◖

Their exams end in May. It is an unusually hot afternoon, and the unlucky ones with papers on the last day are met with spraying soft drinks, streamers thrown on their clothes. Will is one of them. He and Josh had their final further maths paper after lunch, and afterward, they walk out of school together for the last time.

Things are different between them now. For weeks, Josh had spoken to him strictly about maths, as if Will had crossed some sort of line, betrayed him in a complex way that neither of them ever discussed. This bothered Will, for a time. But then he called Darcy and spent most evenings at her house, went back to meeting friends at bonfires on the beach. He upped his shifts at the garage, went for long, winding rides along the coast on his motorbike. Things were good. Things were fine. He was soon to be done with school. Released, the day he got that slip of paper, no matter what letters were on there.

But today, as they leave the atrium and wander down the path and get sprayed with Silly String, the tension lifts off the both of them. They laugh together. People are shrugging off their blazers, shedding their uniforms. The sun is the color of butter, and it melts over everything; the pavements, the parked cars, the sixth formers spilling out through the school gates.

Done, says Josh, dusting his hands together.

Boom, says Will, and Josh throws his head back and laughs.

Boom, he repeats. You know it!

Guys, says a voice from behind them. It's Darcy, and Will's shoulders sag. They'd spent weeks fucking in her house when her mother was out, and in his garage, on the concrete floor, when she wasn't. Not once had she complained, until she'd decided she wanted someone to take her to dinner. Someone to go to Norwich with on the weekends, to meet her raucous friends, buy her froth-topped lattes in coffee chains.

Will was not that someone.

They've not spoken for weeks, but in this moment, with the sun beaming down and school finished forever and everyone drenched in lemonade, this doesn't seem to matter.

Big party at Jessica's tonight, she says.

Cool, says Josh.

I won't be touching you with a barge pole, Will White, she says, but she stares him down, as though by saying this, he'll want to touch her all the more.

Understood, he says.

But both of you are invited, all right? Tell everyone. The more the merrier, or whatever.

What's the story there, Josh asks, as Darcy stalks off, and they continue down the hill.

There isn't one, Will says. We hooked up. Then we stopped.

Such drama, says Josh.

Josh, mate.

Yeah?

Are we okay?

He doesn't realize he is going to say it; doesn't plan on asking such a thing. It just comes out. His heart feels light and open with the sun, or the freedom, and he finds that he just needs to know.

Josh looks at him sideways, as if he's going to feign ignorance, perhaps ask him what he means. But he doesn't. They keep walking. Birds warble overhead, celebrating the blue of the sky.

Course, Josh says, and he bashes his shoulder with his own. Asks if he thinks he'll go, tonight. If he should wear his Hawaiian shirt.

*

Summer comes. It is the longest one they've known, and yet it slides by so fast, the academic year refusing to wait. Weeks of iced coffees shared in the park, clear straws, blue drinks that stain their tongues and turn them giddy and loud and happy. University shopping lists; cutlery, saucepans, printed photos of school friends they're certain they'll love forever, never lose touch with, whom they'll see at Christmas and then never again.

Rosie meets up with Marley. They go for walks along the river, take-away slushies in hand, and she listens as her friend chatters on about Tom. Rosie pretends she's interested and tries not to burst with her own story, the kiss by the sea that she can still taste in her mouth. It still gets her sometimes, when she least expects it, at night as she lies on top of her sheets, or when she's washing her hair, in the bath, and she's naked and wet and alone.

But no. Not allowed.

Not fair, remember, on anyone.

When she's not with Marley, she and Josh spend long afternoons in their garden, listening to her iPod, trailing an earphone each so they can talk, or else listen to the neighbor's shears, the drone of low-flying bees.

They do not speak of what he'd told her.

She tries, once or twice, to bring it up, to see if he's ready to talk more, but he just turns the music up louder.

She has never known him to not let her in like this, and it troubles her, but in spite of the summer holidays, with their exams over and their new lives waiting, they are both continually busy. At their mother's suggestion, they both tutor younger students to keep their brains sharp, and they both still attend their music lessons. Josh trains with his basketball team twice a week and Rosie keeps to her gym regime, so the weeks slip by, results day looming ever closer. And this distracts her. Means the thing that matters, the thing they should really get into, is held at arm's length, like something on her to-do list that she remembers, sometimes, and knows she will have to address, soon. When he's ready.

*

And then the last Tuesday in August rolls round—a Tuesday that happens to be Will's birthday. It is the prelude to his friends' lives changing come September, and his birthday marks something of significance; one last excuse for them to all laugh, and drink, and be young together.

You've got to mark it, mate, someone said to him. I'll bring a keg.

I don't really drink, Will reminded him, which didn't seem to matter.

And so he finds himself, turning nineteen, sitting cross-legged on the grass atop the cliffs at Burwood Bay. Sipping a single beer, and wondering where the months have gone, and how the two people he'd want to spend his birthday with are not here, because they haven't spoken, really, all summer.

They'd both got into Oxbridge, of course. Two out of three who'd applied. He'd seen them hugging on results day, Rosie in tears, Josh holding her aloft like a trophy.

Will had done fine, too. Had folded his letter into his pocket and gone back to his shift at the garage. He'd seen them both at a house party, soon after. Passed Josh, on the high street, the week before, and kept Rosie, mainly, from his thoughts.

But there is something about the light of tonight.

Candyfloss clouds, the sun meeting the line of the sea and melting to liquid gold, and it bothers him that neither of them is here to see it. So he texts them. Says he knows it's been a while, but it's his birthday, and everyone's out, and she replies first, asks where he is.

He types back and leaves no full stop, so it is open-ended and the start of something, though of course neither of them knows this when she says yes, they'll be there, and Will puts his phone away and feels, for the last time in a long time, a sense of having done the right thing.

*

I'm over him, you know.

This is what Josh says to her as they walk past the wetlands, toward the clifftops of Burwood Bay. The sky is a puffed, marshmallow pink, and they catch sight of a barn owl with its silent wings, swooping over the fields.

Really? she says.

Sort of. As much as you can be over your first gay crush.

It is the first time she's heard him say it. The first time he's identified as such, out loud.

Josh, she says, because she doesn't know what else to say; doesn't think he's as okay as he sounds. They are walking side by side but he is a half step ahead, so she can't quite see his face. Just the angle of his cheekbone.

There are two major issues with him, see, Josh goes on.

Okay, she says.

He's not gay, for one thing, he says. Bit of a problem.

Yeah, she says. Scared of saying anything more.

Plus he's into someone else, he says.

Oh, she says. Right.

Her heart rate skitters, and something balloons in her throat, because she isn't sure if he means her or another girl, and either way, it makes her feel dreadful.

There is no wind as they walk; just the weight of summer, the smell of grass and seeds and earth. They ended up sneaking out tonight, because they both have to teach tomorrow, after their own early-bird music lessons.

They had asked, at first. Explained it was Will's birthday, and that all their friends would be there.

You *can* go, their mother had said, but I think it's best you're fresh for your lessons, don't you? And when she'd gone to bed early Josh had said screw it, Rosie, we're uni students now, and so they'd climbed out of his window onto the garage roof, like they did when they were kids, where they would go to watch the stars together if Rosie couldn't sleep.

He'd helped her down with his long arms, and they'd set off, giddy with rebellion; Rosie feeling the slightest bit sick.

That person's still you, Josh says now. In case you didn't know.

Her swollen throat eases, slightly, but her cheeks burn.

Yeah, she says. Breathing in, out. Then she says, who knows why.

Don't do that, Josh says.

What?

Don't be so coy. It's annoying.

I'm not, Josh! He's . . . well, he's Will White, and he could have anyone he wanted.

And he has. Historically.

Well, she stutters, yeah.

Until you.

What do you mean?

Well, you're not together, are you? That's probably pretty hot, for him. That he can't have you just because he wants you.

Rosie doesn't reply to this. It feels like some kind of backward compliment, aggressive, somehow, and she drops her eyes to the ground.

But you're also the best, Josh says, his voice stiff. So maybe he's got good taste, after all.

Thanks, she says, though she still feels somewhat chastised. Things between her and Josh have seemed normal, mostly, since results day. But he has moments when he turns distant, or unfriendly; hours where he lies in his room, or acts uninterested if she tries to tell him about a new song, or a funny thing Marley said.

So go out with him, if you want, Josh says, as he opens a gate, slides the metal bar back on its spring. They pass through, shut it hard against its latch.

Go out with him? Rosie repeats.

Yeah. Don't let me stand in your way.

His voice does not align with his words; every syllable, to her, sounds like an obstruction, solid and with hard edges. She thinks back to catching her thigh on the corner of her bed that morning. The triangular bruise that came after.

You weren't the reason, she says.

Josh has sped up, his strides so long that Rosie needs to trot to keep pace. But he slows, at this, glances round at her with his hazel eyes.

There were lots of reasons, she says. For us not getting together.

Is one of them that you're scared?

Yes, she says, because he's her brother, and he knows it, and she's not sure why he's being so brutal with her, tonight.

Kind of terrified, actually, she says, and this seems to take the spite out of him. He stops walking, turns to face her properly.

You can't be scared of everything you can't control, Rosie, he says.

She shrugs, crosses her arms.

I could say the same to you, she says. Why are you being like this?

You mean why am I being a normal human instead of a bouncing ball of sunshine?

Well, yeah!

Because I'm just working stuff out, Rosie, okay?

I know you are. But why won't you let me help you?

'Cause it's my thing, he says, walking again.

So you keep saying, she says, and once more, she has to hurry to keep up. But you're my brother. And I can't bear that you're hurting.

Rosie, he says, and he laughs, but it's not a good laugh; it stings, like hard spray from the sea. Just focus on your own happiness for once, yeah? Can you do that?

She trails behind him, treading in the trampled grass where his shoes have just been. His house keys clink in her pocket; he always asks her to safeguard them on a night out, because she is reliable, keeps track of things so he doesn't have to. And she's happy to do it. Has never felt like she was interfering, or mothering him, until now.

I'll try, she says. If you do, too.

I'm working on it, Josh tells her. Promise.

That last word sounds more like him; softer, like the long grass beside them.

He had shared more with her, on Christmas night. How he'd never known, like you're supposed to. All those people who just knew, in their heart, in their bones, since they were children; he just hadn't. He'd not felt an attraction to anyone, ever, boy or girl or otherwise, and he'd not worried, or cared, figured it would come with age.

And it did. Flickers, at first, when he was watching a film, or passing someone on the street. And then a boy he sat next to in maths, who suddenly made everything real.

Rosie heard all this, and she held him, and she said she was sorry, she was sorry she hadn't been there, hadn't asked him about it sooner. She'd always suspected, of course. The way you suspect someone will be a great cook, or can hold their drink. Something that's a part of them, but means nothing, really; nothing that changes anything, for you.

Why don't we just tell Mum and Dad, she tries now, as they trail along the path.

Not this again, Rosie.

I just think it might help.

What's going to help, right now, is drinking a lot of cider and sitting with my friends and forgetting about everything until the early hours of the morning, okay?

That's not healthy, Josh.

Oh, and your constant checking is? Don't think I can't hear you creeping around your room half the night, doing those weird things you do.

It is like he has hit her; something shrinks inside her with the shame of it, spoken aloud like that. By him.

The barn owl swoops ahead of them, again. Sandy wings in the half-light.

Sorry, he says. Sorry, Rosie.

S'okay, she says, and they don't speak again as they climb the cliff path, as the long grass gives way to chalk dust, and they start to smell the fire and the salt.

Up on the cliff, the bonfire reaches and spits. There is leftover birthday cake, shop-bought and too dry and still in its plastic wrapper. Someone is playing drum and bass from a speaker, and she sees a couple rolling in the grass, get a room, a guy calls, and gets a middle finger in return. Josh does what he intended and downs three ciders within the first half hour, and soon, all the light has left the sky.

It is like the night she first met Will.

Ink black, and intimate.

When she settles beside Marley, Rosie catches Will's eye across the flames, and he raises a hand, but barely, as if he's merely lifting his drink. She wants to go over, but does not know what she'd say, so she drinks red wine from a plastic cup and listens to people talk and tries to pretend she's not aware of him, over there, so intently not looking her way.

She's wearing a dress, with no tights. Wishes, now, that she'd worn jeans, as her naked knees point toward him.

An hour later, she walks to the edge and looks out at the expanse of ocean, just a dark mass, now that the sun has set. There is a sixty-foot drop to the rocks below. They would have family picnics up here, years ago, and she wonders if Josh remembers collecting ladybugs in their lunchboxes, running from the peril of wasps. So many of them, back then. She wonders where they've gone.

It looks better in the daylight, he says.

Will has come to stand beside her.

She turns her head and tries to smile at him, but she isn't sure where they stand; isn't sure if he's forgiven her, for the awful things she said.

I kind of like it in the dark, she says.

Will takes a mouthful of Coke, keeps his eyes on the sea.

Happy birthday, she says to him.

Thanks.

You had a good day?

Pretty standard, he says.

How disappointing.

He laughs at this, and she gives in, too, lets out her own strained smile.

Birthdays should be anything but standard, she says.

In your world, maybe.

And it is subtle, but enough. An acknowledgment of all that she said to him in the forest: that he is not the right guy, for her; that they are from two different—*too* different—worlds. It storms inside of her, this lie she told, for her brother. A lie Will so easily believed.

I'm glad you came, he says, after the longest silence they have ever shared. Someone squeals behind them; there is the rush of foaming beer, a scatter of people avoiding the overflow.

Me too, she says.

Good news on Oxford, he says.

Oh, yeah, she says. It is.

You're not the tiniest bit gutted about music school?

Rosie's brain slows, at this. Filters through minor details from the last few weeks. The looping around her bedroom, at night. The tapping of her fingernails, the endless counting in one room, and then another. Her music application, still blank, but kept, for some reason, in her desk drawer.

Nope, she says.

That's great, then, Will says. Come have a drink, yeah? D'you think we could try and be friends, maybe?

That depends, she says.

On what?

On whether you can forget all the horrible things I said to you.

Will gives a half shrug; like he's shedding something from his shoulders, hardly acknowledging this thing that she broke, between them.

It was all true, he says.

It wasn't, though, she says, and her voice tremors with feeling, which is not lost on Will, she doesn't think, from the way that he looks at her.

Meaning, he asks, and it is Rosie's turn to shrug. To suggest something without words.

*

Their night turns after midnight, after hours of talking, like friends. Will wasn't sure he could be near her like this, but it is surprisingly easy; a relief, even. And he is wondering what she meant, by the cliff. If things have changed. If it was only a matter of timing, for her, like she'd always said.

People drift away, come back, then leave for good. Someone is sick from too much cider; the cellophane from the cake ends up on the fire and it melts, smelling of acid and bad decisions. Josh gets louder and louder by the hour. He is blackout drunk; worse than the night of the winter dance, even, and it was funny, at first, but soon people are rolling their eyes, or shrugging his hands from their shoulders; Will senses Rosie watching him from across the flames.

I love you all so much, Josh is saying, with his arms spread wide. There's so much love in me, guys.

Someone laughs; a friend *aaws*, tries to tug on his sleeve to have him sit down. He bats them away, stumbles a little.

How can love be wrong? he asks them; the remaining few, by the fire. How can any kind of love be bad?

He begins to pace up and down, and his face is blazing, like the sunset from before; the one that made Will text Rosie in the first place.

Josh, Rosie says, quietly.

I *love* love, Josh says, more loudly still, and he laughs at his choice of words. Someone turns off the music, out of irritation, Will suspects. He watches with detached amusement as Josh meanders through the last few of them, old school friends, people from assemblies and science and homeroom, all looking up at him with affection, or fatigue.

Marley is on Tom's lap, and she says we love you too, Josh, and Josh looks round at her and begins to walk backward, a can of cider in his hand.

You think you do, he says. You think you know a person.

Josh, Rosie says again, and there is a warning note in her voice, and Will hears it, and sits up from where he'd been leaning on his elbows.

You can never know, Josh says. But it's all right. You've made me see that tonight, guys. *All* of you.

He's shaking his head now, and Will wonders if he's trying not to cry, can't work out if he's drunk-happy or supremely sad. Two things, so often the same.

Josh takes one more swig from his can, and drops it. It falls with a thump on the grass.

Come away from the edge, Josh, Rosie says to him, but he doesn't. He keeps stepping back, and then he whirls himself around with his arms flung out, like he's embracing the night sky. People are getting up now, from their places by the fire. Laughter changing to words of God, and shit. Mild intrigue turned to dread.

Someone shouts Josh's name, and Will gets up, his blood, streaming, like a river, and walks toward him with his hand outstretched, says mate, come on, you've had a few.

They latch eyes for the briefest of seconds.

And then Josh opens his mouth to say something but his back foot goes, and it happens so fast that Will isn't sure it's happened, even though he is there, right there, could have lunged for him if he'd tried. People are screaming. Girls, are screaming. And the guys are at the verge and shouting fuck and Josh and there is noise about an ambulance, and the shock has slowed everything, for a moment, the stars out, the sea flat and still and watchful. And Will looks over the edge and he sees it, even in the dark, the angle of those long limbs, the seep of something so wine-

like, so wrong, in the sand. And he turns around and he blocks her, because she is running for the edge, and screaming her brother's name.

No, he says, and he folds his arms around her, presses her into his
chest. No. You don't want to see this. You do not want to see this.

And she is sobbing and yelling and still saying his name, and he falls
with her to her knees, and he keeps her there, like that, as though it is his
sole purpose, to stop her from seeing it, as though this can somehow,
someday, take it back.

after

eight

◖

Will knows he will never again be able to eat potato salad, after today.

It is cold and slimy and turns to mush in his mouth. Tastes of stifled things, like the words, forced out, by his friends at the lectern. The air felt close as they filed out into the cemetery car park, shared cars to the house, saying nothing.

They all stand together in Rosie's living room, in black dresses and blazers in spite of the late-summer heat. Eyes dry, now. Finger food on their plates.

Will watches as people eat. Forks some into his own mouth, despite not wanting to.

Voices are low and solemn, and it is busy, busier than their Christmas party, even, but people give each other more space, talk and touch far less. Rosie's father looks lost, as if he can't remember why he's here, in this room with all these strangers and friends and family members. His wife is upstairs, hasn't been seen since the service.

And Rosie. Rosie is sitting by the window with Marley, who is holding her hand, won't leave her side. Another black dress. Long sleeves, hair plaited, by someone else, he's sure, that morning.

She looks like you'd expect a twin to look at their other twin's funeral. Collapsed into herself, but somehow, still sitting upright.

The world has been slow, and weightless, since the fall. Like nothing sits or stands or functions for any good reason. He experienced a similar detachment when his grandpa died—when he had to say a few words at the funeral, and then, right at the moment when he should, he couldn't.

He let everyone down, he knows.

Tar, in his mouth. The world, sunk, under water.

An hour later, Marley takes Rosie out into the garden. He sees them rising from the window seat, the guiding of one girl through the quiet crowd. One of Josh's closest friends is weeping silently in their circle, and two girls start crying, too, because it's like yawning, involuntary and infectious. Will takes their plates, pretending to be considerate, and carries them through to the conservatory where he can see Marley and Roe through the glass, walking the length of the garden.

Outside, the afternoon is gold on his skin, the sky a soft, cloudless blue.

There is an apple tree, a trampoline. A water feature that's not running. He follows them to where the hedgerows part, to an open view of some farmland. Geese, calling, from the fields, as Marley holds on to Rosie's hand.

He hesitates behind them, but then says her name. Marley's head snaps round, but Rosie does not move. He wants to touch her. To hold her other hand, or, if he's really honest, have her hold tight on to his.

The service was beautiful, Marley says, after the longest time.

It wasn't though, was it, says Will.

Marley turns to him again, but still, Rosie does not look round.

What? Marley says.

It was devastating, he says. And stagnant, like all funerals are. Except it's worse, when someone's young, and brilliant.

Marley is moving her mouth as if grinding her teeth; as if she cannot believe what he's saying.

Because he *was* brilliant, Will says. And interested. And considerate.

His hands feel as if they are shaking. He hooks his thumbs into his belt loops.

Funny, too, he says. But not intentionally. He was just too naïve, too nice, almost, for a guy his age, you know? And *that* was funny, to a lot of people. But I thought he was just . . . so different, to everyone. I felt so . . . relieved, around him.

What are you saying, Marley asks, but Rosie jerks her hand, almost involuntarily, as if she doesn't want her to interrupt.

I can't believe he died, Will says. I can't believe we went to a crappy standard funeral where nobody said anything real about him.

Will, Marley says, and she sounds shocked.

It's the truth, he says. Nobody speaks the truth at these things. It was the same with my grandpa, it'll be the same at mine. Roe, he says again. Roe, will you look at me?

She will not; she dips her head to the ground, and he wonders if she's crying, or simply trying not to.

I don't want that to be your memory of him, Will says. Or think that that's everyone's memory of him. He was so much more than those poems and that reading. And your song was great, Roe, it really was. He would have loved it. But he would have loved an entire album of your songs, right? He would have preferred karaoke, maybe, for you to sing live. And he'd have wanted fried chicken, not finger sandwiches. And Christmas music playing when we all walked out, even though it's September.

Stop, says Marley.

No, he says, and he doesn't know why this is so important to say, but his chest is bursting, so he keeps going. Funerals are as meaningful as . . . the hospital room you're born in. It doesn't matter. But Josh *does*. He was charming and idealistic and sort of clumsy, and he knew the missing verses from *Fresh Prince*, and he doodled stars when he was trying to solve equations, and that stuff matters, Rosie, more than a stupid service.

Shut up, Will!

He pretends that Marley hasn't spoken; raises his voice above hers.

Remember your own things, Roe, he says. The real things. Can you do that?

He is pleading with her for something she cannot give, because she likely wants to die, too, he knows, right here at the edge of the field. Half of her, gone, turning to ash, as they stand here, and Josh does not.

Please, Roe, he says.

And when she still says nothing and does not move, he walks back to the house, with Marley holding her hand and the sun sinking beneath the farmland. His heart feels torn open, exposed. Birds, still singing, in the trees.

He's way out of line, Marley tells her.

The sunset clings on for one moment more and then drops, leaving claw marks in the sky. Coral red, and flaming. Muted shadows of dusk.

He's not, Rosie says, and it is the first thing she has said all day.

Marley turns to her then, takes her arm with the hand that is not holding hers.

Well, he could have been nicer about it, Marley says.

People could always be nicer, Rosie says. Her voice doesn't feel right, but somehow, she keeps talking.

I want to remember all those things, she says. The things he said, that no one else did.

And then something happens inside her, something she'd been fearing and tamping down, all day, and she lets out a guttural sound, and it's like ripping herself down her center.

But I can't, she says. I can't remember anything except him falling.

Her single cry turns to sobbing without tears, the crumpling of herself out loud. Marley shushes her, like a mother might, and she falls apart in her garden, near the trees they had climbed, on the grass they'd scanned for clover, blown dandelions and snowmen, daisy chains and cloud-gazing, and it's true, in this moment she recalls none of it, but Marley says you will, I promise you, you will.

Back in the house, Will cannot leave like he wants to; he has to hang back in the kitchen while other guests linger in the hall. Rosie's mother has clearly come downstairs only to say goodbye to the guests; she stays by the door, as if unable to move, unable to face the remaining mourners in the living room.

He watches as people clutch at Mr. and Mrs. Winters's hands, whisper well-meaning, useless words. Roe's dad heads out into the driveway with a few of them, for air, perhaps, or because he can no longer bear the walls of his own home.

When the last person has filed out, Will makes for the hallway too, readying himself to say something equally hollow. But when Rosie's mother sees him, her face does something he's never seen before. Slackens, then contorts. He sees it twice, in fact, because she is standing by the mirror in the hall, reflected in all her fury.

Get out, she says, when he reaches her.

I already was, he says.

How dare you, she says, and it is like her face is carved from wood; like she can barely move her mouth.

How *dare* you, she says, again. After your pathetic, delinquent party that I *told him* not to go to? Joshua does not do this. Joshua listens to me. And then he meets you, and starts needing help with his maths, and sneaking out the house on school nights.

It wasn't a school night, Will says, and he doesn't know why he says it, when she is trembling all over; still talking about her son in the present tense.

What *the fuck*, she says, and it is so jarring, to hear an adult, a composed woman like her, swear at him like this. It stuns him. His blood runs cold.

He goes to apologize, but then she leans toward him, and he has to take a step back.

You have no decency, she says. To come here, today. Then talk to me, like that. Like you have a problem.

I don't have a problem, he says, and he strains to stay calm, to sound it. But Josh was my friend, Mrs. Winters. And I'm—

But she lets out a terrible laugh.

People like you don't have friends, she says. You have people you use, to get ahead, or to pull them down into the dirt. I knew people like you at school. You think I don't know what you got suspended for? You think I'd let you near my kids, for a second?

There is a tiny bit of spittle on her cheek. Her lipstick, still perfectly red.

You are *bad* for him, Will, she hisses. And for Rosie. Get out. Now. I want you out of my house.

She is looking at him as though Josh did not fall. As though Will pushed him.

Get out, she says, for the final time.

Fuck this, he says, but quietly, and he slips past her, his insides lodged in his throat.

He knows, rationally, that this is the talk of a grieving mother. But the darker side of him, the part that likes to drink and tighten and drag him into the blurry, swirling places where he feels nothing, that part hears it and beds in. Because he could have caught him. He could have not invited them, that night. Josh could have stayed home, and Will could have done something, or not done something, and things would be entirely different.

His friend could still be here, solving equations.

Doodling biro stars.

*

Once everybody has left, Rosie lies awake, with her heart racing, and dreads what the world will look like in the morning.

Her mother does not wail, like she has on the other nights. She is simply silent. Her father is numb; just seems dazed, by the entire thing, as if he does not believe it has happened. And while she cannot understand the pain of losing a child, Rosie burns with the fact that they are not twins. They may have created him, but they did not grow out of the same cells; did not share hearts and chromosomes and a home since before they were human.

In the black of night, Rosie imagines that she will die, too. That she can't possibly live, with this eating her from the inside.

And so she moves into his room, and sleeps in her twin's bed, for days. She sleeps as though she is catching up on all of the sleepless nights she has suffered since she was little; since the clock started keeping her awake, and she started counting, and checking, and making promises to herself so that bad things wouldn't happen, and people would not die.

But he died anyway.

He died and she is tired and her parents somehow carry on, get dressed, leave her be, until it just gets silly, is no longer respectable, or normal; her dad opens the curtains and says come on, now, Rosie, time to get back in your own bed, and she agrees until after dark, when she creeps back to her brother's room and presses her face to his pillow. It still smells of him, a little. Is fading, more and more, with each night.

The morning she is to leave for university, she checks, and checks again, until it is so automatic that she is not sure she even checked right.

Her bags are in the car. Her father is in the driving seat, and her mother is calling her down, telling her it's time to go.

Nothing left, but her curtains, and some pictures.

She texted Will, the day before; asked him to meet her by the lighthouse after dawn. He had not replied, but she went anyway, and he did not come. Unsurprising, she thinks, after weeks of no contact. After she would not look at him, at the funeral.

Now, back home, she checks once more. For what, she does not know. She touches her windowsill, positions her desk chair at the right angle. The right angle. Right. Right. A little more to the left, and then it's right.

Then her mum yells again, and it forces her to leave, to descend the stairs.

What were you doing? her mother asks, as if she is on a deadline; as if she has something more important to get back to.

Nothing, Rosie says.

Don't dally, then, her mother says, and she kisses the top of her head.

There is a moment when they hold on to each other; her mother's hand on her back, pressing her close, Rosie gripping her mother's elbow. They are not used to hugging, and it doesn't feel like a farewell embrace;

it feels like they're talking, through touch, their long, matching fingers saying things for them.

You'll be okay, her mother says, and because she's had to say it, Rosie does not believe her. She thinks about telling her, now, with their faces reflected in the hallway mirror, that she does not want to go.

Her mother kisses her again, brusquer, this time, and lets go of her.

Be good, she says.

Always, Rosie replies, an exchange they've shared since childhood. Her mother smiles, without really smiling, and Rosie walks out of the house.

*

The night of the funeral, Will goes home via Darcy's place.

He fucks her in her garden, because her mum is indoors, and because she wants it as much as he does. I haven't missed you, she tells him, as she bites down on his lip. But I'm so fucking sad, Will.

He turns her sideways, grazes his cheek against the pebbledash of her house, and thinks, as he comes, how he wishes he could say that out loud; admit that he's sad, too, and use it to justify everything. All the wrong.

You knew him quite well, didn't you? Darcy asks, as she untwists her skirt from around her waist. He zips up, tells her they took maths together.

And wasn't it your party? When he died?

She says it casually, as if she doesn't care; as if she is just confirming something she already knows. He looks at her, but doesn't answer. Keeps looking, until she turns crimson, asks him what.

He keeps that answer unsaid in his mouth. While he runs, and showers, and works his shifts. At dinner, as he forces down food, under his grandma's watchful eye. It weighs on him now, as he pulls the weeds up in his own garden, feels it slung and objectionable round his throat. The grass is wet. It has rained, overnight.

He'd ignored Rosie's message, the day before she left. And that feels urgent and inescapable; it haunts him, pulsing through his veins as he shoves his hands into the dirt.

He lines the weeds on the ground, then he scoops them up as one and throws them into the garden waste. He is sweating, breathing hard, his fingernails black with earth. Then he turns and makes for his garage, rooting around behind his toolbox, lifting the bundles of grease-streaked rags he keeps piled beneath the workbench.

He pulls out a bottle of the clear, sharp stuff that helped, before. Takes gulps of it in the dark, because he hasn't bothered to turn on the light.

nine

In many ways, university is what Rosie expected.

Green-lawned parks and circular libraries, seminars where she sometimes feels lost, and other times, interested. Lectures, with takeaway cups of coffee, the shuffle of papers. Intelligent people, and stupid remarks. Pennies dropped in pint glasses, so that the beer has to be chugged, like tap water.

She likes the computer room beneath her college library. How it's always warm, and hums with the whir of the printer. People head there with a purpose. They come, they go, and she stays and taps out her essays, with the feet of fellow students passing above her, as she works underground, like she's hiding.

In other ways, it is not what she thought at all.

She thought things would be fine, somehow, when she got here. Even when Josh died, some hopeful part of her thought her old problems might still retreat. That her checking and sleepless nights would wither in the light of a new place, thanks to the new friends and faces, the facts she'd fill her days with.

In reality, though, the deep sleep of her immediate grief has vanished, and she spends her time avidly, achingly, awake.

At clubs, in the bar, in a friend's room poring over last-minute reading.

And when she has to be alone, she ends up circling her room, touching her clothes, her keys, with just the right brush of two fingers, before she can get into bed. If she goes to the bathroom halfway through the night, she has to do it all again.

She does not know why.

But she has made friends. Good ones. A small group she watches films with, dances beside in nightclubs, calls taxis for when they drunkenly decide they don't want to walk home in the cold.

She starts to drink coffee, because everybody does.

She tries her first kebab, downs her first Jägerbomb.

Has to rewrite one of her essays, for the first time in her life, and cries down the phone to Marley about it, even after everything. Even though nothing like this should matter, ever again.

She tells nobody that her twin died.

That she gets two, maybe three hours of sleep a night, throughout the whole of her first term.

She studies. She drinks. She stops writing songs. She eats very little, and drops a dress size, which she knows her mother will be thrilled about when she goes home for Christmas.

She almost texts Josh to tell him about it.

Then remembers, all over again.

It is early December—Oxmas, they call it—when she decides to stop circling her bedroom and instead leave her building at dawn. She walks around the college grounds in her long coat, watching the mist rise from the lawns.

Some days, she follows the river until her hands turn cold, and that is why she notices him for the first time.

He is on the water, rowing, alone, and she thinks nothing of it, other than how strange it is that someone else is awake at this hour, and she watches him glide by, with his large arms and short hair, his jaw strong and set.

She sees him again, a few times. He catches her eye once, but keeps rowing; keeps puffing air out of his mouth, exhaling on the effort, as focused as she's seen anyone on anything.

She forgets about him.

Goes home for Christmas.

Has a near-silent, terrible time, and breaks in two when she returns for her second term, because everything that was hard before feels harder. She stops sleeping, and her checks increase, keep her up all hours of the night so that she can't remember what came first, the checking or the not sleeping, because one causes the other, and her brain loops, endlessly, at night and all day, in the lectures that she drags herself to, in the dinner hall while she eats with her friends, mostly moving the meat around her plate, eating the carbs, the carrots, the soft, easy-to-swallow things. She feels cold, and shaken, all of the time, like an upturned snow globe. Spinning, and empty, and full.

*

Will has eaten himself sober. It is two in the morning, and he is in the kitchen, picking bread straight out of the cellophane bag, squashing it into his mouth with two fingers.

The hunger had felt real, and sudden. So he came down and started to eat and the world became sharper at the edges.

Hovis Best of Both, apparently.

It's not really the best of anything.

But he finishes his fourth slice, twists the bread back into its bag and drinks some water. That's the key, he knows; drink an implausible amount of water, and everything will be fine.

And things *have* been fine, more or less. He's been working, and running, and not missing school, the routine of registration and lessons and revision he didn't really do, the teachers who pitied him, or fancied him, or treated him with suspicion. He does ad hoc shifts at Moe's Motors, and he runs to rid himself of Josh, and that night, and the sickness in his stomach that doesn't ever go away. When he drinks, the thoughts ease, like the dialing down of volume, or the lowering of a flame on the hob. Still there, but muffled with gin, or vodka, or rum. He drank out of the house, at first. In his garage, or after work, at the beach or in alleyways, like the scum he suspects he might be.

He listens to rock music, afterward.

Wakes, hungry, and still sick, with no desire to do anything different.

Now, in the kitchen, he is about to run the tap for more water when his phone vibrates on the counter. Violently, like someone's drilling through the wall.

He sees her name. After he has tried not to think of her, for weeks. The alcohol helps there, too, like an old, comforting friend who always knows what to say. It's distracting, puts things off for a while, until times like this, when real life comes knocking, or ringing, at two in the morning.

He does not run the tap. He does not think too hard.

Roe, he says, when he answers.

She says hi, after the longest pause. He wonders if she meant to call.

You're up, she says.

Yeah.

I didn't know if you would be.

Another pause, even longer, this time. He takes the phone to the living room, closes the door, and sits in his grandfather's armchair. Dave gets up from his cushion in the corner, snuffles at his knees in hello, before padding back to bed.

You okay? he asks.

Yeah, she says, though her voice suggests otherwise.

How's everything, then, he asks. He was going to ask, how is uni, or how was your Christmas, but neither seemed more relevant than the other. There is so much between them, now. So many months, and so many things. They have not spoken since the wake.

Good, she says. Fine.

Rosie.

Yeah?

Why are you calling?

There is a silence, again, on her end, as charged as a city at night. He can't hear her breathing; there is no scuffle of bedclothes, no sighing or tread of feet.

I can't sleep, she says. I've tried everything.

Okay.

And I don't know what to do, she says.

Her voice cracks then, and she lets her breath go, shallow and splintered.

His heart floods. All of it, roaring out.

Okay, he says. Okay. How long are we talking? Just tonight?

No, she says.

A week?

There is more silence, and then she says since she got here, and he doesn't know if that means since day one, or day one of term two, but either way, it's bad.

He gets up and goes to the window and soothes her with meaningless things. Talks about fitting clutch cables at the garage, and Amber's sudden fixation with being vegetarian. The trees he can see; how bare they are, without their leaves. How wet it's been, all winter.

He keeps talking, because she is not talking back, and he tries to picture where she is, what her room might look like; a single bed and a window, her books stacked tall on a desk.

He talks about a manual he's reading. A band he's discovered, how she might like them, the white noise of the tracks.

At some point, she must fall asleep, because her breathing evens, and eventually, when the milky dawn seeps through the blinds, he drifts off, too.

You look like death, his grandma tells him at breakfast.

Cheers, he says.

What's wrong? Are you coming down with something?

Before he can answer, she presses her palm to his forehead, pushes his hair up out of his eyes. You feel clammy, she says.

Just a rough night, he says.

Bad breath, too, she says, as she opens the fridge. He pretends not to care, but clamps his mouth shut, in case she can smell the ethanol.

Did you sleep down here? she asks, nodding at the living room door. She places butter and jam on the table, a carton of juice, and he has a sudden, intrusive flicker of the snow day, when Josh gathered the toppings for their pancakes.

Will?

Yeah?

I asked if you slept down here?

Didn't really sleep, he says. But yeah, I was down here.

His gran hums her understanding, but asks nothing more. She has been gentle with him since Josh's death, and for that he is grateful, and somewhat furious. Like he needs to be handled with care. Like it changes anything. Like he wouldn't rather have her usual, hard-nosed criticism, have life back the way it was.

I'm out tonight, he says, as she slides crumpets under the grill.

Again?

Yep.

Who're you going round with, these days?

People, he says.

No girls?

Lots of girls.

She sighs, and, almost unbelievably, takes this exact moment to mention her, after months of silence and tact and unventured questions.

You lost touch with that Rosie, then?

After her twin died on my birthday? he says, with such a flare of heat, his skin feels ice cold, afterward. Yeah, I did.

Willyum, she says, and she sounds both sympathetic and reproachful, and he stands up, says he's not hungry.

Rosie starts calling him every night.

Around eleven, when he is in bed, or walking back from drinking on the beach. Wind up, stars out. The sea roaring, somewhere, behind him.

He talks, and she talks back, sometimes, but more often than not she slides into sleep, and he keeps going, for a while, to make sure she stays there.

He tells her so many things. He likes doing it; likes the time with her, even though she is there, and he is here, and the whole thing is sort of messed up. He finds he waits all day for that moment, when his phone will ring. Feels both a sadness and gutting relief, because it means that she still needs him.

After a few weeks, when the frost of February laces the grass in the mornings and he can see his breath when he wakes, she breaks the routine and calls him at dawn.

Where were you, she asks him.

He is rising out of sleep, not following.

I waited for you, she says. The day I left.

He stares up at his ceiling, at the outlines of the old stars. Artex, swirled above him.

And why didn't you say goodbye, she asks. At the funeral.

Will remains very still. He never thought he'd have to answer these questions; thought it would just be something between them, that they could pack down, like dirt.

You're talking me to sleep every night, she says, but there are other things that need saying. Things we should talk about.

He keeps looking at his ceiling; at the shadow of sun on the brush-work. When he doesn't answer her, she nudges, don't you think?

And so he has to go there.

Too much has happened, Roe, he says. I want to be there, okay? I want to help you through this. But I can't see you. I can't just talk to you about normal things.

Normal things, Rosie repeats. *All* you talk about is normal things.

What's normal would be to acknowledge this fuck-off elephant in the room, Will says, and there's that anger, again, so rife and white hot.

Okay? And that is?

That your brother *died*, Roe, he says. And that I have to fucking live with that.

An intake of breath, so subtle.

He can hear Amber brushing her teeth in the bathroom. The gush of the tap, grate of bristles in her mouth.

How *hard* that must be for you, Rosie says, and it is waspish, unlike her, and their rage meets like waves crashing on sand; necessary, and inevitable. The silence that follows stretches and holds.

Neither of them hangs up.

His clock, ticking. The sound of the boiler down the hall.

It wasn't your fault, Rosie says, eventually. Relenting.

I'm sick of that, Will says, and his voice tremors with that sickness. Don't try to make me feel better, for Christ's sake.

She says okay, okay, and she is the one trying to soothe him, now, and he doesn't want it, feels suddenly, insatiably furious with her.

I didn't say goodbye and I didn't come to the lighthouse because I didn't want to, he says.

Okay, she says again.

Is it, he asks. *Is it* okay? Because it seemed like it was okay for you to play games, Roe, to decide when and where you wanted me, to not even look at me, that day, but now you're ringing me at ungodly hours and interrogating me about those same decisions.

She doesn't answer him, so he keeps going.

I just don't think this is a good thing, anymore, he says. If it ever was. You were right, Roe. Just focus on Oxford and grieving, yeah, get some proper help, maybe, and I'll go back to doing what I was doing.

He is sitting up now, his body pulsing.

Okay, says Rosie, and she thanks him, for God knows what, and he stares at the phone after she hangs up, wondering what the hell happened, why he said all those things.

He goes for a run. Tries to put her from his mind.

And that night, she does not call.

*

Rosie meets the rowing boy on a night out.

It is a normal, unremarkable evening, where they end up seated beside each other at a pub, and he buys her a drink, says ah, you're the early bird. He's noticed her noticing him on her walks by the river. He is big, almost unsettlingly so; arms and legs shaped for slicing oars through the water, a nose broken, years before, on the rugby pitch.

He is older than her. In his second year.

He asks for her number, and they go on a date a week later, for a coffee in between their lectures. It is a Wednesday. His name is Simon.

He reminds her of a bear, with his wide skull and large hands, his ready, deep laugh that sounds so certain and full. He drinks no alcohol, eats a lot of chicken and egg whites, tells her about his love of racing and the water. He talks about how easy it is, for him, to get up before dawn, how he's in bed by nine, and his friends all laugh at him for it, but it's the way it goes, when you're on the team, the way it has to be.

He asks her about her own interests and her studies. Takes her coat and hangs it on her chair, like a grown-up. He pays for the coffees. Asks her out, again; this time for dinner, at a place he thinks she'll like.

It is easy, with him. She finds herself folding into his life the way a baby bird might beneath a mother's wing; for comfort, and shelter; out of necessity.

Marley calls her every fortnight, give or take. She is studying medicine like she always wanted, and she works hard and parties harder, sounds like she has a head cold every time they speak.

She ended things with Tom before they left for university, and hasn't had a sniff of romance since, unless you count her getting off with guys in the student bar, and that, she says, is the least romantic thing ever.

What's he like, she pleads, when Rosie tells her about Simon.

He's nice, Rosie says.

A bonus, says Marley.

Better than nice, she corrects herself. Really kind. And good at two-way conversation. But he doesn't ask too many questions, you know? He's like, the opposite of intense. Just really sweet. And kind.

She has said kind twice.

He sounds great, is all Marley says.

Rosie agrees, and looks out of her bedroom window, across the college grounds. There is a pigeon on the windowsill of the old library; cornered, with its wings folded. Like it's waiting for something.

And how's everything else, Marley asks her.

Rosie considers the question. Just yesterday, in the Bodleian, she saw a boy who looked a little like Josh. Her heart had rocketed into her mouth and she'd returned to her desk and written a line of her essay before she went to the bathroom and sobbed, silently, in a locked cubicle.

Everything's fine, she tells Marley.

Yeah? You're sleeping better?

Yes, she says, because it's the truth, and because she'd have given the same answer even if it wasn't. So many people, Marley included, have shown her such concern since Josh died—her school friends, her parents, distant relatives, even, checking in with her—and she knows she should feel loved and appreciative. Instead, resentment spreads in her navel, like that pigeon stretching its wings.

Cool, Marley says. That's good.

Where're you at with your cadaver, Rosie asks, moving things along.

She did not sign up for a single music class at the Freshers' Fair. She walked past the choir stall, the orchestra stand, the callouts for a capella and Philharmonia and swing band.

Nobody in her new life knows that she sings, or plays.

That music was a part of her, before.

When Will stopped talking her to sleep—stopped talking to her, full stop—she had to find another way to get through her nights. So she started writing poetry again, for the first time since Josh died; only in bed, and only at strange hours of the night.

She found she could combat them both, that way; the sleeplessness, and the throttling of each day, by taking her pen and writing down the unsayable things. Things not made for music, or human eyes; things she can't believe she is thinking, and feeling, and somehow finding the words for.

Ink spots on her sheets.

When she writes, she cannot check things, or grieve.

Cannot think of anything else.

*

Will starts doing more work at the garage, because he asks to, and because he needs the money. He fits batteries, changes cables, but when he asks to be made a proper mechanic, Moe says it wouldn't be fair.

I can't pay you a mechanic's wage, Moe tells him.

Why not?

Because I've got a business to run.

But I've been on the same wage for three years now.

And I never promised you more than that, did I?

So, all year, Will cleans preservative off the new, ready-to-collect bikes. He picks up overalls from the launderette. He greets customers and sweeps the floor and rinses mugs and makes so many coffees he almost asks Moe to cut back on caffeine, seeing as this alone could allow for a pay rise.

He puts all of his wages, bar a little that he gives to his grandmother, into his bank account for a plane ticket. Because he is going, this summer.

He is half gone, already.

He picks up odd jobs around town, fixing things, cleaning gutters and mowing lawns and painting walls. He learns to sand floors, varnish skirting, lay loft boards and wire plugs and do whatever he needs to do to fill his time and earn his way out. In the evenings, he does as he always has; he runs, cooks, a little, when his grandmother does not want to, and he reads and drives and drinks.

No phone calls. No texts or party invites.

None of his old friends are around anymore, anyway. Even Darcy went away to some college somewhere, got the points to study health and social care. He snorted when she told him this, mainly at the idea that she could take care of anyone.

He screws women like her, most weeks, one from the launderette, barmaids and baristas and teaching assistants he meets in the pub.

He fights hard to focus on these girls, while he's with them.

Tries to listen when they talk.

On bad days, he lets himself picture Rosie. When he's with a girl, or simply lying in bed with them afterward, windows open, the curtains lifting with the breeze.

They would lie like this, he thinks, before he can stop himself. Clothes on the floor, clouds skating past the blinds. Her mouth, imprinted, on his water glass.

Ridiculous.

He gets in from a ride one summer night, his hair swept back with the speed, his heart stilled with the risk and the stretching, empty roads.

He decides to eat before he showers. Wonders what his gran will have left him, as they so rarely eat together these days; he is never home at the right hours for that, despite her asking him to try. She's usually in bed when he gets in, all the lights off in the house.

Tonight, though, she is in the kitchen. Seated at the table with her hands laced together.

All right, he asks her, and she raises her eyes.

He is about to ask her what's up, why she's looking at him like that, when she reaches down beside her chair and lifts a bottle onto the table.

She does it again, and again, until there are five part-drunk bottles lined up in front of her. Glass soldiers with long, bone-like necks, catching the kitchen light.

Are *you*? she asks him, and her eyes do not leave his face. Are *you* all right?

Will's mind suddenly feels full, and slow; like someone's blown smoke into his ears, fogged him up from the inside.

When did you start drinking spirits again, she asks him.

He thinks about denying it, like his younger self would have, but then he shrugs and asks, does it matter?

Yes, it matters, she says, and her voice wavers, just once.

After the funeral, he tells her.

Which funeral?

Whose d'you think?

Which funeral, Will, she asks, each word like a hole punched through paper.

Josh's, he says.

His grandmother remains very still, but he sees something release in her face. Just under a year, she's thinking. Not an irreversible habit, which it perhaps would have been, if he'd been drinking in secret for years, since his grandpa's heart gave out in the bathroom one morning, his toothbrush still in his mouth.

I want you to pour these away, his grandma says. Right now.

I could just buy more, he says.

Don't do that, she says, and she grits her teeth to keep from crying, and he burns with the sight of it, every ounce of him blaring with shame and hate and fury, for her, for himself, for what she's about to make him do. Don't you dare threaten that, Will. Promise me. On my own withering heart. Right now.

It won't change anything, he says.

We'll get you help, then, she says, and she stares straight at him with her wrinkled, raisin-like eyes. They shrink, when she is sad. Everything about her gets harder, and larger, except her eyes.

They are the eyes she used on his mother.

I don't need help, he says.

Then pour these away.

Gran.

What?

That won't make a difference.

Yes it will, Willyum.

It won't! You haven't got a fucking clue.

Don't you *dare* speak to me like that in my own house, she says, and she stands up, and she is huge and loud and the woman who raised him, and she knocks one of the bottles, slightly, with the arm of her chair.

Shall we take this outside, then?

How can you *joke*, William, right now? How?

Because, he says, and he shrugs.

They continue to stare each other down. She is breathing too deeply, and he finds it strangely, jarringly calm. It is as though real feelings have deserted him. Like he's stepped back, out of his own body, to watch this scene play out.

If you won't stop drinking for yourself, his gran says, then do it for me.

That won't work either, Gran.

I'm not pulling on your heart strings, she snaps. I'm being practical.

Oh yeah?

He leans against the door frame now; lets the hinge dig into the small of his back.

I might need you to drive me to some hospital appointments, she says. Very soon.

Why? What's wrong?

I'll tell you when I know.

But why have you made appointments?

Just promise me you'll be able to drive, if I need you, she says.

You're lying, he tells her, and he can't believe this of her, can't believe she'd play so dirty. She doesn't deny it. He turns his back on her and walks upstairs, and she lets him go, the bottles still lined on the table.

*

Rosie has run out of paper.

She's been writing on discarded scraps from the printer, but there's none left, and she has more to say, so she takes her pen and writes the rest across her wrist, down the entire length of her arm.

The nib tickles.

It feels thin and light, like the end of a feather, and this prompts another memory, another sentence, a time when she and Josh discovered there were real bird feathers in their pillows. Duck down, she knows now, and she writes a whole song about it, for the first time since Josh died, about the softness and the sharp edges, the rain of white fluff stolen from things once living.

In the morning, she does not scrub it off.

She goes to lectures with long sleeves hiding her skin, crammed with the stories she cannot, it turns out, forget.

———

After a date one night—though is it a date, she wonders, when you are a couple, when you have slipped into each other's lives without discussion—Simon asks her about the songs on her skin.

They have been for dinner, and to see a film. Something mainstream and high budget and dire; Rosie cannot remember much of it. Now they are in his room, with the curtains drawn, his desk lamp bent low in the corner.

She is cross-legged on his bed. He sees the words, peeking out of the gap in her sleeve, the small teardrop of skin beneath the button at her wrist.

What's this, he asks her, and he nods his large, kind face down at her hands clasped around her tea. Chamomile. No caffeine, anymore.

She tries to retract, but he reaches out and lifts her forearm to the light, turns it over so he can see. She waits for him to smile. To crease with curiosity and questions, but he simply shrugs and says, arts students, before he gives her arm back.

*

It is raining when Will bumps into his sister in the hallway.

His grandma is watching television in the lounge. The mournful clarinet from one of her soap operas winds up the stairs, as the drops slash hard on the windows.

Oh, Amber says. You're home.

Yeah, says Will. He was heading downstairs for some water; she is on the top step, blocking his way.

We thought you were out, she says.

Well, I'm not, he says.

She still doesn't move, and this is unusual, the most time they've spent together for nearly a year. They have an unspoken agreement; they never go into each other's bedrooms, and have always maintained a healthy distance. It works.

Gran's upset, Amber tells him.

Why? Did someone die in *Emmerdale*?

No, she says. Because you're drinking vodka again.

His heart snaps, like a band, against his ribs. The rain is deafening against the windows.

I . . . didn't know you knew about that, he says.

I know, she says.

He looks at her then. Properly, for the first time in a long while. She seems older than her eleven years. There's a speckle of acne on her chin, and an intensity in her eyes that reminds him of no one; none of the girls from school, not their gran, nor their mother.

She shouldn't be telling you this stuff, he says, when neither of them goes to move. You're too young.

Gran never tells me anything, Amber says. I'm just not stupid.

His eyebrows rise, at this.

No, he says. You're not.

You are, though, she tells him, and he folds his arms, waits for the why. You're actually quite bright, Will, she says. And good-looking, apparently. All of my friends say so.

What's that got to do with anything?

It means you can do things, Amber says. If you wanted.

She sounds like his grandmother and he wants to tell her so, but she keeps talking, raising her voice above the rain.

You could do more than clean bikes and drink yourself sad, she says, and he stares at her, for the last part.

I know you liked that girl, his sister goes on, and that she went away. And I know that boy died on your last birthday.

Dark cloud, beyond the glass.

And that's why you're sad, Amber says. But while those things might *feel* like they're killing you, Will, it's the drinking that will *actually* kill you. Eventually. I read about it. I can show you pictures.

No need, Will says, when he realizes it's a genuine offer.

Okay. If you're sure.

I'm sure.

Take my word for it, then, she says. And make up with Gran, will you? she adds, as she finally moves out of his way. I want a sleepover with Abbie, but she needs to be in a better mood before I ask.

Right, Will says, because despite all that she's said, all the things she's seen without him knowing she was watching, she is still only eleven years old.

He tries to stop.

He does.

He pours the contents of the bottles down the sink, like his gran asked him to. Throws them in the recycling and flinches when they smash. He goes for longer runs that strip his lungs of breath and leave his glutes flaring, and he drinks lots of water, smokes a cigarette when he feels the need, for something to do with his hands.

He lasts three whole days.

Then he takes his wages to the off-license, buys the cheapest spirit he can find and drinks it in the alleyway behind the shop, hating himself because it feels so good.

He walks around afterward, unable to go home, and ends up in the car park. The one in the center of town, where things went so horribly wrong, when he was a kid and hanging out with bad people, doing things he shouldn't, because his parents had left him, and his grandpa had died, and now, after all of it, Josh has died, too.

He starts to run; does a lap of the empty parking spaces, looks like an idiot in his cheap shoes, his nonwicking, too-tight shirt. The lights are on in the corner shop across the way. He knows it's catching him on the CCTV. Knows he looks different, older, than when it caught him before.

He ends up in a bar with a pint, and a coaster that he tears into pieces.

A girl makes eyes at him, but for once, he doesn't look back. He can't stop, he has realized. He's always been able to, before. Not wanted to, but been able to. This feels different, more desperate, and heavy. Like he needs to climb out of it before it crushes him; and because he can't stop, he must act.

So the next day, he buys his plane ticket.

Asia, first. Thailand. He likes pad thai, and the flights were cheap, and that is as much thought as he gives it. He buys them using the computer in the town library, prints the tickets using the huge, red-flashing printer. He shoves the paper tray back and forth a few times, and then it's there, ready and waiting, still warm to the touch.

As he walks home, he realizes that he is due to fly the day after Josh died. The day after he turns twenty.

Coincidental, he's sure. A strange, stupid old world.

ten

(

The deathday rises gray and wet, like it knows.

Will has been braced for the chest pain, and because of this, it is absent. He gets up. Finishes packing his rucksack, checks he's got his passport, his ticket, his sunglasses.

He has said goodbye to his grandmother and his sister. Amber is back at school, some early-bird summer camp for science nerds. His gran left at lunchtime for her book club, kissed him roughly on the cheek, held him for a hard, strange half minute. They do not hug. Not even when his grandpa died, or when his mother left.

They have barely spoken since they both lied to each other, since it all came out in the kitchen. Since she said she needed him for her elusive hospital visits. Since she found his secret liquor stash, and shamed him, pried him open.

So they had their uncomfortable non-hug in the hallway, and she asked him to let her know when he landed, and he said he'd try, and at the door she said Happy birthday, Willyum, before she left him in the hall.

He spends an hour waiting.

Checking the clock, and his bag.

He is traveling into London that night, getting a train to a cheap hotel beside the airport. He is due to leave at three, was going to walk to the station with his rucksack on his back, but it begins to rain, so he books a taxi. Checks his bag again. Sits at the kitchen table, toggling on his phone, with nobody to talk to.

There is an uncut birthday cake on the table.

A single card, from his gran and his sister, propped open by the fruit bowl.

And then, at a quarter to two, there is a knock at the door. Two light taps with the knocker. It is still raining, streaming down the windows in sheets, and when he opens it she is standing there and soaked through, her hair drenched, her shirt transparent with rain.

I couldn't go home, she says.

He stares at her, as if to check she is real, then tugs her in by the arm and takes her bag, shunting the door closed with his foot.

I couldn't go, she says, again, each word strained between her breaths.

And he drops her bag and presses her to him, feels her warmth through the wet of her clothes. She seems smaller, to him, wren-like, even. All wrists and spine and bent wings.

He makes her mac and cheese. She needs salt and dairy; something thick and unyielding, something to weigh her down. He gives her an old T-shirt and a pair of his sister's leggings to change into, and she sits at the kitchen table and watches him cook. He grates nutmeg and dices bacon and pours milk with the utmost care, as though it is her he is touching.

She stops crying somewhere between him adding the mustard and grating the cheddar. He grates more than the recipe says, watches it pile like wood shavings on the plate.

Do you want a drink? he asks, but she shakes her head. He pours them both some water, anyway, boils the kettle for tea. He hasn't spoken another word to her, and on some level he cannot believe that she is here, in his kitchen, today of all days, but in some ways it feels inevitable, somewhat right.

He puts the macaroni in the oven at three; the exact time he should be leaving for his train, and tomorrow's flight. His heart turns over in his chest, like a stone in his hands, considering it. But it does not feel like a choice, anymore. He does not want to go. Not now. He wonders, vaguely, if he'll regret it, but turns to see Rosie at the table with her rained-on hair and her swollen eyes and knows he would swap her for Thailand tomorrow, and the next day, and he can make a decent pad thai, anyway, and the world isn't going anywhere, right, so he puts it from his mind.

They sit quietly while the pasta bakes. When it's ready, he carries the dish to the table and gives her a fork. They eat together, directly out of the Pyrex, the cheese stretching white and hot from the pasta to their mouths.

Don't burn yourself, he tells her, and she nods, picks at the edges. The kitchen is warm, feels almost damp. The windows steamed up from the heat.

I'm sorry, she says.

Don't be, he says.

You said you couldn't see me, and I came anyway.

Will sinks his fork into the food, and it feels both soft and dense.

Things change, he tells her.

She does not ask him if she can stay, but after they've eaten he leads her upstairs, lets her sit on the end of his bed.

So this is your room, she says.

Impressive, right?

I like it, she tells him. I'd always wondered what it was like.

Were you close?

I knew there would be CDs, she says, nodding at the piles beneath the window. And mess.

It's not *mess*. Everything has its place.

Its place on the floor?

As good a place as any.

I like your cactus, she says, as she shifts back on the bed and props herself against the wall. It is a small, potted thing, and try as he might, it continues to live.

Amber bought it for me last Christmas, Will tells her. Said it reminded her of me.

Rosie frowns, as if she cannot see the resemblance.

A prickly bastard, he says with a shrug, and this throws her, and she laughs, sort of, as if wondering whether she can.

Try and rest, he says, and she nods.

At the door, she says his name, and he turns back, his hand on the frame.

Happy birthday, she says.

Thanks, he says, and he looks at her in his childhood bedroom, each as small as the other, one unexpected, the other so ordinary. Her hair, still damp, shines in the light.

*

When Rosie wakes, she does not know where she is, at first.

Small room. Pine forest smell. There are clothes on the floor, a hoodie and some balled-up socks.

It has stopped raining. The morning spills under the curtains, and she never wants to get up, never wants to leave this warm, still space where nothing has to happen. She lies like this, under Will White's duvet, for she doesn't know how long. Then there is a soft knock, and the door opens, and his grandmother walks in.

She puts a mug of tea on the bedside table, opens the curtains.

Morning, my girl, she says, and Rosie sits up, keeps the duvet close.

Mrs. White, she says.

Elsie, she says. Unless you'd prefer Miss Winters?

No. Rosie's fine.

Did you sleep well?

I did, she says, and she sounds surprised, almost scared to admit it.

Now, I'm not asking you this because you aren't welcome, Elsie says. Or because I want you to leave, or have any issues whatsoever with you being here. As far as I'm concerned, it's no trouble having you to stay.

Rosie waits, because there is a but in there, and Elsie sits down on the bed.

Do your parents know you're here?

Rosie shakes her head.

Don't you think it would be best to tell them?

They think I'm at my boyfriend's for the summer, she says.

Elsie nods, once, so deeply that her chin almost touches her chest. Rosie chews over that word. Boyfriend.

So they won't be worried, or calling the police, or putting your face on a milk carton, Elsie asks. And when Rosie looks confused, she tells her that's what they used to do with missing kids' faces.

I'm nineteen, Rosie objects.

And still their child, Elsie says, and she lays her hand on Rosie's knee, on top of the duvet. It's a hand covered with moles, years of weather and toil and hardship. Wrought with lines, like a tree stump showing its age.

I won't be here long, Rosie says, though she has no idea how long she'll be there. She hadn't planned to be here at all. Had got off the train to go home, to do the right thing and be with her parents on the anniversary of her brother's death.

Couldn't do it.

You can be here as long as you like, Elsie assures her. It won't hurt Will to stay on the sofa for a while.

Rosie wants to say thank you, to ask her why. You don't even know me, she thinks of saying. But the old woman looks at her like a granddaughter, squeezes her knee through the bedspread.

Drink your tea, she says. So she does.

Rosie spends the long days with Will in his grandma's house. Watching television and reading her books, and eating eggs and toast and roast chicken. The living room smells of furniture polish and the earthy, outdoor smell of a dog's paws. Dave takes a liking to her and often sits by her feet, or lies across her on the sofa.

Dave's a funny name for a dog, she says, as she rubs his wiry head.

Davidstow, says Will, without looking up from his phone.

Is that a place?

A cheese, he says. My grandpa's favorite cheddar.

Rosie smiles, and she feels out of practice; her teeth feel misaligned, her lips cracked and tight. They talk about cheese, for a while. Get into a debate about Stilton, and whether the rind is meant for eating.

The rain is continuous, but they get out for short walks when they can. Stick to the back fields and forest trails, without having to voice that they need to avoid the town center, in case they run into her parents. They think she is in Oxford, still, working a summer job. Staying with Simon at the weekends.

How's your mum doing, Will asks her one morning, as they traipse through the trees, the ground damp underfoot.

Rosie doesn't answer for a while. She looks at the backs of Will's trainers, the wet mulch stuck to the rims.

She's herself, she says. Times a hundred.

Okay.

She's cold, she explains. Colder, and more distant. For self-preservation, you know.

Yeah.

They keep walking, twigs snapping beneath their shoes.

And your dad?

Heartbroken, Rosie says. He's on antidepressants.

Are they helping?

I don't think so.

God.

There is no God, Rosie says, and it is dramatic, she knows, but also true, and Will doesn't disagree or call her out or say come on, now, Roe, and she loves him, right then, as if she didn't already; it is the moment she knows for sure.

But she puts this away, in the drawers of herself. Remembers Simon, as she follows Will down the forest path. Separating this from that, and all the things that came before.

Tell me about your friends, Will says, one night. They are in his bedroom, with their backs against the wall. Playing cards. Or pretending to, while talking.

My uni friends?

Yeah. I want to know.

That surprises me.

They're in your life, he says, with a shrug. I like knowing about your life.

Okay, she says, and she watches as he collects up the cards, begins to shuffle the deck. There's Lydia, from my course. Really smart, really scatty, really into chocolate milk. She has it on her cereal.

Weird.

I know. But I kind of like that about her. And there's Henry, who lives on our floor. He's studying Biochem, and really looks like he's studying Biochem, you know?

Glasses?

Yep! And this intensely thoughtful resting face.

No preference for chocolate milk?

No, exactly. He eats toast every morning.

I love that you assess what everyone has for breakfast.

It tells you a lot about a person, Rosie says, and there's a lightness in her stomach as he teases her, asks her about the life she's built, without knowing.

She tells him about her college friends and her lecturers, and she almost doesn't tell him about Simon, but she has to, and there is a stilled, suspended moment as he deals out the cards, when she wonders how it will feel; whether it's a good idea.

And Simon, she says, eventually.

Yeah?

He's really sweet. He's a bit older than me. He rows.

That's cool.

Yeah. He is. Well no, he's not cool. He's actually a little dull. Not dull—no—I meant he's just really by the book, in a good way. He goes to bed early. He eats really well, and exercises every single day, and he's a great listener and he just knows what he wants. Which is so great, isn't it. To know that. To be so sure, even now.

She is chattering, and nervous. Will feels it, too. Has slowed his dealing of the cards.

He looks after himself, and everyone around him, she says. You'd like him. He has clean hands, and nice hair. And he's, uh. Well, we're together.

There. She said it.

It hangs, tangibly, in the bedroom air, which smells of her own sleep, her own breath and skin and borrowed clothes.

Right, says Will, and it's not right, it doesn't feel right, and she immediately regrets it, every last choice of the past warped, just bearable year.

What about you, she asks, desperate for reparation.

What about me?

Anyone on the scene?

He glances at her, once, and then drops his eyes back to dealing.

You know me, Roe, he says.

I do, she thinks, and I don't. And either way, it doesn't answer her question.

*

A few weeks into her visit, Rosie tells Will that she wants to be elsewhere. Not because she doesn't want to be here, with him, he understands; but because living in her own life is taking everything she has.

Where d'you want to go? he asks her.

They are sitting in his living room, as is their habit in the evenings, while his gran cooks and Amber stays out of their way upstairs. Will is in his grandfather's chair, Rosie with Dave on the sofa, gazing at the painting on the wall. An old mill, and a river. Reeds, tangled, in the foreground.

Just away, she says. Anywhere.

So let's go somewhere, he says.

I don't just mean the lighthouse or the forest, she says.

I don't, either.

She takes her eyes off the painting and looks at him.

We could be at Norwich airport in two hours, he says. A door closes upstairs; his sister heading to the bathroom, or perhaps the wind catching it through an open window. She lets out a small laugh; a shuffle of her breath.

We can't do that, she says, when he doesn't smile.

Why not?

Because.

Because?

I don't have any stuff.

You have your passport, right?

Yeah. My passport and my bank cards and my toothbrush.

Then we can go.

Where? she asks him, after she's held his eyes, seen that he isn't joking.

Away, he repeats back at her. Anywhere.

They book five days in Montenegro because it is the cheapest flight that has two seats left, and they both know, roughly, where it is.

Rosie may have packed her passport out of anxiety—too precious to leave behind, even in a locked room on campus—but she has little else. Nothing for the blazing sunshine and oven-hot heat of the tent Will has packed. She buys supplies at the airport; bright flip-flops, T-shirts blazoned with flag-filled hearts, a pair of sunglasses that flick high at the edges and, Will tells her, make her look like a bug.

She puts them back, and he says no, in a good way, and she asks him how looking like a bug can be a good thing, and he lists all the beautiful insects he can think of, right there in the aisle of the Sunglass Hut: butterflies and queen bees and dragonflies and she says okay okay, and takes them to the till.

The flight is smooth and Rosie sleeps while Will stares out of the oval window. He has only been on a plane twice before; on a school trip to Scotland, and a family holiday to Portugal that he barely remembers. There was a fish market, and the unwelcome paste of suncream on his face. He ate a lot of spaghetti. Looked at some boats with his grandpa.

He was absorbed by the view from the plane then, too. That sense of being so high and moving so fast, without actually moving at all.

When they touch down, they hire a small, scratched-up car, and they drive the thirty miles to a village where Will has read there is a lakeside campsite, which turns out to be no more than a scrubby field shared by three raggedy sheep. There is a toilet block with one working cubicle and insects spattered to the mirror and a single tap for drinking water which, a hand-written sign informs them, doubles up as a spot where they must wash their feet. *NO SAND IN MAN'S TOES*, it says on the door.

There must be a beach somewhere, then, Rosie reasons, as Will un-rolls the tent, starts to clip the poles together.

Just over the mountain, he says, and he nods toward the hills.

*

The ocean calls to them; they agree that's how it feels. They read by the lake and eat the biscuits they bought at a corner shop on the way in, and then they pack a bag and walk the long, shady route up and over the hill to get to the Adriatic Sea. It is just before noon. That way, Will explains, they'll spend the hottest part of the day out of the sun. Rosie is surprised he has thought of such a thing, and she lets him lead the way, because she has never had that before; never had someone plan things for her. She has always been the planner. The worrier. The watch-for-sunburn-type organizer. She likes that she is unexpectedly here, in a European country she never thought she would see. She likes that she is not having to think. She likes the shade of the trees and the airport clothes that don't fit her and the way she is hungry, again, at unscheduled times of day.

It occurs to her that she should text Simon and tell him where she is, but then she'd have to tell him she is not at home with her parents.

That she's with an old friend.

She doesn't want to worry him, and everything feels so removed out here, so foreign, so far away from everything back home. She is not a liar, but she is exhausted, and relieved, and so warm and soothed in the shade of the trees that look so different out here. She inhales the scent of pine needles, and cones. Switches off her phone.

On the beach, there is a shack where they buy lemonade and figs and sandwiches. They eat and drink and swim and talk, sometimes, but don't talk, mostly, letting the sun trail across the sky, relying on it to tell them what time it is, when to move. She lets the warmth dry the salt on her skin, on the fine hair of her arms.

It is so hot. Almost airless, back in the tent. But she can breathe.

*

They drive to a mountain viewpoint, pass a cobbled village with a car park and a rubble of old ruins. They don't discuss it, but instinctively change their plan; Will pulls up, pays for parking, and they walk up the hill, looking at the market stalls, the trinkets and spices and swathes of painted scarves.

It is like they have crossed out of Europe and into the Middle East.

The heat is closer up here, and soon their top lips are beaded with sweat, the cooking smells from the tavernas as heady as the sun. Will sees Rosie touch a necklace of brass and turquoise, something handmade and imperfect, and she smiles at the lady who offers it out to her, shakes her head, thank you, but no.

They wander through the ruins of the long-gone village and then sit under the terrace of a taverna, order sparkling water which comes with mint and ice. There are fresh hunks of bread in a wicker basket. Lemon slices, salt shakers. They order tomatoes that glisten like rubies, diced cucumber drowned in yogurt.

I like it here, Rosie says.

Good, he says.

Don't you?

I do.

Good. It worked out, then. This spontaneous plan of yours.

I'm not sure something can be a spontaneous plan, he says. Bit of a contradiction, isn't it?

Rosie raises her glass in acknowledgment, takes a sip of her water.

Well, I'm glad the non-plan worked out, she says.

I never plan things, Will says. And life more or less goes okay.

They don't say anything for a while, because they're both musing on how this isn't entirely true. How the worst thing, the most not-okay thing in both of their lives, occurred, because the world is cruel and unpredictable and things just happen, sometimes, and their understanding of this is what brings them back together, over and over, in spite of it.

I think about him, Rosie says.

She says it without emotion. A fact, like how the rain is coming in, that night.

Every day, I'd imagine, Will says.

Every second, it feels like, Rosie says. Unless I'm with you.

Will lifts his eyes to hers and they look at each other for too long and then she blushes, her cheeks flooding with color. Like a plum, or a peach.

He has a chance, here, in this moment, with the light and the lemons and this opening between them, and he does not take it.

Oxford's not a distraction? he asks.

And Rosie, too, takes the way out, because it is less complicated, and because too much has happened for them to undo, and she says sort of, but it also gives her a lot of time to think, you know, a lot of alone time in the library and her room and watching really bad student theater.

I sort of zone out, sometimes, she confesses. I know I should be concentrating on the essay, or the play, but I just find myself going over things, like what it would be like, if he was here. Or, just, things he said. Things I never told him.

A hoverfly hums over their bread basket, and the heat seems a degree warmer despite the shade of the terrace. Sunlight dapples through the overhead vines, makes the water jug glint on the table.

There can't have been much you didn't tell him, Will says.

Rosie isn't looking at him anymore; her eyes are vacant.

Not a lot, she agrees. But there are . . . some things.

What things, Will asks, and she smiles, even though she is sad, and doesn't answer him right away.

He'd have liked this, she says.

Yeah?

Sitting here, with you, she says.

Her voice is strange; far out, like her eyes. Will shrugs, his chest loosening as she pours him more water.

I'd tell him about my OCD, she says.

The hoverfly is back, and Will tracks it while listening to her every word.

I'd tell him that's what it is, she says. The thing he knew about. The thing that got worse, and better, but was kind of constant, since we were kids.

Like hand washing? he asks her, and he keeps his voice even.

No, she says. Nothing like that. It's subtler.

Light switches?

No.

Okay.

A lot of counting, she says. A lot of straightening things, and checking things are there, or locked, or off, or how I left them. It keeps me up at night, sometimes. I went to the doctor at uni about it. And he said that's what it was: obsessive compulsive disorder.

Yeah, he says. A kid at my primary school had it.

Really?

Really.

Well, she says. Her face is still pink from earlier, her hands folded, in her lap, like she's afraid he'll try to hold one.

Is it, he tries. Then he tries again. Is it . . . stressful?

She takes another mouthful of water. Puts her glass back down.

Not really at the time, she says.

No breeze. Condensation, streaming down their glasses.

But over the years, she says. It's got . . . exhausting.

Will nods, because he doesn't need the full picture to understand. He thinks of telling her about his numb days, and his drinking, and the dull pain in his chest, even the thing that happened in the school bathroom that he tries not to think about, but instead he tells her something else, something not quite as bad, but still awful.

I robbed a woman, he says.

Rosie's eyes seek his out, slowly, like she doesn't connect these words with him.

Well. He recalibrates. I was there, when a woman got robbed, in a car park. I knew it was going to happen. They'd planned it, the guys I was with. And I didn't do anything to stop it. The police came, and they all ran, and I didn't.

Why not, Rosie asks, after a pause. Will takes his time to reply, holding himself abnormally still.

I deserved to be caught, he says.

But you didn't do anything.

Exactly. I did *nothing*. I didn't even try to help her. They took her bag and her dignity, Roe, and I don't care if I was just fourteen, I should have said no, or gone for help, not just kept watch, like they asked.

Who were they?

Just some guys I got mixed up with.

Bad guys.

Really bad guys.

A rare breeze channels through the street, lifts Rosie's hair at the ends. Their empty plates gleam on the table.

You're not a bad guy, Will, Rosie says, and she puts her hands back on the table, as if in surrender, so he could take one, if he wanted.

They both drink more water, parts of their selves now out and floating in the close, ever-thickening air. The tomatoes, when the waiter brings more, taste startlingly sweet.

Her bag and her dignity, Rosie says, with a slight smile. Who even talks like that?

At night, they sleep together without sex, and it is the most intimate thing he has ever done with a girl. He can feel the heat coming off her on the roll mat beside his. She is sleeping through the night, and this, to him, is a quiet triumph that they don't acknowledge. She snores, a little, and clacks her teeth, hard.

Do I snore, he asks her, and she looks panicked and says no, do I, and he lies and tells her no. That she talks, a bit, sometimes. What do I say, she asks, and he smiles and shakes his head, all the better to let her wonder.

The shower is more of a dribble, and the cubicle is mostly occupied by insects, so they bathe in the river. Don't look, she says to him, and he promises he won't, and pretends not to as he lays out their towels on the grass. She lifts off her vest and stands in the water in her underwear, washing her underarms, her legs, round her neck.

The sheep watch her, too. Chewing their grass.

Will goes in afterward with his trunks on, and there is no splashing or swimming together, no romantic notions of this turning into something more than what it is.

They wash, walk, drift in and out of sleep.

Exist, in tandem, and ask nothing more of each other.

*

They overdo it, one afternoon, and get sunburned so badly that they struggle to sit on the chairs at the beach café. The backs of their thighs feel raw, like uncooked meat, which is ironic, Will says, seeing as they've actually been roasted.

They'd been reading on their stomachs all day, and while they'd been careful to apply suncream first thing, they'd become lax, were too absorbed in their books, too bronzed and relaxed to care. It had crossed Rosie's mind, at one point, that the backs of her legs felt sore, that perhaps her lower glutes were burning. But she couldn't reach those spots properly, and she wasn't about to ask Will to touch her there; even though he'd do it, she was sure, if she asked.

She had to reread the same page of her book three times, after that. Had to focus on moving on, from wherever her thoughts were leading.

She's got very good at this, over the summer. Shutting things down, and thinking of Will as something more than a friend, but unromantically so, an attractive second cousin, almost. Someone off-limits, but still nice to look at. And that was allowed, surely. She's certain that Simon will have spent his summer at the rowing club, noticing the girls in their short dresses and sunglasses as they cheer him on, flirting over their Pimm's and their picnics, their freckled, sun-kissed legs.

That's normal, she thinks, as she watches Will fold his beach towel and place it on the plastic seat. Completely fine, she decides, as he does the same for her, and they both sit down, gingerly, the pain more bearable against the cotton.

We'll need to buy aloe vera or something, Will says, after they've ordered their drinks. To put on the burns, later.

Rosie is wondering how they would apply lotion to one another's skin in such places when the barman arrives, puts their drinks down in front of them.

You want to eat, he asks, in his broken English, and Rosie says we always want to eat, and the barman laughs, the full-bellied noise they've heard every day since they've been here. They order a tuna salad to share and the barman says you here on honeymoon? Or just summer break?

Rosie splutters, and the barman is teasing, she can tell; simply wanted a reaction. Will takes a sip of his drink. His hair has turned lighter in the sun.

Surely he marry you soon, he says, turning to Will as he takes the menus. Girls like this? Not so many of them, no?

Um, says Rosie, just as Will grins and says sadly, she's not his to keep.

The barman laughs again, but then seems to understand what Will has just said.

You're not, the barman says, pointing between the two of them, ah, what is it called?

We're not together, Rosie says.

Not in the love? the barman says.

Not in the love, no, Will says, and laughs. Rosie feels something flash inside her, at the sound, or the sentence that came before.

This makes no sense to me, the barman says, and he clatters off, toward the next customer.

Will and Rosie's eyes meet across the table.

Well, Will says.

Yeah, Rosie says back.

You're just not my type, he tells her, and she stares, but then laughs herself; balls up her napkin and throws it at him.

*

I think you're my best friend, Rosie tells him, on their last night.

They are lying side by side in the tent. It is stiflingly hot, their skin tight from the sun and the sweat.

Don't tell Marley, she says, after a while.

Will snorts, says he wouldn't dare, that he's a little bit scared of her. This makes her laugh, and then she is crying, and he has no idea why, and he sits up to touch her and she says no, don't, can he just get her some water, please, and so he leaves the tent and does as she asks. He fills up a plastic bottle, the same one they've been refilling since their flight over, the stars thrown like salt across the sky.

He gives her a moment and then heads back.

She is on her side, facing away from him, and when he settles inside the tent she says that she's had the best time, and she didn't know she could have that, still, and she feels so relieved and so guilty, and how can she be both?

He gets it, and says so, as he lies back down beside her.

It's okay, he says, and she says, just before she falls asleep, that he's lying, that he always makes her feel like things are okay, when they're not.

He says he's sorry, even though he isn't, and soon, her breathing changes. She doesn't snore, for once. Hasn't touched the water he brought her. He listens to her breathing and thinks of her awake and looping, obsessive and hurting and trying to cope, and the love he feels is bigger than anything he's felt before, bigger than his anger and his pain, his desire and his fury, and this, to him, is entirely new, and the right thing, he knows, is to keep it to himself.

eleven

❨

It is still raining when they get back to Will's house; has been raining for the full five days they've been away, his grandma informs them. And then, one morning, shortly before she is due to go back to Oxford, it stops.

She is awake in Will's bed, listening to it on the paving slabs outside, when there is suddenly silence.

She decides right then that she is not going back. She is seized by the certainty, feels like something is pouring out of her, and before she can rethink it she phones her mother.

Darling, she answers, like always.

Hi Mum, she says. How are you?

Busy.

Yeah.

Are you just calling for a chat, Rosie? Because I might call you back tonight, if I can?

Rosie pictures her in their home kitchen, making coffee. Scrolling through overnight emails with her long nails.

I just wanted to tell you I'm not going back to Oxford, Rosie says.

There is no emotion in her voice.

But you're in Oxford, her mother says.

I'm not, actually, Rosie says, because she wants her to care; wants her to know, for a cruel, unexpected shot of a second, that she has been a bad mother, all year.

There is a pause. A recalibration.

Where are you, then?

With a friend, she says.

Not with Simon?

No.

Rosie, her mother says, and she finally seems to have her attention. What's happened?

Nothing, she says. I made friends, I studied, and it was fine.

But it's killing me, she does not say.

There is a hard silence on the other end, so still and clear, she thinks for a moment that the phones have disconnected.

You're being ridiculous, her mother says, eventually, and Rosie feels her throat swell, everything she wants to say rising and lodging. Her mother waits for her to crack.

Mum, is all she can manage.

Where are you? her mother asks her, again.

A friend's, she repeats, because she does not know which word she would use for this house, this place, this boy she keeps returning to.

Right, her mother says, and she tells her to wait, which is ironic, because that's all Rosie feels like she's doing these days—waiting for something, though she does not know what.

*

Will wakes to the September light slanted on the living room floor.

He has slept downstairs the entire time Rosie has been here, although all he has wanted to do is sleep beside her.

He almost did, a few times.

Thought about getting up, in his boxers and T-shirt, padding up the stairs and letting himself into his own room. She would be awake already, or perhaps she would stir. She would see him, and shift up toward the wall, and he would lie down beside her and his fantasy would end, because that, in itself, was enough.

But he stayed on the sofa, mainly because his grandmother would kill him if he didn't. And because Rosie has a Simon.

Simon. So biblical, like a bored, irrepressible exhale.

He loathes him, mostly in the dead of night, when he tries to picture what he might look like. Fights him, in his head, in empty car parks.

In the daylight, though—in the morning, with coffee and clean teeth and no streetlight shadows—it makes sense, to him, that she would have someone.

Someone gentle and good, and university educated, who did not invite her brother to the cliffs that night. And if he and Rosie are destined for never—destined for friendship, and card games, and annual, undiscussed visits around his birthday—he thinks that maybe that's okay.

Maybe that's better, for the both of them.

He is frying eggs for breakfast when there is a violent jab at the doorbell, three, four times, so it resounds for far too long in the hall.

He hears his grandma shuffle to the front door, then the tight, recognizable voice he'd know anywhere.

He turns off the hob. Waits to see if he can hear what's being said; briefly considers slipping out of the back door. But he steels himself and moves through to join his gran, whose shoulders are hunched in defense.

Where is she, Mrs. Winters says, as soon as she sees him.

You should know, Will says, and his gran shoots him a look.

She's upstairs, she tells her.

When she said she was at her *boy*friend's, I didn't think she meant here, Mrs. Winters says. She is dressed in a long coat, despite the late-summer warmth.

Mrs. Winters, his grandma says. Why don't you come in? We can go and fetch Rosie and—

I do not need you to *fetch* my own daughter, she says. She can come downstairs with her things and I am going to take her home. Tell her I'm here, Will. Please.

Seeing as you asked nicely, he says.

He ignores, for one ruthless moment, that she is a mother who has lost her son; he wants her to hate him that little bit more, because it is savage, and satisfying, and he has nothing to lose.

Please come in, his grandma repeats, as he turns and heads up the stairs, and he hears her refuse again. He feels strangely calm and controlled as he ascends. He has not drunk a drop of alcohol since the night that Rosie arrived; hasn't felt the need to.

He opens his bedroom door without knocking and stops when he sees Rosie's midriff, the curve of her left breast. She is getting dressed—her arms reached high, a vest skimming over her stomach.

Shit, he says, turning his face away. Sorry.

It's okay, Rosie says, and she sounds like it really is—unbothered that he might have seen things he shouldn't have. She is tying her hair up while looking at him, the morning pouring through the window behind her. A drained, white sky. No birds or breeze.

He momentarily forgets why he is here, and then remembers, like a needle in his side.

Your mum's here, he says.

She lowers her hands, her hair high in its unfinished bun.

My mum?

The very one.

How did she know I was here?

I assumed you told her.

Well, I didn't.

Sixth sense, maybe, he says, and he's joking, but Rosie nods.

I guess I should go, then, she says.

Do you want to?

Rosie lifts her chin and doesn't look him in the eye. She glances out of the window instead, at the wide garden with its scrubby patch of grass.

No, she says.

Then stay.

I can't.

Why not?

Because—I don't know, Will, because you're sleeping on the sofa? Because your grandma needs her house back?

We don't care about any of that, he says.

You will, she says. Eventually. It's already been weeks, Will. I'm sorry, I should have gone ages ago.

Do you have somewhere you'd rather be?

That's not what I mean.

What do you mean, then?

That it's not right, is it? Hiding out here, like this.

That's what you're doing? Will says. Hiding?

Rosie takes her eyes from the window and shrugs, like she doesn't know. She looks better than she did when she knocked on his door in the rain. Fuller around the face and eyes. Rested, and more like herself.

I have to go, she says.

Then go, he says.

*

The drive from Will's to her own house is short, but feels long. Eight stretched, hard, silent minutes, with her mother's windscreen wipers swiping back and forth.

When they stop, her mother gets out without a word and heads up the driveway, and Rosie sits in the car and looks up at her house. It is much the same as when she left it a year ago. A blue front door. Potted olive trees and a perfect lawn and her own bedroom window beside her twin brother's, staring at her from the first floor.

Inside, it smells of home.

The same photos on the wall.

Lock the car, will you, her mother calls, and Rosie takes the keys from the dish on the side, points and presses the button so that the car doors clunk.

Then her mother says her name.

It's not angry or impatient or relieved. It sounds like a question, almost, so she walks into the front room, sits down.

You're tanned, her mother says.

A bit.

Not from the Norfolk sun, I doubt?

Lydia's house in France, she says, because Montenegro is her secret; something she never wants to share. And so she lies by omission once more; a new habit of hers, since Josh died. Since things broke, and no one could fix them.

Why were you with him, her mother asks.

Rosie does not expect this question. She was braced for why she isn't going back to Oxford, or why she didn't come home this summer, or why she was only eight minutes away, for weeks, and didn't even tell her.

All these things, and yet she asks her about Will White.

He's my friend, she says.

Rosemary.

What?

Let's be adults here, she says, and it's her favorite phrase, a sentence she's used since Rosie was by no means an adult; eight years old, maybe, and asked to grow up and be reasonable.

Okay, Rosie says. Isn't it possible for two people of the opposite sex to be friends?

Oh, Rosie, I'm not an idiot, her mother says.

I don't know what you want me to say, Rosie says.

I want you to tell me why you were with him, her mother says, and her voice is fired up now, full of the feelings she tries so hard not to show. Why, Rosie, after everything? After that night? After you've moved on, and met Simon, and are handling everything so beautifully?

Rosie looks at her mother's strained face. Her cheekbones, so pronounced.

It wasn't his fault that Josh died, she says, and her mother simply stares at her, for so long that she has to speak again. Josh was . . . he wasn't himself.

You think I don't know that, her mother asks. You think I wasn't aware?

Rosie's throat swells. Fingers, tingling. She wants to ask her, *you know?* but she cannot dredge up the words.

He was distracted, her mother says. And miserable. Ever since he started revising with that boy. The Joshua before William White would not have snuck out the house, drunk himself to oblivion and fallen off a cliff edge. I just know it.

Her voice, still ablaze.

Rosie's heart on fire.

He was gay, she says, aloud.

Her mother's face slackens, for half a second.

What?

He was gay, Mum. He told me. And he was just—adjusting. That's why he was acting so different. It was nothing to do with—I mean, his dying, or the drinking—had nothing to do with Will.

Why are you defending him, she asks, and Rosie cannot believe she is asking this, after what she has just told her.

They sit in the living room, after that, for too long. Her father is not home; Rosie realizes this after an embarrassing amount of time, and even then she does not ask where he is. She feels hot and sick, as if she's colossally betrayed her brother.

Wonders if you can betray somebody who's dead.

Gay, her mother repeats, eventually, with less ferocity in her voice.

Yes, says Rosie.

He was miserable, she says. I was . . . right, about that.

Yes, Rosie says. And then, because she wants to vouch for him, her imperfect, joyful human of a brother, she says that he wouldn't have been miserable for long. He would have been fine. He would have told people, when he knew what to say, and he would have found love, and been happy, and even more himself.

I thought he *was* himself, her mother says.

Rosie remembers the way the walls seemed to shine with a new light; folding back on themselves, shadows shrinking, when Josh told her the truth. It didn't matter, one bit, but she wanted him to know that, to feel it. In the same way, right now, she leans forward and grasps her mother's hand.

It was bad timing, Mum. That's what I think. And I've thought about it a lot.

Her mother is rigid. Holds herself like a rock.

You can't leave Oxford, she says, eventually. Rosie cannot believe it. She feels as if the floor has dropped out from under her, and something is opening, beyond the window, a sense of space rushing between them.

It seems they will not revisit the gay thing, or the Will thing, or any of the things that need revisiting.

Think of all the things he can't have, Rosie, her mother goes on. You've worked *so hard*, for so long. You can't let anything get in the way of that.

Rosie holds her eyes, acknowledging the truth of this.

But you won't, her mother says. I knew my son, and I know you. Even after this past year, I knew you'd be at that boy's house, if you were not where you'd said you'd been. I should be angry with you, for that, Rosie. But I'm not.

Rosie swallows, even though she is the one who is angry, and she wants to say so, throw it all out of herself and into the room, but she cannot grasp where to begin.

You've been through a lot, says her mother, in a softer voice; a voice reminiscent of migraines. I know that. I'm so *proud* of you, Rosie, and I know I don't say it a lot, but it's a given, and you're doing so well. D'you know, when I'm struggling to get up in the mornings, I just remember how you're coping with it all, how mature and diligent you are. And then I put my suit on, and go to work.

Rosie blinks at her. She feels caught between two different conversations with the same person. So burned and hurt, but full of such love and tenderness, she could melt.

You struggle to get out of bed? she asks, after a moment. Her mother gives a one-sided shoulder lift.

My son died, she says.

And Rosie watches as she breaks, in front of her, for the first time since the funeral. Her mother's face crumples, for one, surreal moment, and then she is straight-faced and staring at her, hard, as though trying to keep it together.

Mum, Rosie says, and she goes to put her arms round her, but her mother shakes her head so fast it's like she's hurt her.

No, she says, please don't, Rosie.

So Rosie doesn't. She leans back, lets her mother collect herself, her own throat tight with tears. She has often wondered how her mother has managed through all of this, because whenever she's tried to ask, she just moves the conversation on, or says something vague, and clipped, as if Rosie has insulted her by asking. But Rosie has always hoped that she's coping, somehow. Hoped that she allows her father, at least, to care. To hold her at night, and reassure her, show her she's not alone.

Except she is, Rosie thinks, as she runs her thumb over her mother's fist. When it comes to the one and only thing that matters, she is entirely on her own. Just like Rosie is half of a twin, now; here is a mother, without her son.

Stupid, her mother says, after a while, dabbing at her face. She didn't even cry, not properly, but her color is up, her cheeks blotched with pink.

It's not, Rosie says.

What were we saying, her mother asks her.

I don't even know, Rosie says, and they share a rare moment of peace, the light mellow, on the wall. She is still holding her mother's hand.

You do what you need to do, Rosie, her mother says, and her voice is normal again. Rosie's heart skips with uncertainty, or triumph; she cannot tell.

You can *think* you don't want to go back to Oxford, her mother goes on, not looking at her. If that's what you need, for a while. But you will. Because you do the right thing. And it's the right thing, Rosie. You know it is.

Rosie absorbs her mother's words, then slowly takes her hand away.

Something sinking in her, like a stone.

She calls Marley, that night, and tells her she's home. She comes straight over and they lie on her bed and talk, with their feet up against the wall, like they used to, and Rosie is startled that her friend's hair is dip-dyed an electric blue, but that she is otherwise, reassuringly, the same.

Her mother pauses in the doorway on her way to bed and asks Marley how med school is going.

It's going, Marley says, with a shrug.

You don't like it?

I love it, she says, but it's a lot to learn. I can't help thinking I'm going to kill more people than I help.

There is a strange, fluid quiet between the three of them.

Nature of the job, Rosie's mother says, after the most delicate in-breath. Goodnight, girls.

Shit, says Marley, when they are left alone again, after her mother has closed the bedroom door. I didn't *think*.

It's fine, says Rosie.

I joked about killing people in front of a mother who just lost her son, Marley says. It's not fine. I'm a moron.

You aren't, Rosie says. And she didn't just lose him. It's been a year.

Marley turns her head to look at her. She has a Drumstick lolly in her mouth, and it makes her look young and vulnerable, like a child sucking her thumb.

A year isn't that long, Rosie, she says, with her tongue around the stick. It's still going to hurt like hell.

Rosie feels the retorts rise in her throat, but she lets them go, because it's easier, and she is too tired to be angry. Of course it's going to hurt. Of course every hour without him is going to siphon the cells off her, but she's trying, goddamnit, and she wishes the world would let her.

So, Marley says, after an awkward and loaded moment, where she pulls the lolly out in one long string, like gum. Do I get to meet Simon soon?

If you visit Oxford, then sure.

You could bring him to Edinburgh. I could take you to all the cool curry houses and we could listen to folk music and eat deep-fried Mars bars.

Do they actually do that in Scotland?

No, but we could if you wanted to.

They listen to the rain on the window. It is late, and it sounds louder now that her parents are both in bed; now that the rest of the house is in darkness. The light from her lampshade bathes them in pink, everything blurred at the edges.

Folk music sounds good, Rosie says.

Let's do it, then. But I'll come to Oxford, too. You like it there, right? Your friends are nice, and—you're—you know.

Rosie waits, because she does not know. Marley clears her throat, puts the Drumstick back in her mouth.

As happy as you thought you'd be? she says. After everything?

As happy as I thought I'd be, Rosie repeats, and she says it aloud to see if she can understand what Marley means, but instead, her friend takes it as an affirmation.

Good, she says. That's good.

Yeah, says Rosie.

The rain taps, like feet, on the windows.

Simon calls her the next morning while Marley is still sleeping, her mouth parted, curled hair spread on her pillow. Rosie has been awake since four, listening to her friend's deep breathing.

She slips out of bed and leaves the room before she answers, wondering why he's calling so early. They usually speak just before bed; a warm, sleepy exchange about their days, before they say goodnight. Simon has presumed, for the last few weeks, that she's been staying with her parents, and Rosie hasn't been able to bring herself to explain otherwise.

Hey you, she says, once she's accepted the call.

Morning sunshine, he says, and his voice is too loud for the hour, for the silence of her house. You know what day it is?

No, she whispers, in an attempt to make him do the same.

It's the day before I get to see you.

Oh, right. Yay!

She has never said yay in her life, but it felt appropriate, though she feels suitably stupid afterward. Simon doesn't seem to notice.

What time are you coming back, he asks. I'll meet you, help you unpack the car.

Won't you have your own unpacking to do?

All done, he says. I got here yesterday. Wanted to get some training in before lectures start.

You have the whole of noughth week for that. Lectures don't start till first.

Thank you for explaining how our terms work, Rosemary, he says. I'd forgotten, being in my third year and all.

Sorry, she says.

I'm joking, Rosie.

I know.

So what time?

What time what?

What time are you arriving tomorrow?

Oh, she says. I don't know. I haven't really thought about it.

Well, when you do, he says, can you let me know, please? I want to see you. And to impress your parents with my undeniable charm.

Right, she says, because she's forgotten that he hasn't met her parents yet.

Rosie, he says again.

Yeah?

You're away with the fairies, he says, and her body turns to water, because that is something that Josh used to say.

*

Will does not drink when Rosie leaves. He does not book another plane ticket, either. Instead, he gets a job at another garage in town, and Moe is so annoyed that he rings him up and offers him a step up, with more cash.

You should've said you were getting itchy feet, he says, and Will shakes his head, disbelieving.

But he takes Moe's offer and trains, finally, as a mechanic. He knows things, of course, knows more than he has ever let on, because his grandpa taught him, and because he's been building engines since he was old enough to make tea, and watching his grandpa do it before that.

He is soon earning a good enough wage that he can leave his grandma's house. He views a flat without telling her. Closer to the coast, in a block that looks derelict from the outside. If he leans really far out of the kitchen window he can see the edge of the harbor. There is seagull shit streaked down the panes, Coke cans wedged in the gutter. It comes unfurnished, but with a working oven and an ancient, crackling fridge.

He says he'll take it.

He speaks to Rosie roughly once a week. She talks a lot, he thinks, without managing to really say anything, so that he's always left filling in the gaps. He tells her stories about the garage and she tells him about her friends and her weekends, and he pretends to be blithe and engaged and not in the least bit jealous.

He misses her singing, and he tells her this one night, when she's home from a date with Simon, is pouring herself some water in the shared student kitchen. He hears the tap running, the fill of it in the glass.

I don't really do it these days, she says, and he hears her moving from kitchen to hallway.

You did at mine, he says, remembering her quiet voice in the shower, the hum of her passing between rooms.

Not properly, she says. I don't . . . sing properly, anymore.

I knew it, he says.

How did you know, she asks, and he thinks she's smiling, even though it must be uncomfortable, the fact that he's caught her out. That she's made a choice, and it's wrong, and he's not being polite about it.

I could tell, he says.

Yeah, but how?

You won't believe me if I say it, he says.

Go on.

I'll tell you if you'll sing for me.

No, Will.

Why not?

Because firstly, she says, and she lowers her voice, so that he knows she's right outside her door—in the porch that links with another person's room. He hears the scrape of her keys, the thick clunk of her lock.

Door shut. Voice back.

Firstly, she repeats, it's close to midnight, and everyone is asleep.

Sing quietly, then.

And secondly, she says, as though she hasn't heard him, it would be weird singing to you down the phone. Like one of those sad cat mums who asks for the phone to be held to her cat's ear when she goes away, so she can sing it a lullaby.

Cat mums, Will says, and he laughs because it's ludicrous, and because he still sort of knows what she means.

She is mute on the end of the phone, but he is sure he can hear her smiling now; feels it stretching through the receiver.

Those aren't good enough reasons, he says, and the silence that follows is indecipherable, this time. He waits.

I just don't want to, she says.

What, sing to me?

To anybody.

He hears the gentle knock of glass on wood. The flump of her body on her bed.

Well, if you change your mind, he says, and they move on.

They talk like this, nowadays. Like friends. And between their calls he does his best to forget her, to live a life she isn't part of, day to day, which, he reminds himself, she isn't. She chose to go back. She chose to stay with Simon, the guy he asks after, to sound interested in her life and uninterested in her, and she tells him almost nothing while somehow still answering his questions. They send each other photos and songs and texts at normal times of day. She sleeps, it seems. Sometimes in Simon's room. And Will brings women back to his own apartment, with a fridge stocked with Coke and ketchup and protein shakes. He flips through television channels and walks into town in the evenings, sometimes, to watch the seagulls and pretend he has somewhere he's going, somewhere he has to be.

*

Rosie has been dating Simon for two years. Two years of lectures and essays and skipped lunches. Late nights, shared pillows, films half watched.

Two years of him not knowing about Josh.

It is a Sunday when she tells him. They are lying in bed together, and it is his rest day, which means he is not out on the water, for once. His arms are around her, holding her to his chest. Hairless, and smooth, like the hull of a boat.

She'd had a bad dream. Woken up and thought, momentarily, that Josh was still alive, and Simon asks her what's wrong, and so she tells him everything.

Or at least, the everything she can bear to tell.

That she had a twin brother. That she loved him like she hasn't ever loved anybody, and that he died, one night, just before she came here. Dead before he made it to the hospital. Dead as soon as his skull smashed on the rocks, so far back from the tide.

She talks like it is all she is able to do. No emotion and no pause; a river, pouring out of her, until it isn't.

Simon lets her run dry, and then he says my God Rosie that's terrible, and he just holds her, and asks no questions, and it is then that she thinks she might marry him.

*

Will's grandmother comes over, unannounced, most weeks, with some groceries and judgments and any excuse to check up on him.

I can shop for my own lunch, Gran, he tells her, as she unpacks tins of soup onto the counter.

Pot Noodle is not a lunch, she tells him.

I don't eat Pot Noodle.

You do. I saw it in the bin last time I was here.

So I had one Pot Noodle, once. After a night out.

Well, there you go, then.

I smoked pot once, too, he tells her. Does that make me a pothead?

Will, she says, with a sigh. You're so contrary, you know that?

So I've been told.

Never been any different. Just like your mother.

There is a stilted quiet after she says this; one of her accidental slips that she makes, sometimes, when they have more or less agreed never to speak of her. His gran opens a cupboard and starts stowing the soup cans inside, and he pretends she said nothing.

Are you busy Wednesday afternoon, she asks him, when enough time has passed that her voice is normal, the soup all lined in a row.

Working a shift at Moe's, he says. Why?

Any chance you could shuffle?

Probably, he says. How come?

I might need you for something, she says.

Okay.

So just keep it free.

You'll have to give me more than that, Gran. I don't think my grand-mother needing me for some secret mission will go down too well with the boss.

Moe knows I'm the boss, his gran says, and she winks and puts the kettle on. It begins to rattle almost immediately, too little water to boil after his morning coffee.

I'm having my first round of chemo, she says, as though she's merely pointing out the seagull sitting on the roof.

Will is taking out a teaspoon for their drinks. He will think, later, that if there was ever a time to drop some cutlery, that would have been it. Fingers numbed, the clash of metal on the tiles. But he just holds it in his hand, the cheap, plastic handle unremarkable against his skin.

Chemo, he repeats.

I'm afraid so.

For what, he says.

Oh, Will, you know what chemo's for.

What kind, he says, and she sighs again, as if he's being difficult, and he can tell she does not want to talk about it, that her whole body has closed off the way it does when she is sad, or tired, or thinking about his mother.

Lung, she says. Which, if you ask me, is the most ridiculous thing about it.

But you've never smoked, he says.

I know. That's why it's ridiculous.

I never smoke in the house, Will says, and the terror is so real and red and tidal that he has to sit down—to grab the chair from his tiny fold-out table and fall into it, so hard that the wood creaks with his weight.

No, his gran says, gently. You don't.

There is another moment of quiet—not stilted, this time, but stretched, skin-tight. The seagull outside the window takes flight, its wings huge, pterodactyl-like.

How long have you known? he asks her.

Not long, she says. I knew something wasn't right, so I've had lots of tests. Been passed from pillar to post, actually, for months. But now they know.

Will nods, feels his guilt fall, then rise.

Could it have been Gramps's cigars? he asks.

She sighs, again, but this time without sound. He sees her shoulders sag a little lower, and then she turns to him, and her eyes are resigned.

Could have been, she says. But more likely, Willyum, it's just one of those things.

He swallows.

Nobody's fault, she says.

When he doesn't move, she steps toward him and prizes the spoon from his hands. Asks if he wants sugar in his tea.

*

Rosie has put off introductions for too long. Her parents tell her this every time they speak, and Simon brings it up, too. I'm starting to think you're ashamed of me, he says, with a playful wink, and she laughs, and simultaneously panics.

So when she goes home for the weekend of Mothering Sunday, she takes Simon along with her.

They'd packed their bags, caught a train. Held hands up the driveway as they approached.

He has been polite and gracious and complimentary about her childhood home and her mother's cooking and her father's crime fiction collection, and she feels like screaming with the niceness of it, with how much she wants, for some strange, inexplicable second, to have violent sex with him on her bedroom floor.

This thought comes to her at dinner. As Simon smiles at her over the salt and pepper mills, passes her a dish of carrots.

She shoves her chair backward.

I have to go, she says.

Darling? Her mother raises her eyes, her own fork halfway to her mouth.

I ordered something for dessert, she says, and I've just realized I forgot to pick it up.

But I have dessert, her mother says. I bought a trifle.

Yeah, but—it's Mother's Day weekend, and I thought I'd do something special, Rosie says, and she's walking to the hall as she says it, taking her coat from the cupboard by the door.

Darling, her mum says again. We're eating.

Can't it wait?

Her dad, this time. Paused as he's topping up Simon's wineglass.

No, Rosie says. I won't be long. I've had enough, anyway.

You've barely touched your beef.

See you soon, she says, and she takes herself to the front door, hears their nervous laughter, her father saying she's always been this way, I'm afraid, Simon. There's no getting through to her, when she gets something in her head.

She traipses to the bakery, because she has lied, and now she has to come back with something to cover that lie. Her rage, her hot, rising waters, have subsided again, and she almost laughs at herself. There is no air in that house. There hardly ever was, but the small talk and the clinking forks and Josh's empty chair drive her near crazy, now, every time she comes home.

She thinks she loves Simon, and she knows he loves her, but sometimes she wants him to look at her like he could eat her; wants him to touch her in a way that means she feels wanted, instead of just cared for. But he sips wine and talks and smiles with all his teeth and passes carrots across the table.

She does laugh at herself now. Wonders whether it's hormones; what Marley would say, if she told her. I wanted him to fuck me upstairs, with my parents eating their roast beef on the good china, she would say. On my flowery childhood rug.

She tries to hold on to this image, now she's outside.

He would never. And she would never, either.

The day is mild, even warm; there are flowering trees and picture-book clouds, families walking by as she heads to the nearest line of shops. A hair salon, and a café that's rarely open, its faded laminate menus stuck to the door. She stops outside the bakery to assess the window display. Pink cupcakes. Farmhouse loaves. Piped celebration cakes covered in roses, the sort of thing her mother would never choose.

She goes in and she buys one.

And when she steps outside with the cake box she almost drops it, because Will White is standing there, leaning on the brick wall between the bakery and the salon. He hasn't seen her, and she cannot fathom why he would be here.

She says his name before she can stop herself, and he looks up, as surprised as she is. She has never seen him look like that. Always so cool and unaffected, so ready for anything.

Roe, he says, and she feels a wash of something warm. Hey.

Hey yourself.

What are you doing here?

I'm home for a few days. Mother's Day, she says, indicating the cake box, and he raises an eyebrow.

Didn't think your mum was the cake-eating type, he says.

Isn't everyone the cake-eating type?

She struck me as someone who would rather abstain, he says, and he is right, but she doesn't say so. She asks, likewise, what he's doing here, and he nods toward the salon.

Waiting for my gran, he says.

Rosie peers through the glass, and sees her sitting in a chair. She smiles at her little frame, her graying, recognizable bob.

How is she?

Will doesn't answer right away, and she glances back at him, impatient. She's conscious that she needs to get home; that her boyfriend and her parents are waiting. And she's annoyed, too, that she would rather stand here in the street, with him, even though they haven't spoken in weeks.

Their friendship has swollen and shrunk and ballooned again, over the past year. Sometimes they talk once a week, and sometimes life gets in the way and they slip into mutual silence before one of them reaches out again. That's how true friendship works, she thinks. Like her and Marley. She is distracted, cutting bodies open and partying until four in the morning, frequently rescheduling their calls so she can spend the day with her head in the toilet.

But with Will, Rosie reflects, things are slightly different. Will might be quiet, sometimes, but he is always there when she calls. Not once has he rescheduled. And now he is here, and holding himself differently; like he's being pulled up from the crown of his head.

Will? she says.

She's sick, he says.

What?

Cancer, he says.

Oh.

Her *oh* is an intake of breath—a shocked, sad, it can't be, but it is.

Oh God, she says, and she wishes she wasn't holding the cake box, wishes she could reach out and touch him.

Yeah, he says.

Is it . . . is she going to be . . . ?

Too soon to tell, he says. She's having chemo.

Well, that's good.

Is it? She's seventy and being pumped full of poison every other week. Her hair's falling out. She doesn't want to eat. She's dropped a stone and just sleeps, constantly. It's like she's a fucking shadow.

Rosie blinks at him.

But it's giving her a chance, right, she says.

Yeah, Will says. Yeah.

She knows it, without him having to say; can see it in his eyes. He has written her off, already. He is waiting for her to die.

D'you want to . . . go to the lighthouse, for a bit? she asks.

He glances at her, and then back inside. She can see him calculating whether he has time. Whether he can make room for Rosie in his life, today, now that everything has changed.

There is a young couple leaning on the railing when they get there. Hands interlocked, nuzzling noses and necks.

How dare they, says Will.

Don't they know who we are? Rosie jokes.

We should leave a sign, Will says.

What, no one near our lighthouse?

Bugger off, basically, Will says, and she laughs out loud, and he smiles, a little, and she is so relieved she almost hugs him, but the cake box stops her. She has some time, she thinks, before she has to head back, so they walk farther on, to a bench that looks out to sea. The ocean is choppy today. Waves, determined and deep blue, rolling fast toward the shore.

I didn't know you were back, says Will.

It's just for the weekend, Rosie says. Family stuff, you know.

Yeah.

Is Mother's Day weird for you?

He seems to consider her question; watches a family picking their way across the beach in front of them. Two young children in bright welling-ton boots. A mother, a father. Hand in hand.

Not really, he says. I think about her at odd times.

She doesn't press him, and so he goes on.

Mostly when good stuff happens, he says. Like when I got my me-chanic qualification, I sort of wanted to tell her. I know that's sad. Just a learned behavior, like when you get a gold star on your shirt at school.

Oh, yeah! Rosie says. I got so excited about those.

I'm sure.

That's not sad at all.

I don't really think about her when bad stuff happens, he says. She made hard things . . . harder. She never even came to my grandpa's funeral. Her own dad.

Rosie did not know this. She feels pulled in two directions—half panicked, thinking she should get back to her own family, yet desperate to stay here, as long as he needs, especially while he is saying these things.

Sometimes I think I see her, Will says. Out on the street, or when I'm running. But it's never her, obviously. Just a random woman. Same age, wrong face. It's not like I'm pining for her, looking for her on every corner, or anything. It's just one of those things.

He falls silent, as if remembering the last time it happened, and in that moment, Rosie really wants to touch him. Wants to hold his hand, or push his thick, golden hair out of his eyes, as if to say, I see you, even if your mother does not.

So to answer your question, he says. No, I'm not thinking about her, right now. Not before you asked, at least.

I bet she's thinking about *you*, Rosie says, and he makes a derisive sound, and she feels hurt by this, his rejection of her empathy. She swallows the lump in her throat, and he says nothing more about his mother.

How are you, anyway, he asks.

Fine, she says, thinking that fine actually means half dead; nothing to report, nothing new or exciting or good.

Just fine?

Just fine, she repeats.

Still with Simon?

Yep.

Still on track for your First?

I think so.

S'all coming up Rosie, then, he says, and she knows she should laugh, but she is still reeling from the news about his grandmother; still hurting, as if she's her own.

Can I visit? she asks him. Can I come see her, sometime?

He looks at her, and his eyes are full.

She'd like that, he says.

They sit together, watching the water. She asks him how Amber's taking it, and he says like Amber; turning to facts and figures, writing numerous lists. She tries to ask him about normal things, too, work and running and a recent album she thought he might have heard, but she gets the sense that he's struggling to respond, so she falls silent, lets him be. The afternoon has dipped to early evening when he says his gran is probably done, that he should go and drive her home.

When they get back to the salon, Rosie says his name. Puts the cake down and hooks her arm round his neck, standing on her tiptoes.

She wants to say, I'm sorry, but she cannot speak.

He cradles her in return and she thinks she feels something slip in him; that height she'd noticed, that pull-up, slackening like a snipped puppet string.

Can we get coffee, before you leave tomorrow, he asks her, without pulling away, and she says yes, of course, without thinking.

*

That night, Rosie texts him to say she's bringing Simon, and is that all right, and it's not, so he doesn't reply.

They are due to meet an hour before their return train. He makes sure to get there first, sits at a booth by the window. It needs cleaning, has handprints smeared up the glass.

He feels agitated, and spreads his fingers on the wood of the table. He wonders how his gran is feeling, if she can be a reason to bail early. And then they walk through the door, him after her, and he takes in the person she says that she loves, the one she lost her virginity to, spends all of her spare time with. He is tall, and muscular, and clean-shaven.

They spot him, and head for his table.

Ah, the famous Will White, Simon says, and he comes forward with an arm outstretched. Will goes to shake his hand but instead the guy folds him into a brief embrace, clapping him on the back. Will is embarrassed that he didn't expect it, and embarrassed that he is embarrassed by it. They break apart, and his face feels hot.

I've heard a lot about you, Simon says, and Will says oh yeah? And when Rosie shoots him a look he says, uh, you too.

All good things I hope, Simon says, and Will wonders if he's being clichéd on purpose; if he's embarrassed, too, or threatened. Rosie is standing beside him, watching Will with a strange expression on her face. Alert, and ready to bolt.

What's up with you, Will asks her, when Simon goes to get their drinks.

What d'you mean?

You've got a little fawn face on.

What?

You know. Bambi.

No, I don't.

You don't know Bambi?

Of course I know Bambi! But I don't have a fawn face.

You can't see your own face.

Will! For God's sake!

What? Why are you so on edge?

I just want you to get along, she says.

Okay, Will says. Weren't we getting along?

It's too soon to tell, Rosie says.

Well, exactly. Give us a chance, at least. Let us drink our coffee, chew the fat.

I hate that expression, she says, and he says he knows, and then Simon is back with the coffees and too many sugar sachets and he bumps into Rosie's arm as he sits down, his frame too big for their booth.

So, Will, he says, as he distributes the drinks. Rosemary tells me you're a mechanic?

Will raises his eyes to his; muddy brown, and, it would seem, genuinely interested. Which annoys him.

What is this, he asks. A job interview?

Simon blinks, then grins. He stirs his Americano, clinks the teaspoon against the cup.

She said you were kind of surly, too, he says, and Will sees Rosie tense as she lifts her own cup to her lips.

Surly? Will repeats.

Excellent word, I thought.

She does have a great vocabulary, says Will.

One of the many things that attracted me to her, says Simon.

Is that so?

Okay, Rosie says, too loudly. Shall we start again?

Both men look at her, if only for a second, before flitting back to one another. Simon is still smiling, though perhaps less genuinely.

I like you, Will, he says. I like that you've got my girl's back.

Will says nothing. He forces himself to remain still, then remembers he can drink his coffee; that this would be a nonconfrontational, even sociable move.

Always, he says, once he's swallowed.

Well, good, Simon says. Anyone who's a friend of Rosie's is a friend of mine. If you want, he adds, and it is boyish and humble and a bit pathetic, and Will pities him then, because he really has no idea.

There is an awkward moment of no talking.

Rosie, looking into her tea.

But if *we're* all good, says Simon, breaking the silence with his booming, private-schooled voice. Then all I need now is Marley's approval.

Good luck with that, Will says, and Simon laughs, and it's a nice laugh, full and appreciative, and this annoys Will, too, because he wasn't being funny.

You don't need anyone's approval, Rosie says.

Nice to know, Simon says, and he takes her hand and squeezes it on the table, and then he asks Will something about motorbikes, and the rest of the hour is perfectly pleasant, though Will's blood beats in his head.

*

He tries to fix the clicking ignition on his gran's oven.

Thinks, if he spends all night on it, he'll crack it.

He does some reading online, adjusts a few things, makes himself coffee after coffee, to stay wired and awake. He finally thinks it's there, at around three in the morning, and he doesn't even question why he started the job so late, why he couldn't just do it in the daylight.

His gran fries up some bacon the next morning, and the clicking is still there.

*

Rosie is true to her word, as he knew she would be.

Weeks later, after a few late-night texts, she comes by the house, alone.

She'd made some excuse and caught a train and knocks at his grand-ma's door, because he told her he'd be there, if she came.

His grandmother is thrilled. They hug, and she says she looks brighter, and too thin, and Rosie says that's what Oxford will do to a girl, and they laugh some shared female laughter and she says let's eat, then, let's eat.

Will cooks for them. Fish and vegetables, cooked in lemon, because he's read that Italian nonnas swear by citrus, claim it's what keeps them alive. His grandma doesn't eat much, despite her own insistence, and Rosie doesn't seem to want to, either, but they pick at their plates for something to do, for an interruption between the questions and the can-cer talk. His gran seems happier to tell Rosie the details that he himself has asked for; she is methodical and thoughtful with her answers, doesn't hold anything back.

The radio is on low. Country music, desperados waiting for a train, as his gran outlines her chances, the odds that she's dealing with.

You'll beat it, Rosie says, and there is a ferocity to her voice that catches him off guard.

Let's hope so, my girl, his gran says, and Rosie reaches for her hand and holds it and Will has to get up to clear their plates.

They play cards by the fire. Dave curls up at Rosie's feet and they stop talking about cancer and things feel normal, for a while, like they did two summers ago.

His gran asks her about Oxford, and her friends, and even Simon, which is unexpected and awkward, though she pretends that it isn't, looks mildly at her and sips some tea from her mug.

He's lovely, Rosie says. And Elsie says well, good. And Rosie reddens and asks her what she's reading, and they swap notes on a book that's too long but worth every page, something about a man and a passport, and he tries to concentrate, he really does, though he wants to drink, or run, or do something he'll regret.

Late in the evening, he walks her back to the train station. His gran said she should stay, but she said she needed to get back, that she has an essay to finish.

She left gifts; a jar of Oxfordshire honey, and sunflowers she put in a vase. So yellow, wide open like faces or planets or ripe, freshly grown vegetables. They seemed gaudy to him. Smug with enforced cheer.

Thanks for coming, he says, as they walk. She really loved seeing you.

I loved seeing her, too, Rosie says. I'm sorry I haven't come by, since, you know. That summer. I'll come more often.

Because she's dying?

No, Rosie says, and he doesn't know if she means no, that's not the reason, or no, she isn't dying. But then she says, because I want to.

They walk in silence along the busy roads. It is a Saturday night. People are going places, doing things. After she boards her train, he will go back to his flat and watch mindless television, maybe call the girl he'd hooked up with last week.

Simon really liked you, she tells him.

Her voice is light, noncommittal.

Huh, he says.

He lets her words hang there, and she seems flustered when they arrive at the station, her eyes bright and her cheeks too pink from the short walk.

See you, then, she says.

Yeah. See ya, he says, and they do not embrace, and for a reason neither of them can quite voice, after she's spent an afternoon with his sick grand-mother, held her hand, made her laugh, there is no gratitude or tender-ness but a disconnection, a pain so deep and private they cannot broach it, and she boards her train and Will turns his back, without watching it pull away.

twelve

Rosie has a nosebleed on her wedding day.

She has only had two in her life. One on the first day of secondary school, during the fire drill, and the other some years later, on the same day she started her period. The school nurse told her it was like her body wasn't sure where to bleed, and she'd laughed at her own little joke, and Rosie felt something else leak out of her, then, something vital and self-preserving.

This third nosebleed is not the nightmarish scene she'd read about in bridal magazines. She is not yet in her dress. It is early, her mother and bridesmaids still sleeping. She is twenty-four years old, and she is still Miss Winters, for now, and she's sitting on the edge of the bathtub watching the light change outside the window, gray lifting to milk-white, when she feels a wetness on her top lip. She reaches up to touch it and draws back, her fingertip startlingly red. And that is it; it doesn't flow or drip or stain the tiles.

She wipes her nose on a sheet of toilet roll, and then her mother knocks on the door, says, Rosie, are you in there?

*

When she'd told him she was engaged, he'd said he was happy for her. Three times.

He was standing in the street, queueing for a bag of chips, his breath white on the air, as she told him the news he'd been waiting for. Then he hung up and took the chips home, let them turn cold in the paper.

His grandmother cried, when he told her.

What, he'd said, and she said nothing, just wiped her face with the tissue bunched at her wrist, her hair wispy but grown back, in patches.

Don't, he'd said, and she'd asked don't what, and he said just don't, and he walked out and phoned a girl and spent the next few weeks in her flat, drinking and smoking and dabbling in things he said he never would, again.

On the day itself, he almost storms the wedding; or at least, he thinks about doing it, and that is nearly the same thing. He knows the ceremony is at two, keeps looking at the clock. He makes a coffee, a long, luxurious version usually saved for weekends or when he has women to stay. He drinks it in his kitchen, looking over the rooftops. Clogged gutters. Lichened slate. It's an astonishingly hot day and it's another hour closer to her vows and something in him is taut, like a guitar string that smells of nylon and rust, the swollen tips of her thumbs.

He was invited. Not to the ceremony, but to the reception at some barn on the outskirts of Norfolk, a relatively short drive away. He was even granted a plus one. He did not RSVP, and Rosie did not ask him to, and he still has not decided whether he is going when the time to shave and dress and leave comes and then goes and he is still in his kitchen, in his jeans, staring at a shred of sea.

He was going to give her the Montenegro necklace, one day. The one she looked at in the market, which he bought, later, when she wasn't looking. He has kept it, all these years, in its creased paper bag. The chain has darkened, a little, but the stone is still the color the sea was, that sum-mer, so he takes it to the beach, when she is probably saying I do or I will or in sickness and in health, and he throws it into the waves, like they do in the movies, and it does not make him feel a single bit better.

He wants to drink. Really drink. But instead he makes a decision, and for once, it feels like a good one. For once, his chest eases, like a valve has opened. Air, escaping, in a rush.

*

Vol-au-vents. So fun to say, she thinks, though there is nobody to share this with, even though the hall is filled with people she knows and loves, and many that she doesn't.

There are roses, and gypsophila, and table runners and sparkling wine and warm-hearted speeches and lemon sole sprinkled in dill. Brides-maids' dresses in royal blue, because that was Josh's favorite color.

It is everything a wedding is meant to be, but Will's absence is like a missing tooth. Something she worries at, all night, without giving it proper attention.

Her dress is beautiful and too tight. Her mother laced it up the back for her, and it should have been a tender moment, but they were mostly quiet, stressed about the fit, and instead of focusing on her husband-to-be in the ceremony she was thinking about how Josh wasn't there and neither was Will, and that was her decision, not to invite him to the first part, to their intimate and graceful ceremony. A harp entrance. Religious readings, even though they're not religious, because it's only right, Simon had said.

She has spent her life trying to be only right, so she did not argue, did not care, even, very much, because the words were nice, and surely that was the point.

All day, they talk and stand and drink. They hold each other for their first tilting slow dance, and she thinks about the night she was seventeen, in the teachers' car park, the current between her and Will and the urge she had to both touch and not touch him. It felt dangerous, and this, she thinks, is the opposite. She feels steadied in Simon's arms. Propped up. With Will, she never knew where she was, how he might make her feel.

She realizes, as she slips off her garter that night, with her husband undressing beside her, that she has spent a lot of the day thinking about a man she barely sees. It must be because she loves him like a brother, she concludes, after all this time. And she's lost one of those already. So she phones him the next morning, while Simon is in the shower.

He doesn't answer, so she keeps trying until he picks up.

Rosie, he says, and he so rarely calls her that, and she hasn't heard his voice in so many months, that she smiles, and tenses, both at once.

Hi, she says.

What's wrong?

Why would something be wrong?

You called me like six times.

Well, you didn't pick up.

He says nothing. Light falls through the blind, skirts her splayed fingers on the bed sheets.

What's wrong *your* end? she asks him. Why wouldn't you answer?

Rosie, he says again, and he sounds tired.

I just wondered where you were last night, she says.

The silence weighs them down, like snow.

I just couldn't, Roe, he says.

Oh, come on, she says, and her heart quickens, and she reaches for humor like a life raft. I know posh food and string quartets aren't your thing. They're not really mine, either. But it was my wedding day, Will.

Silence. Snow. Cold hands, not so long ago.

Right, he says.

It was . . . weird that you weren't there, you know?

Weird, he repeats, and she thinks she can hear him raising his eyes to his ceiling, opening his mouth as if he's angry, holding something back.

Will? she says.

I think we're done, Rosie, he says. I'm leaving.

Leaving?

I'm moving, he says.

Where to?

The North.

How rugged.

I guess. Rent's cheap.

She hears Simon shut off the shower in the bathroom. The water, faltering.

Are you going soon? she asks him, ignoring what he'd said, before. Can I see you before you go?

I don't think so, Will says, after another pause. Like I said, I . . . think we're done.

Shadow, beneath the bathroom door. A cabinet, opening and closing. Simon does not emerge, and she does not hang up.

Take care, he says, and she says wait, and he does, and she says what do you mean we're done? What . . . were we doing?

The sun pales on the bedspread. Clouds, moving, beyond the window.

I don't know, Roe, he says, and it's the name he gave her, and the same small thrill lights in her stomach, before he says, I really don't know. Do you?

*

He follows his plan and goes to Leeds, but he doesn't like it. It's busy and cold and full of people he has nothing to say to, kind of like Norfolk, but with more rain.

He soon moves to a town in the Yorkshire Dales, instead, and that is far better. Still cold. Still wet. But quieting, and with quiet people, and a job he lands with a garage owner who asks no questions and likes his handiwork and pays him a decent wage.

It's just for a while, he'd told his gran. For a change.

Her chemo was over, and she had survived, and she understood and let him go and he knows nobody and drinks one-off ales in the local pub and volunteers for Mountain Rescue after two weeks, not knowing what he's letting himself in for. But he hears them chatting by the bar, sees the hills outside his bedsit window and thinks, why not. He runs. His legs are strong. He has time to kill and nothing to care about.

He needs to pass some kind of test, which he brazenly thinks will be easy. But the inclines are steep and the ground is pocked with rocks and he has to train his body to move differently, to endure in an entirely new way. They make him carry heavy packs, force him to revisit navigation, after the little he'd learned from his grandpa. Safety is paramount in the hills, which is a new concept, to him. It is, oddly, not a place for risk-takers; they try hard to make this clear.

After a year, he is made a prospective member, and called out mostly for sprained ankles, tourists walking in plimsolls who get tired and em-barrassed and emotional. He gives them flapjacks and hot tea and they make it down the mountain and he goes home and reads cookbooks and looks up new running routes on his Ordnance Survey maps and his heart feels fine, for a while, as if it's beating beneath a drawn curtain, taking time to rest.

One time, when the weather is bad, the sky as white as the hilltop fog, they take a while to find the couple who'd raised the alarm. Eventually, though, they reach them. Two women in their late forties, one of whom has slipped on the scree, and he flares up when he sees them, because one of them looks so impossibly like her.

He spends so much of his time unseeing Rosie Winters, he had forgotten this nostalgic fear—the jolt of seeing a person, of around the same age, who looks like the woman who birthed him. Same shade of red hair, same limber arms. Never, ever the same face.

Sometimes, when he thinks about her, he wonders if she's died.

And he doesn't know how to feel about that.

One night, he is ordering a round for his rescue team, his face fired with the wind burn from the hills, and there is a girl at the bar.

She looks at him like a lot of girls do, so he knows she'll say yes if he offers to buy her a drink. She has short dark hair and sharp, even darker eyes. A twist of jade at her throat, looped on a piece of twine.

It's from New Zealand, she tells him, when she catches him looking.

You're Kiwi?

I wish, she says. I spent a year there, after uni.

Skydiving and stuff?

God, no. Just living. I sold tickets for boat tours.

Sounds thrilling.

It kind of was, she says, shrugging. I like boats. And anything's better halfway across the world.

He tips his drink at her for that, and sits beside her on a bar stool, ignoring his friends as they jeer at him from behind.

She can drink. He nurses his single pint, but she doesn't comment on this, which makes him like her, and they talk about travel and home and underrated things that make them both laugh, a little. She likes cats, and late nights, and horror films. She doesn't eat meat or coriander. Tastes like soap, she tells him. She has a sister, and a mother and a father who are separated, but still live down the same street.

Is that weird, he asks her, and she says people who make vows and then never see each other again is weirder. She is pale, like milk. Reminds him of the weather up here.

What's your story, then, she asks him, as the bell rings for last orders. You got a mum? A dad? A one-legged dog?

No to all three, he says, and so he gets into it, and she's so interested and matter-of-fact that he keeps going, and he even tells her about Roe, spilling all of it to this woman he doesn't know but senses he can trust. That he moved here, really, to cut loose, and he wishes there was another reason but there it is, the truth, stark and bent like the dead trees on the side of the Yorkshire roads. She listens to every word, swirling her wine in its glass.

So you're in love with a girl you've never even slept with?

Worse than that, he says. With a girl I've only kissed once. Eight years ago.

He does not repeat the start of her sentence.

I'd say you just love the idea of her, then, she says. You're pinning everything on something you've never even had. Something that's not real.

You reckon? he asks, and he stares at her, desperate for this woman, this stranger, to be right, so he can suddenly, finally, in his midtwenties, become unstuck.

I do, she says, and he knows as he watches her tip her drink back, the way her fringe falls to the side, that she will be important to him, somehow.

Her name is Jen. She has a tattoo of a fern on her hip bone, he finds out that night, as they remove each other's clothes, and she tells him that is real, and that, and that, as she guides him to touch her in places that make him crave and blur and forget all other things.

His sister comes to visit for the first time since he moved up North. She has spurted upward like a bean shoot, all elbows and kneecaps and shoulder blades.

You're a teenager, he says, and she says obviously, and he goes to hug her and she says, um, what are you doing?

Greeting my little sister, he says, as the train eases out of the platform and trundles onward.

Then greet me, she says. No touching.

How are those intimacy issues going? he asks, and she rolls her eyes, says she's hungry, that he'd better still be a good cook.

She seems to like Jen, as much as Amber can like anybody. They live together now, which he hasn't told his gran yet, and the evidence of living with a woman is everywhere; her razor on the side of the bath, the low-fat yogurt in the fridge; clean, dry tea towels, folded on the kitchen counter.

At first, Amber says nothing, though he sees her taking it all in. She slopes off to the guest room and seems happier at dinner, when Jen shows an interest in her studies, and she gets a chance to show off about her grades and her swimming, and her new plan to be a human rights lawyer.

Or an oncologist, she says, and Will looks at her across the table as he tears some bread with his teeth.

Because of Gran? he asks.

Because it pays well, Amber says. And I'd be good at it.

Jen is looking at her, too. She swallows some wine and then asks if they really have the same parents, and it's meant to be an affectionate joke, a compliment, which works on Amber—she snorts, and takes a half-shy, half-smug glug of her lemonade—but Will is quiet for the rest of the meal.

In bed that night, Jen asks him what's up, what she's done. Will exhales, wondering if he can be bothered to share.

We have different dads, he tells her.

Jen's eyes search his own. She is facing him in bed, her hair fanned black on the pillow.

I didn't know, she says.

Amber doesn't, either, he says. She's too young to remember that my dad had left, already.

Jen touches his face and asks if he wants to talk about it and he says no.

I didn't know, she says again. I'm sorry.

No need, he says, and he means it. He rolls over so he's lying flat on his back, scoops his arms behind his head.

She's a good kid, she says. You did a good job.

My grandparents raised her, he says. I did nothing.

Rubbish, Jen says. She idolizes you.

He actually laughs at this.

Seriously, she says. All these things she says, and does. She's trying to impress you.

She's trying to outdo me, Will counters.

She wants to make you proud, Jen says, and he finds this hard to believe, but he doesn't say so; lets her have her sentimental family vision, if it's what she needs to see.

Love you, Jen says, when she is close to sleep, and he is still looking at the mildew on their ceiling. He tells her he loves her, too, because it turns out it only takes practice, and meaning it—and feeling it—has nothing to do with anything.

They take Amber out walking. See the skylarks on the fells, climb over stiles, order tea and cake in small, slate-roofed cafés. She takes photos of unremarkable things like thistles and phone boxes and sheep, and asks him about Mountain Rescue, and talks, mainly, about her friends and her coursework and her desire to study at Warwick.

The morning she is leaving, she asks him how he's doing.

How d'you mean? he asks. He is making them both coffee in his kitchen. Jen has left for work, and it is the first time all week that they are properly alone.

Like, how are you *doing*? Amber repeats. Are you drinking?

Socially, he says, after a pause.

That's all right, then.

Yeah, he says. It is.

Gran worries to death about you, she says.

Don't say that.

Why not? It's true.

The death part, he says.

He grins at her to show he's only joking as he puts her cup down in front of her. He can't quite believe she drinks coffee now. That she's nearly as tall as him.

She's still in the clear, Amber says. She has another check-up soon, but she's good. Cooking casseroles and baking bread. She's even whistling again.

Oh dear, Will says.

I know. It's infuriating.

I remember.

But I do kind of like it, now.

I know what you mean.

I heard you talking through the wall, she says, out of nowhere. She holds her coffee up to the light, as if checking to see what brand of mug he has in his cupboards. Details she'll report back to his grandmother, no doubt.

Okay, he says.

And I already know we're half siblings, she says. At least, I'd assumed.

He cannot look at her. He doesn't like how casual she sounds; how untroubled.

Right, he says.

I don't think it matters, though, she says.

No?

Nope. Both our dads are absent, so fundamentally, they mean nothing. And our mother is absent, but shared, at least. You're pretty much
all I've got, she says, thoughtfully. Apart from Gran, and she won't be
around for long.

Ambs.

What? You need to get used to the idea, Will, that people die.

I know they fucking die.

You don't! You don't confront it, or properly let it in. It's why you
drink and run like a madman and try to kill yourself on that motorbike.

What?

I saw you, sometimes, she says. Taking corners like you had a death
wish. People from school called you Suicide Will.

Will stands up so fast he cracks his knee on the table; he feels the
bruise burning around the bone, the creeping of his blood.

I'm just saying, Amber says, as he turns away, runs the tap for something to do. I feel like you need to—I don't know—*process* things. I'm doing
Psychology A Level, and—

Process things, he repeats, and his voice is high, disbelieving. Christ,
Amber. I'm a fucking adult. Some shit things have happened, okay, but
I'm fine. I'm all right.

But are you *happy?*

Water running. Fingers, underneath, to check the heat.

No one's happy, he says.

That's just not true, Amber says. For goodness' sake, Will, this is what
I mean. You can't go through life like this. You need to talk to someone
about Mum, and Grandpa, and your friend who died.

I talk plenty, he says.

I saw her, she says, changing tack so quickly he can't grasp what she means.

Mum? he asks.

No, not Mum, she says. Your girl. Rosie.

A pause. Sun, stilled, on his shoulders, as he stands with his back to her.

Rosie is not my girl, he says.

Well, whatever. She was home with her boyfriend.

Husband, he says.

Whoever. They were at the pub with some old school friends. You'd probably know a lot of them.

I don't care about any of this, Amber.

You don't care about Rosie Winters?

Why are you telling me this?

Because, Amber says, and she takes a deep breath, and is quiet for so long that he has to shut off the tap. It has filled the washing-up bowl. Teeters, on the edge, water slopping into the sink.

I was saying that you're all I've got. And I was saying that I want you to be okay. And I feel like the only time I've ever seen you close to okay was when that girl was around. Not that I liked her much, she adds.

Something sparks in him.

A fuse, blowing out.

She was mopey, Amber says. And so *floaty*, like she wasn't really there.

Her brother died, Will says.

Yeah, Amber says, and she has the decency to pause, again, to pretend that must have been hard for this girl she barely knows.

But when I saw her, Will, I felt like I should tell you about it, and that's why I came all the way up here. Not that it's not been nice to see you. Sort of.

Will has his hands in the sink water. It is so hot that it scalds.

Is she pregnant? he asks.

No.

Another spark. He takes his hands out of the water, slowly, sees the raw, meat-red of his skin.

She's miserable, Amber says, and she waits, lets that hang in the air.

Her eyes are *hollow*, she goes on. And she's stick-thin. She wasn't drinking wine like everyone else—she had water, and when she went to the bathroom, she was in there for ages, Will. Like, ages. I almost went to check on her.

Why are you telling me this, he asks, again.

I thought you'd want to know, Amber says, with a shrug. Clearly, I was wrong.

Clearly, he says.

I just think, she says, and she stands up, takes her empty coffee cup to the side, that you only get one life, you know? So what's the point in spending it miserable, or inert?

Inert, he repeats.

Yeah. Good word, isn't it? I am soon to be a tertiary educated young woman, Amber says, and she looks smug again—but also different. Something else in her eyes.

So get over it, she says.

What, you being smart? Or me being miserable?

Both.

She smiles at him then, without teeth. Just hitching her lips on one side.

And for the record, she says, as she retreats, heading to the hallway to start packing her things. I did really like Jen.

He notes her use of the past tense as she stalks into the next room, but there is no spark, no fuses blown, no flame in his stomach.

He upends the bowl. Watches the water flood, then drain away.

*

Rosie does not go far, once she's married. She and Simon did not want to live in London but craved the lights and youthfulness of a city, so they settled for the center of Norwich; close to home, but different enough.

Different from what? Simon had asked her.

The place where I see Josh on every corner, she'd not said.

And so the place she could not bear to leave.

She gave him some vague answer, and Simon thought about it, said it was like a bigger, less beautiful Oxford, why not, and so they bought a penthouse flat, wide and glassy with a view of the river and a feasible commute to the airport, the capital, the rest of the country, for all the adventures they planned to have.

He has a senior position in investment banking, and Rosie, somehow, ends up in management consultancy. Unplanned, but stimulating enough, with long hours and high wages, a good pension and health benefits, and family days where all her colleagues have picnics or ride go-karts or play badminton in tennis whites.

She does Pilates and cardio classes and counts calories and cooks, badly, for Simon and sometimes their group from university who have remained close and jovial, and connected only, it seems to Rosie, by their ages and their salaries. She buys chia seeds and soy candles and antiaging cream, on her mother's orders. She fits into clothes she never thought she'd be able to, and she puts them on and feels exposed and unlike herself, instead of sexy or beautiful like she expects. She has dabbled in therapy. She cannot meditate, though she has tried. She checks things, still, on a loop. She is a wife and a daughter and no longer a sister.

Wonders if she can be a twin, still, without him.

She still writes on her skin, in private, when she's waiting for a client to join a video call, or if she's traveling in a taxi back from the office and something comes into her head that she will not be able to hold on to. This is her favorite part of any day, this stealing of a moment. Crafting a sentence, or stanza, and feeling, for a time, like she's standing in sunlight.

She means to write it all down properly, to transfer it to a notebook, and sometimes she does, and sometimes she forgets and the poems or scraps or lines, whatever they are, smear off her arms in the shower. Ink washing down the drain with the grime from the city, the sweat from her treadmill sessions, the shower crème she lathers all over her strong, bony, unrecognizable limbs.

Sex, with her husband, is sometimes nice, and occasionally awkward, and often makes her shiver in the wrong kind of way. He is away with work a lot. He is sweet and tender when he is home, and for this, she feels grateful and guilty as hell.

One evening, after she has shaved her legs in the bath, she is rubbing moisturizer onto her calves. Simon is out at a conference, and she has to make herself dinner, without him. She thinks, briefly, about slathering her body butter onto a cracker, and biting into it. How thick and creamy it would be.

It has been so long since she has tasted sugar.

So long since she has allowed herself anything that even remotely resembles love.

Marley calls her every month. She is pregnant, now; seeing another doctor, a neurologist, in fact, and living in London and taking on that eclectic, caffeine-laced energy that all Londoners have, a fast-walking, tube-catching, ramen-eating verve that makes her friend feel like a gust of swirling wind when they speak. She is ambitious and direct and still interested in Rosie, but Rosie feels like she can't keep up with her; like she's observing her through those brass opera glasses you get in theaters, simply watching from far away.

Her friend seems happy, if incessantly busy. Rosie wonders if she's satisfied, if all their hard work and rule-following and good grades at school have paid off, for her. If she even gets time to think about it.

Rosie is the opposite. She has too much time to think now, after a time when things just happened, when she wasn't herself, and she let things play out, without thinking.

Most unlike her, she muses, sometimes, in the dead of night, or when she's walking to the gym in the rain. But it's not all bad. She's writing. She's earning. She's got floor-to-ceiling windows that let the sunlight in, and a good husband who smells of soap and brings her tulips and says he loves her, every day, before they turn out the light.

She does not feel satisfied, but she feels safe and calm and poised, and that's okay, because that's what she'd needed. What she needs.

She gets a text near midnight, when Simon is home and sleeping beside her. She wasn't tired when they got into bed. Has been writing her poems down, the ones she washed away earlier that day and is now trying to retrieve.

When her phone buzzes and she sees Will's name, she does not open the message right away. It has been so long since she saw it, like that, on her screen. They have not spoken since she got married, and he told her they were done, which sometimes, she thinks, is completely fair, and at other times, makes her so mad she wants to stamp and scream like a child. Like a broken-hearted teenager. Even though, she reminds herself, her heart was not his to break. They were close friends. They were not meant for more. She knows this, now, and is happy with Simon. Happy with her lot.

So she ignores the text for a while. Observes, as her therapist would advise, what happens in her body; what spins and pulses and rinses her out.

She finishes writing, thinking that maybe she won't read it until morning. Closes her notebook. Stares at the moonlight, on the wall.

Wonders who she's kidding, and opens up the message.

She scans it too fast, at first, has to slow down and reread. He asks her how she is. Says he's thinking of coming home to visit, and would she and Simon like to get together. That he's bringing Jen, who he lives with now, and who he's sure she'll like.

It is the most ordinary message, so she doesn't understand why it infuriates her. Why she has to get out of bed and do a core class down in the living room on her laptop, holding herself stiff and tight and clenched.

Will wants to see us, she says at breakfast.

She says it casually. She does not care. She sips her sugar-free juice.

Will White? Simon says, not looking up from his magazine.

How many other Wills do we know?

Simon doesn't answer; he takes a mouthful of his smoothie and keeps reading. She marvels, then, at how much he reminds her of her father doing his crossword. Letting important things pass him by.

What should I say? she asks him.

What do you want to say, he asks, and she wants to throw her juice at him for being so reasonable and companionable, all the time.

I don't feel like I know him anymore, she says. I don't think I care about seeing him.

Then say we're busy.

But could we conceivably be busy for the whole week he's down? Is that rude?

Rosie, Simon says, and he finally looks up. You're overthinking this.

Sorry, she says, because apologizing is a reflex, like flinching away from an open flame.

Would a drink with him be so bad?

No. It wouldn't be bad.

It might be good. Clear the air between you both.

What do you mean, she asks, and her whole body hardens, until he says you know, since he let you down with the wedding, and all.

Yeah, she says.

He might even want to apologize, he says. For missing it.

A few years too late, she says.

Better late than never, Simon says, turning a page. So she says maybe, and dithers about it all week long.

Her cowardice takes over the day Will is due to leave, and she finally texts him back. Says she's sorry that she'd missed his message—that Simon was away and she was on a conference but next time, yes, definitely, it would be nice to see him, no kisses, a pause, then a follow-up text, two small letter Xs, either affectionate or canceling out her lies, she is not sure, and he himself does not reply this time, and for that, she is relieved.

*

Quiet things ensue. Calm days. Marriage, and partnership, and restful, regular sleep. Will falls for the landscape of North Yorkshire, even more than the coastline back home, and Rosie likes the routine and certainty of her days, a newfound strength she thought she would never find, but here it is, without her realizing, one morning, and still there, the next and the next.

There are good days, and not so great days. Rainfall, in Yorkshire, that lasts a full week, and cold snaps in Norwich that turn Rosie's hands numb, make her think of things she doesn't want to think about, snow days and lighthouses and storm-gray eyes.

I love you, you know, she says to Simon, when this happens, a thread of panic wheedling through her.

I do know, he says back, and they carry on, this way, and everything is steady.

*

It is a raw winter's night when Will gets a call.

A thirty-four-year-old male is reported missing, was last seen heading for the hills. He's not in good shape, they're told, so Will heads out into the sleet with his team, carrying ropes and survival bags and warm gear, the urgency driving them uphill more than the strong winds behind them.

His team does not seem worried, and so he isn't, either. It is first thing in the morning, and the dark is the opposite of dark—a whiteout of unfallen snow, weighing heavy in the clouds. Will's own heart rate is up because of the weight of his pack and the force of the gale, but he is not struggling; he is focused. Pumping with the edge that running gives him; that hit of speed and danger, like clear, hard alcohol, which he has not touched since that rainy knock on his door, so many summers ago.

His own foot skids on a sheet of rock, and his heart jolts, but he rights himself.

All right? asks Jim, the officer behind him, and Will says yeah. Because he is all right. At this moment, everything is all right. They take another nine, ten steps. The wind is roaring, ocean-like, and the sleet has finally stopped.

He does not hear or see a single thing to warn him. He is in front, and it has already happened. The man had made the decision, tied those knots, taken the step that was required. A single step. A single tree branch.

One moment, Will is looking for a missing person, and the next, he is not.

Dammit, Jim says, under his breath, but Will hears him, and realizes he must be stupid for not having expected this. For not expecting it to stare him in the face, one day, in some form, in a different county under a different sky, but with the outcome successful, this time, for the person who wanted it bad enough.

Terror. That thing he has always felt, but kept down.

It comes for him, on the hill.

Things get numb and blurry, after that. He wants to drink, desperately, but he tells Jen in a moment of clarity and she does her utmost to prevent it. He spends his days in the flat, and goes to work and completes his shifts with as little interaction as possible. In the evenings, he takes his motorbike out, because it is the only thing that makes him feel anything at all.

He thinks about what Amber said.

What they called him at school.

He thinks about that day in the school bathroom, with the smashed mirror and his cut head. People assumed he'd attacked another student, and that was easier, more understandable. Nobody, least of all himself, would know what to do with the truth. That he had cracked his own skull multiple times against the glass, to see what would break first.

He thinks about the woman they robbed.

Josh, and the edge.

His mother left. His father was never there. His grandpa died, and his grandma will, and the missing man, with his khaki trousers and unlaced boots, the man they did not find in time—he was gone, too, and nothing Will did or could do would stop any of it.

So he rides, and he lies in bed, and he says very little, and he lets whatever it is inside him take him down, down, down.

*

Rosie goes to see Marley and the baby. She takes an assortment of gifts from herself and Simon but also her parents, wrapped in tissue paper and dotted with ducklings. Marley asks her to open them for her, sunk into the sofa cushions with her tiny person nestled on her chest. She looks exhausted. Content. Disheveled, like a bud that's late to open.

She tells her in detail about the birth, and Rosie holds the baby for a while but is so startled by the weight of her that she soon hands her back. Sunshine tips through the windows and warms the room. Rosie takes off her jumper, refreshes their drinks.

I can't believe you're a mother, she says, at some point.

Me neither, Marley says. I wasn't meant to be until I was thirty-three.

Oh, really?

Yep. I had a plan. A Rosie Winters plan.

Rosie smiles as she lifts her lemonade, tells her to go on.

I was going to marry Trev at thirty, Marley says. Finish my residency and start trying. I figured it would take me roughly a year to fall pregnant. So yeah, I'd be popping her out at thirty-three. Not twenty-nine. This is all a bit . . . soon.

What happened, Rosie asks.

Skye happened, Marley says, looking down at her little human. She seems unconcerned that it is too soon, that her plan had a timeline of its own.

So will you marry Trevor, anyway, Rosie asks her. They are both staring at Skye, her sleeping face and hammy hand, resting on Marley's collarbone.

Someday, Marley says. If he asks.

Of course he'll ask.

There is a pleasant silence. They listen to the sigh of traffic outside, the shuffle of the blinds in the breeze.

Did you feel any different, when you married Simon? Marley asks her.

Rosie takes another mouthful of lemonade. Different how, she asks.

I don't know. You tell me. I always thought a wedding would be necessary, you know, and special. But now we have Skye, I just wonder whether anything can be more special than this. More binding. You know?

Sure, Rosie says, though of course she does not know, because she does not have a child. She and Simon have talked about it, once or twice. She feels no desire to be a mother, though she has never admitted such a thing, hopes that it'll set in, one day, without her noticing.

So did you feel a change, when you got married?

Yeah, of course, Rosie says.

Marley waits, and Rosie drinks more lemonade. It is tart and already flat, leaves a film of sugar on her teeth.

It solidifies your commitment, she says. It was nice to do that out loud, in front of everyone.

Nice, Marley repeats. She is watching her in that way that she does.

Wonderful, Rosie corrects herself.

Rosie, Marley says.

Yeah?

Are you all right?

. . . yeah? Why?

No reason, she says. You're just so . . . on edge.

Haven't I always been?

They smile awkwardly at this, thinking that it's both sad and true.

Skye mewls and Marley rearranges her on her chest, and soon, she falls asleep again.

You're skinny, too, Marley says.

Finally, says Rosie. Marley pulls a face; not denying it, but not approving of her response, either.

It's just Si's healthy lifestyle, Rosie says, with a false laugh. It's hard to be married to a rower and still eat dairy and bread.

But you're all right, Marley says.

I'm completely fine, Rosie says. Really.

She goes over this lie as she rides the train home. Because the fact is, she has never been completely fine; can't remember a time she was ever fine, and that was even before Josh died.

Josh.

His name, like a lost lucky charm. Still shining with hope and good things, but also laced with something irretrievable; a yearning that gets her nowhere.

She sees him in the mirror, sometimes, in the shape of her own ears and the angle of her jaw. Both of them a little funny-looking; he, with limbs too big for his body, sure to grow handsome and refined with the years he was never given. And she, never quite right. Eyebrows too thick. Forehead too broad. Almond eyes, blue, but sad.

She misses him like a vital organ.

Sits up, sometimes, in the middle of the night, because she thinks she can hear him coming down the hall, even though he never set foot in her apartment, would have probably hated all the granite and the gray, the lack of plants and music and cushions.

When she gets back from Marley's she skips dinner, brushes her teeth because that makes it easier to convince herself that she's eaten. Then she checks the windows are closed, three times—a smooth night, really, all things considered.

Once she's in bed, she phones her mother, without thinking about it. A reflex, when she feels down, or confused, even though it so rarely helps.

Darling, she answers, and Rosie says, Mum.

Are you all right?

Not really, she says.

Oh! What's happened?

Nothing. Nothing.

A silence.

I think that's the problem, she says. *No*thing has happened. I think I'm bored, Mum. I feel stuck. And tired, all the time.

Are you eating properly? her mother asks. Do your breasts hurt?

I'm not pregnant, Mum.

Are you sure?

Yes. That's not why I called.

You called because you're tired?

Rosie holds her breath, looking at her drawn curtains, the scattering of face creams on her dresser. She wonders where her books went. Her records and notebooks and her stacks of Post-it notes.

Yeah, she says. I guess.

Well get an early night, darling, her mother says. And just watch it. It could be anemia, or something. You might need some supplements.

Maybe, says Rosie.

Darling?

Yeah?

You're just bored because you're bright, she says. Start looking for new jobs, if you need to. You've been at your company long enough. You probably just need a change.

Rosie agrees. She thanks her mother, though she doesn't know what for, and hangs up. The face creams seem to stare at her, like they don't know what she expected. So judgmental, standing in their straight line.

Soon after, Simon texts to say he'll be late, that she shouldn't wait up, and even though she is already in bed she feels a flash of righteousness, like she's allowed to be angry at the man who loves her and cares for her and plans their weekends with the diligence he shows almost everything: rowing, sex, weight-lifting, Scrabble. He touches her wrong, but it is still touching. He supports her through her quiet grief and her constant checking, and holds her strange, tapping hands when she is nervous because something bad is happening on the television.

In time, she slips out of her anger and sleeps, dreamlessly. The same way she moves through her days.

long after

thirteen

☾

Seasons of good, and bad, and totally fine.

Sleepwalking.

Routine-making.

Life passing like cars. Smells of petrol and bleach and instant coffee. Chest pain, fresh tulips, calories burned and units consumed and late-night noodles out of a pot.

Good sex; bad sex. Rude waiters, and crying women, and long phone calls with relatives that expect it but have nothing to say, talk only about the washing, the neighbors, the things outside the window.

They do not think of each other. Often.

They do not.

Until, one bright day, at the top of a hill he has climbed, Will takes a photo of a view he has never seen before. Like he used to when he was a teenager, on his long runs by the coast. Photos of clouds and silhouetted seabirds, and sunlight doing bold things. This time, the sky is the clearest blue he's ever seen, so clear he can see as far as the Irish Sea, which hasn't happened in all the time he's lived here. He captures it, for Rosie, without pausing to think, and feels good, and light, for one clear moment.

He is hiking back down, the summit behind him, when the weight returns to his chest. Because he will not send it to her.

They have not spoken for nearly two years. He does not want to draw her in again, doesn't want to go there, even though he so badly wants to hear from her, to read her words on a screen, and he is furious with her, for that. For making him want something he shouldn't. So he keeps the photo on his phone, a reminder of the good things, the light things, that they must not share.

Last time they'd been in touch—when he'd reached out to check on her, more than anything, after what Amber had told him—she had ignored him. Or seen it, and opted not to respond until too late. Either way, he feels quietly enraged at her cowardice, or worse, the fact that she no longer cares. So he fumes, and stays silent, because he doesn't want to know her reasons, is not sure he could handle it if they were to cross texts, or send Christmas cards, in case he finds out she's happy without him in her life, moved on and married and detached. So he says nothing. Just rages, day in, day out, apart from the odd occasion he sees a sky like that, and things feel right for a while.

It is all less beautiful, on the way down.

Rosie plays on his mind, like the sunlight on the stream beside him, running parallel to the edge.

He knows this thing between them will always hold some temptation, some kind of magnetic pull that neither of them can quite break. An addiction, he thinks, as he descends, passes another lone hiker who nods to him, says morning. And like any addiction, you have to learn to manage it. It's a moment of weakness, when he sees something and wants to share it with her, an urge that crops up out of nowhere, even though he is calm, and managing, and getting out every day, as if he can walk off the bad feelings, because Jen says it is good for him, that she notices a change in him if he does.

He does it to please Jen, more than anything. To stop her worrying. And because there are seconds—literal seconds—when he is walking, stopping to drink some water or watching figures atop the opposite ridge, when he does feel a change, and it is such a relief, so pure and real, that he knows feeling numb won't last, that things are going to be okay.

The urge to send Rosie photos comes, and goes, like this.

Out on the fells, he can make these kinds of choices. To see, and not send. To think, but not do. Back at home, in his flat with Jen, everything feels too bright, and hard. The sun, catching the edges of the TV screen. The unwashed bread knife on the chopping board. Fork tines. Nail clippers. The nick of Jen's dental floss, cutting at her teeth in the mirror.

After the night on the hill, he quit Mountain Rescue. He works and socializes and walks alone, like this, to make it through each day. Nobody presses him about anything, the way they did after that unspeakable time at school, and the year after Josh fell. His gran, his friends, his girlfriend—they all let him function as he needs to, without questions and without criticism. His depression—because that is what it is, he knows now, what has plagued him since his early teens, the need and the numbness and the chest pain—has finally got a reason for being.

The doctor put him on medication.

It hasn't changed a thing, but he's living, and he's cohabitating, and he's not one of the bodies on the mountain and that, he thinks—on his better days, when the lights are dimmed and the noise is level, and he finds small flickers in things like the smell of Jen's hair or the thick buttering of bread or the call of the larks in the pale morning—that is only a good thing.

He has a ring that he keeps in his sock drawer. Something his gran gave him that belonged to her late sister, or some other meaningful relative he'd never asked about. I'll trust that you'll give this to the right person, she'd said, handing it over when he'd last visited. I meant to give it to your mother, she'd said. But, you know. Someone else works, too.

He does think about proposing to Jen, sometimes. But they've been together for more than four years now, and she's often scoffed at the concept of weddings and marriage, all that tradition and paperwork. She wouldn't like the ring, anyway, he knows; too delicate, too fussy, with its interwoven strands and deep-set white stone. It doesn't look like her.

She takes him into the hills, most weekends. They walk and scramble and boulder, in the wind and rain and rare, pollen-heavy heat. She swims, too, in the cold, shallow tarns, often going in completely naked, calling back at him to join her, though he never does. He just watches from the shore, listens to the splash and dives and shrieks of her, as they carry across the water.

She is proactive and, it seems to him, always in motion, in a way that keeps Will moving, too, stops him from thinking too much.

In the evenings, they play cards together and watch box sets and he even stops running, to spend the mornings in bed with her. Hiking doesn't keep him in quite the same shape, though he finds he has no energy to care. Much of him wants to give up and get fat and start smoking again.

Don't you dare, Jen had said, when he'd shared this desire with her. My friends are jealous, and I like it that way.

As she'd said this, she'd moved her hands down toward his groin, slid them across his lower abs. They were still there, beneath a soft layer of skin he'd never had before. That's the meds, he'd said, his voice bitter. That's turning thirty, Jen had said, before she took him in her mouth.

He does not know how she knew this. He'd been with Jen for more than two years when she suddenly clocked that she did not know his birthday, and he'd told her that was because he didn't celebrate it. How woke, she'd said, and he'd said nothing, let her believe it was because he was too cool, or unsentimental. Anticonsumerist. Clinging on to a golden youth he would actually much rather forget.

*

Simon goes to the kitchen cupboard and takes down the first-aid kit while they argue, again, about nothing. Arguing with Simon is a quiet and stalled activity; to an observer, it would hardly look like they were fighting at all. To Rosie, it is exhausting, and endless.

He removes some ibuprofen from a pack while she badgers him, swallows two tablets before he pours himself a glass of water.

I just don't see what's wrong with it, he says to her, again. I thought you liked your parents.

I *do* like them, she says.

Then what's the problem?

The problem is I want to spend some alone time with my husband, Rosie says, and she cannot believe she is having to explain this to him, yet again. We need that, Si. Don't *you* need that?

I don't feel like I do, he says, and I suppose that's the issue, Rosie. I feel as in love with you as I always have.

That is not what I'm saying.

What, then? What's wrong with inviting them along?

When you said let's celebrate our anniversary, I thought you meant me, you, maybe some wine. Not a family gathering where I need to worry about how revealing my dress is, or whether I can order a cocktail.

Why couldn't you order a cocktail?

I could. But if I didn't, she'd think I was pregnant. And if I did, she'd raise her eyebrows, or mention the calories in the fruit juice.

I'm confused, Simon says, and he's rubbing his temples now, as if the pain has intensified. Does your mum want you to order a cocktail or not?

This is a hypothetical cocktail. We're not even at the restaurant yet.

I know, but hypothetically.

Simon, this doesn't matter!

You're the one that said—

I'm *saying*, she says, that I don't want to have an anniversary meal with my mum and dad, okay? I want to go with you. Alone.

Simon looks at her over his water glass.

But I've asked them now, he says.

Right. And we can't un-ask them.

Well, we can. I can say there was a misunderstanding.

No, you can't. It's done.

Sorry, Simon says, and he sounds so helpless, so dazed by one of his frequent headaches, that she decides to let it be.

To Simon, it seems, six years of marriage calls for an upmarket restaurant with too many forks; dauphinoise and jus and some sort of three-bird special, the greed of which turns her stomach. Rosie looks down at the menu and doesn't want any of it. She thinks about how she would rather be cooking a vat of spaghetti at home. Throwing it at the wall, to see if it would stick. Eating it with a spoon and a twirling fork and getting ragù down her chin. Someone kissing it off her. Garlic and heat, and unwashed pans in the sink.

That's what she thought sharing a life might look like.

Moments of need, and lust, for each other, and places, and books and food and music. But she and Simon do not even listen to the radio. And they have never really been anywhere; he is always too busy with work, too tired at the weekends. She is not sure he even knows that she was a musician, once. That she still writes songs when she can.

The waiter brings over a bottle of sparkling wine and they order their starters. Her mother lays her napkin in her lap and her father asks her husband about the hours he's working and Rosie slips her heels off under the table, because the straps are cutting into her toes.

How's Marley, her mother asks her. The light drops from the chandelier, glitters off their wineglasses.

Good, Rosie says. Struggling a little, in this heat.

They say your second is always bigger, her mother recalls, nodding. She'll be the size of a whale soon.

Don't write that in your New Baby card, Rosie says, and her mother laughs, a forced tinkle like a fork on china.

What about you, she asks her.

What about me?

How are you, Rosie. You don't really tell me anything these days.

Rosie reaches for her water. She lets the surface of the glass moisten her palm, which feels slick, and far too warm. She'd chosen to wear a high-necked dress, and regrets it.

There's not much to tell, she says.

You look good, her mother says, and this surprises Rosie so much that she glances up at her, to see if there's a catch, or a but.

You look good, her mother repeats. But you don't look as though you feel it.

Tired, Rosie says, shrugging. That's all.

Are you sleeping?

Depends.

Do we need to get you to a sleep specialist again?

No, Mum. It's fine.

I do worry about you, darling.

You don't need to. I'm fine. I'm . . .

She considers finishing her sentence truthfully. Perhaps it is the low light, the safety of her husband in deep conversation across the table;

perhaps it is the rare moment in which her mother has asked her a real question and seems to want a real answer.

But then the waiter arrives with their tiny wide-rimmed bowls, ceviche and gazpacho and tartare.

I used to play piano, Rosie says that night, to the bedroom ceiling.

Simon is in their bathroom, doing whatever it is he does before bed. She has already shut off the light, and the gold spills from their en suite across their new carpet, just touches the foot of their bed.

I know, he says, his voice measured around his razor. She hears the swill of it in the sink, before he raises it back to his skin.

Do you?

Sure. There's that photo, in your parents' hall.

She realizes he is right; a shot of her as a five-year-old sat on the piano stool, her feet not yet touching the floor.

Well, I miss it, she says.

Oh yeah?

She doesn't respond. Waits until he comes out of the bathroom, flicks off the light and eases himself into bed. He smells of shaving cream, their bergamot hand soap.

You should play, then, he says. I'd love to hear.

Would you?

Of course.

Why have you never asked, then?

Because you never mentioned it?

Rosie sighs, because she is angry, and she feels bad about it.

Happy anniversary, then, Simon says, and despite everything, he falls asleep within minutes. Light breathing, catch of air through his teeth.

She glares at the ceiling. She can't help it. So much about him annoys her these days. It annoys her that he gets so many headaches. That he weighs himself daily. That he brings her tulips, even though she doesn't particularly like tulips, the way they droop one by one, like they've given up, their necks broken over nothing.

There was a time when this was a good thing.

She remembers telling Marley, over a glass of wine, that this was one of the reasons she was marrying him. Because he got rid of the sad tulips, without her having to ask.

The sad tulips? Marley had asked.

Yeah. The ones that droop. He takes them away, leaves just the happy ones standing.

Oh *stop*, Marley had said. That's too adorable.

But now, this beautiful thing, this kind, understated gesture that they'd never even discussed, annoys the hell out of her. Like he's trying too hard. It bothers her that he is a better cook than she is, even though he never makes dinner, and that his breathing is nasal when they're watching television. His chest, once so wide and safe, seems to have shrunk, which makes her feel wrong, too big.

He sleeps well, and Rosie tries to.

She counts the light switches while she lies there.

Thinks about how he is still gentle and patient and loving, but he does not hold her hand, so much, anymore, when she taps and clicks and has to check they've locked the front door six times. Seven, maybe eight.

Everything's fine, Rosie, he tells her, with a strain in his voice.

Everything's fine.

*

The doctor is looking at him over his glasses.

Will looks back, because he's not sure he heard the question.

I asked if you'd consider counseling, the doctor says. I know we've discussed it before, but it's an avenue you're yet to explore. Worth a go, perhaps. I can get you twelve sessions on the NHS, in this same surgery.

Will nods, as if he's considering it.

Maybe, he says.

The doctor sits back; steeples his fingers.

How are you sleeping? Any nightmares?

Fine, and no, Will says.

Are you sleeping more than normal?

No.

Do you know what's normal, anymore, Will?

It seems a rude and accusatory question, so he doesn't answer. He lets out a puff of air, like he's offended, but not bothered.

Are we done? he asks. Look, Doc, I'm grand. I'm not wanting to overdose or hang myself off trees. Progress, right?

He is trying to keep his voice even. The doctor eyes him as he speaks.

Progress, he repeats, after a long, clock-filled silence. There is a metal ball apparatus on his desk, and Will has the desire to lean forward and get it started—to watch the steel knock on steel, make something move, fly through the air.

You appreciate, the doctor goes on, that we need to be mindful of a person with a history like yours. And if the medication isn't enough—

It's enough, Will says.

But if anything changes, the doctor says. If you begin to feel worse, or have any of those old urges. Any thoughts, even.

Like throwing myself off a cliff? Will asks.

Well, the doctor says. Or cracking your head against a mirror.

Will crosses his arms.

That was once, he says.

And still a concern, the doctor continues, looking back at his screen.

Using his index finger to scroll through all the godawful details, no doubt, the story that Will wants to delete, or forget, but which gets dredged up every damn time.

Yes, Will says. I attempted suicide in the school bathroom. I was young, and stupid, and I failed. So here I am. Taking my meds. Feeling fine.

You're feeling fine, the doctor repeats.

As ever, Will says. He reaches over, this time, lifts the silver ball and lets it fall. They both watch it start something; watch the other end raise and knock back, tiny noises, like nails on wood.

Glad to hear it, the doctor says. He types something on his keyboard.

Jen is waiting for him outside.

All good? she asks. She has shopping bags in both hands, is wearing sunglasses so he can't see her eyes. He's always hated that.

Yep, he says.

Any updates?

Nope.

Talk to me, she says, as they turn and head for home, past the grave-yard and the kebab shop, the traffic lights, the square. It is a quiet day in town. Retired folks ambling about; no bikers or hikers or tourists.

I am, Will says.

No, you're not. You used to. But now you're all . . . clammed up.

Well, I'm feeling clammy, he says.

He takes one of her shopping bags so he can link his hand through hers. It is not like him to do this, but he knows it'll get her off his back.

It works. She shakes her head and drops the subject. They walk in si-lence the rest of the way home, and in the flat, the sunshine is bright, bounces off their wooden floor.

It's like a greenhouse in here, Jen says, as she unloads the shopping, so

Will opens the windows and closes the blinds. He lies on the sofa and shuts his eyes and pretends he's fallen asleep while Jen witters on, and he thinks she finally buys it because, after a while, she goes quiet.

But then he feels her shadow. She sits on his chest, wraps her legs either side of him, and he gets an erection, in spite of himself.

Jen, he says. I'm knackered.

Too knackered for this? she says, and she takes off her top and her bra and amuses herself with his jeans for a while, and it is good, and distracting, and it is all over in fifteen minutes, quick and dirty and raw. Her heart flutters against his own as she lies on top of him afterward.

Now, she says. Talk.

Jen, he says, and he struggles up from beneath her, but she is strong, clamps her calves down around him.

What did the doctor say? she asks. If we're partners, Will, and not just roommates, then you tell me this stuff, okay? That's the rule.

I didn't know we had rules.

Well, we do. I'll just be your roomie, though, if that's what you want.

He doesn't answer. The sunlight stripes across the floor, through the gaps in the blinds, iridescent as it catches the brass wheels of the furniture.

Look at me, Jen says, so he does.

What did they say, she asks him, again.

They checked I was fine, he says. And when she keeps looking at him, like she knows there is more, something blows in him—another fuse, another implosion—and he goes there, decides to give it to her, if that's what she so desperately wants. See if she can handle it, the fear, the terror, the distaste of all that he has to say.

He has never told anyone. Not even Rosie. But Rosie did not need him to say it.

I tried to kill myself, Will says. When I was a kid.

Jen says nothing.

Not properly, he says, as the shame tightens in his chest. I tried to smash my head on the mirror in the school toilets, after taking a few too many painkillers.

She is still looking. Still straddled, across him.

It's why I was suspended. Except it wasn't really a suspension. It was time off, to recover, or whatever. Everyone at school thought I'd attacked someone and got in serious trouble, and I sort of preferred that story.

Sun, barred, on the floorboards.

The fridge heaves behind them in the kitchen.

So he was just checking, I guess, Will says. That this depression isn't going down that route.

And is it, she asks. Her voice is normal, somehow.

Nope, he says. It's why there was nothing to say.

She is still looking at him, but he won't meet her eyes; looks instead at her pierced ears, the mole at the base of her neck. There are parts of her he still doesn't know. As if he looks, without seeing. Struggles to remember the small, incredible details of a person who matters, but doesn't seem to know him, either.

And mostly, that's been a relief.

Jen swings herself off him, after a while, and sits beside him on the sofa.

For what it's worth, I'm not surprised, she says. I can tell the difference between sadness and real shit.

He shrugs.

But I hate that you've felt so much pain, she says.

It is an abnormally emotional thing for her to say; they are well matched, because they don't share their feelings, don't show affection unless they're having sex—sometimes, not even then—and it is jarring. Like accidentally biting down on a fork, the metal hard between his teeth.

It's not really pain, if that helps, Will says. More a sort of . . . nothing.

Even with the meds? she asks.

So far, he says.

Maybe you need a higher dose.

Jen, he says. Please leave it, all right? I'll figure it out if I need to.

But—

If you want to be *just roomies*, he says, then keep pushing.

It is cruel and unfair of him, but it has the desired effect. She gets up and leaves him to his fake nap on the sofa, his jeans still around his knees.

*

Rosie finds herself staring up at her mother's office block. She has not been here since she was a child, when she was too ill to go to school one day, and her mother brought her to work. Sat her on a chair, gave her a book, and told her to be good and quiet. She managed it, for an hour or so, and then vomited in the waste-paper basket.

She squints at the glass doors. Remembers the acid, the half-digested cereal. The chrome finish of the bin, so cool beneath her hands.

It is a tall building, with floors of lawyers and bankers and insurers. Important people with important jobs, and important leather furniture. Orchids in the lobby. Brass buttons on the lift. She presses floor 5 and waits, her heart thrumming like a sparrow's wings.

Her mother is where she expects her to be, in her glass-walled office sealed off from the rest of the floor. She moved in when she made partner; Rosie had helped her pick out her lamp and potted plants and rug, things to make it her own. It had been an exciting time. Her mother had seemed happy and fulfilled. She was kinder, for a while. Asked good questions.

Right now, she is on the phone, and Rosie waits for her to finish, watches as she turns to her computer and clacks on the keys with her long nails. A mousey girl in a crumpled suit rustles past with papers and wired, caffeinated eyes. A phone rings somewhere down the hall. Then she bumps her fist on the glass, watches the reaction as her mother looks up. Her face goes taut; she rises from her desk as Rosie pushes open the door and closes it, gently, behind her.

Rosie, she says. What's wrong?

Nothing, she says.

Your dad? Simon?

Everyone's fine, she says.

Are you pregnant?

God, Mum, Rosie says, and she lowers herself into the chair in front of the giant desk. The view out of the window is wide and lustrous. More glass buildings. More people at more screens. And farther out, a hazy fade of the city; the river somewhere, beyond the concrete.

I am not pregnant, Rosie says. That's sort of part of the problem.

You're infertile, her mother says.

Jesus, Mum.

Well, why else would you show up at my office unannounced?

Because, Rosie says, and she raises her voice, unintentionally. Because I wanted to ask you about divorce.

She does not look at her mother's face as she says it.

The city traffic roars beneath them.

For a friend? her mother asks.

Yes, Rosie says. Then, no. I don't know.

*Rose*mary. You can't be serious. Every couple has difficulties. That's what marriage is—it's compromise. It's living through the worst. It's binding.

Says the divorce lawyer, says Rosie.

It's a last resort, her mother snaps. And you don't exactly strike me as someone at the end of her tether, darling.

Rosie looks up at her, completely astonished. Her throat swells; that old pressure against her voice box.

What's going on? What's changed?

I don't know. That's just it.

Talk to him, then, her mother says.

I've tried.

Then try couples therapy. Have a baby, even. If you need IVF, your father and I—

That's your advice? Have a *baby*?

Lower your voice, Rosie. You're giving me a migraine. I just thought, if there was an underlying issue—

But babies are the issue, too, Rosie presses on. We should want one, by now, shouldn't we? And we don't ever discuss it. He doesn't even want to go on holiday, but he seems so stressed out, all the time. We're just on this hamster wheel, Mum.

What's the exact problem, Rosemary? You need to tell me that before you come here asking for a divorce.

I'm not *asking* for a divorce, Rosie says. I just wanted to talk about it. To find out our options. See how often it works out, maybe. In your experience.

Her mother sighs and raises her bony hands to her temples.

He's so miserable, Rosie goes on. He's always tired and bored and uninterested in me.

That's marriage, her mother says, and it takes Rosie a second to realize that she's not even joking.

It shouldn't be, Rosie says.

Well it is. It's managing.

I don't want to just manage, Rosie says.

Oh, Rosie, her mother says. You always were an idealist.

Just like Josh, they are both thinking, though neither of them says it; and he, her golden boy, was never criticized for it.

Her mother turns back to her screen and clicks her mouse. Rosie resists the urge to walk out, keeps her feet rooted to the floor.

Your father and I aren't happy, her mother says, eventually. Haven't been for years.

Rosie stares at her.

But nobody is, she says. The *successes* are the ones who choose to stick it out. And you're not a quitter, Rosie. You never have been.

You and Dad aren't happy?

We tolerate each other, her mother says. Which works, for us. He's a good man. He respects me. And I like him, most of the time. Wanting anything else is a fairy tale, Rosie; I've been in this business long enough to know that.

You're not happy with Dad, Rosie repeats. Something seems to crumble, every time she says it. She knew her parents weren't the best of friends. But she thought, after all this time, there must be something she didn't see. Hands touched, under the duvet, at night. Whispered stories about their days. Comfort, and grief, and unity.

Happy is what you make it, her mother says, and Rosie looks out of the window, at what little she can see of the sky.

Look, Rosie, her mother says, and she sounds impatient now. Why exactly did you come here? You didn't really come to ask about divorce papers, did you?

No, Rosie says. Still looking at the sky, the impenetrable cloud.

Well, then. Promise me you'll work on it.

More work. More effort. It looks as if it might rain, and she waits for it, just for a few more moments. When it doesn't fall, Rosie slides her bag back over her arm, stands up from the mesh chair; the one that she'd helped her mother choose, all those years ago.

———

Simon is in bed when she gets home. It is early afternoon, and he is hot, the duvet flung back.

Feeling rough? she asks him.

Yet again, he says.

Maybe it's stress. Can you take some time off work?

Work doesn't *feel* stressful, he says.

Then . . . is it us?

No, Rosie. Why would you ask that?

She feels terrible for suggesting it, then. For feeling the opposite.

Just thought I'd check, she says.

That's very polite, he says, and he rolls over to rest his head on her arm, his cheek stubbled and prickly. He has no idea, she thinks, and the guilt feels like a sword sheathing itself inside her; huge, and pointed; put away.

Maybe you should see a doctor, she suggests. Could be a thyroid thing.

He makes a noise of agreement, and they lie together in the low daylight. Their bedroom smells of their marriage; folded pajamas and hand cream, bed sheets she should wash more often.

Do you want dinner, she asks him, at some point, and he murmurs no.

Do you want *me*, she asks, and he snuffles, rather than laughs; doesn't answer. She waits awhile, lets the darkness encroach across the carpet.

I want things, she says, into his hair.

Like what? he asks her. He sounds as if he's near sleep.

I want to leave management consultancy, she says.

Okay, he says.

I want to play music again.

All right.

Piano. And guitar. I think I want to teach.

Then teach, he says.

It is as easy and as complex as that. No arguments. No questioning, or discussion, or conflict. She does not know what she wanted. Some kind of fervor, or fire, she thinks, beyond his body heat.

You should row, she says.

He snuffle-laughs, again, before his breathing changes, and then he sleeps on her arm, like a child. Pins and needles, tingling, in her palm.

*

Will is at work when he gets a call from his sister.

He is changing the oil on an old Triumph. The radio is on, and he will never again be able to listen to the surf guitar and close harmonies of the song that is playing. The potato salad of the music world.

Will, Amber says. It's Gran.

She okay?

She died.

Two words. Two words he'd expected, all those years ago, when the cancer got her, when she fought and her hair fell out and the light mostly faded from her eyes. Two words he does not expect now. Not while he stands here on the oil-marked concrete, with his coffee going cold on the workbench.

What, he says.

It was painless, Amber says. In her sleep. Old age.

But she wasn't old, he says.

Will.

Are you sure? Have you called an ambulance?

His sister ignores him, says, just get here, okay, and there is something in her voice that means he cannot argue; cannot check or confirm or deny. He turns off the radio. Says he's coming. But as he leaves the garage, he still does it, can't help himself; he dials his grandmother's number and listens as it rings and rings and rings.

The house is too quiet. There had always, irrefutably, been sound; the fire in the grate, the television on low, the ignition clicking or the wind clattering against the blinds. But the windows are shut. The oven, the TV, the fireplace, all dead.

Dead.

It is a word that does not feel like a word. Like when he reads something, over and over, and it just stops looking right.

He and Amber had parted ways at the hospital. She had a seminar the next day and needed clothes for the funeral, so she caught the train back to Warwick. I'll be back soon, she'd assured him, her eyes holding on to his. Like she was the older sibling. Like she would guide them through this.

He moves through the house, checking for clues to construct his grandmother's last hours, but there is nothing untoward. Her bed clean but unmade, where the paramedics had lifted her out. Her book on her bedside table. He picks it up, opens it to where her bookmark is wedged against the spine. It's a story about a girl and a long-lost love. Bad dialogue. An even worse cover. He touches the page where she would have done, before she turned out her light.

He has a missed call from Jen, checking on him, he's sure, on her lunch break. But he does not call back. He goes to the garden and pulls up weeds, trims back the little tree where Dave was buried, all those years ago. He remembers his gran calling him, so choked she could barely speak, as if Dave were a child, and not a dog. He snaps twigs, snags the skin of his hands on the bushes as he cuts them back, because it is what he would do, for her, whenever he came over.

It is so wet outside, he thinks, which is weird, when it hasn't been rain-ing. So wet and goddamn aggravating, getting in his eyes.

Amber is true to her word and catches a train back to Norfolk a few days later. The funeral is soon. Too soon, it seems to Will, mainly because they did not ask for a postmortem. It won't change anything, Ambs had said, and he guessed she was right. She was nearly eighty, and she died in her sleep. Nothing more to it than that.

They have to do all the things you do when someone dies. Go through her things. Her drawers, her paperwork, her stash of old records to select music for the service.

I've no idea, Will says, as he stares at the vinyl in his hands.

About what? Amber asks, not looking up from her screen. She is craft-ing an email to the funeral home, answering questions about flowers and coffins and things that don't matter, because she's dead, but for some reason they need to try to care about such details.

What songs to choose, he says. Do we want happy, or mournful? Her favorites? Or something bland and funeral appropriate?

Definitely not the latter, Amber says.

No, he says. No.

What about the song she danced to at her wedding?

How do you even know what that was?

I asked once, she says, with a shrug. Will nods, and swallows. He never asked her those sorts of things.

So I have a question, Amber says. She closes the laptop lid and looks at him.

Yeah, he says, expecting something about finger food, or poetry read-ings, or where to host the wake. Here, he thinks, so they don't have to pay for a badly lit hall with cheap carpets and smoke-stained ceilings.

Do we invite Mum, Amber asks.

A silence. A car heaves past the window. Diesel, instead of petrol; he knows by the sound of the engine.

Why would we, he says.

Because she's Gran's daughter, Amber says. She should know that she died, at least.

She didn't come to Grandpa's, Will says.

And she might not come to this one, either, Amber says, and she starts to plait her hair, splitting it into three before overlaying each strand. But it's not our choice, I don't think. It's hers.

Why even ask me, then, Will says, and his heart is kicking.

Because we don't *have* to invite her, she says. If you think it's a bad idea.

I think it's a nothing idea, Will says. I wouldn't even know how to get in touch with her, Ambs. So go ahead, if you think you can.

I have her email address, Amber says.

He looks up at her, at this. The records feel heavy in his hands. His sister looks right back at him, waiting.

How? is all he can manage, after a moment.

Gran, she says.

She was in touch with her?

No, Amber says, and she finishes plaiting her hair, starts to undo it right away. She just had the email, and said I could use it if I wanted.

When?

A few years back. She said it was my choice, at the time. And I think this is Mum's.

Big of you, Will says.

What is?

Giving her a choice. Like she deserves it.

Amber turns to the laptop again, opens the lid and tells him to think about it. He says he doesn't need to; that she should do what she wants.

The day before, he goes running, for the first time in months.

He runs through the forests and along the roads and across the wind-strewn cliffs. He sweats, and swears, and hates how hard it feels, and listens to his own breathing as it rips through his lungs and catches in his throat. He runs on the wet sand on the beach. Pauses at the lighthouse, which feels all wrong, and makes his heart thud faster as it looks at him with its glass eye and asks him things he doesn't have the answers for.

When he gets home, he lies in the bath until his fingertips turn soft, and he looks at his nakedness and he thinks of all the things he never asked her, the woman who actually raised him, scolded him, loved him in spite of all he did and didn't do. And he wonders what the hell he should do next, beyond this bath, and the funeral, and he dreads the life he's built and how little he cares about it, and he sickens himself with the contempt he held for his grandmother's own shoebox days, with her books and her casseroles and her accidental second family, but at least she had some-thing, he thinks, at least she had things she thought she wanted.

He pulls the plug when Amber asks him, through the door, what's wrong. Says that he's been in there a long time.

I can't believe she died, he says.

The suck of water, clouded with soap.

I know, Amber says.

They stay like that, on either side of the bathroom door, as they listen to each other and say nothing.

fourteen

◖

The day is overcast, at first. Bleak cloud, diluted sun.

Despite feeling like it, Will does not wear black. He has asked the guests not to, either. Instead, he buttons up a blue shirt, something his gran bought him one Christmas, and he combs his hair, like she would want him to.

He and Amber get a taxi to the crematorium because neither of them feels like driving, and both of them feel like drinking, later. His stand-alone beer awaits.

They get there first, as planned, and the guests arrive in pairs or alone, elderly friends from her book club or her old job, a few even from her school days. She never left Norfolk; she grew up, lived and died in this town. Raised children, twice. Made friends. Met her husband, and lost him. Kept going, because that's what you do.

Jen pulls into the car park, looking oddly out of place, to him, outside of Yorkshire. She has driven down this morning, taken time off work to be here. They embrace, and he smells the tea tree aroma of her hair, the vague, lemony scent of her car freshener.

You're okay, she says, a reassurance, perhaps, or a question he can't answer. She takes his arm like a girlfriend should and they walk in together, the two of them and his sister, and the room seems so small with its wooden benches and pinstriped carpet, and he wishes they could have the service outside. It is mild enough. Scudding clouds, sun breaking through before it withdraws again. Birds, and mown grass, and trees.

There are no windows in the crematorium.

Amber goes to talk to the celebrant while Will thinks about the name, and how inappropriate it is. Because this is not a celebration. He hates it, and he hates himself for agreeing to it, he needs air, and he tells Jen he's going to the bathroom and he breaks out of the windowless hall and he finds a bench, hidden from the car park and the entrance and all the faces he should know but does not.

He puts his head in his hands and decides to miss the service, to just have his own memorial right here, with the daisies speckled at his feet and the wood pigeons shuffling across the grass, no hymns, no sad, meaningless overview of her life measured in years and jobs and paragraphs, but Amber comes to get him, says it's time. He wants to ask her if their mother is here, but at the same time, he does not want to know.

He looks up at her as if to say, do I have to, and in the strangest moment, though perhaps not so strange for the occasion, his sister holds out her hand.

He takes it and stands.

Her palm is cool, like his own. Chewed fingernails, and split lifelines.

It is mostly a blur, until the end, when something happens. They have sung—mouthed, mostly, in Will's case—the final hymn, something about sunrise and shadow, and then her name is called.

Will is in the front row, beside Jen, who is beside Amber. A sad show of family, he thinks, as he tries not to look at the coffin.

And now one of Elsie's young friends, the celebrant says, is going to sing a little something for us. If Rosemary Winters would like to come on up?

A slow-down.

A shift on his own axis, while everyone sits and waits, looking down at the order of service, or else watches this woman tread down the aisle with her guitar, her wide, doe-like eyes beneath her fringe.

His heart halts.

It is like seeing a ghost, or a mirage, and he does not believe it right away.

He wants to say something, but the words are stuck, so he turns to his sister, who is looking straight ahead and holding herself oddly still.

She knew.

She knew, and he does not know what to feel.

Jen looks at him sideways, and he turns his face to the front. Roe is arranging herself on a chair, takes a moment to tune her guitar.

The room watches her take a breath. And then she begins to play.

Will has never seen her with her guitar, before. Her fingers flow over the frets, and he waits, unable to breathe, himself, until she starts to sing.

She looks different. Fuller, and softer, than he remembers, her hair chopped and shaped. But her voice—that voice—is the same. Still touches him in a way he didn't think possible, now, on medication that numbs the numb, leaves things muted and bearable and bland. But it lights something in him. That same old match, struck.

She is wearing a blue dress.

No earrings in her ears.

He does not recognize the song. She sings about early mornings and apples, something clear, hanging in a window. He suspects it is one she has written, especially for this moment, and it is beautiful, and haunting, and it comes to an end too soon.

Nobody applauds, because it is a funeral.

But the stillness does not break, even as she returns to her seat. No shuffling of papers or clearing of throats. No focus, anymore, on the celebrant's closing words. Everyone taken in, by this girl and her voice and the lingering quiet.

Will cannot believe her.

Cannot believe what's inside him, today, of all days.

The wake is at the community hall down the road; a shabby square of a building that smells of stale beer and snooker cues, the sweaty peel-back of cling film. It is a joyless, shadowy space, but many of her friends' wakes were there. Her husband's, too.

We won't want to host, Amber had told him, and he'd argued with her about it, but now, as the guests stand to leave, he is grateful. Bodies creak and shuffle. He can't imagine having them crammed in the house; touching her things, outstaying their welcome. Taking up all the air.

He stands, too, but tells Amber and Jen he'll meet them at the hall. That he just needs a minute. Jen protests, says she'll stay, but Amber takes her elbow and guides her out, still, he notes, not looking at him.

When the room has mostly emptied, Will sits back down and waits. Because she has waited, too. She has waited, and she comes down the aisle, settles herself on the row behind him. Breath of blue, like the sky they cannot see.

The coffin hasn't moved. They did not opt for that moment where the curtains close or the turntable spins, and there is a definitive end to the proceedings. Just leave it where it is, they'd said, and so it is still there on the table, with its polished wood caught in the room's flat light.

Who makes coffins, he asks, and Rosie shrugs. He sees it out of the corner of his eye.

A carpenter? she ventures.

You don't think there's a niche form of carpentry for it?

I guess there must be.

A coffin-maker, Will says, and Rosie says yeah, that maybe it's a nice job, really. Crafting something so personal, for a stranger.

She has chosen a chair one back and two down from his own. They both look at his gran's coffin and try to form words, until the celebrant says he's sorry, folks, that there's another service in ten, but to take all the time they need.

All ten minutes of it, you mean, Will says, and the celebrant looks confused but then laughs in apology, stammers in a way that Will is used to, when he does this; when he asserts himself, like that.

Let's, says Rosie, and she nods to the door.

A familiar, slight dip of her head.

It is spring, but still cold, like the season hasn't quite found itself. If seasons could have voices, Will muses, then April would be a whistle, light and noninvasive, like the tight-lipped buds on the trees.

Your song, he says, as they settle on his bench from before.

Yes, she says.

Did you write it for her?

She looks at him, as if surprised he's had to ask. Her pupils are so wide and black, he can see his own face reflected back at him.

Of course, she says.

He has to swallow, at this. Has to turn away.

I'm so sorry, Will, Rosie says, and she puts her hand on his own, after the shortest deliberation—he feels it hover and then lower, the warmth of her palm as it closes. Her hands are so delicate, still. Such thin, lovely fingers, and he never even thinks of words like lovely, and it embarrasses him, and he feels pathetic, and angry, all of a sudden.

I didn't know you were coming, he says, as he takes his hand away.

Rosie blinks.

Really?

Really.

Oh. Well, Amber invited me.

Did she ask you to sing?

Of course. I wouldn't have . . . presumed.

But you didn't think to tell me you'd be here?

I figured you knew I was on the invite list, Rosie says, and there is a heat to her voice, a disbelief at how accusatory he's being. I assumed you'd have other things to worry about, without me . . . messaging you hello.

Sparrows flit in the hedgerows. A mower, somewhere beyond the graves.

She died, Rosie, he says.

I know.

If any time called for a message, he says, it was then.

I'm sorry, she says again, and her voice is like breath, the wind in the elms. He does not want her to say sorry. He wants her to hold his hand again. He wants her to leave. He wants her so badly, he thinks his heart might give out.

Roe, he says, and he is not looking at her.

No yes, or murmur of assent. More breath; more wind. More of everything, when she is around; white sun, blinding his view.

I'm so fucking glad you're here, he says.

You are?

You're the only person I wanted to see. I actually thought that, this morning, when I woke up and realized what day it was. And now you're here.

She is quiet for the longest time. The mower stops, then starts again. The sparrows have gone, and he wonders if she will get up and leave, too.

Let her, he thinks. Let her go.

Why is it so hard, to let her go.

You said you didn't want me in your life, she says to him, eventually.

I never said that.

You did.

Think back, Roe. I did not say that.

You didn't *not* say that, she says.

Stop avoiding what I've said.

What, that you're fucking glad I'm here? God, Will.

What?

Even when you're saying nice things, I feel like you're angry, she says.
I never know what you want from me. Just like when we were seventeen.

Are you kidding me?

What?

You're the one who didn't want *me*, he says. Remember?

I've never not wanted you, Rosie says, and she seems to say it without
thinking, not intending to put it out there, so raw, in the clear April air.
The words hang between them, like forbidden fruit. Bruised, but unripe.

I don't get you, Will tells her.

And I don't get you, Will, she says, and her voice is trembling. Aren't
you with Jen?

And aren't you with Simon?

No, she says, and that single word is strong, and fierce.

Come off it.

I'm not, Will.

Since when?

Since recently.

But you married the guy.

Yeah. We're still married.

So you *are* with him.

What are we even doing, she says, and she stands up now, in a gust of dress and long coat. You're with Jen. We're adults. We haven't spoken in forever.

Twenty-nine months, Will says.

What?

We haven't spoken in twenty-nine months.

She stares at him like he's sworn at her again, called her something inexcusable. His sudden anger has soared into something else. He cannot explain it. He is at his grandmother's funeral. His girlfriend is half a mile down the road, eating crudités and making small talk with cousins he's never met, for him, and only him.

We can't, Rosie says, and her voice is strained, like water being wrung from a cloth. He lets it fall, all that she does not say splashing at their feet.

I didn't say we should, he says, and he looks around, at the grass, at the headstones set deep in the earth. Something ruptures. He wants his gran. Wants to talk to her about this, or have her talk some sense into them both.

I just wanted to tell you, he says. Just once.

And still, he does not tell her, but it seems she does not need him to.

I should have told you every day since I knew it, he says. But I was young and stupid and scared and I'm still a lot of those things, Roe.

She is quiet again.

Roe?

I don't know why you're yelling, she says.

I'm not.

You are. It sounds like you're furious with me.

He looks at what he can see of her face, her hair grazing her cheekbones. He wants to tell her that love and fury so often feel the same, to him. That his skin burns for her. His blood crawls, and that doesn't feel safe or nice or quiet; it feels like rage.

I'm not yelling, he says.

Not anymore, you're not.

This wasn't the way this was meant to go, he says.

What, today? The funeral? Or us?

All of the above, he says, and something thaws between them, then. Birds, singing. Shift of sun through the cedar trees.

Will, Rosie says.

Yeah?

I . . . I think we should talk about this. But not now. Not here. It's Elsie's day, you know. Let's just go and remember her.

He feels so much toward her, then, that he nearly spills over. He draws his hand around his face, says the wake isn't far from here, and Rosie nods. They rise from the bench and begin walking in silence toward the car park, but then there is a noise, like footfall, which makes Will turn back toward the bench.

Someone, approaching.

A woman, of the right age. With the right face.

*

Rosie takes sandwiches and cocktail sausages and stands in the corner and picks at her plate. She has felt herself soften, these past few weeks, as she takes in bread and pastry and puts sugar in her tea. So many years of nuts and proteins and low-fat alternatives, but now she feels the closest to nourished that she can remember. She is not thinking about calories, or hardening, or lessening, or holding on for five seconds more. She is thinking about how she is teaching, now; her students, and her songs. How she's writing on paper again.

She recognizes faces at Elsie's funeral. People from her hometown, the library, the bakery. But she doesn't truly know anyone except Amber, who seems intent on speaking to everyone but her. She doesn't mind. She works her way around her plate, waiting, because she left Will in the car park with his mother.

Her gut feels knotted. She keeps watching the door, hoping that he will walk through it and be all right, or at least something close to that.

Three miniature sandwiches down, and still, he has not shown, and that is when Jen comes over and says hi.

Hello, Rosie says back.

Her blood simmers in her veins. She feels guilt, and dislike, and shame for both.

Your song was decent, Jen says, and Rosie hears Will's inflection in her voice, the way you mirror the words of someone you live with, without meaning to.

Thank you, she says.

So nice to have proper music, and not just hymns.

I'm glad, Rosie says. She lifts a sandwich off her plate, then puts it down again.

You're Rosie, right?

Yes.

Will's best friend?

Not sure he'd say best, she says. But we were friends. A long time ago.

Jen watches her, and Rosie is about to comment on the weather or ask about the breadsticks when Jen cuts to it, and Rosie sees the kind of woman she is.

He talks about you, you know, she says.

Rosie raises her eyes to Jen's; this woman he shares his life with. Solid black hair and narrow features, a twirl of jade at her throat.

Does he, she asks.

Not a lot, Jen says. But enough.

There is a ripple of laughter from near the bar, too loud for the occasion, and both women look over to see two men clapping each other on the back. They keep watching the strangers, and Jen keeps talking, her voice level.

I know he had a thing for you, she says.

Rosie burns red; takes her focus away from the bar and drops her eyes to her plate.

I just don't know if he still does, Jen says.

And Rosie's throat closes in on itself, like it does when she has no idea what to say, when there is no right or wrong, and no room to be either. She tries to swallow; reaches for her water glass on the side, when there is a shunt of color and noise and they see Will storm into the hall, heading toward Amber. Oh shit, says Jen, as Rosie thinks the same, and then his girlfriend is gone from her side.

Rosie puts her plate down. A few people are looking, because the commotion is tangible, even without any shouting; Will is angry, and he is saying things in a low, rough voice, and Amber is holding her chin high, as though she'd been braced for a fallout.

Rosie makes a choice and heads for the exit. She strides past Will and his sister and the funeral guests, wide-eyed and watching, and then she's out of the hall and in the car park, and the air is colder than before. It smells of frost and wet tarmac. Ashen sky, in puddles on the ground.

And as she walks toward her own car, she sees what—or whom—she had hoped to see. The woman who abandoned her son, because life was too much. Bailed, because it was easier, because it was wild and freeing and the opposite of how Rosie has learned to be. She watches as this wild, absent woman with her long copper hair turns the keys in her car, so that the engine growls alive. She watches as she keeps both hands on the steering wheel and places her forehead, oh so briefly, between them. She watches as she cries, for a while.

*

Jen takes him to a bar. She gives Amber the keys to her car to drive home, and the two of them get a taxi to a country pub in the middle of near-nowhere, on a road out of Norfolk, with brick walls and local draft ale and low, twilight-style lighting. So dark, it's near impossible to read the menus.

But Will does not want to eat.

Double vodka, he says to Jen, and she says no, he can have one beer, or a soda and lime, and he wants to smash his fist into the small wooden table they're seated at, but instead he stares at his hands.

So much, for one day.

She comes back with his soda, her own glass of wine like a fishbowl in her hand, and they sit and drink, the murmur of the pub washing over them. Not being numb, for once, is unsettling for Will. Things poke at him like needles, and he's trying to figure out what hurts the most when Jen speaks.

I met Rosie Winters, she says.

I met my mother, he says back.

She lowers her eyes at this, and he's jabbed with another needle, violent satisfaction, he thinks, then a stab of guilt, because he told Roe some things he did not intend to, today. Implied, maybe. He does not know what he was doing on that bench, nor does he know what he's doing here with Jen.

D'you want to talk about it, Jen asks. She is swirling her wine the way she did on the night he first met her.

There's nothing to say, he says. She came. We talked. I told her to go.

Laughter, and voices. The shove of the pub door.

Was it . . . awful? Jen asks.

It was what I'd always expected, he says. She wanted to hug me, at first, then she got defensive and tearful, like I owed her something, like I was an arsehole for not collapsing into her open arms.

That's shit, Jen says. That's really shit.

She said she thinks about me, Jen, he says, and some spittle flies from his mouth, like an old man, and he doesn't care. She *thinks* about me. As though that excuses every fucking thing.

It doesn't, she says.

I'm not even talking about missed birthdays or Christmases, he plows on. I'm talking about *years*. Holes, in my life, where I didn't have a mother. And what that felt like, after my dad had already left. Jesus *Christ*.

He slams his fist on the table, and some men at the bar look over, and he wishes they'd start on him, wishes he'd have a reason to break something, a glass or a bone or a nose.

Amber knew, he says, his voice snapping, like a guitar string. She knew she was coming. My mum replied in advance, for the first time in her bloody life, probably, and Amber could have prepared me—she *should* have prepared me—but she thought it was *better not to tell me*.

If she had told you, Jen says mildly, would things have gone any different?

Don't take her fucking side.

I'm not. If there is a side to take, Will, I am on yours. Every time.

She is calm, and he feels his insides simmer, at that.

I fucking hate her, he says.

So you should.

I hate her, he says again, and he is being a child, he knows, but Jen nods.

They drink some more. Will downs his soda and feels that chasm open in his gut, an endless, unfilled well.

One vodka, he says.

Not a chance, Jen says.

More murmuring; more burning; pins in his hands and feet and eyes.

Can we talk about Rosie now, Jen asks.

Will takes his empty soda glass and rolls it around on its base. It leaves a ring of water on the table, and he keeps rolling, drawing a wet arc onto the wood.

If you want, he says.

I'm just going to say it, she says.

Okay.

I saw the way you looked at her, she says. While she sang.

Okay, he says again.

And I don't think I can go on hoping that you're over her, she says.

He keeps rolling his glass. Look at her, he urges himself, but he can't. His rage settles. They have changed gears, now. Upped their speed; a new focus required. He lifts his eyes to her face.

She is trying not to look at him, either. He has so rarely seen her cry, and he realizes he has always liked this about her; appreciated her stoutness, her unsentimental way of moving through the world. It's pacifying, and uncomplicated. He likes her skin, too, its near-translucence. He often wondered, when the morning bled through their window, how a woman could be so pale, so paper thin.

Strong, somehow, but transparent.

I don't need to know any details, Jen says. But I can see it in your face, Will. And at the risk of sounding like a goddamn diva, she says, her eyes flaring, I just, you know. I want someone to look at me like that.

Will stops rolling his glass.

And I'm not coming between that, either, she says. She deserves to know how you feel, still. After all this time.

He cannot believe it is unfolding like this. He was prepared for anger and accusations, an argument that saw her storming into the car park so that he had to follow, or order a drink at the bar. But this: this steals the breath out of him.

I'm so sorry, he says, because that is all there is to say. They sit together with their empty glasses and the low-lit bulbs in their domes, the mirth and hubbub of other lives happening all around them.

At least we never got married, Jen jokes, raising her glass to him.

She did, though, he says.

And while she doesn't answer him, he sees the hurt in her face. That even now, as they're ending, he doesn't have anything to say that isn't about Rosie. He feels a sudden, wrenching sadness. Wants to reach out and touch her, apologize, change the things he cannot change.

I had a ring, you know, he says, after a while.

I know, she says. I found it in your sock drawer.

And you never wondered why I hadn't asked you?

Not really, she says, cupping her glass with both hands. I knew your heart wasn't in it. I knew, when we started all this, that you were in love with someone else.

Somebody laughs, elsewhere. Doors swinging, waft of hot chips.

Bit of a red flag, I suppose, Will says.

Yeah. I think I liked the challenge, Jen says. Thought I could change your mind. Which was arrogant of me, I guess. But it would've been *so* sexy, if I'd managed it.

To undo my undying love for someone else?

Yeah, that, she says, and he's relieved to see that she is no longer near tears. But also, to just . . . set you free from it all.

He has no words, for this. He knows he should buy them more drinks, but he also doesn't want to stand and break this thing they're cradling; this fragile, near dying thing they've passed between them for five whole years.

Would've been fucking hot, he agrees. She gives a wild laugh, but it sounds like something else, a cough, or a sob, maybe, and she puts her wineglass down and stands up and leaves, all too fast, all coat and boots and noise.

And that's it.

That's it.

*

It is disquieting, to Rosie, being in her childhood bed. It feels too narrow and she cannot sleep without the mass of Simon beside her, the familiar, habitual weight of him. They have not spoken, as they'd agreed. She packed a holdall and came to her parents' house, in some stupid, broken outreach of yearning that only made her feel worse.

You disappoint me, Rosie, her mother had said, when Rosie had told her why she was there.

A voltage of pain, and something harder, like a nail, passing through her.

Upstairs in her room, she did not unpack. It felt easier and less permanent not to. She will get her own place soon, and decorate it in her favorite colors; have a musical instrument in every room, and books, lots of books.

She sinks toward sleep with these pinboard plans, and then she jolts awake, like she's forgotten something.

She gets up, checks that she has her purse, her passport, her keys, then she gets back into bed. Watches as the night lightens to dawn, the shapes changing from deep mauve to the fairest cloud-like blue. And just as she's drifting off, she jolts again, and this time it leaves her burning, like someone has tipped molten wax on her skin.

It is then that she reaches for her phone.

You said I never wanted you, she says, when he answers. And I was a stupid, scared teenager, too, Will, for reasons that don't even make sense

to me now. I know it doesn't change anything, but I just—I needed you
to *think* I didn't want you back. That's why I said no, that time, in the
forest.

There is background noise; some sort of muffled wind, as if he is
outside.

I shouldn't have said what I said, she says. I didn't think it would
have such a lasting impression on you. It was just easy, to play the good
girl card.

What are you saying, Rosie, he asks her. It still sounds as if he is in the
thick of a crowd; on a high street, or at a port, somewhere bustling despite the early hour.

Rosie takes a breath, looking at the teenage posters on her wall; three
faces who sang about colliding and still believing.

I'm saying it was a lie, she says. And I just wonder how things would
have gone, sometimes. If I hadn't said it.

There is a short silence. She hears a shuffle, as if Will is moving the
phone from one ear to another, or finding a more sheltered place to
speak.

You're talking about that time you told me I was the wrong kind of
person for you?

Yes, she says, and she feels her chest clag with the cruelty of it, even
though she remembers her reasons. Josh, crying, in her arms. And something else, something sterner; a hook, in her heart, that holds her back.

More noise. A squeak, like shoes on a hard floor.

That was a lie, he repeats, as if he's checking what she's said.

Yes, she says.

But your brother dying was not, Will says.

I know, she says. But—

You couldn't even look at me afterward, he says. I know why, Roe. I
get it. And we can try this thing, we can pretend it's okay and that you

don't see him when you look at me or that you want to be over it, we can *try*, but I swear to God, Rosie, it won't work. He died, and it was because of me, my invite, my birthday, no matter how you try to spin it, and that's why we dance around this thing, that's why I never chased you and why you never wanted me to and why you're still not sure, even now, that this is what you want.

Rosie breathes into the receiver. His voice is tightly wound, about to break. So brittle, after holding back, for so long.

That's what you think, she says. But—

No, he cuts in, again, and she hears the chiming over a loudspeaker and realizes he's at an airport. No, Roe. I ended things with Jen, last night. I fucking ended things with the woman who's stuck with me through depression and my gran dying, and for what? Because she knows I'm not over someone who doesn't even want to *be* with me?

She tries to cut in, too, but he keeps going.

I will never, ever be okay with Josh dying like that, Rosie, he says. And you won't, either. So let's just stop whatever this is, between us.

I do see him, when I look at you, Rosie breaks in. She is breathless with adrenaline, with the need to finally say it.

Right, he says.

No, she says, and she shakes her head, violently, forgetting that he can't see her. I see him when I look at you, okay, but not for the reasons you think.

He finally, mercifully, does not respond.

He was gay, she says, and it is some sort of joyful, heartfelt firework of truth that she sets off down the phone.

What?

Gay, she says again. He'd only just told me. And he—uh—he'd fallen for, well—you. Obviously.

She is sitting on her bed, her bare feet beneath her. She feels cold, but she cannot move; holds herself still, in the moment that's unfolding.

And I just wanted him to be okay, she says. I wanted him to figure that stuff out, first. Before we broke his heart, you know? And then he died.

She says it, just like that; as hard and clear as the fact of it.

He died, she says again, and I . . . I didn't know how . . .

He was gay, Will repeats.

Yes.

More silence. More white noise from the airport. She wants to ask him where he's going; wonders how long he's going for.

You were protecting him, Will says, after a while.

I should have told you sooner, Rosie says.

Yeah, Roe. You should have.

Would that have changed things, she asks.

What things?

A question for a question, she says, and he says don't joke, Rosie, not now, and he sounds distant, is still processing, she thinks, on the other end of the phone.

I'm so sorry, she says. For not telling you. It just . . . didn't feel like my secret to tell. You know?

Will does not respond to this, and Rosie waits, too long. Another fluid, female voice sounds over the loudspeaker at the airport, announcing something she can't quite make out.

Roe, Will says, and she says yes.

Thanks, he says. But I have to go, now.

And he hangs up.

fifteen

☾

The doorbell rings.

She is alone, the duvet tucked beneath her arms as she stares at the ceiling and thinks. Her parents left for work hours ago, and still, she has not got out of bed.

It rings again and she curses the postman and his packages and his insistent, infuriating desire to do his job.

Leave it on the damn step, she says, aloud, and immediately feels rude and embarrassed, even though nobody can hear her, as she pads down the stairs to the door. She turns down the handle and swings it open and goes to say thank you to the uniformed man with the outstretched parcel.

But it is not the postman.

He is standing there, in his leather jacket, with his harsh cheekbones and his bronze hair and his burning, endless eyes.

They share a single heartbeat and then he says he'll never travel the world at this rate, and he steps forward and takes her face in his hands, those rough, mechanic's hands, and he keeps looking at her like that until she pulls him into her, with her mouth on his, and he tastes, to her, the way he did before.

*

They end up on her parents' staircase. The carpet burns their backs and there are teeth and sighs and nails, but a softness, too, a melting.

The colors of them, beneath their clothes. Skin that nobody else gets to see, and wanting the other person to touch it, so badly, to have it as their own, and it is teenage years and lucid dreams and desire that feels so raw and real that it cannot be allowed, surely, it can't. They say each other's names, just once, and then again, and they both half laugh without sound, as if they'll scare it away if they are anything less than silent, but they can hear each other, still, and that's all they want, all they have ever wanted, if they are honest, if they cut through the noise that came before this, all of this. Her hair, like willow, falling between them. Strong arms, and bent, soft, downy legs, unshaven and uncaring.

She presses her mouth to his collarbone and he groans, softly.

Shadows, from the trees, on the wall.

They cradle each other, and between their rushing blood and their thrumming hearts there is something neither of them has known before. That unreachable, implausible place. Bonfires, crackling. Imploding. The sun rising, permanent, and blinding, if you look straight at it, if you're so bold, so wanting, so goddamn, unbelievably lucky.

And then quiet.

Perfect quiet.

We can't stay here, Rosie whispers, afterward.

She is wrapped around him, the midmorning light grazing their foreheads, catching the copper-gold of his hair.

No, he says. He kisses her again, so long and drawn-out that she thinks she might come, right there, but then he draws back, says he knows a place they can go.

＊

Will stirs, for the next few days, as if in a dream he does not want to wake from.

He lies still and tries to hold on to it, but then he hears Rosie breathing and his heart launches upward, like a whale out of water, sudden and graceful and huge.

They are sleeping in his old single bed. Neither of them felt right moving into his grandma's room; not until they can change a few things. Rosie insisted they buy new bedding, at least, and he agreed, though they have not yet left the house.

It has been days of drifting, and discovering. Making coffee but drinking only half of it. Mapping each other's skin, the soft, hidden parts of it, and tangling their limbs and hands and hair in bed, in the shower, and once, on the kitchen table.

This is, Rosie says one time, breathless in his ear.

Happening, he says, and she shudders into him, and he thinks he might die with the pleasure of it, and he dares not think beyond the next touch of her, the next note from the birds outside; the crests and the sparrows and the geese they can hear, sometimes, in the slipstreams over the house.

＊

He was gay, he says, one night, as they're facing each other in bed. Imprints of her, all over him. Her eyes look like orbiting moons; pulled into his, wide and white and unearthly.

Yes, she says.

I had no idea, he says. But now you've said it, I can sort of believe it. You know?

Maybe, she says, her favorite word, and it is like she has retreated from him. No real movement or pulling back, just something less than before; she seems reticent, and he curses himself, inwardly, for raising it.

Did you know? he asks. Before he told you?

I'd wondered, she says.

He nods. Watches her face fall, as if remembering things he was not a part of.

I don't think he'd mind, he tells her.

Mind what, she says.

This, he says. Us. If that's what you're worrying about.

What made you think I'm worrying about it?

Because of what you said, he says, and he props himself on his elbow as she rolls away from him, tucks her long, dark hair behind her ear. About not wanting to break his heart.

I'm not worried about that now, am I, she says. He died.

He looks at her looking away. Moonlight falls through the still-open curtains, the room shifting between silver and shadow.

Aren't you, he says.

He doesn't say, I know you. And I know this thing you've carried for years does not suddenly lift, in spite of everything. In spite of getting all you knew you'd wanted, but thought you could not have.

Maybe a bit, she says, and her voice is hoarse with the strain of not crying. He gathers her hair, laces it over her shoulder. Leans in to kiss her collarbone, the shallow, pooling dip of it.

She is more rigid than he has ever known her to be.

I don't think he'd mind, he says to her, again. But I still feel sort of weird about it.

She nods, and sinks back down again, the pillows creasing beneath her. She smells of soap and duvets and breakfast tea.

I guess I feel bad, he says.

I do, too, she says.

Both of them thinking, all of the time, and folding in on each other.

*

After four or five days, Rosie makes them leave the house.

We need air, she says. Supplies.

So they walk into town for milk and eggs and other basic things, though they crave nothing but each other, and she feels giddy, like the seventeen-year-old that first fell for him, and it is stupid and embarrassing and so all-consuming that she doesn't even care.

They talk about school, and dinner, and terrible television. The sun pours over the pavements, creamy yellow, like buttermilk. So warm, for late spring.

It is in the supermarket queue, as Rosie unloads the groceries onto the conveyer belt, that she realizes she is still wearing her wedding ring. There is a shift in the speed of things, for just a moment; as if someone is taking something from her, and she has to try and hold on to it.

She packs it all into her tote bag, pays, takes her receipt. She walks down the exit aisle, thinking she should process the divorce, soon; they'd both left the paperwork, because there was no rush, and it was exhausting, to separate, to even make that choice. I'll be in touch, she'd said, and Simon had said yes, he would, too.

Outside, she asks Will to get some bread from the bakery and while he's in there, she twists the band off her finger, zips it into the coin pocket of her purse.

The sky is a graze of gray.

Her reflection, in the glass.

She waits to feel shame or regret but there is nothing, nothing she confronts beyond the golden-haired, wolf-toothed guy who comes out of the dinging door with a loaf in his hands and says ready? and she says yes, yes I am.

Tell me something, she says that night.

About what?

Anything. Something that happened while we weren't in touch.

That's a lot of things, he says, and he closes the cookbook he'd been reading, slots his bookmark in place.

It should be easy, then, right?

Okay, he says, and he puts down his book, raises his hands behind his head while he thinks. She wonders how he is even more attractive than when he was eighteen. Tucks her arms across herself, and watches him. He has not shaved in several days. There is honey-blond dandelion down, all along his jaw.

Well, he says. I was chased by a badger, one time.

A badger, she echoes.

An angry badger, he says, and she laughs, a tremor of disbelief and alarm.

You were not.

I was. On a Mountain Rescue call.

Rosie laughs properly, now, and it makes him laugh, too, and they stay horizontal on the sofa, tickled by the story or each other. When they settle, she asks him why it was angry.

Aren't badgers always angry?

I don't know. I've never met one, she reasons, which sets her off again. Her ribs ache. She feels bruised, out of practice, and so relieved. His calves, pressed against hers.

Your turn, he says. You tell me something.

I wasn't chased by any woodland creatures, she says.

Disappointing, he says. But not essential.

All right, she says, and she's still smiling, doesn't think much about it when she says, um, I lost my appetite, at one point. I don't know why. And I did some therapy. It was sort of helpful, and sort of awful.

Will holds her with his eyes.

In what way?

Lots of ways, she says. I went because of Josh, obviously. But we barely spoke about him, really. It was mainly about goals and my mother and what I did and didn't eat, and my OCD, and everything. Which I suppose was important.

Will is not touching her, apart from his legs leaning on hers. His hands are still behind his head, elbows out, as if he's sunbathing in the lamplight.

I think we were meant to be unpeeling things, she says. Layers, you know. But I was too impatient. I wanted to jump straight to Josh, and be fixed, and get out to my spin class.

Spin class?

Another thing I did, for a while. Which was also kind of awful. I remember one time, the instructor was yelling at me to pedal harder, and the lights were flashing, and I thought, wow, I really hate this. I stopped going, after that.

Thank God, he says, and she says yeah, and they are momentarily quiet.

He is still looking at her, with his hands behind his head.

Did you do anything that wasn't awful, he asks her. In all that time?

She half smiles, at this, though she doesn't think he was joking.

The wind roars, outside, like the sea. It is due to storm around midnight. She has been looking forward to it; the noise of it on the windowpanes, later, when they go up to bed.

Sad, I know, she says, after she has no answer for him, and he touches
her properly, then; leans forward, takes both of her wrists in his hands.

You're a lot of things, Roe, he says. But sad? No. No way. Even after
everything, you're a light, Roe. A goddamn beam of light.

She feels embarrassed under the intensity of his eyes and his words.
She burns, all over. Her face, and neck; between her legs.

Who even talks like that, she says, her voice like breath against his.

Laughter, again, between them. Softer than rain, the cloth of their
bookmarks.

*

He does not wear pajamas to bed. Just boxers. She starts to wear his
clothes without asking, takes a T-shirt from his drawer, pulls bed socks
up to her shins.

He asks her how she can sleep with socks on.

She asks him how he can't.

It is like being at school again, the pull and the fizz and the heat of it
all, when it is just them, in a different decade, the way they always were.

*

Summer brings the tourists. The coast is littered with families and fish-
ermen, and still, after two months of being together, they go to the lighthouse, most days.

I'm singing again, she tells him, as they walk along the seafront
toward it. Driftwood lies like bleached bone on the shore. The air smells
both fresh and rotten, all foam and washed-up weeds.

So I've heard, he says.

Not just in the shower, she says, and she laughs, and it is so easy and she thinks of how different she feels, right now—not weighted down or boxed in, but torn open.

And not just at funerals, she says. But at work. They've asked me to take on the choir.

She left her consultancy job just before she and Simon parted, began working as a music teacher at a Norfolk girls' school. She teaches piano and guitar, helps with the admin of school concerts. It is not world-changing work, she realizes, but it feels life-changing. For her.

When she told Will she was playing again, and getting paid for it—albeit badly—he looked at her like he wanted to swallow her whole.

That's so great, he says now, as they pick their way across the sand.

It is, she says. It feels kind of right, you know? It was my choice to quit music, obviously. Even though it didn't feel like a choice. It was like I had to learn to breathe differently, if that doesn't sound too weird.

It doesn't, Will says.

But now, it just feels like . . . how has this not been my life the entire time?

The sand crunches beneath their shoes. Grains, pushed sideways, leaving their footprints behind them.

He says he knows, and she is embarrassed suddenly, because she real-izes what he means. Her cheeks redden and she stoops down to pick up a shell so that he doesn't see her blushing.

She watches him as he walks on, turns, waits for her. He is so tall, so strong and weathered. William White, on his medication, with his hurt-ing heart and deep, sad eyes. Hers. Every splintered, scar-healed part of him.

She keeps the shell. Puts it on their bathroom shelf.

When they get home, windswept and with cold hands, Will boils the kettle for tea, and then he leaves her, to go and trim the garden hedges.

I didn't have you down as the hedge-trimming type, she says to him, and he shrugs, says it's for his gran, and she nods.

She still does senseless things for her twin. Or with him in mind, at least. Too many things. She still buys his favorite cereal, and goes to see films he'd like, ones she couldn't care less about. Sometimes it's hard to untangle where Josh ends and she herself begins, what she really thinks and feels about something, whether she is trying to honor him instead of herself. It was like this when he was alive, and has become blurrier since he died.

Just little things.

But it's those things that make up a life. That make up a person.

She hears the back door shut, out in the kitchen. It is strange, being alone in the house without Will, and without his gran or his sister knocking around upstairs, like the summer that she stayed here. She listens. Settles in the armchair by the window and does nothing except look through the open curtains. Absorbing the quiet, like a warmth, on her skin. A mother walks by with a pram. A man, with a whiskered dog in a coat. It is a clear bright day that matches her heart, as if everything inside her is lifted.

So she takes a pen and begins to write.

It is so rare that her songs come so easily, and she feels young again, a person with no mistakes or tragedy in her life. Something flowing through her, from some other place. It is like floating in water, or standing in the sunlight or the snow.

The snow.

There's Josh, again, and she wonders where exactly he comes from when he's attached to these strands, thinks there must be something separate to the mind, the heart, the gut. And is it memory, or is it the soul, and what might a soul look like, if you could touch it, if you could dance with the light and the dark of it.

She keeps writing, as the hours fall. When Will comes in from outdoors and begins to cook dinner, the oil shimmering and spitting in the saucepan, drawers rolling open and closed, water running, knife on wood as he chops.

You like spinach, right, he calls to her. She says yes, without really registering what he's asked, because she is elsewhere, even as she's in the armchair, in this house that saved her all those years ago, and is saving her again.

She finishes it, before they eat.

Wishes she could play it for Will, or for Josh, maybe, if she really believes he is watching, somehow, up and away or between worlds, because he loved physics, after all, and he knew there was more than just life and death, didn't just ponder, but knew. Yes, she'll play it for him, or that part of him that is her, so maybe, just maybe, she'll end up playing it for herself, after all.

*

Something has changed, or begun, or simply begun again. Every moment that Rosie is not at work, or sleeping—or not sleeping, with him—she is writing.

Will watches her without comment, with her sheet music and her fountain pens, the cheap notebooks filled with graph paper so she can draw out her own staves. It feels as though he's been given a window into something private, and he knows if he questions it, even with well-intentioned interest, that nothing good will come of it. He is happy to exist around her, when she is writing. He cooks and cleans and takes himself off for hours at a time to tinker in his garage. That is his own personal art, in a sense, though it does not remove him from the world in the way it seems to with Rosie. Mechanics root him in the here and now. But with Rosie and her songs, he sees a transcendence. A change.

She has always been an attentive person.

It's what caught him at the bonfire. The way she looked deep into him and listened, even though she did not know him then. And that attention has never wavered, until now. Because when she is writing, all of it falls away. The focus she reserves for everything and everyone else just disappears, and he thinks that, actually, this is a side to her he has not yet seen. All that energy going where it's supposed to.

She hums, sometimes, or moves her lips.

Hair tied back from her face, legs tucked sideways as her fingers tap, or count.

She goes somewhere he is not able to follow, and he lets her, and it is a joy, a privilege, to be able to give her that space and time and make no demands of her. He loves it even more, he thinks, as he turns a page of his cookbook, or puts a mug down by her elbow. That version of her. Before she returns, blinking in a daze, as if coming back to earth and reminding herself of the world. His feet up, crossed at the ankles. Her novel on the coffee table. Them. Their things. Night sky, velvet beyond the blinds.

Rosie brought her guitar to his gran's house, and she has her voice, but something seems to be missing. She starts staying late at the school, sometimes, to make use of their piano, play her songs the way she intends them to be played.

Is that okay, she asks him, calling him up when she's meant to be leaving and he's got water boiling for dinner, oil glopped in the pan.

It concerns him, that she thinks she needs to ask.

But it does make him wonder. He has an idea, and it is hard to let go of, so he takes to the internet on the nights she's still out, and after a couple of weeks he finds just what he's looking for. It's only a short walk away, cash in hand, a thanks mate, be careful with it, yeah, and he wheels it all

the way home, up the curbs, across the roads, as if it's a completely normal thing to do, to roll an old piano down the street.

It needs restoring, a little time and care. The woodwork is deeply
scratched, and pools of ancient candle wax, spilled long ago, have hard-
ened on its lid. He takes it into his garage and touches the keys to try its
sound, and while he knows next to nothing about music, it's clear that
it is desperately out of tune; the keys feel stiff, and slow, click like joints
beneath his fingers. The overtones are impure, as the seller had explained,
but somehow, that didn't seem to matter.

He knows she'll love it.

The swirling design on the wood panels, and the delicately turned
legs, which remind him, loosely, of the candlesticks he made in sixth form.
The deep brown of the wood, so different to the shiny black of the piano at her parents'. He digs out his toolbox, spends hours watching vid-
eos online to understand how to take it apart, remove the front panels, get
to the soundboard and the tired strings and the hammers and dampers
and pins.

It looks forlorn inside. The metal rails are dull and tarnished, the felt
withered in places. He spends a long time just looking, and figuring things
out, like he did when he would watch his grandpa with the engines, when
he had nothing to contribute, no skill or experience, but a desire he couldn't
articulate.

Just him, with a project, in his garage.

An itching in his palms.

When he hears Rosie's key in the door, he throws a sheet over it, just
in case, though she rarely comes out here, is scared of knocking his bike
over. He turns off the light and heads inside, where she kisses him hello,
shoes off, hair down, and they eat dinner and talk about their day and he
burns with silent pleasure at the thought of her piano waiting for her, on
the other side of the wall.

*

The days slip into late August, toward the day they both dread, every year. Will's birthday; the day that Josh died, and their lives split into before and after; what should have been, and what was.

They do not talk about it. Will gets up, earlier than usual, and goes running, and Rosie pretends she is asleep when she has in fact not slept all night, not properly, has been drifting in and out of dreams since dawn.

When he's been gone a good while, she gets up and makes breakfast. Something a little special, jams and croissants and fresh juice, Will's favorite biscuits on a plate. She calls her parents, as she always does on this morning, and her father answers. Hard day, she says, and her dad says isn't it, and they share some things about Josh, his habits, things they miss or still remember. The smell of his socks, after a basketball game. The way he would crack his knuckles, or hide his vegetables under his knife, when he was little, as if no one would notice he hadn't eaten them.

They laugh, the only way they are able to on this day, and at Christmas and Easter and any other occasion he is no longer here for: quietly, and with so much love and hurt in their hearts, it feels like they might choke on it.

Shortly after she's hung up, Will gets home, his face red with effort and the early, already-hot sunshine. He walks into the kitchen and sees the breakfast things and asks her what she's done, and she says nothing, really, that it's just breakfast, for his birthday. But he shakes his head, says no.

No? Rosie repeats.

I don't celebrate my birthday, he says.

Will.

No, Roe. I never have, after everything, and you *especially* don't need to make a thing of it, just because you're here. Seriously. Let's forget it.

Will, she says again, but he backs out of the room, starts up the stairs for a shower.

Rosie sits at the table for all of three seconds and then pushes her chair back to follow him. He is already under the water when she heads into the bathroom, no steam, because he still showers in the cold.

Josh would hate that you don't mark your birthday, she says.

Will is squeezing shampoo into his hand, runs it through his hair. It looks so long when it's wet. Turns a dark, dirty blond, like the pine-pocked Montenegrin sand.

I'm sure you're right, he says, as the water pours all over him. Down his back, between his strong, runner's thighs. Rosie watches him from the door frame.

So let's do something today, she says.

Can't, Will says. I'm washing my hair.

Don't be annoying, she says, and she watches him rinse, lather up, rinse again. Then he shuts the water off, rubs it out of his eyes.

Pass me the towel, will you, he says, and she does as he asked, watches him wrap it round his waist and step out of the tub. She has a moment, even though it is the day that it is, even though her heart aches like a cracked rib, where she feels elated. Because she is here, in this bathroom, with Will White, and he is the most beautiful thing she has ever seen. She actually thinks that to herself, and nearly laughs out loud.

Will sits on the edge of the bath and says that she can't change his mind on this. That he's thought about it a lot, and it's better this way. Unless she needs to acknowledge it, somehow. Not his birthday, she understands, but her brother.

The bathroom window is cracked open, and she can hear a bird rasping in the garden. A magpie, she thinks. So harsh, and unlovely.

I think about him daily, she tells Will. So today isn't any different.

Right, says Will.

A normal day, then, Rosie says, and Will looks so relieved, so grateful, that her heart aches even more. She stands aside, lets him pass her into the bedroom, and thinks how all the old songs are true, how love is so often just pain, still four letters, the flip side of the same feeling.

*

After five months together, they are walking to the beach when Rosie grabs Will by the arm and pulls him into the doorway of a high street shop; some place filled with hanging signs and seashell frames.

What, he says, as she peers around him, her nails dug into the crook of his arm.

She shushes him, and holds still. An elderly woman comes out of the shop so that they have to step to one side. Treated myself, she says to them, holding up a paper bag and continuing on her way. She has a walking stick, and Will watches her hobble away from them until Rosie steps back, looking flushed.

Who did you see, then, he asks her.

My dad, she says. Which means my mother's probably nearby, too.

Right, he says.

God, Rosie says, and she presses her palms to her eyes. Sorry. It was a reaction.

It's okay, he says.

No, it's not. I'm such a coward. We're not doing anything wrong. They know that Simon and I aren't together.

But they don't know about me.

No.

Does anybody?

She tilts her chin upward, as if sighing at the sky. Someone else moves into the alcove, asks if they can get past, and Will gestures toward the pavement. Rosie steps out of the doorway and they walk back the way they came; in the opposite direction to her father, he presumes.

I'll tell them, she says. I promise.

I don't actually care whether they know or not, he says. Unless it would change anything, for you.

In what way?

If they're unhappy about it, would that mean you would leave?

She stops, midstep, and looks alarmed.

Of course not, she says. That's not—no. Of course not.

He leaves her to mull over his question, because her repetition shows she has not actually considered it. He keeps walking, and she follows. The light is clean and fresh, a day for drying linens on the line. A sheet-stripping day, his grandma used to call them. Bright sun, a steady breeze.

Nobody knows about you, either, he reasons, as they edge away from town, rejoin the backstreets that'll take them toward home. But I never told anyone about anyone. I figured it's nobody's business.

No, Rosie says, as if she's trying to agree.

You didn't keep Simon a secret, though, he says.

No, I didn't.

And how'd that work out for you?

Rosie doesn't say anything, and Will bumps into her side, as if to bring her back.

Rosie, he says. It's okay. I'm saying it's fine.

I should tell people, she says. I want to. But I also just . . . don't want to ruin anything.

I get that, he says.

And not because I care what they'll say, she says. My parents, or my friends, or whatever. But it's just not been that long since Simon. And none of them will understand that it's been even longer, for us.

A red kite sweeps low overhead. It cuts behind the rooftops, disappears.

They'll assume this is just a fling, Rosie goes on, when it's not. And I feel good about being happy, and I just want to enjoy it a bit longer. I'm so scared of it going away. So the fewer people that can interfere, or disturb this . . . this thing that we have, is just a good thing, I think. You know?

Will knows. He thinks he should tell her not to be scared, that there's no reason to be, but he knows too well how she feels.

D'you know what I mean? Rosie prompts, misreading his silence. Another bird, then. A blackbird scoots from the top of a flint wall, flits along the grass verge.

You're saying I'm not your rebound, says Will.

You're definitely not my rebound.

Well, okay. We might need to regroup, in that case.

Why?

I thought this was just a casual thing.

She laughs, then, her sparkle laugh, and loops her arm through his own. Leans against his shoulder.

I've not even told Marley, Rosie says, as they follow a bend in the road. But she's been so busy with the new baby, and everything.

You'll tell her, Will says. When it's right.

He knows this is what she needs; openness, and space, without imposed timelines or rules. It has felt like one long summer since they found their way back to one another, and that is no time at all, really, not after all the years he has waited.

And besides, he has kept Rosie a secret, too, which is easy when he and Amber aren't speaking, and he's meant to be off traveling the world. In Vietnam, by now. Yet here he is in Norfolk, again, with the same girl, again, rushing nothing, just letting life happen. He's applied the same, unhurried strategy to the question of her divorce. Hasn't asked her when, or how; just assured her she'll know when it's time. It is unsettling, being so stimulated, so eaten up with desire, for a woman he really cares for. He wants to shield her, and shelter her, but let her find her own way, too, with certain things.

They are turning down his grandma's street when he sees that she is smiling to herself, her arm still in his. He asks her what, and she shakes her head, a little jerk, no. But he presses her, and she shrugs, a shy smile still at her mouth.

I wish I'd done everything on earth with you, she says.

The street is quiet. No cars, or closing doors. Just them, and her voice, on the linen-dry wind.

It's not mine, she says. The quote. But it's beautiful, isn't it?

He nods, but barely, because he is not used to such talk.

And I feel it, Rosie says, still with that smile of hers. I was just thinking that I feel it.

*

Will got home early, has been waiting by the living room window, and there she is, walking down the pavement, her school satchel in hand, her hair tucked beneath a scarf so it looks like she has a short bob instead of her long, wild mane.

He takes a breath.

His feet are tingling. He laughs, a little, because he wonders if this is what it would feel like to propose.

He has a vision of the ring his grandmother gave him, but then Rosie's key is scraping in the door and he feels his heart ricochet in his ribs, and then she's by the lounge doors, putting her bag down, loosening her scarf and turning to him and then stopping.

She is still, for just a moment.

What's this, she asks.

It's yours, he says.

She says his name, the sound higher than her speaking voice, a note
of both shock and joy. It is a wonderful sound. He has an image of her as
a girl at Christmas, or wandering into her first music shop.

Come and look, he says, and he touches the top of the piano in invitation, and she comes forward, still holding her scarf. He takes it from her,
frees her hands. She looks and looks and says nothing, and his excitement
begins to waver.

She reaches out and traces the design on the panel. Something Vic-
torian, vines and whirling leaves, which he had conditioned and then
stained. He'd reupholstered the piano stool, too, bought a new fabric he
thought she might like, filled all of the scratches and dents and sanded
them back to smooth.

He is proud of it, if he lets himself think about it.

But Rosie isn't saying anything.

I know it's old-fashioned, Will says. But I read that early 1900s was a
good time for pianos, that they got a bit mediocre after that? And the guy
said this one was 1920s, so I thought it was probably decent. Not that I know
anything about pianos, obviously. Maybe I should have asked you first.

Still nothing. Her hands, trailing across the lid.

It wasn't in great shape, Will admits, but I've tried to restore it as best
I can, and it had good bones, you know. The strings needed replacing,
and it's got new felts and keys, so the soundboard's back to how it should
be. Apparently the bass is better in these pre-Depression pianos, because
they're that bit bigger. And this one's like fifty-four inches, or so. So yeah.

He swallows. She still has her coat on, has stopped touching the wood;
is standing with her hands by her sides.

Don't you like it? he asks, and she turns to him and her eyes are full ·of tears and light and she says his name again, and he watches her, wants to see her, remember her, like this.

Color stained in her cheeks.

I, she says. I don't even know what to say.

Just play, then, Will says, and she looks stunned at this idea for all of five seconds, and then she unbuttons her coat, sits down on the stool and lifts the lid.

He watches her take in the keys, for a moment. Sees her lay her hands in place, as if checking that they can be there.

A pause.

And then she plays.

*

How did you know, she asks him, later. They have eaten dinner, showered, are lying in bed with the duvet folded around them.

Know what, Will says, into her hair. She is pressed into him, her back curved along his stomach, his knees tucked alongside her calves.

What I needed, she says.

Will is not sure this is a real question. He thinks it might be her way of simply telling him what everything has meant to her. Not just the piano, but all that time apart, the months where they did not speak, gave each other space, tried to heal in their own, separate, fruitless ways. How he never forgot her. He never knew they would find their way back to one another; never dared hope it would happen. But life continued, and there she was, and here he is, for her.

He was right; she does not need an answer, because she falls asleep before he can respond. Lying with her reminds him of their last night in the tent, the night she cried, told him life could be good again, and that she did not understand how.

*

Half a year of this.

Hours of talking, and eating, and piano playing, shopping and sleeping and not sleeping. They have moved into his grandmother's room; redecorated, changed the bedding and the curtains.

He makes her coffee before work, milky and with a half spoon of sugar, his own black and bitter. They drink it in bed with the blinds open, the sun falling on the opposite wall. We should put some pictures up, she suggests. I prefer the sunlight, he tells her, and she smiles, says nothing. Lifts her coffee cup to her lips.

He kisses her, deeply, at the front door, every day before her short commute to school. It leaves her breathless, leaves him hard, and they have sex most evenings, as soon as she gets home. In bed, on the sofa, and again on the stairs, which gives him a fairly severe carpet burn one time. I'm too old for this, he tells her, as he inspects it in the bathroom mirror that night. Just making up for lost time, she says, and he grins at her, marveling at how much she can surprise him, still, with the things she comes out with.

It is all too perfect, of course.

Too right, for a life of wrong.

She gets a phone call one day, six months after she moved in. He is making eggs. Stirring slowly at the hob, wondering whether he should start to make his own bread. Fill their home with the smell of whole grain and comfort, when he hears her on the stairs, and he knows it, already, from the fall of her feet.

Simon, is all she says, when she walks in.

He turns the gas off and puts the spoon on the side. Turns around to look at her.

What about him?

He's ill, she says. Really ill.

A roaring, in his ears. He is a terrible person; he wants to tell her he doesn't care about this man, this fellow human being who once loved the woman he always has—that nothing matters, now, but this, but them, their kitchen and their eggs and their mornings drinking coffee. Simon can die, for all he cares, and it's ruthless but in that moment it's true and he wants to say it to her, to make her feel the same.

He asks her what she needs to do.

I need to . . . go to him, she says, and her voice isn't apologetic, but firm. I'm still his wife.

Technically, Will says, and she nods, repeats the word. Technically.

Do you have to go now? he asks, and he knows it's meaningless in light of everything but he gestures at the eggs, at the plates he's laid out on the table.

I should, she says, and she won't look at him, won't even meet his eyes, and he is suddenly so angry he cannot speak. She leaves the kitchen and he grips the side of the counter, waiting.

Prisms, splintered, on the chrome of the sink.

The burn of it in his eyes.

And then she is back, with her bag at her feet. He leans against the countertop, watching her. Takes his coffee mug from the side. She comes over, folds herself into him, and he holds his breath. Won't inhale. Won't smell her hair or her skin or her early-morning sleepiness, a smell he has come to rely on.

I'm sorry, she says into his shoulder, and then she is gone, and he waits until he hears the front door close before he throws his coffee cup to the floor, watches it shatter into a hundred shards, the explosion of it on the tiles.

sixteen

Rosie goes to him, her husband. The man she has not spoken to in seven months.

The man she spent night after night with on a single university mattress and in their queen-sized marital bed, who soothed her to sleep in his large arms and bored her with his endless kindness and commitment and unwavering certainty about how their lives should go.

They would spend hours at the gym together; toning, strengthening. Him running in front of her along the river, telling her to keep going, that she was doing great.

With him, she was always doing great.

And she is sickened with herself now, and the euphoria she had found outside of him. With Will. With the breakdown of the structure they had built since that first coffee Simon bought her in the Student Union café, when she was still so sick with grief, so unendingly awake. He took her hand, and her coat. He propped her up. And so she goes to him, and she shuts down everything she is feeling about other things, and other people, and she climbs back into that tight, wraparound skin she knows so well, before she knocks on their old front door.

———

Simon tells her about Hodgkin's lymphoma in their living room, with a teapot on the table, something herbal, the color of urine. She wants milk and sugar and Yorkshire tea. Custard creams. She cannot stop thinking about biscuits, and she is queasy, with how surreal it all feels. Her sofa. Their sofa.

This man she should know, sitting on it, with his dulled, red-rimmed eyes.

They drink their tea and he lists things like enlarged lymph nodes and extreme fatigue and how he thought it was stress, at first, because of—well, them—but when the night sweats started he got the blood-work done and the scans, and that was it, his diagnosis, and all Rosie can think of after the custard creams is the artist she studied at school, Howard Hodgkin, who painted Mumbai weddings and raspberry crumble and red mornings, and she should be asking Simon smart, attentive questions, but all she sees are streaks of color, artworks she'd not understood. Brain, looping. The touching of windowsills; tilting of internal chairs.

Simon is calm all afternoon. Matter-of-fact, his gentle self. But after dark he tells her he is scared, and he cries, and she holds him in her arms and is reminded of the time that Josh came out to her in his bedroom; that similar loss of what to say, but an instinct to show up, so fully, that there is nothing, no one, that would see her anywhere else.

She thinks about Will's grandmother.

How she beat it, and died anyway, after all.

You're young and fit and you're going to be fine, Rosie says, for herself as much as him. Numbers glare at her from his fitness watch. It has been hours; has felt like hours. He twists himself round to look at her.

When I found out, Rosie, the first thing I thought was, why on earth did we do this?

She wants to hang her head, but she forces herself to look back at him.

I'll cut my hours, Rosie. We can sell up, move to the country. Move to Bali, even. Whatever you want. We can have kids, or not. I'll make more time for you. We'll be like us again. I promise.

We were always like us, Rosie thinks, in the dark.

Simon, she says, and she tries to extricate herself, peel back from the weight of him.

I love you, Rosie, he says, and for the first time in their years of knowing one another, his voice is fierce. I should *never* have let life get in the way of that. So I'll survive this, and I'll put it right.

Simon, she says again.

Yes?

We were apart for a long time, she says. We ended things. And. Well.

You're not wearing your ring, he observes.

Her heart freezes over; spreads like frost down her spine. Shame, burning cold.

We both thought it was over, Simon reasons. We'll have both . . . done things that married people aren't supposed to.

He folds his fingers in hers. They feel clammy, like the backs of her knees.

Let's agree not to go there, he says. I love you. This is just about the worst thing I could imagine happening, and all I could think was, why is Rosemary not here?

But—

I get it, if you don't feel the same. I get it, if you don't want to be married to me. To this, and all that it comes with.

Simon. It's not that.

Then give me a chance, Rosie? Give us one more chance?

He is still looking up at her, and his face is so pleading and good, and she has loved him for so many years, and she made a vow, and he could be dying, and there is no question of right or wrong, here, for her. She knows what she wants to do. Who she desperately wants to be.

In sickness and in health, she says.

Till death do us part, says Simon, and she says oh, God, please don't.

The days after are leaden, and slow. She endures them, booking chemo dates into her diary, pouring herself into laptop research for outcomes and statistics, but then, inevitably, she calls him.

She can't not.

The fear and the regret and the sinking of it all is suffocating, and she needs her best friend, as selfish and awful as that makes her, her skin crawling with the plague of it.

He does not pick up, so she tries again.

In the end, she leaves a voice mail.

Will, she says. I know I'm the last person you want to hear from right now. So hang up, if you need to, okay? But I just need to talk, to someone. To you. It's cancer. He has cancer. Lymphoma. And I can't actually believe that. I can't be*lieve* it. My brother died, and your gran, and now this? How much bad luck can one person witness in a lifetime?

She gives a stupid, strange laugh, and she is trembling, really trembling. Her hands don't feel like her own.

He's my husband, Will, she says. And I know we parted ways, and I know that . . . we . . . but I just can't, anymore. He might be dying. And I have to stand by him. I have to be his wife, you know?

She pauses, as if he is listening, to give him the time to absorb.

I have to do this, she says. I do. And I don't want you out of my life,
Will, I never have. But it's your call. Okay? Okay.

And she hangs up.

Marley comes as soon as she asks her to, with her toddler in a pushchair,
the new baby in a sling, and most importantly, a takeaway menu in hand.

Order whatever you want, she tells Simon.

I don't really feel like eating, he says, and she says all the more reason
to order what you want, Si.

Then she asks questions and listens and reassures them both, dan-
dling the baby on her knee, telling them exactly what his own doctor has
said, echoing the figures and recommendations and timelines they expect. Skye plays on the carpet with what looks like a pair of balled-up
socks, and the streetlights come on outside as they eat noodles and sticky
rice and chicken drowned in coconut cream.

If you're going to get cancer, Marley says, then this is the one you
want to get.

So they say, Simon says.

He is twirling his chopsticks around, barely touching his food. Rosie,
by contrast, has devoured bowl after bowl. Something cavernous has
opened inside her since the not-quite-divorce. She wants salt and comfort and soft, warm things to fill herself up with. She listens to Marley's
words as if they, too, can nourish her, as though knowledge and facts
can somehow bolster them against this, like they can build an immunity
among the three of them, here, in this living room, with sheer revision
and repetition of numbers and body parts and stages and cells. Rosie is
good at exams. She is good at knowing all there is to know, and putting
in the effort that's required for the best outcome. She believes, for the

short, quiet time that it takes them to eat dinner, that things are actually going to be okay. And okay is all she wants. All she should ever have wanted.

How are you doing, Marley asks her, as she shrugs her coat on in the stairwell, and Rosie buckles Skye into her pushchair.

Just—trying, Rosie says, as Skye kicks out. There!

She clips her in, and Skye pouts.

No, Marley says, as she buttons up her jacket, one by slow, tortoise-shell one, the baby still asleep in her sling. How *are* you. With all this.

Rosie looks at her friend from her squat by the floor, Skye now tugging at her hair.

I don't really know, she says. I guess I feel . . . focused. Like I just need to get him through his first chemo, and then we can go from there.

Good, Marley says. That's a good way to think.

Good, Rosie echoes.

But I didn't actually mean about the cancer, she says. I meant that you guys were separated. And now you're not. And I get why—cancer changes things.

It really does, Rosie says, as she tries to disentangle her hair from Skye's fist.

Just know that I'm here if you need me. Not as a doctor, or a second opinion, though obviously I'm here for that, too. But I'm still your friend first, Rosie. I'm here if things are hard, all right? Outside of cancer.

Rosie glances into the flat, at what she can see of the kitchen; Simon is clearing up, stacking the dishwasher with plates, banging around as he always has, with his large limbs and heavy hands.

Shall we, she says, and she nods at the lift doors, and between them they guide Skye's pushchair inside, take the seven floors down to the lobby. Outside, the night is clear and strewn with stars. Their breath clouds silver in the air.

Rosie waits for the glass door to close and feels the truth rising like a cough, up and through her, and then she turns to her friend and says that she slept with Will White during the separation. Not just once. A lot. That they were sort of, together, she thinks. For months.

Marley's eyes get wide and her mouth slackens. Rosie puts the heels of her hands over her eyes, presses them into the sockets.

What do I do, Marl, she asks.

Okay, okay, back up, says Marley. Will White. From school. Who you sort of stayed in touch with but then lost contact, because he didn't come to your wedding, 'cause he was still utterly in love with you—*that* Will White?

Yes. Though I'm not sure about the love part.

Whatever, Marley says, and she shakes her head, as if to clear the warm, sleepy fog of too much Thai food. So, you were together. For *months*? How many months?

I don't know. Like five or six. I was kind of living with him.

Kind of living with him.

Yeah.

How do you *kind of* live with someone?

What do you—

Did you have a spare toothbrush in his bathroom, Marley asks, or did you rarely go back to your own place?

I didn't really . . . have my own place, Rosie admits.

I thought you were staying with a colleague, after you left Simon?

I didn't leave Simon. We left each other.

Marley waves her hand like that's insignificant, then shushes the baby, who has started to mewl.

But no, Rosie relents. That was a . . . cover-up. I went from my mum's, straight to Will's grandmother's house.

Mamma *Mia*, Marley says. After all this *time*?

I know.

It's like a movie, Rosie!

A movie where the husband gets cancer so the heroine stamps on the hero's heart and walks out?

Marley's smile fades.

Right, she says. Right.

What do I do, Marl? Rosie asks again. Should I tell Simon? I wanted to, but he said he's been with other people, too, and we don't need to talk about it.

Well, then. I think you're fine.

But it's Will, you know? Not some random guy.

He's definitely not some random guy, Marley says. He's *the* guy.

Stop it, Marl.

You're the one that called him the hero!

There are no heroes, okay? There is just me, and them, and the right thing. And I'm with Simon. I married him. And he's—he's got to be okay.

Her voice cracks, like glass, under the night sky.

Okay, Marley says. I get that. I do.

Rosie's arms are bare, and she feels cold, but she welcomes it. She wants the discomfort, the reminder that it is not so much effort to endure, after all. This life of cold hands and long falls and wanting, so much, that it burns.

Cinders, in the grate of her.

Rosie, says Marley.

Yeah?

Are you . . . is this what you want?

Rosie doesn't look at her friend; she stares upward, instead, at the pinpricks of white so far above them. Light years away. Looking back in time, at millennia gone by. Josh told her all about that. The physics of it.

I have to put Simon first, she says. I want to.

But do you love him, Rosie?

Yes, she says, fiercely, and without pause.

Okay, Marley says. I just needed to ask. But it's okay, Rosie. Don't.

Because apparently, Rosie is crying. She brushes at her face, rubs at her stupid, leaking eyes.

Okay, she says back, and she wants to stamp her foot in fury, tug on her own hair like Skye, and scream, with her face tilted upward and the apartments hushed around them, people looking out of their windows, alarmed, by the noises she would make.

Okay, she says again.

Marley grips her shoulder with her steady surgeon's hand.

You're okay, she says, and it is as if the word has lost all meaning, and yet still Rosie holds on to it, like a life buoy, a truth they can speak into being.

*

Her songs do not dry up, this time.

They gush out of her, like broken waters, as soon as Simon is sleeping. And he sleeps a lot; in the day as well as through the night, and for the whole weekend before his first chemo, which is plenty of time to write. Plenty of time to sit on the windowsill of their flat and bleed lyrics under the gaze of the city lights, the traffic moving below.

Will is probably awake, too, she knows.

He kept similar hours to her.

An early bird, and a seasoned insomniac, both led by the things in their heads.

She makes a list of what she thinks might keep him awake.

She writes a text, and deletes it.

She drinks water and coffee and stays wired and functioning, with her pen nib fused to her notebook, the lamplight on the not-blank pages, the crossings out, the found words and rhythms that flood out of her. Oceans of it. Outpouring.

*

Will thought about taking a bottle of vodka to the cliffs and drinking himself numb. But that was it: a thought. He paces the house, instead, battling the urge to head to an off-license. There is no drink in his grand-mother's house; Amber emptied the cupboards as soon as their gran died. He hates her, for this, and is unequivocally grateful. Roams around the living room, like an enclosed big cat.

He hasn't slept since she left.

Wonders if she's managed to.

But after he's thrown himself into his grandpa's armchair and his eyes are closing, just as he finally gets near to some kind of shutdown, his phone rings and he lurches up as if there's been a break-in, his heart thundering in his ribs.

It's an unknown number. A scam, or cold call, he thinks, as he presses the green button and waits.

Hello? a woman's voice says. Hello? Is this Will White?

Speaking, he says.

Oh, cool, she says, and a shot of recognition goes through him, the sound of a schoolgirl he once knew. It's Marley, she confirms.

Marley, he repeats.

Rosie's friend.

I know who you are.

Right, well, I'm sorry for calling so late. I just wanted to touch base.

Okay, he says.

I know about you and her, she says. She told me, tonight, and she's . . .
she'll hate me for ringing. It's none of my business.

No, says Will. It's not.

You never liked me, did you, she asks him, and her voice has changed,
mild curiosity mingling with distaste; like the time he tried caviar.

You never liked me, either, he says.

Not really, she says. But Rosie did. Does.

Will says nothing. He sinks back into his grandfather's chair, stretches
his legs out in front of him.

For all the good it does, he says.

I know you know her like I do, Marley says. Better, even, I'd imagine.
So I know you already know she's just trying to do the right thing. She's
so moral. Like, annoyingly so. What she wants . . . doesn't really count.
Not even when we were kids. When we had sleepovers, right, she wouldn't
eat any midnight snacks because we'd already brushed our teeth. She's
that kind of person, Will. She has rules that rule her. And it doesn't dic-
tate how she feels about you. Just what she does.

Will is looking, unseeingly, at the living room he grew up in. The
wood floor and downtrodden carpet, with its tasseled rug, ravaged by
the dog. There is dust on the fireplace. Thick, slanting cobwebs, cloak-
ing the poker and tongs.

I think what she does is the most important thing here, he says.

Marley is quiet. He hears a baby crying in the background.

Just don't be too hard on her, she says eventually. She's so hard on
herself already, you know?

Thanks for the advice I didn't ask for, he says.

He hears her sigh. The baby cries louder.

Nice talking to you, Will, Marley says. As ever.

Will snorts, hoping she catches it before she hangs up. Then he throws his phone across the room where it bounces, uselessly, on the opposite armchair. His grandmother's, with her tartan blanket still draped over the side.

*

Rosie rubs Simon's back as he vomits into their toilet bowl, the fan flicked on and the window open. It is cold outside, but they need the air. The taste of sky and wind and good things.

All she can do is soothe him with her hands, these small gestures of opening windows, saying it's all right, over and over. His shoulder blades feel like bird bones under her fingers. Delicate, and unhuman. Like the seagull skeleton she and Josh found, once, on their local beach. They buried it, gave it a funeral.

Simon heaves once more and then groans, lowers his face to the floor.

Let's get you in bed, Rosie says, and he says no, he wants to stay here.

Then let me put some towels down, she says. I can try and make you more comfortable.

He says no, again, and his eyes are already closing. The first round of chemo had seemed too easy, almost jovial. They'd taken magazines but not read them, instead opting to talk to the other patients, learning their first names, hearing their stories. It was an oddly optimistic atmosphere, and Simon had felt fine.

Two days later, he did not feel fine.

Now, Rosie looks at him curled on the bathroom tiles. Then she stands quietly and leaves him to rest, with the noise of the fan and the sounds of the October night carrying through the window. A dog barks. Car horns, scuffing leaves, and low, distant engines.

She makes a cup of tea and doesn't drink it. Chooses a book, only not to read it, and is staring into space at the kitchen table when she hears another sort of engine. A deep, growling sound, the guttural revs that still, even now, flip her stomach. She has one of those moments where she knows something is about to happen, and she watches time, as if it is a tangible thing; sees it seep through the lamplight and the shadows cast by her furniture, nothing moving, holding its inanimate breath.

Her phone rings, and she answers, says his name.

Which number d'you live at, he asks her.

What?

Which number flat, he says. I'm outside and I don't know which buzzer to press.

You're outside?

Yeah.

You want to come in?

Or you could come out, he says.

She hesitates, though stalling is the last thing she wants to do.

I won't touch you, he promises. If that helps.

I'll . . . buzz you in, Rosie says, and she does, and then she immediately regrets it and takes her keys and walks out and down the stairs.

He is already halfway up. Wearing his leather jacket and carrying his bike helmet, and looking okay, and sober, and calm. His steps are long and sure, even in his heavy boots. The boots she knows and loves, somehow, and how can you love someone else's shoes, she wonders, as she watches him ascend.

When she is close, he hears her and stops, one floor below. Holds her still in his eyes, and then shrugs, like the eighteen-year-old version of himself.

Wolf teeth. Unshifting gaze.

Sorry, he says to her.

What for?

For taking so long, he says.

They eat cereal in the kitchen, just like they did before, when Josh was alive and the snow was falling and they barely knew one another. It is inconceivable, to her, that there was a time when this was true. She has never especially wanted a child, but sometimes she wonders, if she did, how it is that she does not know them yet. And it is like this with Will.

Tonight, they keep the lights low, their voices even lower.

He's sleeping, Rosie tells him, and he nods.

Has he started chemo?

This week, she says.

Shit.

Yeah.

I can come back, he says. Another day.

But she shakes her head, passes him a coffee. His hands seem cold from the ride; they look red and a little swollen.

You should really wear gloves, she tells him.

You should really sing for a living, he says.

Huh?

Don't tell me how to live, he says, and I won't tell you, either.

Wow, she says. You got cranky.

I've always been cranky.

No, you haven't.

I have. When I was young and attractive, it just seemed more appealing, I think. Seductive.

Is that right?

But it's actually been crankiness all along.

You are a prickly bastard, she says, remembering the cactus, and she splutters at her nerve, and the memory. It takes Will by surprise, too, and he grins, then snickers at her own laughter. She thinks she wants to cry.

I know it's weird, he says, and he pours himself more cereal, the rush of grains raining into his bowl. But I'm trying to be a better human. More like you. Or Josh.

Rosie nudges her spoon around. She wants to tell him she is trying so hard to be good because she is not; that it is not effortless, for her, like it was for her twin. That she wants things she shouldn't, and makes terrible choices, and hurts people despite trying not to.

You're already a good human, she says.

Thinking, the one that keeps me up at night.

In all the right ways.

Will crunches with his mouth closed, looking at her across the table. Then he tells her he's going to be there, for all of it. Whatever she needs, or Simon needs. He knows they have closer friends than him, but he's flexible, with his shift work, and he can drive, and he has no ties, no girl-friend or family. So he can be a friend. He wants to be a friend.

Traffic breathes through the latched windows. Rosie puts down her spoon and takes his hand, with the day dying around them, the burn of auburn clouds. And when he shifts away, she lets him go.

This is bad cereal, he tells her, after a moment.

I know, she says. Sugar free.

They both take another mouthful, chew and swallow.

It's Simon's, she says.

He nods, and they keep eating.

She does not explain to Simon about Will; simply says to him, during his next round of chemo, that he's going to drive them both home.

We got back in touch, Rosie tells him, while he's hooked up to the wires, the life-saving poison flowing into his veins, and he accepts it without question. Afterward, he greets Will, tired but smiling, says it's good to see him, and then he sits quietly in the back, looking out at the roads as Will drives them back to their flat.

He says thanks, as he gets out of the car, and Will says it's no problem.

There is a moment when Rosie senses Will wanting to say something else. She sees his eyes in the rearview mirror, drinking in this new man, so different to the young, muscular one he met in the coffee shop, when she hoped they'd be friends, all three of them, when she thought life would go another way.

Call if you need, Will says, and she says she will. She does not invite him in, this time. She takes the lift up with her husband—something they'd not done once, in all the years of living there, unless they had suitcases and were coming back from the airport—and she makes him decaffeinated tea and they do easy things like sitting, or napping, the television muted in the background.

One day, though, he is so sick that she is frightened.

He cannot even keep water down, and his skin is like paste, but she has back-to-back lessons that day, and she's already missed enough work as it is, and he tells her to go, that he'll be fine. She wants to call his mother, but he says no. A family friend, then, his best man from their wedding, but he refuses that, too, says he doesn't want anyone to see him like this. That everyone's busy, has work, their lives. That, again, he'll be fine.

I might call Will, she says, from the door. Simon makes a sleepy noise, an agreement or another refusal, she can't be sure. But he has nothing to lose, with Will. They don't know each other; there will be no emotion, no pitying eyes or obligation, which she knows is Simon's worst fear. And so she calls, on her way down the stairs. It is a blanched day, everything dull and fallow, the stairwell mordantly cold.

It's a lot to ask, she says, as soon as he answers. But could you come over? I've got work, and he's in bed, but just in case he needs more water or something happens, I just—

I'll be there, Will says.

And she says okay, and he says okay back, and then he's gone and she's out on the pavement, and her mouth feels too full of teeth.

*

Will knocks on the door, thinking that if Simon's awake, he'd probably rather answer it. Five seconds. Six. When nothing happens, he takes the key from under the doormat, as Rosie instructed, and lets himself in.

He hadn't really looked around their flat, before. It is spacious and expensive-looking, larger than his gran's whole house. Floor-to-ceiling windows let in more light than he is used to, the River Yare gleaming like a silver ribbon below. Their furniture is shiny, and hard. A city dweller's pad, filled with glass tables and chrome handles and a television screen wider than his kitchen table.

He stands by the door for a while, listening, but Simon does not seem to be up. He walks forward, swears, then doubles back, takes off his shoes and leaves them on the mat. He looks out of the wide windows. Peruses their DVD collection, finds nothing he'd be remotely interested in watching.

And though he does not mean to, he ends up snooping; looking in their cupboards, the fridge, the bathroom cabinet beneath their marble-set sink. Gold taps. Pearly-white hand sanitizer. It reminds him of a hotel, which leaves him feeling sad, and strangely, somewhat satisfied.

At lunch, he makes them both sandwiches, a task he doesn't expect to be as difficult as it is. There is some seeded bread in the freezer that seems older than the margarine he finds at the very back of the fridge, so yellow and smooth, it's as though no knife has ever been near it. Sundried tomatoes in the bottom of a jar, and a block of cheese with fine grate marks, clearly only ever used for cooking. He slices it up and toasts the bread, trickles the tomato oil over the top to turn it golden and oozing and less cardboard-like.

Two plates.

Butter knife, left in the sink.

He pads down the corridor to the bedroom and taps on the door with his foot. When he pushes it open, he finds Simon sitting up on his pillows, looking at the wall. There is another television in here. Paintings of blue things; abstract splashes and coiling waves, bordered with mounts and thin frames.

You're up, Will says.

Oh, Simon says. Hello.

Rosie told you I was coming, didn't she?

In a roundabout way, I think, Simon says. I'm not very good at listening, these days.

I made lunch, Will says, and he hesitates in the doorway, some deep disinclination keeping him out of this man's bedroom. He thinks about shoving the food across the floor, leaving him to it. But he is sick, not in prison, he reminds himself, and so he crosses the threshold and hands him the plate.

A sandwich, Simon says, and he sounds bemused.

Yep.

I don't . . . he says, and then he falters. Takes it from him.

You hungry? Will asks, as he seats himself in a chair by the dresser, his own plate balanced on his knee. He watches as Simon inspects the bread, takes a bite, then visibly relaxes.

Must be, he says, through his mouthful, and Will raises his own sandwich in a false toast and they eat, teeth gnawing, the air thick and smelling of sleep.

Will looks around as he chews, without really wanting to. Some dark fascination takes over, like needing to look at a car crash, or a wild animal attack, despite everything that's wrong about it. Simon and Rosie's bedroom. Their private space, with its sage walls and photo-filled frames, mostly snaps from the wedding he never attended. Her dressing gown, on the door. Contraceptive pills on the nightstand.

His heart is beating too slowly. He realizes, as he takes his final bite, that he does not know what Simon knows, about anything.

How d'you feel? Will asks him, when they're done.

Like I have cancer, Simon answers.

That bad, huh?

I wouldn't recommend it, he says, but he smiles, and Will sees the stretch of square jaw from all those years ago, the pleasant face of this pleasant guy he's spent so many years loathing.

He has wished him dead, many a time.

Which troubles him less than it should.

So nice that you and Rosie got back in touch, Simon says, and Will braces himself. Wipes his mouth with the back of his hand, the oil lucent, like spilled water.

Yeah, he says.

It'd been a while hadn't it?

Years, Will agrees.

She missed you, Simon tells him. She never said, but I could tell. I'm glad you got over, you know. Whatever it was.

Me too, says Will, after the longest, most dreadful pause.

Rosie isn't a proud person, Simon says, sinking back into his pillows. But she's principled. She feels things deeply, and takes a long time to forgive. I like that about her, though. She's sincere, you know? And I like sincerity.

Yeah, Will says, though he doesn't know why Simon is telling him this.

So she might have been distant, Simon says. But she came back. She reached out, when times got tough. And that means more than the distance, I think.

Right, says Will. Then, just as it looks as though Simon might close his eyes, he says, I do know all this. It's why I'm here.

So nice she has you, Simon says, his voice fading, already, into unconsciousness. He mumbles something that sounds like the word brother, and Will stands up, takes the plates, and pauses at the door. He wants to tell him he is not the brother, here. That nothing about him is brotherly. A savage, boorish part of him wants to say that Rosie has never been a sibling, to him, that he's read it all wrong, and it's embarrassing and pathetic and he wants to see the carpet burns he has, the white scars of them on his glutes from the sex they had in the house they shared, more than once, where she'd borrowed his shirts and cut his hair and laughed with his grandma in the greenhouse. Geese, calling, in the mornings. Her hair, like apples, after a shower.

But he doesn't. He leaves him to sleep.

Goes to wash the plates, in their giant marital sink.

Later, they play cards. When Simon emerges from the bedroom and says oh, you're still here, and Will says he promised Rosie he'd stay, that she'll be home soon.

I can look after myself, you know, says Simon.

I know, Will says. But he does not move, and so Simon shrugs, and there is a pack of cards on the shelf of the coffee table, staring at them

with its smug, cobalt-blue outline of a king. Shall we? Will asks, and Simon says sure.

Will shuffles the deck. He likes the logic and order of card games; it
reminds him of maths, in a way, or the maintenance of an engine. Such
a variety of outcomes, but with resolutions, definitive ways forward. He
used to play with his grandpa. And his gran, when she was having her
own chemo, so long ago now, though he can still smell the rust, the sour-
ness, of that time, the coppery odor of blood and bodies and split fruit.

Simon does not smell like that, yet.

His eyes look bruised, and his hair is mussed from the hours in bed,
but otherwise he seems himself, though Will realizes, as he deals the
cards, that he has no idea who that is.

Rummy? he asks him.

Simon says sure, again, and Will wonders if he ever has an opinion on
anything, and they play in silence for a while, the slap and scuffle of the
cards the only sound as they sit on opposite sofas. The living room floods
with the setting sun, warms their wrists as they play.

What's with the art, Will asks him, when he feels he has to speak.

Hmm?

Simon looks up, and he sees that it has taken every ounce of his concentration to be able to play their game. He has not read their silence as
awkward, or loaded. He is simply struggling to focus.

In your room, Will says. All the water.

Oh, he says. I used to row. And sail.

You don't now?

Not since Oxford.

Will says nothing. It is a familiar story. One he abhors, and one that
makes him a hypocrite. He still has travel brochures in his old flat, the
pages folded down, circled treks and waterfalls and ancient wonders he's
never seen.

Why not? he asks, when he can't help himself.

I got a job, Simon says. And a mortgage, and a wife. I want to teach her to sail, one day; I always said I would, but it never happened. No time. City living, you know.

Will does not know, because he has only lived on the coast and in the Dales, and his time outside the garage was spent hiking and rescuing and running in the mountains, along the cliffs, in the rain and the shining sun.

Like Rosie's music, he says, after a long pause. Another card laid on the table.

Her music?

Yeah. She stopped, didn't she. For years. No time. City living. All of that.

I suppose so. But she's teaching again, now, I think.

You think?

His voice is harsh, sarcastic, and he should recover it, but he can't. He doesn't know what to say, or how to take those two words back. Simon may be sick, but he is not stupid. He lowers his cards and looks at him, and Will waits.

You still don't like me, Simon says.

What?

You didn't like me, when we first met. That much was obvious. And then you and Rosie lost touch and I figured it didn't matter. But now you're here, and you still don't. Can I ask why?

The sun falls through the high windows, like molten brass.

I'm genuinely interested, Simon urges.

Will exhales through one cheek.

Okay, he says. There's a list.

Blimey, Simon says. After just one coffee?

Well, Rosie and I talked a lot, remember, he says.

Simon nods, his face mild, as though this is only fair.

I thought you were—are—hugely privileged, and a bit of a drag, Will says.

Simon stares at him, and then his face breaks. Will steels himself, thinking he must be offended, angry, even, but then he sees that he's laughing.

A drag, Simon repeats.

Yeah, Will says. Just a bit dull. Nothing to you, really. Beyond your money and your manners.

I do have money and manners, Simon agrees, and he's still grinning. What else?

This is weird, mate, Will says. You really want me to keep insulting you?

Simon has put his cards down, and he rubs his hand along his jaw, stubble like lichen on his chin.

People don't tell me how it is, Simon says. My parents are wealthy, and privileged, like you said, and they're great, but they're also people who never, ever let me believe I couldn't do anything I wanted. All I had to do was ask. Live. Then I went to public school, where my teachers projected the same message, and then Oxford landed me a job that meant I was earning a lot of money, very quickly, with a team of people who do what I tell them. I've never had to think about that not being the norm. Ever. I've never had to think about life not being plain sailing, because it has been, so far, and with relatively little effort.

Will hates him, a little more, despite his self-awareness.

I think I'm an all right guy, Will, Simon says. I care about people, and things. But I'm only just starting to realize how . . . *blinkered* I am.

Because you got cancer, Will says.

Exactly, he says. And because my wife left me. Well. Maybe we left each other, I don't quite know how we got there. But that wasn't plain sailing either. And I didn't know why. Because nobody had prepared me for that. Nobody ever tells me what they really think.

Forgive me if I'm all out of sympathy, Will says, and Simon grins, again.

What else, he says. I want to hear it.

Will pauses, and then relents.

I thought you were smug, he tells him. And patronizing, but because you were nice, it was a subtle sort of patronizing. Not arrogance, exactly, but an ignorance, almost. And I thought you looked at people without really seeing them. You saw a pretty, intelligent, pocketable wife in Rosie, I think.

He stops himself before he says more.

I did, Simon says, and his grin has faded now. That's true. But I see a lot more than that, too.

Do you?

Of course.

What do you see, then?

That's pretty personal, mate, Simon says, and Will shrugs, stares him down. I love her, Simon says. I really do. I don't need to explain why.

But you let her live a life where she's not herself, Will says.

What do you mean?

She doesn't *create* anything, Will says. She doesn't sing or play or write.

She never expressed an interest in those things, Simon says.

It doesn't matter, Will says. You let her get smaller, and thinner, and even quieter than she was. I bet the in-laws love you.

Simon sits back, his face no longer genial.

They do, actually, he says.

I don't know why we're even talking about this, Will says.

I asked you why you didn't like me, Simon says. And you were kindly answering.

There's nothing kind about this, Will says.

Actually, Will, Simon says, it's the kindest thing anyone's done for me in weeks. I've been getting a whole lot of nothing from everyone. Old friends, and colleagues, and family members, who are scared to even look at me, and don't know what the hell to say.

Will gets the impression that it's the first time Simon has said hell.

And I get why, because they're in that same bubble, Simon explains. Where they don't ever have to face things. Where things don't go wrong.

News flash, Will says. Things will always go wrong.

There is another pause. A plane beelines through the dusk, streaking a neon trail across the windows.

Thank you, Simon says. Honestly.

Will looks at him, trying to work him out, when he realizes he is still holding his cards. He puts them down, leans back on the sofa.

You're more interesting, now you have cancer, he tells him.

Every cloud, Simon says.

*

Rosie is walking home. She never learned to drive, and she didn't want to wait for the bus, and when she calls Will he says they're fine, that she needn't rush.

This is a new concept, to her. She feels like she's always rushing.

She walks through the city, past the cathedral, looking up, out of habit, to see the peregrine falcons, but they're not there. She keeps walking. She has to stop, at one point, and tap her foot three times on the curb, and then she curses herself and walks on, under the cleft autumnal clouds.

What'll happen if you don't tap or touch, her therapist had asked her, once.

Nothing, Rosie had said. I know it makes no difference. But that doesn't stop me feeling like I have to do it.

Or what, the therapist had asked, and Rosie had clamped her mouth shut because, once again, she wasn't being heard; because she knew the outcome changed nothing. So she left, and kept touching and tapping and stepping when some internal force told her she needed to. It happens less, in adulthood, she's noticed. But since Simon's diagnosis, the urges come out of nowhere. Touched windowsills and tapped door handles and syllables, counted, in her head.

She is minutes from home when her phone rings. It is her mum, who so rarely rings her first that she assumes the worst. A dead dad, or another cancer, this time in her mother's bones or breast or blood.

Mum, she says.

Hello darling.

What's up?

Nothing's *up*. I only wanted to see how you were doing. How Simon is.

Really, she asks, and there is a confused moment between them, her response not what her mother expected.

Really, she says, after a while. How's the chemo coming along?

Fine. As fine as these things are, I guess. He got sick this morning, just like the doctor said he would.

But you still went to work?

Learned from the best, didn't I, Rosie says.

A bus rattles past; the bus she could have caught, if she had waited. It is so noisy, all fumes and wheels and rumbling engine, that she does not notice the prolonged silence down the phone.

Was I such a bad mother, her mum asks her. Rosie has just reached the door to the flats, and she pauses while searching for her keys.

No, she says, as a reflex. Why would you say that?

I know I'm difficult, her mother says. I know that, Rosie. I know I pushed you, and wanted the best for you. But I always thought you understood that.

I did, Rosie says. I do.

Then why are things like this, she asks, and for the first time, Rosie hears a hint of something new in her mother's voice. Sadness, or desperation. Panic, pushed down, between the edges of her words.

Rosie turns back to the street and watches the bus trundle onward. The cars, moving. Pavements, coppered, in the dying sun.

It is her instinct to deny and smooth over and reassure, but she looks at her hands, one clutching the phone, the other holding her bag, a satchel she'd found buried in a secondhand shop. It is so battered. Permanently bruised, where patches of the leather have rubbed away.

Because I came to you about Simon, Rosie finds herself saying. Before his diagnosis. And you just turned me away.

Another silence, stretched between them.

I gave you advice, her mother says. I told you what I would do.

It was bad advice, Rosie tells her.

Well, her mother says, flustered. Rosie battles herself, for what feels like several minutes. Stones, bulging, in her throat.

How's Dad? Rosie asks, eventually.

Fine, her mother says.

Simon'll be fine, too, Rosie says, and then because there is something wild in her now, something that thinks to hell with it, she tells her that Will's been with him all day.

Will White, her mother says, slowly.

The very one, Rosie says.

I didn't know you were in touch.

It's a recent thing, Rosie says. He's being a friend, to us. Me and Simon.

That's good, her mum says, and it sounds like her mouth has got really small, like her words have to find their way round her teeth. Rosie knows she's dying to say that surely they have better friends, people who know Simon intimately who could be there with him, but she doesn't, because that's the whole point.

I also got a new job, Rosie tells her. The air is warm with exhaust fumes and the lack of wind, wrapped around her as she speaks it all aloud.

Oh?

I'm a music teacher now, she says. Classical guitar, and piano. Some singing. That's why I was out, today.

Oh. Rosie. That's—that's lovely.

It is lovely, she says. It's really lovely. The pay is terrible. Like, god-awful. But I don't really care. No: I don't care one bit.

Why are you doing this, Rosie, her mother asks, after no silence, this time; a hardening, instead, a refusal to play this game.

Why was I not doing it, Rosie asks back. The sky, so red, above her, as her mother does not answer.

*

Will gets to know Simon in a way he has never known another person. He learns what sort of light will make him feel lethargic, and requires him to close the curtains. What color he likes his bananas to be, before he'll eat them. He finds out exactly what temperature the heating should be set to, at varying points of the day; he is overly warm in the mornings, and often too cold after lunch. He wears slippers in the house, like an old man, which he insists he did even before his diagnosis. I hate getting stuff on my feet, he explains, when Will mocks him for it. And when Will asks what he means, he says you know, dust or hair or water splashed on the floor, and Will says wow, you do have problems, and Simon says he reckons he'd take cancer over dirty feet and they laugh about it, together, in the kitchen.

He finds out other things, too. That he takes honey in his chamomile tea, but only past midday, as if sweetness is a treat reserved for afternoons. That he is an only child, and is scared of heights, and reads a lot, about politics and philosophy.

What do you read, Simon asks him, when he's scanning his bookshelves, one day, Will boiling the kettle from the kitchen.

Not a lot, Will says.

Come on, Simon says. Everyone reads.

I read motorbike manuals, Will says. And cookbooks.

Simon nods.

And travel guides, he adds.

You like to travel?

Will just smiles at him, for this. Turns his back to pour the boiling water into their cups, wondering if he can like something he's never done, put on hold, missed, perhaps, altogether.

I don't, really, Simon says. I know that's kind of dull.

I'd expect nothing less, says Will, and Simon grins, tells him he's a bell end, and the term takes them both by surprise, throws them back to school, and they snicker, at first, and then laugh so hard that Simon says oh man, it hurts, which makes them both laugh some more.

*

And this is how it goes. Weeks of a sick husband, and a best, unexpected friend, coming to spend time with him when it's needed; to drive them both to and from the hospital, to stay with them, sometimes, for dinner, or to hang out with Simon while she works.

She is so grateful she feels like her heart might rise up and out of her. Organs held out to him, like offerings.

He asks for nothing, except better butter. She restocks the fridge and watches him, sometimes, when he smokes on their balcony, wondering how he never smells of tar or tobacco, but pine trees and soil, a faint trace of petrol.

She remembers the clarity of him; how he tasted of fresh water.

The hills they climbed in the shade of the Montenegrin trees, and the tomatoes they popped in their mouths, the removal of real life as if it had been cleaved off, for one week, one summer.

You're smoking again, she says to him once, at the door.

Not really, he says. Just sometimes.

Simon says he likes him. That they've found the opposite of common ground; intrigue, and a grudging respect, and Rosie turns to him in bed and says she doesn't want there to be a grudging anything, and Simon laughs, touches her face, tells her she is the sweetest person he knows.

This is a word used to describe her, so often. She is beyond bored of it.

*

Will ends up going to chemo with Simon, one Thursday. Rosie has a school concert that she can't get out of, even though she tried, apparently, asked if she could skip it—but Simon insisted she go, and Will, for once, agreed with him.

He knows the drill; spent a lot of time in a cancer ward with his gran. They don't play cards, or read, or even listen to music, because Simon is too exhausted. This is his fourth treatment, and his hair has thinned, his eyebrows shed into pale lines.

They simply watch the room and the patients, the pools of daylight on the hard floor. It has been a wet winter. So much rain and wind.

D'you know what's funny, Simon asks him.

What's that?

I think, all things considered, you're probably my best mate.

Will feels a sharpness go through him, as if the poison has been hooked up to his own veins.

I know we don't share stuff like that, Simon says. But cancer makes you sentimental, so just give me this one.

All right, says Will.

It's funny, isn't it, Simon continues. We barely know each other, and you're Rosie's friend, really. You didn't even like me. Don't, even. But I'm just sat here, and thinking, that actually, apart from Rosie, there's nobody I'd rather be sitting here with. And maybe that's a bit sad, I don't know.

Will just looks at him. He has no idea what to say.

My parents came over, last weekend, Simon goes on. And I love them, you know, but they were just awful to be around. They made me feel like a kid again, or like I was elderly and incapable, like I'm a feather they mustn't knock down. And my actual best mate, Jon, he calls, sometimes, and it's awkward, and he asks how it's going, which is nice, but we don't talk anymore about the things I want to talk about. The rowing, and the rugby, or even his kids. Like cancer is catching, or something.

Will is still looking at him. He has some color in his cheeks, while he tells him this. He's styled his hair, for chemo, made an effort that Will can't understand. A little gel, so that his hair sweeps to one side, like a lifeguard, a pretty boy from a different life, on the water.

But you're different, Simon says. We can talk about anything. And nothing. And it doesn't feel uncomfortable, whether we're at home, or here, or wherever. You know?

Will simply nods. One slow dip of his chin.

Either way, Simon goes on. I guess I'm saying thanks. And no matter what happens, with all this, I hope we can, you know. Stay in touch.

Simon is observing the room while he speaks, as if his request was simply asking for a glass of water, or getting Will to slant the blinds shut, keep the sun out of his eyes.

We can do, Will says, when he finally finds the words.

Good, Simon says. And Will thinks he should tell him, right then, about him and Rosie, and not just the shared house and the carpet sex but all of it, every year of it, the bonfire and the dance, how he was there when Josh fell, and how it's kept them apart and together for all this time, because Simon deserves to know all that before he thinks he's his friend, but it's too late, it seems, and he is a coward, and he ends up staring at the scuffed shoe marks on the floor and feeling, for the first time in a long while, like he does not know himself, or what he cares about, and it is unnerving and disloyal and he wants, desperately, to run. And keep running.

I take pills, he says.

Simon takes his eyes from the other patients.

Really? What for?

Depression, or whatever, Will says. They keep me on a level, I guess.

Sure, Simon says, and he nods.

You should row again, after all this, Will says. If you can.

You're all about other people pursuing their passions, aren't you, Simon says, and Will doesn't like the way he looks at him, then.

I preferred it when you were dull, Will tells him.

Simon laughs, but barely. More of an inhale. They stop talking after that, and watch the room, and Will feels warm, and sick.

Will stops at Rosie's school and picks her up on the way home from the hospital. She is bright-eyed, her cheeks pink. She looks happy.

How'd it go, Simon asks her from the back seat.

*Won*derful, Rosie says, and she's breathless. They sang *so* well. The solos were near perfect. I feel so—I don't know. Proud.

Will had been thinking, alive, that she looks alive, but he drives in silence as Simon says you *should* be proud, Rosie, and he drops them off and declines their invitation for dinner, says he'll see them again soon.

It is as he's driving home that he has the urge to talk to someone.

Someone who knows him, and might care.

Her number is the first in his contacts, and he calls her on the hands free, sat in the Norwich traffic with the night closing in. Bright red and green of the lights. Engines, biting, near stalling.

Hello, his sister answers, and she sounds uncertain.

Hi Ambs, he says.

Hello, she says, again. He drives. She waits. He clears his throat.

Been a while, he says, eventually.

I'll say, she says.

Sorry about that.

No, she says, as if she doesn't want to hear it, or it simply doesn't matter.

How's the PhD, he asks.

Good, she says. And then, are we speaking, now, then?

Looks like it.

He imagines her nodding. Recalibrating.

I have a question for you, he says.

Go on, she says.

Do you think everyone has a thing? Like, something they're meant to do? I don't mean some grand vocation, or anything. But do you think we all need something to, I don't know . . . anchor us?

Amber is quiet, for the shortest of moments, and then she says well, obviously.

Huh, says Will.

But that's the quest, isn't it, his sister says. People don't always know what that is. And that's why they run. Or drink. Or gamble. Or have affairs or switch careers or suffer from anxiety.

That's cheerful, Will says.

Well, you asked, she says. And you've done a lot of those things, to be fair. But you know your thing, Will. You always have.

Do I?

Think.

Ambs, all I do these days is think.

Think harder, then, she says.

Will has merged onto the dual carriageway now. Cloud hangs like fog, concealing the stars.

Just ask yourself what feels like home, Amber says, and he says okay, but doesn't; he just keeps driving. He can hear her typing in the background. A sentence, then silence, before another. Shuffle of pen on paper.

He drives and she works. The road slips behind him, headlights and red brakes and empty hard shoulders, when he asks her, eventually, how their mother is, and she says oh, who knows, that they only check in every few months, that she's gone to India, or something.

She's the kind of woman who gets elephant tattoos, she tells him.

Got it, Will says, and they share a moment of muted laughter. Silence, taut and punctured, knowing smiles between siblings.

Half siblings.

As if it matters.

He wonders, as he turns off the motorway, why he is no longer angry with her, and then decides not to question it.

He has spent his life feeling angry.

It has eaten him up.

Why're you asking, anyway, Amber asks, as he pulls past the sign to their hometown, streetlights glowing along the pavements.

About Mum?

No. About anchors.

I . . . don't know, he says. I just . . . don't know anything, anymore. I don't know what I want, or what to do next. And that's never bothered me before.

Amber is no longer typing.

Jen's gone? she guesses.

Long gone.

And Rosie?

He remembers the funeral, Roe up front with her guitar, the way his sister would not look at him.

Back with her husband, he says. Her dying husband. Who is, incidentally, someone I quite like now, even though I still despise him, in principle.

Amber clucks her tongue.

Tricky, she says.

A pickle, he agrees, as he pulls onto his grandmother's drive, turns the key to kill the engine.

Couldn't you have just married that awful girl? Amber says. At least you knew where you stood with her.

Who d'you mean?

You know, what's-her-name. Dolly, or Vanessa.

Those names are pretty different, Ambs.

The one with the nose piercings and lacy thongs.

How do *you* know she had lacy thongs?

Gran found some once, in your jeans pocket, she says. I remember because she told me no self-respecting woman ever wears anything less than sensible pants.

That's true, Will says. And chastity belts, remember.

Will, she says. I'm twenty-four years old.

And still a practicing virgin, right, he says, and she sighs, says whatever.

Everything—and nothing—has been said, but he does not end the call. He sits with his sister, who is miles away, and she sits with him awhile longer.

I should, she says, when he keeps sitting, and not talking.

Yeah, he says. Okay.

And when they hang up, he rubs the knot in his chest, sitting in the darkened driveway, alone.

seventeen

◐

Cancer free.

The doctor has said these words, and Rosie has made her repeat them, three times. Simon laces his hand in hers and they sit there in the oncology office, married and stunned and hardly daring to feel the euphoria of what it means.

The chemotherapy has been as successful as we'd hoped, the doctor is saying, and she is smiling, and calm, and Rosie thinks how strangely similar the slowing of the world is at these words, the same, somehow, as the endings and the lost, irretrievable things she is more accustomed to.

As we said all along, the doctor goes on, with her white teeth and her bobbed hair, you're strong and healthy, Simon, and we caught it early. You'll still need to finish your chemo sessions, but it's—

But you got it all? Simon says, and it is the first time he has spoken since they sat down. The cancer's gone?

It's gone, she confirms, and she is patient, explanatory. But it's like finishing a course of antibiotics; you'll still complete the other sessions, and we'll need to see you every eight weeks after that, to check in. But this is good news, Simon. This is the news we wanted today.

So . . . I don't have cancer anymore, he says, and the doctor says that's right, and they cry, the both of them, on each other, and the doctor sits behind her desk and Rosie loves her, this woman she does not know; in that moment she loves her more than Marley, and her mother, and Will's gran; she is indebted and in love and Simon is living, undeniable and permanent, in her arms.

Outside, the day is fair and bright.

Cold, beyond belief.

We should celebrate, Simon says, as they walk down the street, arms looped, half dazed. They feel jet-lagged, or as if they've both woken from a prolonged, shared mirage. That can happen, Rosie has heard. Married people can hallucinate the same thing, in bed at night. When their REM sleep cycles align, somehow, like the intertwined roots of their lives.

Of course, Rosie says. What shall we do?

Dinner, Simon says. And wine.

Done, Rosie says.

With Will, too, Simon says. And we should go to my parents' place, this weekend. Surprise them. And when the chemo's over we should go away, just you and me. Somewhere hot. We could go back to Mauritius, even? Have a second honeymoon?

He is animated, talking with uncommon speed, and Rosie is relieved, finally, to hear that energy back in his voice. She always liked that about him. The joy and the ease of him; his enthusiasm. Things she had missed for so long.

The springtime sun is high and hazy. Pigeons scatter as they walk, their shadows short beneath them. She should talk back, match Simon's delight, but all she can think about is how he wanted Will there, first and foremost, and what that means, and how much harder this just got, despite being all she'd wanted.

———

The restaurant is high-ceilinged, all linen tablecloths and gleaming cutlery and domed, copper lighting. Small, delicious plates descend the length of the menu, and Simon says he's ordering all of it.

But you don't eat red meat, Rosie reminds him, as the waiter retreats from their table.

You do, though, he says. And Will does, I'm guessing.

He's coming, then?

Who knows, with that chap, Simon says, and he gestures for her hand. She passes it to him, and he rubs her thumb with his own.

It'd be nice for him to meet someone, he says, and it is a vague comment, a conversation starter that, she realizes later, is the end of things.

Or perhaps things ended, long ago.

Why? Rosie asks, and Simon looks puzzled.

Because it would be nice for him, wouldn't it? He wouldn't be the third wheel then. And we could do more of this. Go to dinners. Be real friends.

We are real friends, she says. He took you to chemo when everyone else backed off. He drove us to appointments, and he switched shifts, and he put up with a hell of a lot, actually. More than we can ever thank him for.

I know that, Simon says, and he is frowning, a little. Still holding her hand. I'm just saying it would be nice to do more stuff with him.

And why does he need a partner for that?

He doesn't, I guess, Simon says. I was just . . . thinking out loud.

Rosie is about to answer when the waiter brings the bread basket. Warm rolls, seeded and seasoned; this was their favorite restaurant, when they first got married, a place for special occasions, and on special occasions, Rosie would allow herself to eat bread. She would smell it, first, before taking a bite.

Tonight, she takes a roll and splits it open and pulls fingerfuls of the soft dough from its center. She wants to stuff the feelings out of her. Stifle the unsaid things with a cotton-like gag of the mouth.

Did you and Will ever, you know, Simon asks.

He is watching her eat the bread, and she knows he sees it, the frenzy in her hands.

What do you mean, she asks him, and the darkness of the restaurant seems suffocating, suddenly, and she wishes the lights were up, that she could look him straight in the face, burst up and out of herself, for once.

I mean, did you ever have a thing? I sort of thought you might have.

When did you sort of think this, she asks, and her voice is tight, and Simon sits back, because it has answered his question.

I'm not accusing you of anything, Rosie, he says. I don't mind.

Well, I mind, she says.

A candle flickers between them in its glass orb. Floods their tired, drawn faces.

She opens her mouth and then Will says hey, sorry he's late, the traffic was murder, and he drops into the chair between them, at the side of the round, white-clothed table.

Simon lets go of her hand.

No problem, he says. We've only just ordered.

Will nods, says it better not be a salad; that he hasn't driven all the way to Norwich for a couple of radishes on rocket leaves.

He is teasing, Rosie knows. Gently ribbing the man he has come to think of as a friend; something that both troubles and pleases her.

The food's good, Simon says shortly, and Will glances her way, then. She avoids his eyes and pours wine. Slops it, accidentally, onto the tablecloth.

So, any reason we're having dinner in this fine establishment at one second's notice, Will asks, after the waiter has taken his drinks order, and still, neither Rosie nor Simon has spoken.

Yes, Simon says, and he smiles, but without showing his teeth, and Rosie can hear his energy has gone, once more; leaked out of him, like the oil from the olives on the table.

Will raises his water glass to take a swig, but pauses when Simon does not go on. A group arrives at the table beside them. Chairs grind along the floor. Sequins and high heels and low laughter, invading their non-saying of things.

I'm, uh, Simon says, when they're seated.

You're . . . ?

I'm an idiot, I think, he says, and Rosie says Simon, please.

Will puts his glass down.

What's—

Tell me, Rosie, Simon says. Because I was just curious, before. But now I'm more than curious.

It's not interesting, she says. Can we just do this another time? Why don't we talk about what we're actually here for?

Because, Rosie, Simon says, I've lost a lot, over the past year. And I'm starting to wonder whether it's more than I'd actually realized.

Rosie knows that Will is watching the two of them, though her eyes are fixed on Simon's face. She knows he is wondering what he has walked into, and she wants to think of a way through this, a way that is right and kind and inexplosive, but her mind has turned to water. Clear and still, like that in her glass.

Okay, she says. Okay.

Okay what, Will asks, and neither of them looks at him, and he says that maybe he should go.

You might want to stay for this, Simon says.

And then the first courses arrive. Small ceramic plates, gold-flecked and catching the candlelight, a question of more wine, shaken heads. Will's soda and lime is placed beside his napkin, still folded on the table.

I was just asking my wife here, Simon says, when they are left alone again, whether she and you were ever more than friends.

And Rosie can't help it; she stands up.

We were, she says. Okay? We were. But we're not now, because I chose you. And you only chose me back because you needed me, Si, and you know what? That's fine. Because I need you, too; but not like this. Not with drama in a restaurant, when Will is a good friend, and came all the way here for us, and today is a day we've all been hoping for. So let's not ruin it, okay?

You keep saying okay, Simon says. But it does not make it okay.

Look, mate, Will says, and Simon holds up his hand to silence him, and for a staggered, whirling moment, they all find that it works.

What bothers me, Simon continues, is not the *fact* of the thing. It's that neither of you told me, which says there was a reason not to.

It was just, Rosie says, and she shrugs, still standing, her hands splayed flat on the tabletop.

She wants to take back time.

Take back all of it, and none of it.

I'll meet you at home, she says. I'm not doing this here.

And she does the boldest thing she can ever recall doing, and walks away, even though she is wrong, even though she owes Simon everything and the man next to him even more, and she gets her coat from the cloakroom and she heads down the many flights of stairs, alone, lets the maître d' bid her goodnight and begins the cold, star-strewn walk home, her breath white on the damp air.

*

Will looks over his unfilled wineglass at the man whose wife he's had.

Or who has the wife he was meant to.

We should eat, Simon says, and it is the last thing Will expects, but after Simon lifts a plate, scrapes some onto his own and starts to pick at it with his fork, he follows suit. The food is rich and buttery, and the restaurant is oppressively dark. He hates it when he can't see what he's eating.

I don't want to argue, Simon says. I'm too tired for that. I was never good at it, either. And I sense that you probably are.

When the mood takes me, Will concedes, as he pushes a paste-like something around his plate. Simon forks something into his mouth. Chews, and swallows.

Rosie's easy to read, Simon says. Always has been. She's a terrible liar, and she shows her emotions in her eyes. Have you noticed that?

Like a deer, Will says, and Simon says yes.

They eat more small things. Take small bites, and say nothing for a while.

The bread's good, Simon says. Did you have any?

Will shakes his head, and Simon says he'll catch the waiter's eye, get the basket refilled.

This nice guy thing is really starting to grate on me, Will tells him.

I thought it might, says Simon. He shifts some sauce onto his fork.

Can we just say whatever needs saying?

And what does need saying?

Don't do that, Will says.

Do what?

Answer questions with questions. Rosie does it.

Does she?

Can we just . . . have it out?

I don't want to have it out, Simon says. I want to enjoy the nice meal I'd booked to celebrate being cancer free. And then I want to go home to my wife of seven years and tell her that none of this matters, because it's nicer for all of us. But I've realized, Will, that even though you've essentially lied to me, for weeks—my God . . .

He rubs his eyes, takes a moment.

All this time, Simon goes on. You've lied, skirted the truth, insulted me, actually, without me knowing. But there's one thing you did say that's true.

Which is, Will asks, after a tight pause.

That things go wrong, Simon says.

They have stopped eating. Laughter, and voices; the hum of enjoyment around them. Will runs his index finger along the edge of the table. Back and forth, and back again.

Look, says Will. Things went wrong with me and Rosie years ago. Several times. It's sort of . . . a thing we do. We fail, but we stick around, because she's . . . well, I'm . . . we're friends. Good friends. I tried not to be, for a while.

Simon does not say anything. He's staring at his plate, as if willing it to refill.

You could try and be friends with her, too, Will says. If this is too much, the lies, or secrets, or whatever. But I don't think you'd have much luck.

Simon meets his eyes, for the first time all night. His white wine gleams in its glass.

You love her, he says.

Will holds his gaze.

Tells him he has tried not to.

Their plates sit, untaken, on the table, and Simon drains his wine, pours more. He offers him the bottle, and Will declines. Droplets perspire down his soda glass.

I just thought you were like siblings, Simon says. That's how it seemed to me.

That's because you don't pay attention, Will says.

Don't be an arsehole, Simon says, and Will feels a savage triumph, because he wants the rage, welcomes it, even, can handle fire with fire. This is all so placid. So disconcerting.

If anyone's the brother here, Will says, and he lets it hang.

What d'you mean?

You're just like him, Will says. Sort of.

Like who?

Oh, come on, Si, Will says. This is your *problem*, see? *Every*thing comes back to Josh. You know, her twin brother, who died? Fell to his death? Smashed his skull and bled out on the beach right below us, nearly half our lives ago?

Simon says nothing. His face has gone slack.

It's destroyed her, Will says. And you don't even know it.

She, he says, and he clutches the stem of his wineglass. Twirls it in his fingers. She . . . never wanted to talk about him, much.

Right, says Will.

Oh God, Simon says, and he drags his hands across his thin, cancer-lined face. Will watches him do it, and his anger dies. Things slow, for a long, rolling moment.

She chose you, Will says, even though it kills him, and he wants to upturn the table, to throw the tiny plates at the solar-shaded windows. Simon keeps his face in his hands.

I've never met anyone like Josh, Will goes on. But you're pretty close, Si. Friendly. Unassuming. Kind, and fair, and full of this, sort of, relentless energy. Annoying as hell.

You think she married me because I'm like him?

I don't think she realizes it, if that helps.

The waiter appears then, to take their plates, asks them how everything was. They both say good, though Will remembers none of it; he has no idea what he's eaten, and is hungry, still, for something he cannot identify.

Like I said, Will says, when they are alone again. Nobody's quite like him. But you fill a hole, for her, I think.

He stands up, because there is nothing more to say, and as he turns to leave Simon says, just tell me, Will, when it was. Was it years back, or more recent?

Will asks him why that matters, and Simon shrugs. Says he's not sure that it does.

Both, Will tells him.

He should apologize. He should say sorry, to this man, this good, well-groomed, just-about-living man, sitting alone at the table with his warm wine and his ruined evening. But he will never apologize, for her. No regrets, his mother used to say, and it is the one thing he has tried—failed, indubitably—to live by.

Oh, Will says, as he makes to leave. Congrats on, you know. The cancer news.

Simon raises his glass, in acknowledgment.

Broken things, between them, that Will cannot—even if he wanted to—take back.

As soon as he steps outside, Will starts to run.

The air is the brittle cold before snow; he had not checked the weather for the drive home, but it doesn't matter, because right now, he is running, and he thinks if he knows anything, he knows where to go.

It takes ten minutes to reach the riverbank and then he speeds up, dragging long, heavy breaths of the night air as his heart pounds with his feet. He feels something hot and joyous flowing through him, which seems wrong, after all that's happened, but it's Rosie, and it's him. Currents, fast-moving, like the river gushing beside him.

He catches up to her on the bridge. She's standing at the parapet, looking out.

I told him, he says, when he reaches her.

She's wrapped in her coat, her hands stowed beneath her arms. The river flows fast and steady and black.

Told him, she repeats, as if from far away.

About us, he says.

The river, rushing, like the tide.

I also told him he fills a hole, for you, Will says, because he wants her to bite, wants her to disagree, to finally tell him the things she hasn't.

He doesn't, though, Rosie says—and it is there, she has said it, at last. She keeps her face turned toward the river, away from him, and he finds he wants to shake her. Grab her arm and force her to look at him, speed up this long, arduous thing between them.

He doesn't?

No. I thought he did. I wanted him to. I really, really wanted him to.

She takes her hands to her forehead, tugs her hair behind her ears. She is still, and upright; like a dancer, he thinks. He sees her mother in her then, for a second; that strength, that hardness.

I'm half a person, Will, she says.

No, you're not.

I am. The moment the doctor told me he'd died, I felt it—I felt something detach, and I'm half empty, and nothing helps. Eating doesn't help, and starving doesn't help, and therapy and marriage and music and cured cancer—none of it ever *helps*. I don't know who I am, or what I want, or what anything means, anymore.

How theatrical, he says, and she says fuck off, Will, and then she finally looks round at him, surprised.

Sorry, she says, immediately.

Don't be, Will says, and he's angry, but also kind of laughing. Jesus Christ, Roe. You're the person you always were. Believe me.

Cars pass on the road behind them. White noise, in their ears.

I don't know what I'm doing, she says, so quietly, he can barely hear her.

Did you ever?

Well, yeah. I thought so.

Getting good grades doesn't count, he says. Nor does marrying a nice, boring boy who doesn't eat real butter.

Don't, Rosie flares, and there it is again, that triumph, flaming inside of him—he wants her to yell, and he wants to yell back. He wants contact, and raised voices. He is sick of tinkling spoons on ceramic, shared cereal at night, unanswered texts and false friendship.

Goddamnit, Rosie, he says. Why the hell have you stayed with him? Can you tell me that? I thought, after everything, he must have something—and I figured I could live with that, maybe, if it's what you really wanted. But if you're standing here and telling me he doesn't, after all these years? Then *why*, Roe?

I don't know! she says, and she seems fraught. He's—*good*!

Good, Will repeats.

Yes! He's good and kind, and there needs to be more people like him, she says, and she sounds feverish now, her words coming fast and deliberate. And it's not his *fault*, Will. It's not his fault that it's not enough.

So it's not enough, Will echoes, and it shoots through him, the fury and white-hot joy of it, but Rosie's face crumples, and she asks him why isn't it, Will, what's wrong with me?

He should not answer, but he is angry, and cold.

A lot of things, Roe, he says. You're indecisive, for one. You let other people choose for you, over what you want, and that's not just sad, Rosie, it's fucking spineless, which is the opposite of what you actually are. And you have this false perception of what's good and, I don't know, *proper.* Like it matters. You don't live your life the way you should. You never speak out, to anyone, least of all your mother, who frankly could do with being put straight. You don't sing, anymore. You deny yourself every-thing. You rob yourself, Roe. Every second of every hour, you're forcing yourself into some kind of box, and it's fucking painful to witness, but you do it anyway because you don't know any different, and nobody's ever told you not to.

Snow is falling now. It drifts down, lands in her hair. She is looking at him as he rants, her hands back beneath her arms.

But in spite of all that, Will says, there is not a single thing wrong with you, Roe. With any tiny part of you.

Her eyes, on his. Blue, and ocean-deep.

I made a vow in a church, she whispers, as the snow floats around them. He says he knows she did. And then she says he's her husband, and she loves him, and he says, not in the way you should.

He does not say all that he wants to. That she is meant for more. That she should have someone who burns for her; who crawls beneath her own skin.

I think, he says, that you need to figure some things out, Roe.

She looks at him with her fawn face; it breaks him, a little, but he can't not do this; can't keep doing it, either.

I'm not saying choose between us, he says. You need to work out *what* you want out of life, Rosie. Not who.

They stand there, in the sifted dark. Lights glimmering on the water.

And through his anger and relief, he finds he still wants to kiss her. His hunger so real and cavernous that he wants to take her inside him, somehow, to drink her up; swim deep in the low, dark red of her.

Instead he says, this thing we do, Roe. Let's not do it, anymore.

Will—

No. I tried to be a nice guy, just your friend, or whatever, but I can't. I'm sick of waiting, and hoping, and thinking about you all the goddamn time. Not just these past few months. Ever since that bonfire.

Her eyes are as open as her mouth, and he steps back, because he wants to consume her, or cradle her, or both.

I'm serious, Rosie. Go be married, or not. Go write music, or not. Sing, don't sing, open a fucking late-night cereal café, for all I care. Just figure out what you want. And I'll go and do the same.

But—

Stop, he says, more loudly than he intends to. Just stop, he says, and with everything he has in him, every last good fiber or breath or feeling, he turns and he walks away, from her, from them, from all of it, and he knows, deep down he knows, that it's finally for the last time.

eighteen

☾

It is a long night, after the river.

A long few nights.

Rosie goes back to Simon, though she knows she cannot go back in any real sense. They talk, for days, and she tells him everything. He expects her to move right back in with Will, but she can't, not after all that he said; not now she knows that he's right, about all of it. She always thought she knew what she wanted, but it turns out she'd just been following rules and structures and ideas put on her by her mother, by Marley, by old movies; some sense of right and wrong she formed so long ago, she can't even remember doing it.

She can't keep it up, she knows.

Can't let this life be her own.

Can't keep using Will as a comfort blanket, like she always has, the boy with the wolf teeth and the rough hands and the bad birthday.

She'd told him, by the river, that Simon wasn't enough, and rather than take her in his arms he'd told her he was done; and that, strangely, was the most freeing thing he could have said to her. No need to choose between one thing, or another.

No right, and no wrong.

Things are broken open, and waiting, and she knows, now, what she has to do.

When she and Simon finish talking, she moves out of her marital home, for the second and final time.

Late nights, and tears. Emptied drawers and sodden shirts and things packed into bags. Books, dog-eared and faded from the sun on the shelf, squashed into a holdall and brought with her, like children she cannot be parted from.

I am doing this, she tells her mother, when she moves home, just briefly.

I am fucking doing this.

She has never sworn, aloud, in front of her.

She has never done a lot of things.

This time, she stays with her parents for two nights, while she gets her things together. She tells the school she is going, and they are kind and supportive and she has to resign, because they can't cover for her, can't hold her job indefinitely.

That's okay, she says, and it is.

She touches the photograph of Josh in the hall, before she leaves. Wishes he could come with her. Wishes she could hear his voice, if only for a second. She would give so much of herself, just for that, still, and that is why she knows she is doing the right thing.

*

Will begins to dream about his grandfather. He did this a lot, when he first died. They do things that they never did in real life. Things like fishing off the side of a rowing boat. Building things, together, out of wood and hammers and nails.

They do not talk, in these dreams.

He thinks he's forgotten the sound of his gramps' voice. Wishes he could forget Rosie's, too, if he could have a say in such things.

He dreams, and he wakes, and he goes to a group, sometimes, when the days are hard, when he wants to turn to the bottle or something worse. Things embedded in his past, mostly. But there is a line, he knows, a thin, pliable line, like the fishing wire he twists round the hooks in his sleep, and he does not want that line to unwind, despite all his years of tightening.

It's not like the TV shows.

No, I'm Will, and I'm this. No heartfelt storytelling or revelations. Mostly, it's a lot of listening, and allowing. Making eye contact, sometimes, with people he does not want to.

There are biscuits at the break. Orange squash, watered down like at school, and he laughs at this, at the supposed circle of life. Everything leading him back to sour milk and cheap cookies and tea and coffee and juice that nobody wants, and yet everyone drinks, because it's what you do, isn't it. It's what you do.

*

Rosie has always loved the mornings, even when she wasn't sleeping. Especially then, perhaps. The light so liquid and gentle, as if saying, it's okay, you can get up now.

But now things are different, and to her surprise she has found an affinity with the late nights in Vienna. A romance, almost, when the day bleeds to dark, and the cobbles start to shine in the streetlights.

It is then that she lines her eyes with pencil, slips on a dress and walks down the iron stairs in heels that make her feel like a woman who knows what she wants. At this bar. In this place. Making up for lost time.

Before she begins, she always closes her eyes, a ritual that is not obsessive, but necessary. And then she plays, and the diners either listen or they don't, and she finds that she does not mind, has stopped noticing, even. It's just her and the grand piano.

No dead twin. No ex-husband.

Her hands, finding themselves, all over again.

When she is not working, she walks, and she thinks. Exists, in the city of music, as if breathing here is healing, and harmonious, as if the daylight itself will soak into her skin, the way it touched all the composers who lived here before her, crossed these roads, turned their faces to the same sun. Centuries of music, hanging in the air like heat. She had never dreamed of living abroad, but there is something about the pull of this city that felt right when everything else collapsed.

She returns to her favorite restaurant most nights, the one that clings on to the sunlight at the edge of the square, horses' hooves and Bavarian and wine pouring, all around, as she reads or drinks or writes or eats. Some days, all four, together.

Mostly, she sleeps in after her shifts in the bar, then spends the late mornings in the coffeehouses with her books and her sheet music. She eats strudel, daily. She takes her shoes off in the museum quarter and treads in the grass and does not visit any exhibitions. She goes to so many concerts she loses count.

She calls her parents, rarely, and Marley, often. She even rings Simon, sometimes, and they talk naturally enough, about his checkups and their divorce papers and his mother, and her mother, and she is glad to do it, but she is gladder when they hang up.

She writes in real, leather-bound books now.

Not on her wrists, or on loose paper, or on napkins that she loses. The poems tumble out of her like fallen leaves, flying every which way so that she has to chase them, almost, catch them with her pen.

It is some kind of magic that she had once forced herself to forget.

So many things, forgotten and found.

So much to fill herself up with.

There is a man, even. A gorgeous, olive-eating, dark-eyed man who is younger than her by a couple of years, who waits tables and plays violin and does not kiss her in the daylight. They get coffee, and go to concerts, and then they go back to his or hers and blur between the sheets in a strange, satisfying tangle of sex and cigarette smoke, in his hair, on his skin, along his jagged back teeth.

She says no, when he offers her one, afterward.

He smokes in bed and they might kiss, for a while, as if they're both somewhat hungry but unbothered about eating. And then he dresses and leaves her, and it might be several days, or a week, until they do it again.

She sleeps well, once he's gone. Or she writes about it. The smoke smell. His pointed chin. The pegs of her, stretched and held.

*

Will tells Rob to book in the Honda, that there's space out the back, but to be careful with it.

Rob nods, and Will sees in his young, unshaven face that he wants to tell him he's always careful, that he doesn't need to say it. Will does, though. He can't help it. It is his own name on the line now; these early days rely on word of mouth and reputation, and any scratch, any dink, could be the end of his good run.

And it turns out he cares about that.

He logs the customer's details and is about to follow the kid into the workshop when the door goes, again, and his sister walks in, tall and skinny and bare-ankled. She looks like she could be working in his garage. Leather boots and patched overalls, *dungarees*, she tells him later, when he comments. Glasses with lenses so thick, it's a wonder she can see.

Amber, he says. Hi.

Am I interrupting? she asks.

No customers right now, he says, and she says that's not good, is it.

I've had plenty all morning, he says. D'you want to see the books? Check my finances from the last twelve months?

That won't be necessary, she says, and she's looking around now, at the limited stock he keeps, the engine oil and spark plugs, the bulbs and brake cables and inner tubes.

I don't know what any of this is, she says, and he tells her she doesn't need to. She also says that it smells weird.

That'll be the exhaust fumes, he says.

Want to swap petrol for paninis? she asks, and he looks at his watch, says all right, to just give him two minutes. Out the back, he washes the grease off his hands, tells Rob to watch the shop for an hour. The kid looks at him, terrified, but determined not to say so, and Will likes him a bit more, for that.

Outside, the wind is low. Clouds layered like basalt.

So, how is it, running your own business? Amber asks, as they head down the gravel path toward town, their shoes crunching on the stones.

Good, Will says. Busy.

You named it after Grandpa, she says, and her voice is light, offhand. He shrugs, says yeah, and that is all they need to say.

She never questioned him staying in Norfolk either, after they'd sold their grandmother's house. He couldn't have told her why it felt right, even if she'd asked. Something to do with the proximity to where his grandparents were buried, perhaps. Where he'd realized he had roots, after all, after thinking he'd had none.

They find a table in the café on the corner and order sandwiches with mugs of tea. Old boys greet him by name, and the waitress winks at him, brings him extra bacon on the side.

You'll get fat, Amber tells him. You're not eighteen, anymore.

Just eat your roll, he says, so she does, and she tells him about her training, and her new boyfriend, whom she's not sure about because his voice is too loud, and he drinks far too much water.

Yeah, hydration's a turnoff, Will says, and she looks at him and says seriously. He laughs at this, but she does not. She is wiping up salad cream with her crusts. He feels a shot of something like tenderness, or pride, as she does it. A rising, in the pit of his chest.

Where are you staying, he asks her, when they've eaten.

Your place, she says.

Right. A heads-up would've been nice.

I had some leave and thought I'd be spontaneous, she says. Why, what's the problem? Got a woman living there?

No woman, he says. No women.

Good.

It is, actually.

They order more tea, listen to the conversation between the two men at the next table. A debate about horses, and numbers, and luck. They both look out of the window a lot, rather than at each other. The sea is slatelike beyond the window. Seagulls stand on the harbor wall, sardonic and alert.

It's weird, not having Gran's house to come home to, Amber says. She is handling a sugar cube as she talks, angling it between two fingers.

Too weird? he asks her.

No. It's good, obviously. To have the money.

Know what you'll do with yours, yet?

She curls her lips in a don't-know. Says she'll buy a flat, she guesses, when she knows where her training will take her. Put it in an account with good interest, maybe.

Don't go wild, he says, though she does not get the joke, and she puts the sugar cube in her tea and says she doesn't know why she just did that, that she hates sweet tea, and so he swaps his mug with hers, promises he hasn't drunk from it yet.

Amber stays for the weekend, though he barely sees her because he's working. The garage is finally breaking even, and he has been working harder than he can ever remember. He knows full well that it is a distraction in the way of alcohol, or running, or riding his bike so fast he almost comes off at the hairpin bends. But it is not dangerous, this time. It is sustainable. And that's all he wants for himself, it seems; something constant.

They order takeaway and sit up late and talk, because that's what they do when they see each other, these days, and after two nights of it they are done, and she goes her own, academic way and they barely speak for weeks until she shows up again with her news and her watchful eyes and her annoyingly pertinent questions. He sees his grandmother in her, now, and this is both pleasant and strange for him. She is not the kind of woman who would get elephant tattoos. She is not the kind of woman who would walk away.

You found your thing, she says to him, just before she leaves, and he shrugs, says maybe. They are sitting in his car, the rain like spittle on the windscreen.

You seem good, she says. Better.

I'm still on the antidepressants, he says.

I know. And what I said still stands.

He nods, says he is, and she gets out at the train station and he watches her go, wondering if this is as good as it gets, and if so, it's okay, really, it's fine. It's better than a lot of things.

He'd told the truth about the women.

There are none.

He found he did not want them, in the same way, after the carpet burns and the scrambled eggs. After the good-guy act, with the chemo and the sandwich-making and the small talk. Some guys in the pub like to mess with him about going soft, or bent, or dying lonely with a house full of cats.

I don't like cats, is all he says, supping from his single beer, or his soda with its chunk of cheap, too-old lime. So tart, and effervescent, settling only when he swallows.

And don't say bent, he tells them. It's fucking offensive.

And they *ooh* and *err* and he lets them.

He cooks even more, these days, like he's stockpiling for winter, or the end of mankind. Low-cost, stew-like meals, mostly, with glugs of olive oil and blackened skins. Brown rice. Torn herbs. Full-bodied coffee that he grinds by hand and drinks in the morning and at night, and sleeps worse for it, probably, but not so bad that it matters.

And he swims. Every day, in the sea. It's good for his tight muscles, and he can do laps in the shallows before or after work, and it costs nothing and makes him feel strong and wild and a part of something bigger than the seaside town he never left.

He always meant to.

Somewhere along the way, things happened, or they didn't.

So he swims, and he works, and things are.

He thinks of her, sometimes.

Rosie Winters. The girl he lost, several times over, for several good reasons.

She crops up at moments that seemingly have nothing to do with her. When he's pushing his trolley down the supermarket aisle and he sees a burnished tower of apples, red and ripe. When he's pouring milk into a saucepan, or he hears the pitch of a certain note when he flicks past a song on the radio.

He sees her mother, one time, from the car park at the harbor.

She is queuing for the butcher's and does not see him; he stays in the driver's seat for a while, and waits for her to be gone. She is on her phone, her handbag clasped beneath her arm. She looks much the same, just older. Deeper frown lines, he imagines, from a distance.

He wonders if she would know him, if he got out of the car. If the hatred in her eyes would have dimmed, even a little.

He sits in his car and observes her as she waits, with her hard face. Like an elbow, all points and edges. He wonders, not for the first time, how it is that a woman like that could have reared two children like Rosie and Josh, but then he thinks of his gran and his mother, and the unborn seeds of nieces and nephews and sons and daughters he might not yet know, and he lets go of something clenched in his gut as he watches her step into the building, sees her pointing with her elongated nails, the butcher nodding, taking something from the counter and wrapping it for her, gently, in his gloved hands.

———

One night, Rosie finishes playing, with the restaurant near empty and the waiters carrying glasses back to the kitchens, plates in the crooks of their arms. The room sparkles as if it is Christmas, even though winter is ending. Little gold lights and leftover wine, all crystal flutes and mirrors. She savors the scene, for a moment. Then she closes the lid, and is gathering her sheet music when she feels rather than sees someone approach.

You play so beautifully, says a young woman, at her side. She has long black hair and square shoulders. A wide mouth, sincere and serious.

Rosie smiles and thanks her. She does not know what more to do; nobody has approached her like this in all the months she has been playing here. It is her job to serenade, to entertain, while the wine is poured and the food is eaten and the hum of conversation ebbs and flows. But her shift is over. So she faces her, this intent woman, dressed in black. No makeup. A tiny mole, on her cheek.

Rosie will remember this about her.

I am writing my thesis on the last song you played, the woman says. Her English is somewhat stilted; Rosie suspects it is not her first language, and nor is German. She must be a student here, she thinks. She has that sort of look. Curious, and hopeful, and thirsty for things still within reach; Rosie had known that feeling, long ago.

She is thinking this at the exact moment that the woman asks her which arrangement she was playing, by whom, and Rosie feels her cheeks bloom with color. Oh, she says. No one's. Just my version.

The woman blinks.

Are you studying, too, she asks her, but Rosie shakes her head.

Just working, she says.

Did you study, before?

Yes, but not music.

The woman nods.

You should think about it, she says. Rosie smiles at her, again, and they talk a little about the arrangement; she shows her the sheet music, when she asks, says she can keep it, if she likes, that she has plenty of copies.

The woman touches her shoulder in thanks, walks out of the bar with Rosie's music, and later that night, Rosie finds she cannot sleep. She sits up in bed, with the windows open and her phone in her lap, and considers how she has walked past it, many times. The largest music university in the world, with its ocher brickwork and arching doorways, the Schlosstheater she'd so often dreamt about.

Mozart had performed there.

He'd walked these streets, sang and played and taught piano in this city.

And Rosie had come here, thinking that would be enough, to be around such tradition and history and meander through it all. To attend the concerts and write fragments of her own songs, play classical music late into the night.

She hadn't, however, foreseen the students. The best musicians from all over the world, who congregate here, with an openness and a vision and places at the music academy. They are her long-ago peers, she knows. The people she'd never met; the person, perhaps, that she'd missed the chance to be.

She'd felt something she thought was sadness, every time she saw them, but she knows now that she was wrong. That it is not melancholy at all, but a longing. That deep, silent pull she has felt ever since she was a child and her father sat her down at their piano and showed her that she could make sounds with her own hands, magic that matched the music she'd heard elsewhere, in the swirl of the sea, the leaves in the forests, her brother's footsteps, light on the stairs.

So that night, after the woman with the mole and the black hair, Rosie learns everything she can about what she has always wanted. She reads up about the institution she can see from her window. Devours the descriptions of two courses, in particular, writes down the names of the professors, makes notes on the entrance exams, and feels a heat inside her, an inflation, she thinks, all of her molecules bouncing and rocketing and colliding, even when the sky begins to lighten.

She is still in her dress, from the night before.

She puts on a jacket, collects her notebook and pens and locks the apartment door behind her, heading for her favorite place in the city.

It is a fifty-minute walk, and when she arrives, she remembers that it isn't exactly beautiful, the *Leuchtturm*. Iron stairs wrap around the outside, tourists standing before it and zooming in with their phones, their miniature, handheld cameras. Flashes of white, foreign chatter. There is a patched circle of grass, and a nearby bench that's empty, but Rosie settles herself on the ground and sits with her back against the wall. She gets a view of the water, that way.

She sits, and she watches, and waits.

It'll come to her, she is sure.

If she is quiet and patient enough.

She prepares. Plays her way through the nights at the piano bar, with a new, renewed deliberation, as if she's got something to prove, or perhaps, somewhere else to be.

It is like she has growing pains in her hands and feet.

She is thinking about how she could put this into words when Simon rings her, one night, an hour before she needs to be at the piano bar. She puts him on speakerphone so she can continue applying her eyeliner while he talks, staring herself down in the mirror in a way she had, until recently, always avoided.

They say their hellos, and then Simon cuts to it. Says he has found some of her jewelry in a drawer, wants to know if she'd like it back.

Rosie asks him to describe it to her, only for them to realize it is not hers, after all.

Well, that's awkward, Simon says, down the phone. It must be . . . someone else's, I guess.

One of the women you had while we were apart, you mean, Rosie says.

Yes.

I don't mind, Si, she says.

Of course you don't, Simon says. Why would you, after what you were up to, yourself?

Rosie takes a breath, listens to him exhale. He says sorry, and she puts down her pencil, says it's fine. This is what they do, now; try to stay pleasant, attempt some sort of halfway friendship, only to clip each other with hard comments or occasional digs, treading a line that neither of them knows how to walk.

D'you think we should, Rosie says. She doesn't need to complete the sentence; doesn't need to voice the idea that they should stop speaking, now their divorce is through. That it's better, and smarter, even though it feels like they're giving up. Cheating each other, somehow. Again.

Yeah, Simon concedes. I do.

There is a sad, overdue silence between them.

I'm thinking of staying in Vienna, anyway, Rosie tells him, as if that'll make it easier on them both.

Oh yeah? How come?

I want to study music, she says. And this is the best place for it.

Uh-huh, says Simon. Makes sense.

She doesn't respond, at first, but he is quiet for so long that in the end she asks him, what does?

You, wanting the best, he says.

Rosie lets out her breath, unaware that she'd been holding it.

It's a compliment, Rosie, Simon tells her, but after they say goodbye, for the last time, she is not so sure that it was.

*

Will runs the Norfolk marathon, one day. Just like that.

Although it's not just like that, he knows, because he has been training his whole life, without knowing it, and he is fit and strong after years of hiking and running, the daily swims he has come to love.

The water, slicing his skin.

There, every day, without fail.

But he is in the pub when someone tells him they've dropped out of the race, got injured, and before he knows it he's agreed to take his place and he is there the next morning at the start line, in his old running shoes and shorts and cursing himself for not eating properly the night before, no carb-loading or lean meats or whatever the other runners are conferring on, and he thinks screw it, when did he ever eat anything but what he wanted, anyway, and then the horn sounds and the race begins and they all start moving, in a wave, a great surge of nylon and calves.

Nothing matters, when he is running.

Still, after all this time.

He forgets that he didn't eat right and he forgets that he hates jogging beside other people and he just follows the route along the coast, runs from Sea Palling to Sheringham, down the open roads, listening to his breathing, like always, no music or interruptions or clock-watching. His limbs, meeting the earth.

He is used to running twenty miles most weekends, but the final six almost kill him. He actively thinks this, at one point, when he hits the famous wall. That this could be it. He feels like he could drown under the weight of himself, the impossibility of the next step, but it still comes, somehow, and comes again, simply because he won't quit, because there's someone in front and behind him. Strangers, cheering him on, even though they don't know a thing about him.

So he keeps going.

When he finishes, drenched in sweat and every bit of him hurting and feeling fantastic, he whoops, out loud, with the other runners, claps them and thinks, out of nowhere, that of all the people under and above the blue and cloudless sky, he wishes his grandma were here.

He gets a silly little medal, on a silly striped ribbon.

He puts it on the kitchen counter when he gets home, and takes a shower before he cooks dinner, a giant bowl of fresh pappardelle, the radio keeping him company. After he's eaten, he stacks the dishwasher and runs the taps for a bath, even though he's already showered. His limbs and his abdominals ache, almost pleasantly. All he wants is to lie down and close his eyes, soak his muscles in hot water.

He pours a can of Coke into a glass, and is about to head through to the bathroom when the medal catches his eye.

A little lurch, in his chest.

The question of what to do with it.

His gran kept everything, of course. His childhood drawings of cars and motorbikes, Amber's swimming certificates, their school reports; his grandfather's cigar humidor, the hospital bracelets from her own chemo. Books she'd read. Photos, and letters. Pieces of a life, and not just her own; things that made up her entire world. Sentimental, and stupid. She'd have been the first to say so.

Will takes the medal off the side and feels the weight of it in his hand. He can hear the bath running, the water rising in the other room. He pads over to the shelf next to the television, toward the only framed photograph that he owns.

He doesn't know anything about it, really, where it was taken or who took it; how he even came to possess it. It captures his grandparents, young, pre-children, standing on a boat, white railings and a body of water behind them. She is smiling, adjusting his sun hat as he stands beside her, his eyes part-closed in gratitude.

Will looks at the two of them, then props the medal against the frame.

Sentimental, and stupid, he knows.

The months slip by, as they tend to do. He gets up every morning and jogs to the sea, swims and then runs home, showers, makes a strong, tall coffee in a thermos that he drinks on his way to the garage. He services bikes and orders new parts and jokes with Rob and Ryan, the new mechanic he's hired to manage the workload.

He sometimes thinks, as he locks up and lowers the shutters, that if this is all there is, he'll take it.

He considers getting a dog.

A retired greyhound, maybe, who could run with him on the beach.

He checks flights, now and then, wondering if he'll finally do all the things he thought he wanted to, but he has his business now, and it would be difficult to leave it, and Amber might need him, maybe, though she's never needed him in her life, and he forms a long list of excuses that make him feel old, and responsible.

If he's honest, it's because he likes it.

The routine, or the calm, that means he has not felt his heart pain in the longest time. He does not know what has lifted it, exactly. Years of medication, maybe. Or the exercise, or living alone, without a woman, or the peace he's made with the things he did and the people who left and the way the sun keeps rising, regardless.

He misses some things.

Some people.

Knows, though, that that's just the way of things, and he prefers the balance, the rest, unexciting and mundane and, it turns out, all that he seems to need.

And good butter, of course. Decent coffee. He was raised by a woman with priorities.

*

Different days, now. Separate coastlines, split sections of the same sky, but still morning coffee and evening meals, bread toasted when it's gone stale. Scrape of butter, gloss of jam. Moisturizer for their hands. Hers, each morning and night, and his, because they're older and tougher, like animal hide, from the garage and the tools and the grease.

There are things that mean something, friends and laughter and nourishment, and things that just happen, because that is living without tragedy, routine-led, more deliberate. Showers, shaved underarms. Pianos and engines. The one he restored, in his basement, because he didn't know what else to do with it. They think about it, sometimes. Once, even, at the same time, when a song they'd liked plays over the credits of a film they both see, and it leaves them warm, and half sad, and re-flective.

But they are themselves. Full of spaces that don't need to be filled, imprints in the mattress and the carpets of the houses they no longer live in, getting on in ways they had wanted.

Will thinks this to himself, as he locks his garage up one night, and hopes that Rosie is thinking it, too, feeling it, in that period of non-time she'd talked about once, just before dinner and after school or work, where you can't do anything real.

Who even talks like that, he thinks, as he heads to the shop. Picks up some milk on his way home.

*

And then, at the end of summer, that day rolls around again, unnoticed by everyone but felt deeply, like a war wound, when he wakes.

He is closer to forty than eighteen, now, and he counts back, as he does every year. Not in candles gained, but in years that Josh has lost.

He wonders what he might have been, as he grinds his coffee by the sink.

What life would look like with him in it.

Strangely, he finds that he thinks of him as a mid-thirtysomething, too, as though the ghost of him has grown older alongside him. Long limbs, salt-and-pepper hair. Less bounce, more of a slow, seeping appre-ciation in his movements; creases near his eyes, hands trailing along the flint walls of their hometown.

But he wouldn't be in Norfolk.

Bristol. Berlin. Los Angeles, perhaps. Somewhere with color and con-versation and live music; tech centers, with slides and ball ponds and sleep pods.

He would still doodle stars while he worked. Still be curious, about everything.

Will drinks his coffee, skips his swim, and then works through the day, like always. No cards, no cake, no texts from anyone but his sister, and even then, he does not reply. He repairs motorbikes and serves customers and teaches Rob how to check tire pressures and then he closes the shop and takes himself to the seafront for a bag of chips and a cigarette. It is the one thing he allows himself, on this day.

He thinks about dying, for a while. An abstract, undramatic thought, like a low-flying gull; wondering how it might feel, where you might go.

And though he is feeling mostly well, these days, there is a feeling he cannot shake with medication or daily swims or uncelebrated birthdays. He has found it to be true, what people say: that time can heal, but he has also found that it cannot wipe muscle memory. The weight of that dread, the doom felt deep in his chest. So he smokes his cigarette and he digests his deep-fried dinner doused in vinegar and he is wallowing in the sheer pleasure and self-loathing of it all when his phone begins to ring.

And when he answers, he keeps eating his chips, because that seems like the only thing he can do.

It's me, she says, eventually.

It's you, he says.

He looks out at the shoreline, at the waves lapping and retreating. The chips are warm through the paper, and he can taste oil and salt, the off-white grease of the newsprint.

I . . . know I shouldn't be doing this, she says.

Will does not speak. The potato steams hot in his mouth.

But there's this lighthouse in Vienna, Rosie tells him. I go there when I need to think, or write. I've got a thing for lighthouses, I guess.

You're writing?

Yeah. Sort of.

How do you sort of write something?

Well, I don't know if any of it's any good.

It's still writing.

I guess.

What're you writing?

Songs, mainly. Do you. Uh. Want to hear some?

He catches the question as he looks out at the water, and then bundles up the remaining chips in the paper, throwing them into the nearby bin before he takes the steps down to the shore.

I'm listening, he says.

She is quiet then, for a little while. He picks his way along the sand, and the evening is windless, and he waits for her, with his heart too large for his chest. Fragments of shell beneath his feet. Pebbles, driftwood, rope.

This is weird, she says.

You refused to do it, before, he says.

That was back then, she says, and she pauses. And it is your birthday, after all.

Afterward, he heads for the lighthouse, and they talk.

The light is failing. Strips beam from beneath the cloud, gulls flying out to the horizon. So far a journey for so late, he thinks, as she tells him about her piano, and this man that sits, every day, with his cigar and his coffee in the corner of some grand café, how he wears a fur coat and says nothing to anyone. How she's tried to guess his name.

She talks about the rounded sounds of Bavarian German, the pavements, the streetlights, the meat. He tells her about his garage, when she asks, though he keeps it short, would rather she kept on talking.

But he finds, with a little coaxing, that he does want to share things with her. About his meetings, and his swims, how things are enough, but not.

He wants to crack down the center of himself, and launch his phone into the waves, and press it so hard into the side of his skull that it hurts. That line between joy and fury still exists, for him, as real as breath, and bone.

He keeps walking. She is talking about Mozart now, and horse-drawn carriages. Drinking her coffee with cream.

The sky is yellow and pale, a strip of sundown that meets a wall of cloud, like the Rothko postcard his gran kept stuck to the fridge. It feels like it might storm, later. He draws closer to the lighthouse as Rosie talks, and it stands like it always has, tall and white against the dusk. Everything smells of soil and salt, wet sand, oddly sweet. But something feels markedly different, in the way that some nights can: the bonfire, the fall, the night his mother left or his grandmother died or he poured all the vodka down the sink.

And he knows why, before he even sees her.

His heart lifts, without any real reason, and then there she is, sitting on the steps, the railing between her and the sea.

It is Rosie. He knows, even from a slight distance, by the way her legs are bent. The contours of her features, elfin peaks through her hair. He stops walking, watches as she worries about his silence. One moment, two. Then she senses him, looks up, and they both stare at each other for a while, the phones still held to their ears.

Bright eyes. Skittered hearts.

You're here, she says, down the phone.

I am the one who lives here, he says. I thought you were abroad?

I was, she says.

He hangs up and moves closer, but slowly, as if it might have consequences that he cannot prepare himself for. Shatter the semblance of calm he has built. Blow him open. Unquench that thirst he has, for her, and everything he does not have.

She seems thinner, again, her face matured and drawn. More freckles, from the European sun; keen, blue irises despite her late nights. He thinks about her drinking coffee and writing songs by her own lighthouse and he feels that same pride, again, that swell of something so good, it aches.

She puts her phone down.

Hello, she says, as if to restart.

Hey.

I, uh . . . I'm not in Vienna anymore.

I can see that, he says. You visiting your parents?

No, she says. No, they don't know I'm here.

He nods, and puts his hands in his pockets, waiting. She seems nervous. Keeps touching her hair as if to smooth it behind her ear, even though it's already in place.

Here's the thing, she says. I decided I wanted to go to music school. Not just any music school, though: *the* music school.

Okay, he says. Which one's that?

The MDW.

In Vienna?

You've heard of it?

I saw the brochure on your bookshelf once, Will says. He doesn't say, I was looking at your things, when you were out and Simon was in bed, and it didn't pass me by that it was shunted between the sheet music that you never threw away. That he'd pulled it out, seen she'd folded down the pages on voice and piano and composition. That he'd considered, for a long, rogue moment, leaving it out on the coffee table.

Rosie nods, as if it's completely normal that he would have noticed something so private. So tucked away.

Well, I applied, she says. And I didn't expect to get in.

But you did, says Will.

Yeah. I got the email this morning.

He feels a shift inside of him; a light, barely-there wind, changing direction.

That's brilliant, Roe, he says. That's really great.

Thanks, she says. It is.

They hold each other's gaze.

I turned it down, she says.

She does not take her eyes from his face as she tells him this. Hands in her lap, in his pockets. The two of them, blue-black, against the burning cloud.

Why? Will asks her, after the longest time.

It would have meant a few more years in Vienna, Rosie says.

You don't like it there?

Oh God, I love it, she says. It's got such poise and magic and history, in every wall of every building—even the lampposts are pretty. I think you'd like it.

I'm sure.

But I just . . . don't want to live there, anymore.

A beat, between them. The tug of the sea.

He takes his hands out of his pockets and sits beside her, then. Sees the scuffs on her shoes from where she's walked along streets, down iron steps, across bridges he doesn't know the names of.

He can smell her shampoo.

The apples.

He remembers the first time he saw her fresh out of the shower, with her hair hanging long and wet. It is dry now, has grown beyond her shoulders.

So here's the thing, she says, and he waits.

It's been wonderful, she says, and it comes out slowly, as if she's scared of forming the words. All of it—the music, the freedom, the time alone. But you're not there.

Will daren't look at her. He keeps his eyes forward, on the sun.

I shouldn't have left, she says. When things ended with Simon, properly, I should have stayed, and fought for you. But I really believed what you said.

What did I say, he asks her.

That I needed to work out what I wanted. But when I got that acceptance letter today, I just . . . realized I already knew.

His heart has lifted, his pulse fluttering like the wind in the pines. Rosie laces her hands around herself, rests her chin on her knees. Early thirties, and still she seems so young. He wonders how he looks, to her. He feels so much older. Funny, how he's so often thought about dying, but never about growing old.

I don't expect anything, she says. Not after everything I did, or said, or didn't do. But I'm here, if you want me. I'm not going anywhere. I don't need the best music school in the world. I don't want to shoot for things that bleed me dry, anymore; I want things that fill me up, and I don't care what they are, as long as you're there, and I'm there with you. I want to make you breakfast, Will. Meet you at home, every day, and share car keys and toothpaste and surprise you with birthday candles.

She turns her head toward him then, and her face is soft and earnest. He knows that face. He's seen it before. Over shared macaroni, and in a stifling-hot tent. Tickets bought and stairs climbed and doors unlatched in the rain.

Toothpaste, he repeats.

Whatever flavor you want, she says.

She is teasing, trying to soften the strangeness of the moment, but he cannot even think to laugh.

You should go to music school, he says.

I'm going to, Rosie says. Just not in Vienna.

He nods, once, and fights the urge to touch her. Her hand, or face, her slender, freckled wrists.

Never again, he'd promised himself. Never again would he touch her, or get close to her, in case his heart couldn't take it.

But now she is here, beside him, and never has already been broken.

I think about you all the time, Will, Rosie plunges on. And I know I don't deserve to. I know we had our chance, and I blew it. More than once. But I wish I'd just stopped, for one damn second, and realized I was trying to do the right thing for everyone else, which just made everything wrong, in the end, you know?

Will does know. But he hears these things as though he's asleep, and being pulled back to wakefulness. Dragged by the ink of the tide.

I know it seems like I didn't choose you, ever, Rosie says, when all I *wanted* was to choose you. And I'm sorry I never said that to you. Even if we're only ever going to be friends, that's okay, I think, but I just wanted to be able to say it. It's all I can think about, now; that you matter, more than anything, to me. And I never even told you.

Another beat; another wave, breaking on the shore.

I ruined our chance, she says, again.

They keep sitting by the lighthouse, him and Roe. The girl with that voice, the girl who listened, who clawed her way into him without trying.

His hands, on the concrete, are cold.

I don't believe in chances, Roe, he says. I thought you knew that about me.

She unclasps herself, then, and turns toward him. Her eyes are the deepest blue, and he's never told her how beautiful they are, he doesn't think. Never said the things he should have, or asked her the things he needed to know.

There is only what happens, he tells her. What is and what isn't.

And as he says it, her face fills with all that he has dared not look for: certainty, and something else, that word, four letters he has felt and wanted and held, and she reaches out and touches the lapel of his jacket with those slender, piano-playing hands.

So what happens, she asks him.

What do you think, he asks back, though he knows her answer, now, as the sea stretches ahead of them and the geese call from over the trees. Coming home, maybe, or taking off from the nearby fields, two things that are one and the same, really, if he takes a second to think about it.

ACKNOWLEDGMENTS

Firstly, I want to thank my fantastic agent Ariella Feiner, for taking a chance on me and this novel. Thank you, Ariella, for believing in me, advising me so brilliantly, but mostly, for trusting me to write this book. Thanks also to everyone else at United Agents: Molly Jamieson, for her keen insight on the first draft, and the wonderful Amy, Amber, Yas, Eleanor, Lucy, Jane, Alex, and Anna.

Thank you to my impeccable editors: Clio Cornish, my kindred spirit at Michael Joseph, for the letter that changed everything, and for immediately understanding the sort of story I wanted to tell. To Pamela Dorman, for her unflinching eye and decisive, much-needed wisdom, and to Jeramie Orton, for her continued warmth, curiosity and organized notes.

Thanks to all the incredible people at Penguin Random House, both in the UK and U.S., especially Ellie Hughes, Steph Biddle, Kallie Townsend, Courtney Barclay, Emma Plater, Christine Choi, Sara Leonard, Yuleza Negron, Chantal Canales and Marie Michels. To Lee Motley, Elizabeth Yaffe and Lili Wood, for the gorgeous cover art. Thanks also to Louise Moore, Brian Tart and Andrea Schulz, who were behind this book from the beginning, and to the added hard work of Riana Dixon, Emma Henderson, Stella Newing, Claire Vaccaro, Tricia Conley, Tess Espinoza, Randee Marullo, Kate Stark, Mary Stone and Lindsay Prevette. To Shân Morley Jones, for her patience and diligence. Thank you, as well, to all my international editors who wanted to share Will and Rosie with the world—I will forever be touched, surprised and delighted.

Thank you to Richard Skinner and my pre-pandemic writing group, for all their feedback on a previous project which meant this novel could take shape. Special thanks to Gaurav and Kathryn for their kindness, friendship and support beyond the Faber classroom, and to Tamar, for all of this and more.

To the early readers who told me to keep going: Justin Coombes, Kirsten Norrie, Jason Gaiger, Georgia Stephenson, Savannah McGowan, Georgia Taylor, Flic Box, Rebecca Hilsdon and Emily Griffin, among others. Huge thanks to the late Brian Catling, who gave me permission to dream big and write bold, and to Liesel Thomas, who read a lot, cried a lot, and gave thoughtful feedback on the novels that didn't quite make it.

Thank you so much to those who answered my questions: Kelly Degaute, for delving into the realities of Hodgkin's lymphoma; Ollie Henson, for sharing his experiences of Mountain Rescue; and Bella Chipperfield and her father, for their notes on music, wood turning and piano restoration.

I cannot explain how deeply thankful I am for Emma (Lane) Green, for all her love, spirit and happy tears, and to Jessica Lockyer-Palmer, for her guardianship and unswerving encouragement. Endless gratitude to my brother, who believed in me, always.

Thank you, as well, to my parents. To my dad, for his granular knowledge of motorbikes and the many hours he spent on story time (in particular, the blue balloons). To my mum, for the midnight bookshop visits and all those special trips to the library—and to both of them, for the car journeys spent listening to Danny.

Thanks to Elizabeth Gilbert for every single, joyous word in *Big Magic*.

To Kate. For so much.

And finally, I want to thank my husband. For the time and space he gave me to write, in the early mornings, at weekends, on holiday, and during several long, cross-country drives. Thank you, Clive, for never questioning any of it. For ensuring I survive on more than just porridge and tea. For not once dismissing the energy I spend elsewhere, or asking too much, or too little. I would not have written this without you.